Kristyn,
Happy Reading!
Linda Nielsen

Because I'm Worth It

Linda Nielsen

Relax Read.Repeat.

BECAUSE I'M WORTH IT
By Linda Nielsen
Published by TouchPoint Press
Brookland, AR 72417
www.touchpointpress.com

ISBN-10: 1-946920-37-1
ISBN-13: 978-1-946920-37-9

Editor: Kimberly Coghlan
Cover Design: ColbieMyles, ColbieMyles.com
Cover Image: Image 55045251 by malkolm

First Edition

Printed in the United States of America.

For Erik
The Keeper of my heart

Acknowledgements

With much gratitude, I want to thank the enthusiastic dynamics of Sheri Williams and the entire staff at TouchPoint Press for their combination of professionalism and patience because that's what it takes to get a book to press. I am forever indebted to my gifted and humorous editor, Kimberly Coghlan and to Riley, a surprise gift of love, who arrived in the middle of this process. I'd like to include special thanks to my crew of friends; you know who you are—for your steadfast support, feedback and keeping me focused.

Chapter One

Big Sur, California

The family's eccentric stone house stood on a precipice of rock that hung over the Pacific Ocean. While a stiff wind blew across the sea tossing surf high in the air, the Steward family climbed to the ridgeline where they paused to appreciate the views.

Vernon looked toward the southwestern windbreak of newly planted Monterey Pines, smiling at his thirteen-year-old daughter, Melissa. "Your mother and I like to call this planning for the future. When the trees grow tall, they'll keep our home safe from storms."

Melissa nodded. The ties from her hoodie tickled her neck, and she tugged on them as she spoke, "Dad, I really want to paint a picture of the new trees silhouetted against the sky, and I want to add the sun sinking into the ocean." She turned to her mother, "Can you help me do all that?"

"You've set challenges for us. That's good," her mother, well-known artist, Lillian Steward, replied as she pulled up the collar of her coat to keep out the chill. She faced her husband and continued, "The pines have taken to the soil." Vernon inspected his work as she continued. "Now that we've checked on our newest family members," she nodded at the trees and turned toward her daughter. "Shall we all go home and warm up?"

Vernon laughed, "You mean head home to our crooked house that tips just a shade to the right?"

"There's only one," Lillian replied with a knowing smile. "Character comes in many forms."

As the family started down the hill, he joked, "We all know rocks and clay must settle beneath the weight of a structure."

"So true." Lillian laughed as she reached for his hand.

"Yet it stands in spite of this idiosyncrasy." He looked into her eyes and replied, "Shall we agree to call it a quality that can't be duplicated?"

She called out to their daughter, "Be careful. Don't slip on the way down."

"I love our crooked house," Melissa sang out as she danced ahead of her parents.

****

The young artist studied her watercolor with a frown. The softness of the sky flowed into the indigo color of the sea, and her eye had a simple journey across the canvas. Melissa turned toward her mother "Why can't I get it right the first time? Like you do when you paint. This is boring, and it's not very good."

Lillian smiled, "What colors do you want to see?"

Indicating the upper portion of the painting, Melissa added eagerly, "I want to add rose and peach hues here so the trees are framed. Then I want the sky to looks like it falls into the water." She nodded toward the ocean. "See. Just like that." Lowering her hand, she pointed at the bottom corner of the canvas. "And here, right here! I want to paint a sunset and put in streaks of ginger and red." Feeling a flush of heat highlight her cheeks, she paused. "But I don't know if I'm good enough to do all that." Shifting her weight from one foot to the other, she added with a shy smile, "My art teacher wants me to try. She said to make a painting complete, the artist must give it something special. I figure I could add bright colors to my canvas. That's a good idea, right? Besides, when Aunt Helena gets here, she'll ask about my painting, and I want to tell her something really cool. Can you help me make it happen?"

"This is your painting and your idea. Your skill will shine through and she'll see that." Lillian smiled. "After all, Helena is a free spirit."

"But she's, you know, smart and goes around the world all by herself, and she writes about it." She put her hands on her hips and added, "Aunt Helena knows stuff."

"We all know stuff." Lillian patted her daughter's arm and continued, "If you paint what you feel, you'll do fine. I'll help you blend the rose and peach shades. Let's see what happens."

****

A week later Melissa was looking through the series of eastern facing windows that swept across the hill tops of Big Sur. The morning had opened with an inspiring sunrise, and she smiled when she heard a noise behind her. "Oh, Aunt Helena," she called out. "I'm so glad you're here! Mother said you arrived late last night." She rushed forward to give her aunt a hug.

"We're watching the sunrise," Lillian replied with a smile as she poured from a pot of herbal tea.

"I can see that," Helena replied jovially, embracing her niece. She wore baggy tan trousers accessorized with a leather belt that was embellished with a turquoise medallion. A red scarf was tied around her neck: its color accented by the austerity of her white blouse. She dropped a wide-brimmed hat on top of a chair and walked over to the window, her leather boots making a thump sound on the floorboards with every step.

Melissa admired the style and secretly believed her aunt wore the tall boots to ward off snakebites when she hiked through the jungles of the Amazon.

Lillian watched her daughter's open admiration. "Helena has completed her second diary of travel, and as soon as it's published, she'll send us an autographed copy."

"It will be my pleasure."

"That's way cool, Aunt Helena."

"What's the latest in Big Sur?"

Lillian continued, "Vernon has planted the Monterey Pines, and he's eager to show them off."

"Good for him! My brother, the arborist." Helena laughed enthusiastically and turned her attention to the windows. "We've had many a family discussion whether the eastern sunrise is better than the western sunset." She tugged on her niece's braid playfully. "In any event, it's good to be home for a break. And it's even better to see you! My, how you've grown."

"I'm almost as tall as you." Melissa stood at five-feet nine inches. "I'm taller than most of the boys, but mother says give them time, and they'll catch up."

Helena rose to her six foot height. "Both your mother and father carry stature." She winked. "My advice...never stoop. Now tell me, what have you done with yourself this year?"

"Well..." Melissa smiled shyly as she sipped from her cup. "You know that I've always liked to paint pictures of the sea, but this year I discovered that I have lots of different ideas. Would you like to see my new canvas? Mother has been helping me to mix the colors."

Lillian placed the teapot on the table, taking a moment to look through the porthole-sized windows that lined the kitchen walls to the west. They offered a dazzling view of the ocean and she added, with a smile, "Mother Nature is our inspiration. Melissa is learning to paint what catches her eye."

"Yup. Every time I open my water-colors, I want to paint things as I see them." Looking intensely at her aunt, she continued, "Do you know what I mean?"

"Yes. I believe I do."

Melissa sighed with pleasure. She carefully tied a knot in the neck scarf that her aunt had wrapped in tissue and left by her bed. "How does it look?"

"Very good. You have the bravura to wear it." Helena regarded her niece with an expression of pleasure and curiosity. "Now shall we have a look at your canvas?" She grabbed her hat off the chair as she left the kitchen.

The women entered the dining room where a polished slab of burl wood created a long table. Walking past tall cabinets that housed over a century of glasses and dishes, they paused at the entrance to the parlor. Helena smiled at the oddly shaped tables that held mementos ranging from antiques to children's drawings.

A large swan-shaped sofa sat in its full glory on top of a faded rug. Her husky laugh filled the space between them. "Ahh, my favorite part of the house. My parents loved that sofa."

Lillian nodded, adding, "The mélange of furniture is a bit like entering a gypsy caravan."

"Eccentricities, a few kinks but nothing to worry about." Helena paused to observe the intimacies of the room in more detail and nodded gently. "I'd say our pioneer spirit continues to shine...all the way back to the Mexican Land Grant of 1830. We were trendsetters then and remain so today." Facing her niece, she spoke with certainty, "Never settle, Child. Always be yourself."

"That's good advice." Lillian nodded, understanding the words on a deeper level. "We should all heed it." Looking at the brightly colored scarves and tasseled shawls that covered the sagging cushions on the chairs, she spoke happily, "On that note, I'm off to fetch Vernon a thermos of hot tea. It's cold up there on the ridge." Her smile broadened. "You two continue on, and I'll meet you outside."

Taking her aunt's hand, Melissa led her down the hall to a smaller room where an easel was set up. "This is it. Mom and I mixed the colors to create hues. That's the sky getting ready for the sun to set, and the deep green is the tiny trees." She moved forward and pointed at the bottom of the canvas. "Right here, I plan to make a shimmering sunset." She held her breath waiting for her aunt's comment.

Helena hooked a thumb behind the medallion on her belt. Rocking back on her heels, she murmured, "You have your mother's artistic talent." A smile softened her face as she nodded her head. "How fortunate that her expertise was passed on. You have a lot to look forward to." She tucked her niece's arm over her own as they walked toward the front door where a large cut-glass insert allowed light to penetrate the hall.

Melissa pulled on the handle and commented, "It's been damp so it's difficult to open."

"It was long ago, but I recall when the beveled glass came from England as payment for a job that your grandfather had done. He couldn't sell it so, not being one for waste, he inserted it in the center of his own front door. When he realized he had to reinforce the redwood frame to support the additional weight of the glass, he knew he needed help. It's a family story we've told many times. But what you don't know is that I was very fond of the young man he hired. His name was Thaddeus, and he had no family, so while he worked with your grandfather, he stayed with us. They got on very well and did several jobs together."

Helena's face held a faraway expression as she went on, "My favorite part of the day was when I'd make sandwiches and lemonade for our lunch. We'd spread a blanket by the cliffs and talk about books and life." She paused, smiling tenderly. "We were young and had wonderful plans." Her eyes lingered on the etchings within the panels. "But, like many boys..." she sighed, "Thaddeus enlisted in the army. Oh, he sent a few letters to me, but they stopped. That's when I realized that there's always unrest in the world. I never heard from him again. We received a letter many months later that his unit had been ambushed, and there were no survivors. I tell myself that the redwood door swells with the tears of those who never came back." Taking a breath, she added, "Another oddity of the stone house is that it harbors emotions deep within its walls."

Looking up, Helena plopped the hat on her head and passed through the door, firmly pushing it shut. "But life rolls along, and we must live with the hand we've been dealt and learn to play our cards wisely."

Melissa was thoughtful as she followed her aunt outside. "I don't want to make mistakes, but I do want to create really good watercolors."

"Never fear being wrong, child. It's a part of daily life that makes us stronger and smarter. Seize the day, I say! Don't go to bed with a regret of maybe I should have." The ocean splashed loudly below the bluffs, and Helena smiled at her niece. "Shall we find your parents for that promised hike?"

A pair of Irish Shillelaghs, lacquered with a high gloss finish, joined ranks with Scottish crooks and various walking sticks of native wood. All were lined up in a wobbly fashion against a crumbling stone wall. Both women carefully selected the one best suited to her height.

Helena removed her wide-brimmed hat and tucked it into her belt. Her short curly hair, its copper shades filling with the ocean breeze, fluttered about her head as if momentarily confused with its freedom.

"Up here, Helena," Vernon's voice carried down faintly from the top of the tree line.

Leaving the house, they began their walk toward the ridge where ragged cliffs dipped toward the ocean and sunshine sparkled like diamonds on the crest of each wave.

Lillian caught up with them. She was holding a large thermos. "A hike in Big Sur is a perfect way to start a day. Plus I have tea for everyone—and cookies."

"Excellent!" Helena smiled. She cupped her hands and called back to Vernon, "We're on our way."

Lillian looked up and felt the wind caress her face as it chased them along. "Helena, what advice do you have for us this morning?"

Turning toward the sea, Helena paused for a moment before she replied, "My life has taken me near and far, and I've learned that we are tourists in this world, merely passing through. Some days we are blessed with tranquil clear water while other days offer up the chop of a storm." With a quick movement, she raised the hand holding the Scottish crook high in the air and waved it in an arch, giving mother and daughter cause to step back and swallow their laughter. Helena chuckled and continued, "We will all experience what life has to offer us." Using the stick to regain her balance, she added, "In various degrees, of course."

Melissa's whiskey colored eyes sparkled with amusement as her aunt added, "All the fundamentals of living need to be collected, and as the years pass, they will sort themselves out."

****

Atlanta, Georgia

Terri Sue Ellen von Campe, a petite thirteen-year-old with a peaches and cream completion, had finished her swimming class, even though she considered swimming to be an exhausting exercise. Her daddy's chauffer had picked her up from the country club and was driving her to the stables where she would practice her riding.

Such drudgery. She checked her appearance in a small mirror that was surrounded with pearls, a gift that her father had given her for her birthday. She outlined her heart shaped lips with a peach colored pencil and pushed at her naturally curly hair, feeling frustrated. *Just where are mah boobs?*

Everyone else has them. When do ah get mine?

As the stables came into view, she released her breath with a sigh of anger. Dressage required lots of thought about what she was doing, and, if truth be told, she didn't give a rat's ass if the horse moved sideways or not. The flexibility of her hips and the use of her thighs for balance seemed wasted on riding lessons when she'd rather be elsewhere learning about boys and what they liked.

Being the only child of a wealthy, influential father, she wondered briefly how different it would have been if her mother had survived her birth. Still in all, she reasoned, she did have her daddy who showered her with presents, and that was very nice, even though his only answers to her emerging teenage needs were to add more lessons to her life.

The current emphasis was on southern etiquette with belle-of-the-ball manners topping the list and, worst of all, a new ballet class. She wanted to rock and roll, not dance to Swan Lake. Why, with all the extra activities in her life, there was hardly any time left to develop her own style of genteel flirting.

Her sea green eyes blinked in frustration, and her narrow shoulders slumped forward. Soon the day would end, and she could go home to her perfectly pink room, read her movie magazines, and talk for hours to Lisa Louise Maynard about boys and penises and, of course, boobs and sex. *Somehow,* her eyes squinted in thought, *it was all connected in a roundabout sort of way.*

Atlanta, Georgia
von Campe Residence

Silver haired Jackson Beauregard von Campe settled his tall frame into the white wicker chair on the expansive veranda and sipped his early morning coffee.

"You are my little princess," he told his pretty daughter. He enjoyed the hour he spent with her before leaving for his imposing office building where he controlled the operation of several companies. "You favor your mama... petite and sweet, just like her. Why, she would have been so proud of you and what you have accomplished. God rest her soul."

Terri Sue Ellen had heard this all before and was bored but had learned to nod serenely and let her father continue, "Your sweet mama's in heaven now and looks down upon both of us with love in her heart."

"Yes, daddy," she replied automatically. Cleaning her throat, she broached a new subject. "As ah am thirteen now, ah would like to go shoppin' instead of horseback ridin.'" *Ah want to buy me a bra really bad and maybe some tissue to pad it. And mah fondest hope is to see a penis up close so ah know what all the fuss is about. Ah can't do that if ah'm constantly bein' supervised. Shoot! Ah want to get out of the house for a few hours and be on mah own.*

Smiling sweetly, she faced her daddy. "Besides, ah'm not much for swimmin' and it's too hot for tennis."

"Now princess. I don't want you to think I'm trying to run your life, but all aristocratic women from my daddy's side of the German family, as well as southern women from your mama's side..." He raised his index finger to make a point. "See here now—always remember your heritage, Terri Sue Ellen; it will serve you well. All ladies in your position know how to ride and swim and play tennis."

He wondered how much longer he could keep her sheltered from the real world. Boys would be the big problem. She was so innocent.

"Gosh, daddy ah'm sure glad ah don't have to do stitches in a straight line or crochet properly or embroider napkins. That sounds so dull. Ah'm real glad that those are jobs for the housekeeper, our Nellie."

Tipping her head, she watched as her father added extra cream to his coffee. She wished someone would offer her coffee. *It's such a grown-up thing to drink. Why, ah'd add lots of milk and sugar, and it would taste wonderful. And maybe, just maybe, my breasts would grow.* Pursing her lips, she thought, *perchance coffee is the secret. Ah'd best make a note to talk this over with Lisa Louise.*

"All well-bred southern ladies know how to be graceful and diplomatic. They thrive on it. It flows through their blood." Jackson gently reprimanded her. "Nellie was your mama's personal maid and your nursemaid. I promised my sweet Susie Ellen that we would keep her Nellie on. Through the years, she's worked hard and elevated herself to supervisor of our household help. For her years of service, we treat her kindly."

"Oh, ah know that, daddy. If only ah had a paper and pen ah could refresh my memory later with the copious notations ah would be takin'."

"Let me call for some stationery." He turned toward the French doors where Sassy was polishing his desk. "Fetch my princess some writing materials. Put them in a leather binder and bring it on out."

Father and daughter waited patiently until Sassy returned with the items.

"Thank you, daddy. Thank you so much." Terri Sue Ellen made the appropriate notes on the heavy cream-colored paper... a large letter B and the word coffee.

"As I was saying, a proper highborn woman knows how to politely entertain, and that's why Nellie is going to drive you to your etiquette class this morning. Correct protocols speak volumes." He smiled lovingly at his daughter and cleared his throat. "See here now, there is also a skill in knowing how to deal with household help in a firm but pleasant manner. So listen up, little lady. This will be a tutorial for you. Nellie!" He stopped abruptly and lowered his chin. "My error. Shouting is so unpleasant." Reaching for the bell on the table, he rang it loudly shattering the tranquility of the day. "We must remember to use this."

A dark skinned woman appeared on the veranda. She smiled pleasantly. "Yes, Mister von Campe?"

"Come on out here. I want you to see this shirt." He indicated his daughter's freshly pressed blouse. "I believe it needs a tad more starch so it remains crisp as the humidity takes over the day." Lightly touching the Peter Pan collar, he raised his eyebrow at Nellie. "See here. See what I mean? This could droop by afternoon."

Terri Sue Ellen smiled angelically as the conversation moved around her. *If ah had a bra ah could tighten up the straps and nothing' would droop on me. Ever.*

Nellie moved closer, running her finger over the stiff collar and nodded politely. "Yes sir. I'll speak to Sassy about that."

"Excellent! You see, Terri Sue Ellen? When you notice a problem, you fix it."

"Yes, daddy." Chewing on the end of the pen, she thought *the problem is my flat chest. Wonder if there are exercises ah should be doin'?* Removing the soggy pen from her mouth, she made another notation while her father watched with pride.

Waving Nellie off, Jackson said, "Go on. Fetch the car now. My princess has a lesson. And, as you pass the kitchen, you tell Sassy to freshen my coffee and bring me one of those pecan buns hot from the oven."

He watched as the housekeeper walked back inside and noticed she was larger than she should be. *Well, when you feed your help good food and all they can eat, that will happen,* he told himself. But as Nellie had seen his precious Susie Ellen through the illness that ended in her death, it wasn't right to limit her food.

"Ah'm goin' get my purse, daddy. Nellie can pick me up right here." She gathered her notes as she stood.

"Take your time. She'll wait for you. You're worth it, princess." His daughter meant the world to him. Yes, she was spoiled, but she was his only child.

She bent over the pots of blooming geraniums and pointed at the red flowers. "These need more water. Shall I tell Ramos to take care of it?" She indicated the full watering can at her feet.

"You do that," he said with pride. "I so enjoy watching you take on the responsibilities of the house. And if you can't find Ramos, you tell the head gardener. Someone best come out here. Chores must be addressed quick-like. Make a note."

He sighed, thinking what a huge amount of work was involved with being a single father; the list of responsibilities was staggering. Why, just selecting his daughter's friends was a monumental task but had to be done under his astute care. His business partner's little girl, Lisa Louise Maynard, being a native young lady of outstanding upbringing, had proved to be impeccable company.

Of course, he'd directed his social secretary to stay abreast of Who's Who in Atlanta, and from the information she was compiling, he'd be able to put together a larger list of potential acquaintances for his princess. Not to be lost in the shuffle was his unwed sister, Victoria, who was helpful with elite bearing and softy refined speech, qualities that were passed discretely from female family members to other female family members.

Unfortunately, Victoria couldn't be counted on for all the details in a teenager's life as she was often stressed due to her delicate constitution. Or perhaps it was the touch of vodka she added to orange juice to cool her in the heat of the day. It was of no matter. But now, Victoria had told him there was this issue of buying a bra for his little girl. That was not a good sign. She didn't need a bra. She needed another lesson, perhaps piano?

He shook his head as Sassy quietly set the tray with coffee, extra cream, sugar and a warm pecan bun next to him. A heavy serving of fresh butter was melting in a silver dish next to the pastry. Sassy unfolded the heavy linen napkin and placed it in his lap. He glanced at the presentation and thought *No sir, it isn't easy rearing a young lady by myself.*

Seven Years Later
Santa Cruz, California

Melissa Stewart, an art major at UC Santa Cruz, was thrilled at being hired by Ian McGregor as a consultant at his local gallery. He'd put together a new and exciting presentation of students', work and Melissa had been asked to assist at the show's opening. The only flaw, as she saw it, was her apprehension of being able to relate to so many people, on so many levels, and remain relaxed enough to experience the rewards of her job.

The day was warm with only a slight breeze from the ocean that didn't carry as far as the old town where the gallery was bustling with parents and locals, all interested, for various reasons, in what was on display.

Melissa paused, as a frown settled across her face. The remains of a summer tan highlighted her soft golden skin tone, but she felt a flush of heat spread across her cheeks. "It's difficult to know who to talk to first." Her voice had developed a nervous squeak as she spoke to Frances Pepper, the art critic, who had assisted Mr. McGregor with putting together the publicity for the show. Melissa spoke with hesitation, "It's easier to paint a picture than to try to explain it to someone else."

In an attempt to look sophisticated, she had dressed in black, but her long wool skirt was itchy, and her new two-inch pumps felt too narrow for her feet.

"No worries." Frances patted Melissa's arm "Just take your cues from Ian. He's a patient man and won't push you beyond your comfort zone. You know art. Plus you have a natural talent." She gave Melissa a nudge. "And now it's time to mingle."

Melissa didn't move.

"Yes," Frances nodded her head. "Learning to mingle is a part of the job, too. Becoming involved with the energy of the crowd is easy. Watch." She moved toward a group of people admiring a bronze statue of a whale breaking the water's surface and commented on the sculpture. Within seconds, she had engaged the small audience in lively conversation.

Understanding the need to present herself in a favorable light, Melissa took a calming breath. Twisted into a French braid, her reddish-blonde hair felt warm against her neck as she walked into the gallery, smiling timidly at the spirited observers. A woman asked a question, an older man made a comment, and Melissa responded; to her own amazement, she found that the inner play got easier. She directed people to various exhibitions and added informative comments. Her own seascape oil, a tribute to her mother's talent, was on display with a grouping of native sculptures.

Ian McGregor called her to his side, "Melissa, there's a gentleman who is carefully studying your seascape." He nodded toward an attractive young man with long hair who wore jeans and a navy blazer over a white tee shirt. "Perhaps you should talk to him about your work?"

"Okay." Walking over to where he stood, she spoke tentatively, "Hello."

"Hi," he responded warmly, immediately shaking her hand. He bent low over the painting, studying her signature, and then he pointed at her nametag. "Are you Melissa Stewart?"

"I am." She nodded, feeling a blush spread across her face.

"Hey." He sounded happily impressed. "It's really nice to meet the artist." Offering his hand again, he said, "I'm Harm Toppel." They shook a second time, and he pumped her hand a little too long. "Oh sorry." He grinned at her for a few seconds while she smiled back. Shifting his feet, he pulled at the collar of his tee shirt self-consciously. "I like your technique. Oil is a difficult medium."

She noticed that his eyes were a soft shade of grey. *Oh my Lord! I'm staring at him.* Stepping back, she touched the painting. "My mother has the talent for oil. She does flowers and birds and...well, I do water color seascapes, but I did this oil for her. I hope she'll like it."

Realizing she was at a loss for what to say next, she looked down and shrugged her shoulders. *I'm flat out of words.* Glancing up, she found him staring at her. *Are we flirting with each other?* She stood straight, which placed her over six feet in her new shoes and noticed pleasantly that he was still taller. *Isn't that nice?* She felt herself relaxing. *But remember you're at work. This is not a beach party.*

Her voice took on a business-like tone, "Oil is an expressive medium. If you'd like to see some of the other artists' work, I'll be happy to show you." As she indicated the way, she risked another glance back, and he smiled again.

"You have pretty eyes. They're the color of whiskey."

"Oh." She felt goose bumps slide up her arms. "Umm, thanks." *Aunt Helena would say that romance is afoot.*

From the front of the gallery, two young, attractive women suddenly lunged toward Harm, each taking one of his arms in a possessive manner. He introduced them, "Meet Bev and Nancy."

Melissa blinked in open surprise at the sudden intrusion but gathered her wits and responded quickly, "Nice to meet you both." She shook their hands, feeling awkward. *Of course a guy as good looking as this is going to have girlfriends. But two at the same time? That isn't right! And to think that I was about to be number three.*

Donald, the newest employee at the gallery, walked toward the group. "Sorry to interrupt, but there are some questions about a print that you'll need to answer." With his thumb, he indicated Melissa. "She's the one who knows art. Me, shoot, I'm just in the learning stages."

"Sure, Donald. I'll be right with you."

Melissa faced Harm and the pretty ladies who were eyeing her with interest. "Ahh." She shifted her weight and stepped back. "Please excuse me."

"It's okay." Harm tried to reach out to touch her arm, but the girls were firmly attached to him so he settled for a nod. "We can talk later."

The blond girl released her hold and looked at Melissa. "I'm sorry. Really. Did we interrupt something?"

"No, no. Not at all," Melissa replied and looked at Harm with raised eyebrows. "It was nice discussing art with you. Please enjoy the show."

"I will see you later." His grey eyes didn't blink as he held her attention.

"Sure. Of course." She walked away. *Good looking guys are trouble. Especially the tall ones!*

****

When the art gallery closed and she had finished helping Mr. McGregor clean up, she was surprised to find Harm waiting patiently outside.

"I know what you're thinking," he began with a pleasing grin.

"Oh, I don't think so." But in spite of the caustic statement, her resentment seemed to flow away. She noticed that his hair was a pattern of flaxen shades: blond and brown, shot through with white streaks like summer-bleached wheat.

"I do know that you're considering not talking to me, but I want to explain that Bev is my sister and Nancy is visiting her. They both would have given me up. Really fast! " He rolled his shoulders and nodded. "It's true. I'm sort of their unofficial tour guide for Santa Cruz until they find someone else who's more fun and will buy them beer. They're not old enough to drink, but our parents are deceased, and I watch out for her. You know..." He stopped fidgeting and looked straight at Melissa.

"I'm sorry that your parents are deceased." She noticed his grey eyes held tiny gold flecks in the russet light of the afternoon sun.

"It's been a few years and we've tried to make adjustments." He moved a step closer and tipped his head toward his shoulder. "Are we okay? Please say yes."

She felt her heart speed up and blinked at him. "I like the color of your eyes."

"Oh." He seemed embarrassed. "Ah. Thanks!" He ran his hand through his shaggy mane.

She moved closer and raised her hand as if to touch him but dropped it at her side. "There's a blend of shades throughout your hair."

"Okay. Yeah. Must be the artist talking, huh?" He was more at ease with this evaluation. "My sister told me the same thing."

"She has a good eye."

"Thanks. I'll let her know. She was the blond. Me," he jerked his thumb toward his chest and added, "I'm free, completely unattached, and happy to walk you home."

A pleasant sensation fluttered across her body. *Pay attention, Child.* Never having been one to play coy, she replied, "I don't live that far."

Chapter Two

Peach Queen Contest
Fort Valley, Georgia

The auditorium dressing rooms at Fort Valley State University weren't air conditioned, and the outside temperature was close to one hundred degrees, but Terri Sue Ellen von Campe wasn't put off by the heat. She knew she was going to be crowned Peach Queen because her daddy had told her, and her daddy was always right. She even had a perfectly memorized answer for her pageant question because Jackson Beauregard von Campe knew in advance what his daughter would be asked.

It was just too bad that she couldn't have enjoyed a wee bit of vodka before the show, but she had to remain sharp. Aunt Victoria had introduced her to alcohol one day as they flipped through fashion magazines, and she liked the way a drink made her feel.

As she preened in front of a mirror, she admired her full bosom. It had happened all by itself when she turned fifteen, and she'd been forever grateful. Finally, the boys had noticed her, and Clemet Bernard Picket, the son of her father's attorney, had actually taken her to the outdoor movies where he'd told her to call him just plain Clem. She had been so impressed by his friendly ways that she'd practiced what she'd been reading about for years.

She nodded to herself confidently. *Ah can still see his anxious organ standin' straight up when I raised my feet and placed them smack dab on the dashboard of his Chevy. 'Course Clem had to crawl under my legs but that didn't take him but a second.*

Smiling to herself, she let her thoughts roll on. *It was a lot like riding dressage, only more rewardin', plus Clem could even move sideways without direction, and he was ready for another straddle soon as ah finished my cherry snow cone.*

Lisa Louise, it turned out, wasn't that interested in beauty or boobs so their friendship had cooled. She'd pursued the academic life once in college and had moved on to Greek antiquities. *But then Lisa Louise was not gifted with mah breasts. Plus her mouth was turning down into a frown and she insisted on wearin' those thick black rimmed glasses. Why, ah declare, they made her look ever so ugly.*

Her mind returned to how important she would feel riding in the Grand Parade as the Ambassador for Georgia Peaches. Plus, after giving it some thought, she was sure she could hide a flask in her clothes so she could keep the fun going all day or however long a parade would last. Her right hand rose as though it had a will of its own, and she turned it at the wrist practicing a delicate prom float wave. Well, perhaps she'd have to speed it up some, as there would be many people to wave at. Quickly glancing around, she hoped no one had noticed her actions.

Changing the wave to a gesture of pushing at her curls, she took a moment to admire the bleached streaks that her aunt's hair stylist had added to her brunette hair. Over martinis at the salon, it had been decided that lighter hair would emphasize her unique green eyes. Now it looked as if the sun had kissed her curls, and she wondered if the stage lights would pick up their perfect glow.

****

"Mmm-mm. Don't you look gorgeous." Bending over, Nellie felt the discomfort of her arthritis as she spread a sheet across the floor so the white dress wouldn't pick up any smudges when Terri Sue Ellen stepped into it. "There. No dust or dirt for you." Nellie sat on the floor with a sigh. "Could you hand me that pillow, baby girl, for my knees?"

"Oh, Nellie," she moaned. "You try to reach for it. Ah dare not move until you have me firmly in my dress."

Stretching her arm across the soiled floor, Nellie grabbed the pillow and leaned back with a grunt of pain. "Here now." She rubbed her hip. "These old bones..."

"Yes, yes, ah know. Let's move along."

Nellie scooted forward in an awkward movement. "Step into your lovely gown so you don't mess up your beautiful hair-do."

"Oh Nellie, you fawn over me." She patted the maid on her head and smiled as she pulled the dress up. "And ah love it."

"You've always been my baby girl ever since God in heaven called your mama home."

"Ah huh."

Her evening dress was mandatory white, not a good color for some of the girls, but on her, it was perfect, bringing out the creamy softness in her skin. While Nellie smoothed the dress, Terri Sue Ellen applied bright peach colored lipstick followed by gloss. "Ah want mah lips to look pretty." Stepping back, she breathed deeply. She was ready for her walk of fame. "Do you think ah glisten?"

"Oh yes, I do. You are as beautiful as a princess." Nellie pulled herself up using the side of the dressing table. *But you're not a nice person.*

****

Two mirrors away, Betsy whispered to the girls around her, "Y'all know who's goin' to win, don't 'cha?"

"Shush, she'll hear you!" Maribel turned around to stare at Terri Sue Ellen. "She sure has herself a full bosom. Do y'all think there's toilet tissue in there?"

"Nope," Betsy snickered. "There all hers from what ah hear tell. The most visited twin peaks at Valley State."

"Hush now." Annie Lou spoke up. "Just look at her! Why, she's gorgeous and confident."

"You think? Or is it because her father is rich and paid off all the right people?" Betsy put her hands on her hips. "Really, girls, everyone knows that."

****

Jackson Beauregard von Campe sat in the front row and watched his perfect daughter gracefully walk the runway. She appeared to float within a cloud of white as she turned to face the audience on either side of her, blessing them with a flawless smile that radiated charm.

Turning to the well-dressed young man at his left, he said, "There she is, Chucky. My princess. She means the world to me. After winning this contest, she'll have a year of pageant responsibility and then she'll be transferring to Georgia State."

"Yes, sir. Good choice. And your daughter is lovely."

Jackson sat back in his chair. "That she is. She has German aristocratic blood from my daddy's side. And great beauty from her mamma's side."

"A perfect young woman. I would like to have your permission, sir, to meet her."

"You know the new gymnasium at Georgia State? I'm the main donor. My little girl will be graduating in two years with high honors, and seeing as she may need an escort to the many festivities where she will be invited once she's on campus..." He studied the young man sternly. "I can arrange for you to meet her, Chucky, but keep in mind; she's pure as the driven snow."

"Indeed, sir." That's not what Chucky had heard about the princess, but his idea for a consulting firm was about to take wing with Mr. von Campe's help, and he knew he was falling in love with the financier's daughter at that very moment. True love often happened like that, in a flash of light that sparkled from the diamond earrings Jackson had given his little girl just before the pageant.

****

When the winner was announced, Terri Sue Ellen managed to look humble by lowering her eyes and making an "O" shape out of her mouth to indicate surprise...just like her Aunt Victoria had showed her. That was important information to have, and no matter how many lessons her father had insisted she take, that kind of advice hadn't been available.

Raising her eyes up, her chin followed, tilted, and she posed. Blinking innocently, she graciously accepted the two dozen exquisite peach-colored roses. *Ah have arrived!*

A wooden crate, trimmed with a huge bow and filled with perfect peaches, was rolled ceremoniously onto the stage. The fourteen defeated contestants lined up on either side of the runway to allow their queen to walk among them as she handed each girl a rose and a peach, which was the tradition.

When the losers filed off stage, their smiles disappeared.

Betsy spoke in a low voice, "Someone ought to re-think that idea of fruit and flowers. It's stupid." She tossed her souvenir into the wastebasket. "Ah hate peaches. They're sweet and sticky." She looked at Maribel and Annie Lou. "Didn't ah tell y'all who'd win?"

"Well." Annie Lou spoke up, "Lannie Beth is the runner up. I like her." She studied her peach. "These attract flies." She tossed the fruit into a garbage bag. "Ah hope Lannie Beth gets to do somethin'."

"She won't. Terri Sue Ellen von Campe is going to work it for all it's worth—right down to meetin' the Governor and preformin' all her civic duties... and then some. If y'all catch mah drift."

"Oh now. We don't know that for sure." Annie Lou looked toward the other girls for support.

Maribel nodded in agreement. "We mustn't judge too harshly. Did y'all see that gorgeous guy sittin' with Mr. von Campe? That's Chucky Covington."

"Oh, I know Chucky alright." Betsy rolled her eyes. "We dated a couple of times. He's boring as a brick but comes from moneyed parents up in Illinois. He has some crazy idea about startin' an international consultin' firm." She snored, "Like someone is goin' pay him to tell them what to do. Ah declare." Lifting her shoulders in an exasperated manner, she continued, "Those boys from the North are real full of shit."

Maribell gasped, "Ladies don't talk like that." She looked distressed. "You mean boys from the North are full of themselves."

"No. I mean full of shit."

"Oh mah goodness, girls." Annie Lou smiled weakly. "It does seem that Mr. von Campe smiled fondly at Chucky, and that's where we should leave it. The von Campe's do come from a European royalty, and we should treat them with respect."

"Oh fiddle." Betsy looked bored and continued, "That's just a bucket of hogwash. It was something her daddy made up to impress her mama, and now he's stuck with it."

Annie Lou moved toward the dressing table and looked into the mirror.

"Ah got'ta put on my happy face. Mah momma's going to be here any minute, and ah have to act like everythin's alright."

"Everythin' is alright. Unzip me, will ya?" Betsy wiggled out of her snowy evening gown and reached for a pair of jeans. "Soon as our moms are over their disappointment, y'all want to go get a beer and hustle up some guys?"

Chicago, Illinois
Robert and Evelyn Covington Residence

Evelyn Covington, dressed in a stylish St. John knit, drummed her fingers on the arm of her chair. "I have a committee meeting for the Arts Guild in an hour, but I want to take a few minutes to discuss our son. I cannot believe that he's smitten with a southern woman who talks in circles and makes the title of Peach Queen sound regal."

"We only talked to her the one time." Her husband, Robert, sounded busy. "It's difficult to judge someone with limited contact."

"Please. Don't try my patience. She was awful."

"Yes." He looked up and nodded. "The truth is I'm as disappointed as you, my dear. But there is little we can do."

"Oh! He's just impressed with her silly accent. And, mark my words, Robert; she probably screws like a little bunny. There, I've said it!"

"Well, when he tires of the sex, his southern belle will be history."

"I hope you're right. Besides I've talked with Andrea Williams, and her daughter, Tiffany, is a lovely young lady, holds a degree in pre-law, and is a sophisticated girl...an ideal companion for Chucky. I think we should encourage him to meet Tiffany next time he's in Chicago."

Santa Cruz, California
Melissa and Harm

The relationship with Melissa and Harm became exclusive within days of their meeting. Harm rolled with the punches, and his ability to sort through life's challenges impressed her. She learned he'd graduated the year before and was back on campus because he was a guest speaker for a class in journalism.

His work was taken seriously. The *San Francisco Chronicle* paid for his satire on political issues, the *Monterey Herald* published his "Save the Whale" series, and he was actually writing an article for *National Geographic*. She couldn't ever remember being so impressed.

Plus she loved the way he looked at her with a sultry side glance that gave her a happy flip-flop feeling. Though his steely grey eyes combined the many shades of clouds on a stormy day, she felt summer breezes and winter evenings melt together when their eyes meet. She was in love. There was no question about that.

Atlanta, Georgia
Terri Sue Ellen and Chucky

Chucky had escorted Terri Sue Ellen to the Autumn Ball, yet another gala event at Georgia State. Her father had given him the go ahead to ask for her hand in marriage, and this was the night. He was excited; after all, the sex was great, and she was enthusiastic about whatever he wanted to do. Although, when he really thought about it, she was the one who came up with the new ideas.

While he waited patiently for her to change out of her formal dress in their rented hotel room, he thought that only if his folks had liked his southern belle, his life would be so much easier. He wondered briefly what they would think when they found out he planned to marry her?

Terri Sue Ellen emerged from the bathroom wearing a silky purple teddy and a boozy smile. Thoughts of his parents vanished as his heart skipped a beat. She walked toward him swinging a bottle of vodka and then she reached up, slipping a thin ribbon off her shoulder. "Do ya like that?" He nodded as she continued, "Chucky, ah always say liquor is quicker. Do ya want a sip?" She moved seductively to where he was sitting and placed her legs on either side of him. "Ah got me a hankerin' to see your parts. Would it be okay if ah had me a peek?"

Taking a generous swallow, she passed the vodka to him, and her hands reached down to his trousers. She worked her magic and was rewarded quickly.

"Well now," she exclaimed, fluttering her eyelashes, "How do you do, Big Daddy?"

"Will you marry me, sugar?"

"Of course."

His tuxedo pants were on the floor, and he had to reach down to fumble for the ring.

"You know, Chucky, ah love you right down to the very crease in your trousers, even if they are a bit muddled right now." She nibbled his ear and asked, "You goin' tell your parents about me plannin' our weddin', aren't you?"

"I'll call them first thing in the morning."

Yes, she thought. V*ictory!*

He slipped the ring on her finger and reached for the laces that would allow her breasts to spring free.

Chicago, Illinois
Robert and Evelyn Covington Residence
Next day

Evelyn's eyes narrowed in anger as she paced across the antique Sarouk rug. "I can hardly think about anything I'm so upset! Chucky never gave Tiffany Williams a chance. He's going to marry that southern bimbo!"

Robert tried to sound reasonable. "He's a grown man, and we have to support his choice of a wife."

"Excuse me! This Terry Sue Ellen von Campe is a ridiculous excuse for a bride-to-be, and, well, I dislike saying this, Robert, but I believe she already has a drinking problem. You saw how she lapped up the wine when Chucky flew her to Chicago to meet us." Evelyn used her hand to make a small gesture illustrating her point. "Not only does he want to marry the peach queen, for God's sake, but he will not be here to spend Thanksgiving with us, which I point out, we have always shared as a family, no matter where we've been. Instead, he chooses to spend the holiday with that hussy. What do they serve down there... pop tarts and peanut butter?"

"Yes, dear. Washed down with moonshine."

She pursed her lips. "You're not funny."

"Nor am I going to argue with you."

She sat down and sighed heavily. "I just can't believe this is happening to our family."

Her husband removed his glasses and rubbed the bridge of his nose. "I was hoping the job that I recommended down in Atlanta would provide Chucky with the opportunity of meeting new ladies, seeing that he seems so intrigued with southern girls." His face showed displeasure, and he continued, "But I was wrong."

"This is rubbish." Evelyn wound her fingers through the pearls that graced the neckline of her black dress. "We didn't have a chance to say a thing. He was telling us his decision, not asking our opinion."

Robert nodded. "I'm guessing Jackson Beauregard von Camp is involved, and that means there's money on the table."

"What? Our family has plenty of money. Chucky lacks for nothing. We can give him whatever he wants."

"Except for his southern belle."

Evelyn snorted, "So buy him a hooker with a drawl."

"He already has one."

Atlanta, Georgia
von Campe Residence
Same Day

"Oh, Daddy. Ah surly am the happiest girl alive. Ah swear it." Holding out her left hand, Terri Sue Ellen enjoyed looking at her diamond engagement ring. "Why, when Chucky called his parents this morning, they were so thrilled they could hardly speak.

"And ah'm so excited. The wedding can be at the big church or on location, somewhere wonderful, of course. As long as it's big and important and everyone comes and I get lots of presents." She sat down and fanned her face.

"Nellie," Jackson turned to the housekeeper. "Get my little princess some lemonade, and I'll have a shot of bourbon over ice."

"Yes, Mister von Campe. I'll do it right away." Leaning heavily on her cane, she moved slowly toward the kitchen.

"She's a devoted employee."

"Yes, daddy," she replied impatiently. "Ah know all that." Smiling brightly, she continued, "Ah want my wedding dress to be from Paris, France, and ah want to have seven bridesmaids and they all wear colors that ah pick out, like grey or dark blue, so ah am the star of the show, all dressed in snowy white, lookin' pure and virginal." She took a breath and kept talking, "Ah will carry white Cali lilies and creamy gardenias with bright peach colored roses so everyone sees me a'comin'. Just like in my pageant days."

Watching his cigar ash, Jackson thought of the money he had loaned Chucky Covington for his business plan. It was a sound investment in many ways. He looked up at his daughter with a smile. "I've been thinking that Chucky...even though it's a good name, it's got to be changed. Here's a fact; take note now. Right along with starting his new consulting firm, the boy needs a man's name on the letterhead. I propose it be Charles. Of course, you can call him Chuck in private, just no more Chucky. We clear on that?"

I will have a gown with a very low cleavage. Ah'll be wearing a push-em-up bra, and ah'll tighten my straps so it looks like ah'm gon'na bounce right out of my bodice.

"What do you think, princess?"

"Huh?"

"I was saying, and this is important, now. You need to listen up." He looked at the beautiful young woman sitting across from him.

Ah will make penises wag and, oh yes, hearts a flutter 'cause that's the way ah want to do it. She smiled sweetly.

"Princess, sometimes you don't pay close attention."

Terri Sue Ellen snapped back to reality. "Oh, yes ah do, daddy. Ah pay real close attention to what has a direct effect on me."

"Good! I'm glad to know that. And you, my princess, will be on the letterhead, too."

"How nice." She looked toward the house. "Wherever is my lemonade? Ah am simply parched."

"Mr. Jackson, sir, there's a phone call for you."

"I'll be right back princess."

"Why, Nellie, you are getting to be as slow as molasses. Ah need me a drink, pronto." Terri Sue Ellen sounded irritable while she fumbled in her purse for lip-gloss. "Daddy had to take that call, but he'll be back." She glanced at Nellie who was leaning on her cane and smiled kindly. "You need to get more rest. Put your big ol' swollen feet up. Take some of your extra weight off your crippled limbs. Let Sassy do more work."

"Why now. I'll be givin' that idea some thought, baby girl." Nellie moped at her face. "It shore is a steamy one today."

She looked longingly at the fan that was blowing the outside air around. It was aimed at the two people who sat in the deep shade of the veranda where soft cushions nestled in the wicker chairs. She shifted her weight toward her good hip in hopes of reducing some discomfort. Maybe she should ask Mr. Von Campe for a small fan to put in the servants quarters.

"Nellie, are you day dreamin'? Ah want you to dash back into the kitchen and fetch me vodka and lemonade. Be quick now."

"Right away, baby girl. Do you want a glass of ice with it?"

"No. Ah will have it straight up today. Thank you so much." She applied the bright peach gloss to her heart shaped lips and smiled. "That's better. I was parched, and mah lips were dry." *Plus my knees hurt. Ah got 'ta toughen up some 'cause if ah had stayed down just a little while longer last night ah could have asked Chucky for a diamond bracelet to go with my ring.* She waved at the elderly housekeeper. "Off you go. Don't dawdle none."

Nellie moved slowly, passing Jackson as he joined his daughter who continued to talk about her wedding plans.

"Nellie looks tired," he interrupted. "Have you noticed that, princess?"

"Well, yes ah have, daddy. Ah just had a talk with her about how she should get more rest."

Jackson sipped his drink and nodded. "That was kindly. Keeping true to your good nature."

Her drink arrived, and she sipped it eagerly. "Such pressure. Oh mah goodness! I shall of course, rise above it, but ah'm not sure that Nellie is up for this much plannin'.'"

"We'll get you a real wedding coordinator, and you mustn't worry about a thing."

"You are so smart, daddy." She blinked helplessly at her father.

Jackson cleared his throat. "But, let us remember that there is Charles at the alter waiting to take your hand in holy matrimony. That will be the highlight of your day, correct?"

"Of course, daddy. When can ah start shoppin' for my gown?"

Santa Cruz, California

The time had come for Harm to meet Melissa's parents. They were driving to her parent's home in Big Sur, and she realized that, up to that point, their life had not included family members, but that was going to change. In the car, she grew pensive about her explanation of the world he was about to enter.

"It's different you know?" She began thoughtfully, "Big Sur is a state of mind. It's filled with peace and beauty and folklore."

"I'm a journalist, Melissa. That's a state of mind." He laughed and added, "I'm sure that folklore fits in there somewhere."

Melissa grinned. "My maternal grandmother, Grannie June, came from a long line of Cherokee story tellers, going all the way back to the late 1890's when a distant relative ran off with an Indian brave whose father was the tribal historian . A child was born, and the ability for recording legends and history was passed to the baby. Now, mind you, Grannie June came along much later, but she was a descendent of that baby, so folklore was in her blood."

"Yes." Harm agreed with a nod. "Some abilities are passed on to family members."

She leaned over to kiss his cheek. "My mother was born in Monterey but after her father passed away, it was just mother and daughter. Grannie June decided Big Sur was the place to rear a young girl and moved there in the 1930's when the winding journey along the cliffs was only a dirt lane called the Coast Road.

"This story had several translations, but the mythology is as old as the land itself. Grannie June favored the one I'm about to tell you...the Birth of Highway One. Now bear in mind, this could be fiction, but who knows for sure?"

Lifting her hands in front of her, she spread her fingers out as if warming them in front of a fire and began. "Grannie June would ask for a blessing from the moon and the stars then burn sage to allow the wise spirits to speak."

She smiled at Harm's profile. "I learned that story-telling requires the correct mood, so I ask that you imagine a foggy summer night with a musty, minty aroma filling the air. Listen to the small drum that's sounding out a peaceful rhythm in the background." She lowered her voice, encouraging a sacred ambiance to fill the car. "Big Sur was chiseled out of the earth to preserve the intangible quality that is called life. It was the combination of water, sun, earth, forest, and heaven.

"Nature cherished the blue green waters that were bathed by her golden light. Essence ruled the cliffs whose bluffs, rising majestically above the sea, were crowned with nature's shades of ochre. Hillsides dipped into meadows of flowers creating a beauty that bonded with emerald forests where treetops touched the sky.

"Through their love, Nature and Essence produced great joy so the Universe bestowed upon them a gift called Spirit...an entity who could pass between heaven and Earth. It was the only place so honored.

"After many centuries of devoted care, Spirit grew lonely and longed for a mate. When mankind approached her with a pledge of everlasting love, she allowed him to build a path so he could enter her domain. But once he saw the beauty that she had coveted unto herself, he forgot his promise and set about unmasking her purity so that all could see what had been hidden from their eyes.

"Explosives of terrifying power were carried down the dirt road. The sun hid behind clouds in dread as Spirit shuddered with man's betrayal. Nothing could save Nature or Essence, the beauty of their hills and meadows, forests and water. Nothing could preserve Spirit's passageway to heaven.

"The men rammed dynamite deep within the granite of the cliffs, and the Earth screamed in pain as soil was ripped from her womb, again and again. Machines pounded into the knolls, blowing them open, destroying the natural paradise with such brutality that Spirit wept in torment, but to no avail. For out of the slaughter, Highway One was born, and the intangible quality of Big Sur was lost forever.

"Now Spirit continues to search for a new corridor to heaven, and each spring weeps for her mistake and sends the gift of rain to the land in hopes of forgiveness."

Harm inhaled sharply. "Whoa, that story must have scared the hell out'ta you as a kid!"

"Oh, it did!" Melissa blinked and stared out the car window. "If you can imagine, Grannie June was talking about 1937, when the Coast Road became a major highway. She nodded solemnly. "To a little girl listening to an old woman tell the tale, it was really scary!"

"But the truth was, with the completion of the highway, a different life style opened in Big Sur. Restaurants and hotels were built to accommodate the new industry of tourism."

"So what you're saying," Harm's face creased in amusement as he tipped his head, "is that Grannie June's story had merit?"

She returned his smile with a playful look. "Big Sur was a part of the modern world, and everyone had to live with it."

"You've told me that your family's land remained natural."

"My relatives knew that you couldn't stop progress but to not grow was to die." She smiled faintly.

"When my mom was a young artist showing her oil paintings at Nepenthe's restaurant, she met my dad. They stayed and talked after the show and long into the evening, saying they fell in love as the October moon settled over the western sky. They agreed that night to be caregivers to the land that my father's family had inherited in Big Sur. Over the years they've worked with organizations on the state and federal levels, placing restrictions on building." She drew in a breath. "And, of course, there is Grannie June." She glanced at Harm sideways and grinned. "Who knows what stories she would have spun if we let developers take over?"

He reached for her hand.

"It all worked out for the best." She laced her fingers through his, thinking. *Now the sharp curves and imposing hills slow the speeding cars and, while most drivers look out to sea for the view, if they pull off the road at the right spot and look down the ocean side of the highway, they would be charmed by my family's house that sits proudly on a rocky precipice of land.*

"I should tell you about my parents." Melissa smiled as she looked at Harm. "They're not big city people. They're country folk. You know that my father is a wood carver." Raising her chin, she took a deep breath. "I didn't give that enough emphasis. Although my dad makes a few pieces for some local galleries, his furniture is sold throughout the country."

"That's cool."

"Yes, it is." Giving herself a moment for reflective thought, she plunged ahead. "Then there's our house itself. I'll paint a picture for you." Swinging her hands in a circle, she began. "I grew up in a stone house made from natural rocks found in Big Sur. Wooden forms were constructed for support, and cement was poured between the rocks to hold everything in place. This was started back in the 1830's so there's been lots of repair and many remodels over the years. "

Their youthful vitality filled the interior of the small car as she continued, "The first thing you'll notice is the large wrap-around porch with an extended overhang. It leads to the front door that my grandfather carved from native redwood."

She smiled at him, wondering what to say next. "We have a swan sofa. It's sort of cool."

Feeling a silly grin spread across her face, she continued, "Oh heck, I might as well just come out and tell you the whole truth because my grandfather actually built the sofa in the living room."

Settling back into the seat of Harm's Volkswagen Beetle, she took a breath and explained that her grandfather had met his wife by a lake in Scotland where swans were the main attraction. As a wedding gift, he'd created a sofa that boasted gigantic swan necks for both arms.

Sneaking a sideways glance, she noted that Harm was listening attentively. "As a child I loved to stroke the swooping curves of the sofa ends. They have a graceful arch and..." She used her hand to sweep out an airy description.

"I'm looking forward to meeting them," he joked.

"Sarah and Sally." She blushed and added quietly, "I named them as a kid." Her words filled with affection, "Grandpa carved lots of feathers into the back of the sofa." Pushing her thought home, she added emphatically, "It can't be moved because he overcompensated. You see it's too big to leave through the front door so we consider it a family heirloom. I like to think of it as the forerunner to the five-piece sectional, except it's all one piece."

"Hey." Harm tipped his head in thought. "That's sort of neat."

A mischievous expression settled over her face, and she added, "Here's what you need to know. And, by the way, I don't give this information out to just anyone."

"Appreciate the heads up," he replied teasingly.

"Truth is the cushions are very deep so you need to be prepared when you sit down; otherwise, you really sink into the seat. And if you try to pull forward to sit on the edge, you end up on a wooden support. Think you can remember that?"

****

As Harm and Melissa continued their drive down the coast, they passed the city of Marina where golden shafts of sunshine rolled across the sand dunes. A light breeze blew softly as seagulls glided within the pockets of air.

Harm lowered his window. "It's a beautiful day. I'm glad we're doing this." He joked," I got'ta meet your folks eventually, right?"

Melissa tossed him a look bordering on amusement

"Here's a question for you," Harm said. "Stewart is a good Scottish name, and that came from your dad. You have the red hair of the Irish but skin tone that can take some sun. Let's say my intellectual curiosity is piqued."

"My mother is Irish and German, and my dad is Scottish and Mexican.

Lots of nationalities in my family going back to the McPhee brothers...young boys with a sea faring spirit. They left Scotland in 1808 and arrived in the Gulf of Mexico at the Port of Veracruz. Spanish was spoken on the ship, and the brothers learned fast because they knew they'd be on their own very soon." She continued with a shrug, "Secretly they were looking for gold, so once the cargo was offloaded, and they were paid, they jumped ship. "The boys were only twelve and fourteen...filled with dreams."

She uncrossed her legs and attempted to stretch them out as she told him how the brothers learned that gold was difficult to locate and dangerous to mine.

"The brothers had been moving around for two years. They'd traveled the inland trails, first going north, then west, almost 300 miles. It was September of 1810, and they were living in the small hill town of Dolores when Father Miguel Hidalgo made his famous cry for independence. They agreed with the idea of freedom for all and made the decision to join with the Mexicans and fight against the Spanish in the Mexican War of Independence.

"When the war was over in 1821, the brothers were rewarded for their service and given land with the understanding that they were to maintain the new authority of Mexico." She spoke softly, "The McPhees left with their families in the 1830's to settle the acreage in Big Sur. My Scottish and Mexican relatives represent blended people of strength and courage who mark my past."

****

The forests of Monterey lined the highway, and cars slowed as they passed the turn-off to Carmel. Melissa smiled. "There's always lots of traffic. Just stay on Highway One and head toward Big Sur."

Chapter Three

For the better part of the month, Jackson had been listening to wedding plans. Even though it wasn't his favorite subject, he understood his daughter's organizational skills were somewhat lacking, so he had to stay abreast of all events, and that included keeping his princess on-point and happy.

"Oh daddy, ah so want Aunt Victoria there for me, but we all know she can't handle too much anxiety. Of course, keepin' true to our southern tradition of havin' a female family member with the bride, she can be my trusted companion and beloved advisor." *And we can share champagne, which is what ah do believe people drink at weddins' as well as hard liquor and, well, whatever.*

"Good idea, princess. We want to honor and respect the purity of your virtue."

Terry Sue Ellen smiled into her drink. "Daddy, do you need bourbon? Ah was about to send Nellie for a touch more vodka."

"A fine idea." He reached for the old bell. Its abrasive ringing reached the kitchen where Nellie rolled her eyes and painfully rose to her feet.

****

Jackson puffed on his cigar and wondered if his little girl understood the wealth she was marrying into.

"Perhaps, princess, we should invite Charles' parents to spend a long weekend with us. We could eat al fresco on the south lawn under the big magnolia trees. Spread out linen tablecloths and have the servants prepare southern specialties.

"Oh! How they love swanky events!" Terri Sue Ellen clapped

enthusiastically. "What can be more fun than getting his mama down here for a big ol' formal picnic in the heat of the winter when they're freezing up there in Chicago land.

"We'll call it my engagement party! What a brilliant idea. Ah'll buy a new dress...a flashy red one with tiny ribbon straps that fall off my shoulders.

"Even Aunt Victoria could attend. I'll invite all my friends; well maybe they won't all be friends, but they do come from respected families with lots of money and influence, just like Chucky's parents."

"Charles."

"Of course. Charles. Sorry, daddy." She fluttered her eyelashes and continued. "We'll have the servants dressed in uniforms and notify the newspaper so they can do proper press."

Looking at his daughter's flushed face, Jackson paused, "What are his parents names?"

"Huh?"

"His parents have names, princess. What are they?"

"Oh, goodness me, ah only met them once, and it was cold and drafty. Ah have no idea what their names are."

Jackson smiled nervously at his daughter.

"Ah know." She snapped her fingers and replied cheerfully, "That was a test, wasn't it daddy? Well, ah have the answer. Ah'll ask Chucky, I mean Chuck, what his parents' names are." She sipped the icy vodka and lemonade. "Generally he calls them mother and father." She sighed, "Ah suppose we'll have to know more than that."

"Tell you what, princess, why don't you let me find out his parent's names and you can memorize them?" Jackson looked long and hard at his lovely daughter thinking it was a good thing for all of them that Charles found her so endearing just the way she was.

Of course, Jackson knew the names of Charles' wealthy parents; he had looked into their financials and was very pleased with what he'd learned. He winked at his princess who appeared to be practicing her smile as she gazed across the long stretch of green lawn.

Big Daddy is what ah call my Chucky's private parts, and as long as ah make him happy, he won't care whether ah know his momma's name or not. And that's a fact!

"See here, princess," her father interrupted her thoughts. "We should be talking about a wedding present for you and Charles."

Tipping to the left, she replied, "Ah think ah would like a sports car. Bright shiny yellow with plastic covers on the white seats. They're easier to slip across."

"Well, I was thinking more along the lines of something that would be longer lasting and more meaningful. How about the deed to our family home?"

"You're so right, daddy."

"Let that be a lesson, princess. Always permit the man in your life to finish his thought before you interject your opinion." He chuckled. "It makes us feel smart."

Atlanta, Georgia
Investment Firm

Charles felt smart whenever he thought about his fiancée. It was the time he had to spend at the job that his father got him that he resented.

His father, who believed a solid business plan should be put forth to secure money for an investment, didn't understand that his son had already presented his future father-in-law with a conceptual plan that detailed the founding of his company, Tech World International. Jackson had gone through the spreadsheets with a fine tooth comb, making suggestions and promising numerous prestigious accounts with the understanding that his daughter was a part of the deal.

After all, Charles thought, he thoroughly enjoyed daddy's princess. Her creative expertise in the bedroom fascinated him, and when she told him he was her "male machine" and whispered she wanted to see the General, he was thrown into a state of desire he never knew existed. And she always said "thank you" afterward. What a woman! It just didn't get better than that.

His mother had advised him that he would soon tire of her southern ways, but he doubted it. He looked around his cubicle in disgust and knew that very soon he'd have his own corner office and his dream of a consulting firm would become a reality.

Big Sur, California
Arriving at the Stone House

"We're almost there, so now's the time to tell you that the oldest part of the house leans to one side." Harm raised an eyebrow, and she quickly continued, "Oh, not a lot, but just..." she held up two fingers to indicate an inch, "this much."

"I can help. I'm a bit of a carpenter," he kidded, "when I'm not working."

"Good to know," she answered with humor. "Because dad's been trying to fix that for years. He'll appreciate your input."

"Should have told me earlier. I would have brought my tool box."

She wiggled her index finger in warning, "You should also know that very old souls linger within the rooms of the stone house. You can feel them move about in the shady corners of early evening." Peeking at Harm, she asked tongue-in-cheek, "That doesn't frighten you, does it?"

"Nope."

"I didn't think it would bother you." She smiled. "But it was a test," she added mischievously.

"Did I pass?" He bantered back.

"Of course!

****

Vernon and Lillian Stewart sensed from the moment they met Harm that he was a significant person in their daughter's life.

As Harm took in the stone house, his eyes wandered curiously around the rooms. The cave-like feel was warm and secure, and he could see old stones though the interior walls of the house, reminding him of fortifications in an ancient castle. A fresh coat of whitewash had been added, giving a feeling of greater space.

As they moved into the parlor, Melissa pointed to an old spinning wheel. "That crossed the Great Plains in a covered wagon. It belonged to great-great grandma Lillian who used to sing in saloons in San Francisco."

"Hey!" Harm grinned.

"My mother was named after her."

"I can't sing a note." Lillian smiled and offered them a plate topped high with grilled cheese and tomato sandwiches. A bowl of home-made potato chips sat next to a bottle of wine.

Melissa sat on the swan sofa and wiggled into a comfortable position. Harm joined her, sinking into the cushions. *It's like a giant pillow.* He settled in and grinned.

Lillian exchanged a look with her husband and smiled at Harm. "Our daughter gave you a heads-up, didn't she?"

"Yes, she did." As he scooted forward, he noticed many short tables of various heights with weirdly shaped legs.

Melissa laughed. "As you can see, my relatives left behind a variety of handmade furniture. Most of the tables had indentations to hold small objects.

"Now, as a child, I was less inhibited than most children, and if I spotted a rock that I liked, I picked it up, washed it off, painted it, and presented it as a gift." She nodded at her mother and continued, "She had to put them somewhere, so if you reach into the pockets you may find some of my early work."

Harm comfortably kept his balance on the sofa. "I think I got the hang of it." Looking at Melissa, he nodded jokingly, "I'm doing okay. No need to worry about me." He reached for a sandwich. "Thanks." He smiled at Lillian. "These look great."

"Oh, I'm not worried about you." Melissa laughed, "You're doing just fine."

"Told ya I could handle the sofa." Looking at Lillian, he added, "These sandwiches are on sourdough. It's my favorite."

"Good." She turned to smile at her daughter. "You brought me a hungry young man."

"He's always hungry," Melissa joked. She followed Harm's attention as he focused on the stools. "They were early endeavors to create the perfect chair leg. You understand this took place over time?"

"Yes." He wiped his fingers on a napkin. "You can't rush a job like that."

Lillian nudged the bowl of chips toward him.

Vernon laughed, "You better have some of those chips while they're warm."

Melissa nodded at the chairs as Harm reached for another sandwich. He added, "I'm gon'na bet the chairs aren't all carved from the same pattern."

"You're so smart."

"I'm going to check out those indentions in the short tables. You know that. Right?" His head tipped to the side as he grinned and turned toward her mother. "Those were great sandwiches, Mrs. Stewart. And the homemade chips were the best. Thank you!"

"It was my pleasure, and please call me Lillian."

"I'll show you our home." Vernon got up. "Dining room's through these doors. My wife has combined my inherited family dishes with hers." He paused looking for the right words, "It's a collection that's...overwhelming."

Melissa moved toward the tall glass fronted cabinets. "Come have a look." She indicated delicate blue and white dessert plates. "They made it across the prairie wrapped in petticoats. Can you imagine that?" Opening the door on the old cabinet, she pointed. "See, it's just like I told you. Here is etched glass from Scotland mixed in with French wine goblets, and they both arrived in tall sailing ships. The hand-blown glass from Mexico made it to Big Sur in a cart pulled by a donkey named Roberta. And here..." She opened a drawer. "We have pieces of heavy flatware from Scotland, and there is still a golden glaze on the handles of the soup spoons. It's like a meeting of the United Nations."

Vernon added, "The ladies set a fine table."

Harm reached over to brush at a stray hair that had come loose from Melissa's braid. Their eyes met, and he felt a rush of deep emotion flood through him. *I'm looking at a lifetime of happiness, with the woman that I love. And the few eccentricities fit my style!*

Lillian smiled. "Be lots of people to feed tonight...family and friends. They'll all enjoy meeting Harm. You know that you're the first young man our daughter has brought home?"

"I did not know that." He leaned toward Melissa and whispered nervously, "You didn't tell me there would be a lot of people here."

"I know," she murmured sweetly. "I didn't want to scare you."

Chicago, Illinois
Robert and Evelyn Covington Residence

Before the engagement party, Charles flew back to Chicago to tell his parents about his new company and how it had been founded. They'd firmly joined forces and pointed out that, even though his fiancée was sweetly southern and wealthy, she wasn't all that bright. He'd been taken back... along with horny and sexy, those were excellent qualities in a wife.

His mother offered him a sherry. "Son, just because a woman is, how shall I phrase this, agreeable now, doesn't mean she won't become a liability later. Will you at least think about what I'm saying, Chucky?"

"It's Charles, mom."

"Very well." She continued, but her words were ignored until his father took a turn, expressing himself distinctly.

"Taking her father's money was a mistake. It ties his daughter into the company, and, as we have pointed out, Terri Sue Ellen is not, well, she's not an ideal business partner. In a few years, you could have your own firm, under your leadership with your own funding. Let's see if we can't re-visit that decision."

"No, dad. It's done, and I'm pleased with the results. Tech World International is alive, and my job at the investment firm in Atlanta is history."

Charles' thinking was clear; his folks would come around. After all, he was their only child. He stood. "I've got to get to back to the airport. I'll see you both in two weeks at the von Campe home for our engagement party. Remember picnics are big events down there. So, mom, dad," he felt uncomfortable, but knew it had to be said. "Try not to act stuffy, okay? And, mom, get a sun dress. That's what women wear in the South. You'll be meeting lots of hospitable folks. They're all happy for me."

Big Sur, California
Wedding Day

Harm formally asked Melissa's father for her hand in marriage on the day she graduated from UC Santa Cruz. It was decided that the ceremony would be at her parents' home.

The brilliance of the September day spilled golden light through the bedroom windows as Lillian helped Melissa dress. "Here, let me help you." She fastened the tiny pearl buttons and turned her daughter toward the mirror. "Beautiful."

"Oh mom, I'm so happy I could wear your wedding gown. The satin still flows in swirls and makes me feel like a bride. Even the puffed sleeves are perfect." Her voice caught, "And the locket from great-great grandmother Lillian is a gift from long ago. I feel so honored."

"This is a day of celebration." Her mother hugged her. "Your dad and I wish you and Harm a lifetime of love."

****

The afternoon breeze was warm as Melissa held her father's arm and felt herself float into the day. Harm reached for her hand. He looked into her father's eyes imparting a promise to cherish and protect his daughter. Vernon bowed his head in acknowledgement and moved toward Lillian. He held his wife's arm, escorting her across the rocky soil of the bluff to the first row of draped white chairs.

Harm and Melissa turned to face the minister. The sky was a blue bowl filled with soft clouds that dropped into an endless sea. A hush gathered over the wedding guests as the ocean splashed harmoniously beneath the cliffs. The couple read their vows, and the sounds of the day blended with the melodious tones of a flute, soothing to the soul. Then, a marriage was made.

Atlanta, Georgia
Wedding Day

It was the most expensive garden wedding in Atlanta's history. Jackson Beauregard von Campe beamed as his only child repeated the words after the minister. He also sighed with relief that she'd gotten them correct, for she and his sister had sipped a bit too much champagne before the ceremony.

While the guests mingled at the end of the reception line, eagerly waiting for Peach Bellini's, their conversation centered on the bride's appearance. She was indeed a vision to behold in her sparkling tiara and upswept hairdo with spiral curls trailing down the sides of her face. Her chiffon wedding dress overflowed with nosegays of organdy flowers and featured a wide satin sash that hugged her tiny waist. The ends tied into an enormous bow in the center of her back, and the long ribbon streamers trailed down her gown, ending at a wire hoop.

It was agreed that Terri Sue Ellen resembled Cinderella but had cleverly added a deeply low-cut bodice to accentuate one of her better features, thus succeeding in creating a noteworthy appearance.

Several people pointed out that even though the newly married couple made a stunning pair, if the groom bumped into her skirt, the hoop flared out, and everyone could see her white panties. While that could be considered blasphemous behavior, they all concurred that they were being wined and dined in fine style by her daddy, so it was only right they should forgive the profanity.

The bride smiled radiantly as she and her new husband began to move among the guests. Occasionally, her head would tip too far forward, and the glittering tiara would slide off center, giving Charles cause to push both his wife and her tiara back in place. The couple murmured all the right words to everyone, with the bride adding an occasional hand flutter to emphasize a point. It was so sweetly southern, Charles felt his heart melt, even though his mother narrowed her eyes at the annoying performance.

****

"Oh, my Lord," Evelyn snorted. "The bride looks outlandish in that Disneyland costume. Has she no taste?"

"She did pick Chuck," her husband replied logically.

Taking a deep breath, she faced him. "Yes, Robert, to my horror, she chose our son."

****

As the day wore on, Charles felt the need to assume a permanent position by his bride's side as she continued to flit about, handing wilted gardenias to the female guests. He explained to his parents that she was so petite even a small amount of champagne affected her equilibrium.

"She's drunk. You do know that." Evelyn turned to her husband as she fanned her face with a wedding program.

"Yes, dear." Robert replied patiently, "I do know that."

"This is ghastly."

He took his wife's arm. "Shall we socialize?"

"Absolutely not!"

Quietly, the Covingtons moved to the other side of the humid ballroom where an extravagant buffet was being set up.

Evelyn dabbed at her temples with a tissue. "This climate is awful. The heat is unbearable. Where is that breeze everyone is talking about?"

"It comes in the evening."

"And until then?"

He guided her toward by an open window where the scents of many blossoms permeated the area. "This will have to do."

Evelyn shook her head. "Honestly, among the many fragrances these southern women splash on their bodies and the sweet odor of their flowers, I think I'm nauseas."

"No. We can't leave yet." Robert tried a softer tone of voice. "The scent of gardenias is supposed to be intoxicating to your soul."

"Who told you that twaddle?"

"The bride's father."

"Rubbish!"

"Stay steady, dear." Robert smiled. "The day is almost over."

****

A photographer took pictures of the bride and groom in a gold gilded carriage as the guests added their approval with applause. Weddings were meant to be fun, and when the carriage was removed, the couple snuggled together on a board placed behind a one-sided plywood boat, painted white with gold trim. It was set up on an artificial lake with a scenic backdrop, and the people clapped again.

When the lake scene was dismantled, a white horse materialized. It whinnied and tossed its head as Charles climbed on. His bride was handed to him with great care. The wire hoop of her gown spread around the front of the saddle like an organdy cloud that had slipped from the sky

"I can't watch this nonsense anymore. Are all southern weddings this silly?" Evelyn's eyebrow arched, indicating her bad-temper.

"No," Robert replied calmly. "I believe the von Campe's have confused their royal background with a fairy tale."

"Really, Robert? Are you saying that because your new daughter-in-law resembles a story book character and our son is supposed to be her Prince Charming?"

"Yes."

Her voice turned cantankerous, "Have you noticed that her head has too much hair for her tiny body."

"I don't think you can hold that against her."

Evelyn tilted her glass of champagne and squinted at the happy couple. "A porcelain doll with green eyes, peachy-orange lips, and a stuffed body. Yes! That's what she looks like. Something that would come alive at night and eat you while you slept."

Robert paused in thought, not saying anything.

She clipped her words, "Don't toy with me."

He lifted two more champagne glasses from a passing waiter and passed one to his wife.

"Just look at the size of her breasts." Evelyn pointed discriminately. "She could fall forward at any time."

Robert shrugged. "Again, not her fault."

"They're pushed up so high they're spilling out the top." She sighed hopelessly. "Every man here is staring at them. God help our son when he figures it all out." Shaking her head, she asked, "Why is she wearing that tacky looking tiara?

"It's real, you know." Robert looked at his wife with empathy. "Her father gave it to her. She's his princess."

"Oh, for the love of God! When Sherman marched through Georgia, obviously he didn't get them all."

"Now Evelyn. Let's try to be positive. This is a wedding not the reenactment of the Civil War."

"And the humidity! Oh my Lord, how does anyone live like this?'"

Robert sighed. At least his son was happy. How long that would last was up for grabs.

****

The only downfall Terrie Sue Ellen saw was that they would be moving to Chicago because her father and Chucky had invested in a new skyscraper being built on North Wabash Avenue, and Chucky's company would be located there until they could build their own offices. And, oh yes, she must remember to call him Chuck now. Her father had reminded her of that several times. After all, the name made the man, and Chucky had a wimpy sound whereas Charles Terrance Covington, President of Tech World International, had a solid ring.

Of course, it was too bad that Evelyn and Robert Covington didn't appreciate her, but she'd work on them. Oh, she might have to pour it on like molasses if she was going to win over a northern family, but truth was she could do it, and very soon, his momma would be putty in her hands.

Santa Cruz, California

The first year of married life passed swiftly for Harm and Melissa. While she managed the McGregor Art Gallery in Santa Cruz, Harm free-lanced his journalist skills in numerous publications. They wanted a family, and when they were sure of her pregnancy, they decided to share the news with her parents when they drove down to Big Sur for Thanksgiving.

Big Sur, California
Thanksgiving Day

Lillian bustled around the room where a faded oriental carpet covered the old pine floor. Yards of creamy linen fabric had been spread over the marred surface of the old burl wood table. Hand-painted pottery, in an array of vivid colors, sat next to delicate rose shaped plates creating pleasing patterns in front of each chair.

Friends and relatives talked and joked. Offers of assistance were in abundance, and Lillian called back, "Thanks so much, but I just checked in the kitchen, and there were lots of folks helping out. I'll call when I need you."

Returning her attention to the table, she placed saucers under the old stoneware water pitchers. Pausing, she allowed the celebrations of other holidays to float through her mind. Many of her husband's relatives had sat at this table and left behind opinions and emotions. She smiled as she imagined their spirits sharing the day with her and her family. *Fantasy*, she mused. *But you never know for sure.*

Tilting her head, she let the thought idle for a moment before she began to light the numerous homemade candles. The flickering of golden light danced gently across the linen, adding warmth to the stone room.

The new neighbors, Pete and Alice Bailey, a young couple who had recently moved to Big Sur, had offered to bring flowers. Alice was busy arranging late fall roses in teacups and placing them among the candles. Lillian nodded. How thoughtful that no one had to look around a tall centerpiece to see a fellow diner.

Several women were in the kitchen helping with the food when Lillian entered. "Checked the table, lit the candles, and we're ready." Reaching for a brown broadcloth apron, she smiled as her nose picked up the savory aroma of roasting turkey and herbs. "Doesn't this kitchen smell good! Why don't you ladies start to round everyone up, and we'll think about eating real soon."

As the women left, Melissa and her mother exchanged smiles, "It's a good holiday, mom."

"My heart's happy." She handed a matching apron to her daughter. "Do you remember making these?"

"Sewing didn't represent my finest hour."

They laughed, and Lillian added, "As I recall, your first choice of color was a pale rose shade, but Aunt Helena told you that all the food stains would show so you decided on a muddy brown color. Very practical decision," she joked. "Here You'd best put it on so you don't spill the drippings on your good clothes when you make the gravy."

Slipping the large apron over her head, Melissa felt relaxed. "I made one for Aunt Helena, too. I wish that she could have been here, today."

"Oh, you know your aunt. She's in some foreign land eating God knows what," Lillian joked. "Maybe even wearing her apron. We'll hear all about it when she returns for Christmas, but, she did send this." Lillian opened a drawer and withdrew a picture frame that held a sheet of paper with elaborate lettering. "Hand-made. It's a disclaimer for anyone sitting on the sofa." She laughed and continued, "I'm almost temped to put it out, but everyone knows how to sit on the cushions without falling over."

Melissa joked, "And if they don't know, they learn fast."

Lillian eyed her daughter with a look of amusement. "I might get the sign out after we eat. Give everyone a good laugh."

"I love the swan sofa!" Melissa grinned, "I haven't met a soul who's complained about it. There's not another like it. It belongs right here in our family home."

"That it does." Lillian continued wistfully, "You know that our family is getting smaller." She took a breath. "Well, let's keep a happy thought, shall we? It's good that we have so many friends." She hugged Melissa warmly. "And most importantly, I'm so glad that you and Harm are here."

"Mom, what's your favorite time of year?"

"It's difficult to define a favorite part of the year when you live in a house that's perched on a cliff. Let me see if I have an answer for you." Looking through the windows, she spoke quietly, "I do think that November and December are exciting because the grey whales go down the coast. Of course, in March and April, they swim back with their babies." Her shoulders rose as she took a deep breath and released it slowly. "It's the windows that allow us to observe the beauty and rhythm of the seasons."

A movement of air brushed across the room, and Melissa nodded. "Spirits walking. Souls from the birth of Big Sur."

"Yes. That's probably true." A thoughtful expression lined Lillian's face, and she experienced a moment of sadness. "As much as I've enjoyed using the old family dishes, we may have to retire some of them; they're very fragile. I also see the older glassware is chipped in places."

They paused to listen to the November squall as it howled around the house. "Holidays bring out emotions that we keep inside all year." She kissed her daughter's cheek. "My thoughts are swaying within the spiral of the wind."

Smiling, Melissa added, "Aunt Helena would have said that."

"I miss her, too. Your dad's sister is quite a gal." Lillian took a deep breath and faced the kitchen. "Many good reflections are created around a meal. Today we'll tell our family stories over again and make new memories to add to them."

"Mom," Melissa glowed with happiness, "I wanted Harm and daddy here, but this moment is so perfect..." she rested her hands across her middle and smiled. "I'm three months pregnant."

"Oh my!" Lillian grasped her heart. "My child is going to have a baby." She hugged her daughter. "I'm so happy for you, and for Harm, and for me and your dad." Her eyes glistened and she reached for a paper towel. "These are tears of joy."

"I'm so excited!" Melissa put her head on her mom's shoulder. "Can I have one of those, too?" She blew her nose. "Harm is going to be such a good daddy."

Lillian held her daughter tightly. "A spring baby. A lovely season to welcome a child into the world."

She dabbed at her eyes again. "We have a house full of people all waiting to eat turkey and talk and share thoughts, and all I can think of is my new grandchild." Lillian sniffed. "How about that? It sure does make Thanksgiving special!" She dried her eyes and blew her nose. "Now, my baby, go get your dad and Harm, and have them come into the kitchen, and you tell us again. Because we have something to tell you, too."

Lillian tented the turkey with aluminum foil. She splashed water on her face and was reaching for another paper towel when Harm and Vernon entered the room.

"They have some wonderful news," she began as she dabbed at her eyes and moved next to her husband.

Harm pushed at his long hair, now tied in a ponytail, and put his other arm around Melissa. "You told her didn't you?"

"I did. But now you're here, and we can both tell them."

"Melissa is having a baby," he blurted out and grinned. "She's going to be a great mom. We're going to be parents!" He threw his arm around her. "Both of us. Together."

"Yup." She bobbed her head. "At the same time. What do you think of that?"

"My little girl is going to make me a grandpa!" Vernon exclaimed. "And you," he looked at Lillian. "You're going to be a grandma. Don't that beat all?"

Lillian nudged Vernon. "Might this be the time for our news?"

"Sure enough. One family starting and another moving on."

"What do you mean?" Melissa asked.

"Your mom and I have been looking at some houses in Carmel Valley. It's warmer and feels better on our old bones. Plus we'd like to take a trip or two while we still got the get-up and go to travel."

"What your daddy is trying to say is that it's time to deed the house over to you. If you want it?"

Melissa gasped as she turned to Harm, "Could we really live here?"

"I can work anywhere. You'll have to give up your job in Santa Cruz, but with the baby coming, you'll spend less time at the gallery, anyway."

Her voice took on a tone of wonderment, "I can paint every day. And I could get a part-time job at a gallery here in Big Sur." She reached for his hand and he squeezed back. "I love the stone house. I want our children to feel the joy I have for Big Sur."

Harm pulled her into his arms. "Yes, this is where we belong, and this is where our baby should grow up."

Lillian and Vernon nodded. Melissa fell into their arms while Harm watched with pride. Lillian reached out for him, and Vernon embraced them all.

The buzzer sounded. "That sound means the turkey is ready to be carved." Lillian wiped at her eyes again and took a breath. "Now all those folks who want to help can come back in and we'll get the food dished up." She turned to her daughter. "I want you and Harm to meet our newest neighbors...a young couple, Pete and Alice Bailey. She arranged the pretty flowers on the table. And I do believe that I heard she's going to have a baby so you girls will have lots to talk about. "Now we have lots of people to feed."

With that said, Thanksgiving dinner was underway.

Chicago, Illinois
Thanksgiving Day

When Charles learned that his wife was pregnant, he insisted that the holiday meal be catered at the Lake Michigan Commemorated Country Club where, many years ago, his grandfather had been among the founding families. While each colleague had secured the distinguished rights to the coveted membership with a generous gift, his grandfather had excelled by donating the land for the clubhouse.

Even though Charles employed a full-time cook and maid, he wanted Terri Sue Ellen to feel stress-free for Thanksgiving. Of late she'd been a bit cranky in her early pregnancy, and nothing made her feel better than being pampered by the staff at his family's private club.

****

Jackson Beauregard von Campe arrived the day before Thanksgiving with his sister, Victoria, and a small staff consisting of Nellie and Sassy. Charles had them ensconced in a fine hotel.

Terri Sue Ellen had swelled up quickly with her pregnancy, and she loved the attention she received. Her father made much-to-do about the soon-to-be new arrival, while her aunt, who had never married, lavished her with motherly advice while sipping a martini. No Thanksgiving turkey was going to upstage daddy's little princess.

Nellie had been put in a taxi and sent to the condo that morning to assist Terri Sue Ellen with dressing, as her personal maid had quit the day before. Nellie bravely ignored the ache of her arthritis as she rubbed the distended ankles of the princess before helping her select the correct shade of panty hose.

"Ah must look perfect. You understand that, right?" she leaned on Nellie as she pulled her panty hose over her swelling middle.

"Of course, I do." Nellie grimaced with the pain of the extra weight. "Here, let me help you. But lean on this chair. Old Nellie doesn't have the balance she used to."

"That's not fair!"

"Well, baby girl. It's true. Here" She pushed a side chair toward her and continued, "You also need to cut back on the salt some 'cause it'll puff you up."

Terri Sue Ellen popped several peanuts in her mouth. "Ah declare. This is just baby fat, not salt retention."

"And you shouldn't be having that glass of wine. Alcohol isn't good for a pregnant lady."

"Oh, for heaven's sake, Nellie! You don't understand anything. This is just wine, not alcohol." She backed away from the old housekeeper, looking down on her. "Ah have cravins'. Ah am with child." *And ah am very important!*

When the happy couple left for the club, Nellie shook her head in dismay and began to clean-up the dressing room that was strewn with shoes and clothes left in untidy piles. *That one never learned to pick up a thing. It's a blessin' that her daddy's rich and found her a husband who was willing to overlook her sloppy ways. Mmm-mm! Yes, it is!*

****

Nellie joined Sassy later in the day, and they ordered soup from room service. After all, servants didn't join the family for holiday meals—everyone knew that. But Sassy had Victoria's secret stash of vodka so she and Nellie enjoyed a Thanksgiving drink from glasses they found in the bathroom.

Sassy asked, "How was Terri Sue Ellen?"

"Oh Lordy, spoiled as ever."

"Is she getting on any better with Mr. Charles parents?"

"I don't think so. Last week they told him they couldn't make the big Thanksgiving dinner at the families' club because his mama had herself a headache."

"My goodness. A week long headache?"

"Mmm-mm. Sometimes you can feel one comin' on. Tip a bit more of that vodka in here, will you please." Nellie rubbed her hip. "I spend some time pickin' up after that messy girl." She shook her head. "I pity the new maid she hires. I shorely do."

"According to Victoria, the princess has been through four already. Don't that beat all!" Sassy tipped the liquor generously into their cups. "There's no need to worry about Miss Victoria missing any vodka. She'll just up and open a new bottle."

Nellie sat back with her drink. "She's always been a generous lady."

****

Several business associates were invited to the Covington's holiday table, but Terri Sue Ellen was clearly the star of the day. Her main concern was her weight gain and expanding bottom, but one of the Thanksgiving dinner guests suggested she take up golf as soon as the baby was born, as it would be a great way to lose that ugly weight she was piling on.

With a solution in mind, she ordered a second helping of pumpkin pie with freshly whipped cream. Her father smiled indulgently, and her aunt encouraged her to eat, while Charles remained the picture of devotion.

Toward the end of the meal, Terri Sue Ellen leaned over to her father and whispered, "Daddy. Should we bring a turkey sandwich to Nellie?"

"You do my heart proud." He smiled lovingly. "Thoughtful as ever."

Big Sur, California
Baby boy

Skye Harmon Toppel was born on a sunny May afternoon. After a short stay in the hospital, his parents brought him home and proudly nestled him in the cradle that belonged to his great grandfather...the carver of the swan sofa.

Helena surprised the family with a visit. She examined the baby and pronounced him to be perfect...a fact Vernon said they all knew prior to his sister's arrival. He joked that she'd traveled a long way to make her statement, but it was a load off everyone's mind that she concurred with the doctor and that his grandson did possess the correct number of toes and fingers.

Helena offered her husky laugh and told her brother that deeding the house to Melissa was a wise choice. One night she surprised the family by preparing dinner, a dish with warm East Indian spices and vegetables that no one understood, but everyone enjoyed.

During her visit, Helena took Melissa aside and spoke to her confidentially, "You must remember, Child, being a mother is a challenge, and children have a mind set to do what you don't want them to. It's a growing process." Melissa gazed at her perfect son and smiled as her aunt continued. "Don't lose faith. You need to stay quiet when you least want to and allow for change. Children will find their way." She nodded knowingly. "I'm the perfect example. My mother's rigid Scottish thinking never quite got over the fact that I chose a different path but she learned to deal with it, and we grew closer once that happened."

Leaving Skye with a didgeridoo that was longer than his cradle and sheets of hand written instructions on how to play the instrument, she prepared to depart for New Zealand to investigate the rumor that cannibalism had, once again, sprung up on the islands and that the Maori natives were being unjustly accused. Harm explained that the Maori people had a background in cannibalism, but Helena defended them by saying, "That was then and this is now."

Lillian shook her head in disbelief at her sister-in-law's idea, while Melissa nodded in understanding.

Harm spoke with Helena about writing her life's story, but she left before he could start.

Vernon smiled patiently, knowing his sister was given to unusual patterns of behavior. He hoped his grandson had inherited none of them.

Chicago, Illinois

Baby Girl

"Oh mah, Lord! That can't be mah child. She has a face as round as an Eskimo, and she's all wrinkled and ugly." Terri Sue Ellen moaned loudly from her private room in the maternity ward of the exclusive hospital. "Take her away and bring back mah baby. Right now!"

The nurse had heard enough. She picked up the infant and spoke in a sharp tone, "Settle down, Mrs. Covington."

" Ah can't go home with this little troll." She turned sideways in bed and shouted at the door, "Help! Someone help me. Ah've been deceived."

"All newborn babies are wrinkled, and I can assure you this is your daughter."

"No!" Terri Sue Ellen was emphatic. "That is not mah daughter! What's the matter with you?" She glared irately at the nurse and barked, "Mah baby would be gorgeous. You should know that by lookin' at me!" She rose up on her elbows in the bed. "You go on out there and find me a beautiful baby. That's your job! Now where is the hair stylist? Where is mah husband? What kind of service is this? Ah made a shit load of arrangements before comin' here."

Klare had been a nurse in the executive wing for five years so she had seen it all. Wealthy women were used to being catered to, but this southern bimbo topped the list. It was no use talking sense to her so she cradled the baby and smiled patiently. "I'll see what I can do."

"Ah should hope so." Terri Sue Ellen found she was speaking to the nurse's back but continued to issue orders, "Ah was put through hell to birth her, and ah want the right one when ah leave here. Not one that looks like a wrinkled-up potato! That one wouldn't of come out of me! And you, nurse whatever your name is, get me a drink."

Klare turned back to the patient. "Are you referring to alcohol?"

"Yes, of course, ah mean alcohol! What else would ah mean?"

"I'm sorry, Mrs. Covington. You're nursing your baby. Nursing mothers can't have alcohol."

"The hell ah'm nursing," Terry Sue Ellen screeched. "Why would ah do anything like that? That's what mah Nellie was for. Get mah baby a darkie with big breasts, and be quick about it."

Klare closed the door and leaned against it. Taking a deep breath, she shifted the baby to her shoulder. The nursing supervisor passed her and nodded. "That one's a piece of work."

****

A month later, in the professionally decorated nursery, the daughter of Terri Sue Ellen and Charles Covington lie tucked in her picture-perfect bed attended by a Swiss nanny. Delaney Mae Anne was beautiful. Her wrinkles were gone, she had a head of dark hair, and her face was no longer round as a pumpkin.

"She's gorgeous, Chuck. Just as ah knew she'd be. Ah'd go through every labor pain again and again just to give you our lovely daughter."

"She is definitely our little girl. You did good, sugar."

"Thank you, darlin'. But our Delaney Mae Anne should have a black nursemaid so she can grow up as ah did, and my momma did, with a big ol' black face lookin' down on her, every day, all full of love and devotion. It's the southern way of mah family."

Charles smiled patiently. *Not going to happen.* The Swiss Nanny was expensive, but maybe some of her poise and accent would rub off on his little girl. It would be worth every penny.

Wrapping her kaftan around her still too large body, Terri Sue Ellen breathed happily, wondering what dazzling present her husband was going to give her to make up for that disgusting birthing process.

They held hands and beamed at their perfect child, and Charles sent out a silent prayer that she was going to be a smarter than her mother.

Chapter Four

Thirteen Years later
Big Sur, California

Skye had grown up in the hills of Big Sur and attended the local grade school with his nearest buddy, Duane Bailey. When the boys were ready for junior high, they caught the yellow bus that took them into Carmel where Skye began to compare the houses and store-bought furniture of his new friends to the stone house. For the first time in his young life, he recognized a difference in his family's life style and didn't know quite how he felt about it.

He decided to talk to Duane, who lived next door—if you could call two miles down the road next door. Duane's dad, who owned Peterson Bailey's Big Sur Pottery School, and Duane's mom, Alice, were close friends of his parents.

Skye waited until the weekend when he and Duane met early in the morning to build a fort. After selecting the right hill top, the boys started work. Skye pulled vines off the cypress trees and stuck the shiny leaves into the holes of the makeshift form.

"Are you sure about that?" Duane sat back, questioning his friend. "'Leaves of three, let it be.' That's what my dad says."

"I've lived here all my life, and I know what I'm doing. Okay?"

"Yeah, well," Duane looked up and continued, "I've lived here all my life, too, and I'm not so sure you know what you're doing."

"Don't worry. I got this covered." Skye bent over to gather loose sticks and carried them to where the fort was taking shape. "You know, Duane, we've got more important shit to talk about today."

"Why are you swearing?" Duane asked.

"Because you're supposed to cuss when things are wrong,"

"Says who?"

Skye ignored the question and went on with his thought. "Here's the deal. We're not like everyone else, but that's okay." He paused to think about what to say next and raked his fingers through his shoulder-length hair. "I mean everyone knows my mom is an artist, and my dad sniffs out news stories, and people think that's super neat. But I went to Tom's house after school, and it's nothing like my house. It has curtains at the windows—not scarves or old shawls, but real curtains."

"And?" Duane looked bewildered. "So what?" Twisting the sticks together, he filled in more holes with leaves. "I went to Jerry's house, and I noticed that colors in his living room matched the colors in his dining room. It was like, ah, I don't know..." Feeling his brow wrinkle, he continued slowly, "It didn't feel a lot like home."

"Not like our homes, you mean," Skye said.

Duane wiped his forehead and paused. "His mom gave us cookies, but they were from the grocery store. And I could smell chicken, but it was in a carry-out box." He shrugged." It was okay...just different." He went back to examining the foundation for the sticks. "This needs to be stronger."

Skye nodded and asked, "So what else happened at Jerry's house?"

"Well, his mom had a flower garden with roses, but they didn't smell sweet like my mom's roses." Duane wrinkled his forehead as if trying to find the right words, "It was sort of creepy. I thought all roses smelled like roses. "

"See! That's what I'm talking about. This calls for a damn it."

"A what?"

"Give me a damn it, Duane!"

"No," Duane said.

"Okay. But you should know that my new friends cuss." Duane shrugged as Skye continued, "So here's my question for you. Don't you feel odd?"

"Sometimes being your friend is odd, but overall it's okay."

"That's not what I meant!" Skye stood up and stared at the ocean. "We live way down here, and our parents do weird stuff."

Duane looked puzzled. "No, they don't."

"Yes, they do," Skye insisted.

"What kind of stuff are you talking about?"

"Writing and painting and throwing pots."

"That's not weird," Duane said.

"Yeah, Duane, it is!" Skye sounded irritated. "Like they don't work in an office or get dressed up or drive fancy cars. They do creative, artsy-fartsy things."

"Huh?"

"You heard me." Skye shifted his feet uncomfortably. "My teacher told me she hoped I could paint like my mother. I never thought about it much, but I can't paint anything."

"Sure you can. We painted my dad's studio last year."

"No!" Skye rolled his eyes. "Not like that." He sounded angry. "I'm talking about a picture. Something that's really good." He shrugged. "I can't paint like that."

"So?"

"It makes me feel stupid! Damn it!"

Duane stood up. "I think if you're going to swear, you got'ta give it more emphasis." He waved at the air. "Just saying."

"Damn it!!"

"No, still not right." Duane shook his head. "Look, so what if you can't paint a picture? My dad is like a big deal potter, but I don't like to get clay all over my hands." He thought for a moment and added, "My mom is teaching me to line dance. It's fun."

"I don't want to learn county line dancing." Skye's voice was cross. "And, oh yeah, I can't write either! That sucks!"

"Is that supposed to be a cuss word?"

"Sor'ta." Skye looked down and let out a sigh. "I can't us the 'F' word or my parents would ground me. Anyhow," he gathered his hostility and directed it at his buddy, "I'm mad and you should be too!"

Duane put his hands on his hips. "Don't get pissy with me!"

"Well, it's not fair! I got parents who can do things, but I can't, and now everyone knows it." He kicked at a rock. "It was like a secret that I was stupid, and when I started school in Carmel, everyone found out."

"Aren't you going to play football?" Duane asked.

"Yeah. I guess so. Coach says I'll make the team." He knelt and carelessly pushed a few small stones into place.

Duane sat down and dumped out the pail of dirt.

Skye ignored him and continued talking, "I don't want to be like my parents. I really want to be like the other guys and play sports and live in a big house and talk about cool stuff."

"Sounds okay. But you make it seem super important."

"It is!" He held the tree branches straight while Duane tied them together.

"I'm going to get a bucket of water." Duane said as he brushed off his hands and stood. "We should wet this down, and when it dries out, it would be stronger."

Skye asked angrily, "Didn't you hear me?"

"Sure I heard you. It's just me and you out here. Stop shouting!"

Skye wound heavier rope around the make shift support. "Forget the water." Hesitating, he added, "I don't think we should be building a fort either."

"What?" Duane asked incredulously.

"Look, it's a raggedy ass old fort, and besides, Duane, we're too old for kid stuff. We're in junior high now, and we should be playing golf and tennis."

"Huh?" Duane gazed steadily at his friend.

"City people do things like that. We're missing out. You know how our parents get together in the fall and dip candles?"

"Yeah." Duane sounded defensive. "We have fun."

"No, we don't! Not anymore. People go to the store to buy candles. You can buy bees wax candles at the store. Don't you get it? None of our candles are perfect. They're always crooked, and we put them in homemade clay saucers. They sit all over the house looking sloppy."

"Say that when the electricity goes out and those sloppy candles come in real handy."

"The electricity doesn't go out if you live in the city."

"Bull shit!"

"Hey!" Skye looked at his friend. "You said that really good."

"I felt it. Sor'ta like in my gut." Duane hammered the poles supporting the fort and continued, "Truth is, you're misinformed. The electricity does go out in the city."

"Is that so, Mr. Know-It-All?'

"Holy cow, Skye, you're sure in a bad mood today. You're bitching about everything." Duane shook his head. "Art is in the eye of the beholder. My dad says that. I might be using the term 'art' loosely, but I like making candles, and I like making the pizza that follows making the candles. Hey, you always eat your own weight in pizza so you must enjoy that."

Skye groaned, "Well, what about vegetables? It's stupid to grow our own vegetables when you can buy them at the store. And here's something else to think about; it's way more fun to go to the mall than to hike around Big Sur and watch the wildflowers grow."

"I sor'ta like the flowers in the spring but..." Duane looked bothered as he went on, "I also like the mall. It's fun to buy a coke and hang with the guys. But well...it's not a deal breaker."

"Don't you want to party with the popular kids and do the right stuff?"

"Ahh, maybe." He gave Skye's long hair an embellished look. "Like get a real hair cut?" Duane laughed.

Ignoring the dig, Skye continued, "Yeah. That's a start." His voice took on enthusiasm as he spoke, "And get some new clothes, too!"

"We'll need to talk to our parents. We can't do any of that stuff without them."

"Okay." Skye smiled. "That's what I wanted to hear you say! Give me high five!"

"No. You gim'me your hand to hold these sticks in place. This fort won't build itself."

"You sound like a girl."

"You look like one. Why don't you curl your hair?" Duane said.

The boys continued to exchange insults as the morning moved into the day.

That night, when red bumps lined their arms, they realized they had made a fort with poison oak. After chamomile lotion was applied, Duane called Skye to tell him he was stupid and that he wasn't going to listen to him again. When his parents left the room, he added a well-placed "damn it" to end the conversation and hung up.

The skin rash that followed spread to their necks and faces; homemade treatments were put aside when the boys were taken into Monterey where a doctor prescribed medication.

Both sets of parents had been upset but couldn't help smiling that their sons, being raised in Big Sur, hadn't known the difference between green foliage and the shiny reddish leaves of a poison oak vine.

Harm shook his head and looked at Pete. "You think they learned anything?"

Pete nodded. "I'd like to hope so."

****

Adjustments were made in appearance and attitude as the school year continued. New friends and ideas entered their lives, and Skye and Duane embraced the changes in different ways. They felt empowered with fresh viewpoints, yet uncomfortable with their lack of sophistication, but overall, they liked where life was taking them.

Chicago, Illinois

Delaney Covington had just finished third in the Lake Michigan Commemorated Country Club Junior Tennis Tournament. At thirteen, she was a competitive young lady, encouraged by her parents to be the best at whatever she did.

Once in the locker room, she threw her tennis racket down and groaned, "It was his fault. My coach didn't have me properly prepared. I'm reporting this to my father."

The other girls gave her room to move around. Everyone knew who Delaney's father was. Besides, if Delaney really wanted to win next year, she could make that happen.

Miranda frowned when Delaney stepped into the showers. To the other girls, she said, "My advice is, don't get involved with the junior tennis club unless you're playing doubles with her."

"I'm already invested. Plus I'm a much better player then she'll ever be." Kathy smiled confidentially.

"Won't make a difference if her father donates the new tennis courts," Miranda retorted.

"Oh." Kathy wrinkled her forehead in thought. "I don't think he'll do that. Courts cost a lot of money. Besides, my father's brother is a professional tennis player and gives advice to the club's pro shop."

"Really. Tell me, what's more important. Advice to the pro shop or four new courts? Whatever it takes to win is the Covington way."

Delaney called out, "Where's the perfumed oil that's applied to wet skin? It's very special. My mother ordered it from Sri Lanka. It has cinnamon leaf extract and cardamom oil for stress reduction. After that disaster on the tennis courts, I need it. I said, hey! Someone get it for me."

Miranda whispered, "Listen to her, blah, blah, blah." She picked up a small bottle and passed it to Delaney through a crack in the glass door. "Enjoy. It's lovely."

Kathy spoke in a low voice, "It's kept out here because someone in the shower could slip on the oil when it gets on the floor."

"Oh?" Miranda smiled sarcastically, blinking with false surprise, "Good Heavens. I didn't know that."

"And my warm towel." Delaney shouted. "I want a warm towel."

"After you, Kathy." Miranda said and left the door open as she walked out.

"There's a horrible breeze in here." Delaney sounded annoyed, "Hello, hello, is someone out there?"

Big Sur, California

The next year Skye wanted the experience of a business adventure and convinced Duane, after many long discussions, to help him start a summer project, providing gardening services for local restaurants in Big Sur.

Their parents found it difficult to believe that two fourteen-year-old boys had talked seasoned business owners into letting them care for expensive landscaping. After a couple of weeks on the job, one of the restaurant managers stopped at Pete's pottery school with a problem. The boys had removed the wrong greenery, and Harm and Pete had to replace several of the large plants their sons had pulled out; they obviously thought the plants were unwanted foliage.

Skye faced his dad. "I'm really not into shrubbery, and Duane doesn't know squat. Do you?"

"I resent that," Duane said.

"Well, you don't," Skye yelled.

"And neither do you," Duane countered.

Pete commented dryly, "Seems that nature isn't your long suit, boys. You'd both best look for other avenues of interest. Meanwhile, bottom line is that the money you earned is going to purchase new bushes."

Smiling, Harm added, "Upside is they stayed away from reddish vines."

****

The summer passed swiftly, and when school started in the fall, it became obvious that the boys were developing different pursuits. Skye showed natural ability in sports while Duane preferred a more studious approach, favoring his science classes.

Back in Big Sur, the families remained close, and with two energetic teenagers involved in a number of activities, there was little downtime. Shared car-pooling, club meetings, science class shows, football games, dances, and school events filled in the days.

Carmel, California

Toward the spring of the school year, Melissa's paintings, a collection of Big Sur water colors emphasizing her signature splash of light, were on exhibit at the Carmel Library. It was her fourth show that year, and she was pleased with her success.

That morning she'd selected a light-weight cotton skirt in a buttery shade of yellow. It dropped to her ankles where comfortable leather sandals showed off newly painted red toes. Her white blouse was tied at the waist, and she wore a piece of Big Sur jade encased in a silver wire around her neck.

Skye, now fifteen and clearly not interested in art, wanted to spend time with his friends, so he joined his parents for a lift into town.

Melissa felt the comfortable slow swaying of their old truck as they traveled along Highway One. Harm had delivered her paintings earlier in the week so there was no rush, leaving her relaxed and quite happy with her life.

Skye was attempting to stretch out his rapidly growing legs from his position in the middle seat of the cab. His new jeans were long enough now but wouldn't fit him through the summer. He tucked his legs back in place and asked, "Did my grandparents really walk on this road before it was Highway One?"

"It was probably distant relatives who walked along the Coast Trail to worship at the Carmel Mission." Melissa laughed. "It was built in 1793. Your grandparents would be appalled if they thought you considered them that old!"

"But," Skye continued, "the road was just a dirt path way back then." He spoke with an authority recently acquired. "Oh, I know we have a lot of land in Big Sur, and it's been in our family, like forever." He rolled his eyes and continued, "'Cause of some Mexican Land Grant thing." He extended his arms and wiggled his shoulders, trying to wedge out a little more room.

Harm tipped his head, smiling at Melissa as he addressed his son, "Sounds like you have some interest in your family history, Skye." *Thank God*, he thought with relief and glanced sideways at Skye who looked uncomfortable jammed between himself and Melissa. "If you can imagine a wagon bumping over a dirt path filled with potholes, well shucks, son, it makes our truck seem like a luxury vehicle."

Skye looked cross. "Dad, please don't say shucks again. It's embarrassing."

"I thought you liked a little country twang."

"Not anymore," Skye answered and then continued with his original thought. "People had to make a trip to Monterey for supplies. It wasn't like they wanted to." He turned to his mom. "I know you're really into all those old stories, but the truth is people had no choices. Right?"

"We come from tough stock," Melissa joked and lifted her braid to cool her neck. "Monterey was the only outside link to other homesteads. All the supplies were carried back by wagons and shared with other pioneers who were setting up their ranchettes in Big Sur."

Harm's window was half-way down to allow fresh air to flow through the truck. His sun-bleached hair usually needed a cut, and today, it blew across his forehead as if to remind him. "Big Sur was safe from outside development for a long time, son." He glanced in Melissa's direction and smiled. "That is...according to Grannie's June's folklore."

"I don't remember her." Skye pushed his face toward the breeze from the open window. His long hair was gone, replaced by a closely cropped style. "When does the air conditioning get fixed?"

"Soon," Harm answered. "I bring the truck in, first of the week."

Skye spoke thoughtfully, "I don't think I would have liked that."

Melissa blinked at her son's remark and cautiously asked, "Not liked what?"

"Living way back then."

"How come?"

"'Cause." He paused and tilted his head in thought, looking like his father for an instant before the semblance disappeared. "I really like cities and lots of people and exciting things going on." He added pensively, "Living down the coast is okay, but it's not for me. My friends have houses designed by architects and furniture that's bought in stores...not chairs and sofas made by their grandpa or other dead relatives."

"Skye!" Melissa cautioned, "That's being disrespectful."

"Well," he fidgeted with his hands. "They *are* dead, and we *do* have all their stuff." His tone was belligerent, "Besides, it's messy." Glancing at his mom, he saw she looked hurt. "Well, some of it is okay. I guess. Like the swan sofa is comfortable in a weird short of way." He added quickly, "But with most sofas, you don't have to give people directions on how to sit down."

Melissa added meticulously, "I find it to be peerless in the world of furniture. Not many people can say that."

"Nor do they want to, mom."

To divert the conversation down a different path, Harm asked, "What else do you like better about living in town?"

"My friends' parents are professionals, you know, like doctors and lawyers and business people. Joe Campbell's dad owns a bar and restaurant." Glancing at his mother, he hesitated. "Ahh, not like there's anything wrong with being an artist." He focused on the highway and mumbled, "I guess I didn't inherit your talent."

Melissa reached for his hand. "You've never tried painting, Skye. Maybe you'd like it?"

"Nope." He pulled away. "I've tried in art class, and I'm not any good."

"I didn't know you were interested in art." Melissa offered, "I can help."

"Nope. I'd rather play football. I'm a good quarter back, and Joe is a running back. Besides, my new sport is tennis."

"Fair enough." Harm nodded.

Skye's voice carried a vibrant note of excitement. "When I grow-up, there's tons of stuff I want to do. Like start companies—not paint or write." He looked sheepish. "Sorry, Dad."

"No offense." Harm paused thoughtfully. "It takes a lot of different people to make this old world go round."

"Yeah. And lots of them live in big cities where they see and do things... really important things."

Harm leaned back and glanced at his wife behind Skye's head. He saw that disillusionment shadowed her features.

"And I want lots of money to do those things."

Harm waited before he replied, "You know, Skye, it's not what you do with your money as much as what you do with your time."

"Yeah, well dad, you would say that. Being a writer and all. You're supposed to have those thoughts. I get it. They're lofty. And mom is an artist, so she thinks the same way. But in real life, shoot, money buys stuff, and there's nothing wrong with having lots of stuff."

Melissa experienced a feeling of doom as she listened to her son's thoughts play out. "You know, I think that the hours of each day can be rich and shining."

"Exactly!" His youthful gusto filled the car. "I want to be rich and be an executive and have a good time and sail a boat and fly places! And, oh yeah, I want a really cool car...like a Corvette or hey, I got it, a Lamborghini!"

Harm couldn't help but grin at his son's gusto for a luxurious lifestyle, and Melissa let her eyes roll and laughed along with him. That hadn't been what she'd wanted to hear, but Skye was still a teenager. He'd experience new thoughts daily, shedding more than he'd keep. For a moment, the world seemed to stop, and she realized, inside the wind-blown truck, that her son would seek a different path from her and Harm. Of course, it wasn't the end of the world but, as a mother, she felt disappointment.

****

Later that night, when Harm was doing research for a series of articles on the impact that oil drilling had on marine life, Melissa sat outside reviewing the events of her day. Many of her watercolors had sold, not only to locals, but to tourists as well. Skye had been busy with his friends but had reluctantly joined them for dinner at a Carmel restaurant where two of her paintings were on display. It had seemed to embarrass him, and he'd been quiet on the drive home. Now he was now on the phone with Joe.

Harm has sensed her disappointment, and before starting his project, he had told her, "Skye's only had fifteen years on this Earth and hasn't spent much of it thinking about the responsibilities of his family's inheritance in Big Sur."

She knew that was true.

The porch wrapped her home with love, but a sense of fear crowded around her. *Skye's attitude was harsh, but then I might have been reading into that. I will hope that his eagerness for new visions will be tempered by compassion.*

Chicago, Illinois

The Covingtons had returned from Europe after a month of touring. Charles had made some good business contacts while Terry Sue Ellen discovered the joy of sipping martinis. Their daughter, now a precocious fifteen-year-old, had visited the fashion houses of France and considered herself an expert on style.

When Delaney entered her fall term at the private academy, the other students hung on her every word as she told them what to wear and how they were supposed to look, except for Harriet Johansson whose family's business was creating elite sportswear. She often spent her summers abroad and understood the European approach of matching chic design with innovative fabric.

Harriet held court at the private girl's school. "Delaney is bossy and poorly informed. It's a good thing her father is so rich that he can give her a job because she'll never get one on her own. She may look the part, if she has a lot of extra help from a dresser, but she doesn't have the smarts to pull it off by herself."

Phoebe spoke up, "Her mother was a peach queen. You know?"

"Oh. Big deal!" Harriet opened her book to cram for a test in economics.

Phoebe continued, "I believe her grandfather was a count in Germany."

Harriet rolled her eyes. "Bullshit."

Delaney sashayed through the dorm, tossing her Prada handbag on a chair. She fumbled through it and found a hairbrush. Flouncing over to a beanbag chair, she grabbed a fashion magazine. "Phoebe, come over here. I think I've found something for you."

"Ahh." Phoebe snuck a glance at Harriet and replied self-consciously, "Well. Not now. I've really got to study." She offered an apologetic smile. "Sorry."

"Oh, no worries." She looked at the other girls in the day room and nodded, "You, Sarah, and ...I'm sorry what is your name again?'

"Marty."

"Yes, of course. Marty, please join me and Sarah for a fashion session. I've got the most wonderful ideas for new hairdos and shoes. Here, sit on either side of me, and I'll bring you both up to speed," Delaney ordered.

Harriet snickered. "Up to speed? You bring someone up to speed?"

Delaney raised her head and looked at the glasses resting on Harriet's nose. "You need work. More fluff, less boxy styles, perhaps a few ruffles."

"Ruffles? Really? You need to study up to be the queen of fashion. Ruffles are totally passé."

Shrugging, Delaney waved dismissively. "Truly, I'm too busy to deal with you right now. Come ladies." She rose, turning toward Sarah and Marty. "Let us go to my room where we will pursue the good life." She whispered loudly, "I also have a box of chocolates with a liquor filling and chilled coca cola."

Harriet called after them, "It's another of her bribes. Be careful."

"Really, Harriet? Is that all you've got?" Delaney asked.

"You might want to try opening a book now and then, Miss Southern Belle."

"Oh, I don't have to." Her smile broadened as she looked over her shoulder. "I'm naturally gifted with intelligence. It's a family trait I inherited from my mother and my titled German relatives."

"You wish," Harriet muttered as she turned back to her textbook.

Chapter Five

Chicago, Illinois
Robert and Evelyn Covington Residence

Evelyn waited as the phone rang. "Robert, I'm going to put it on speaker, and then we can both talk."

"Delaney Covington speaking."

"Hello dear, is yousr father at home?"

"Oh, Grandmother Covington, how nice to hear your voice. I have some thrilling fashion news for you. Short skirts are the rage, and tube tops are divine."

"Well, Delaney, dear, I may be a bit too old for that."

"Of course. If your concern is aging skin, then I might suggest a sequined face mask. They're still the rage in Vienna, along with little boats that look like canoes."

Evelyn sighed. "How nice that you know all that."

"I'm sorry. I have so much going on in my mind, I seem to have misplaced your question. What was it?"

Evelyn muted the phone and looked at Robert. "You do realize that our granddaughter has many of her mother's traits?"

"I agree. But there is little we can do about it."

With a sigh, she released the mute button and returned to the call. "Your father, dear, is he at home?"

"Oh my, no. Father isn't here right now, but perhaps I can be of assistance. I take excellent notes. Mother taught me. We practice all the time. If you wait a moment, I'll get my binder and be right back."

Evelyn looked off in the distance as she muttered, "It's sad, really."

Robert got up and moved toward the table holding a decanter. "Sherry?"

He smiled woefully and looked at his wife. "Perhaps Delaney will become smarter as she grows older."

"Do you really feel that way?"

"No."

"Hello, Grandmother Covington. I'm back and ready to convey a message. Are you there?"

"Please tell your father I called."

"Is that it? I can write more."

Big Sur, California

Time didn't mellow Skye's feelings about his family's inheritance. When he was in high school, his mother and father embarked on a trial and error approach to help him understand the beauty of the Big Sur Land Grant that would one day be his.

****

Harm turned to his sixteen-year-old son and nodded toward the waterfall. There was hope in his voice. "What do you think, Skye? Big Sur at her finest? Is nature without bounds?" Harm squinted at the sunshine as he pointed toward the sparkling water that shot downward in an eighty-foot stream. It splashed onto the sand in Waterfall Cove. "This is our neighbor."

"No, dad." Skye replied with a frown, his tone bored, "A waterfall is not a neighbor. Well, maybe to you and mom, but not to normal people."

Harm laughed. "Maybe I pushed the point." A thoughtful expression crossed his face. "But my meaning was clear, and I think you understood what I said."

"Dad, I know about Christopher McWay and the waterfall and how it's a year round attraction. But I'm not into nature, and I'm not into spending my life caring for our big-deal land grant, either." He shifted back and forth and added, "Everyone knows we have all this property." He shrugged his shoulders. "Between you and Mom, I come from the best known family in Big Sur."

"Is that a bad thing?"

"It's a lot to live up to." His tone was cross. "I'm always compared to you."

Harm smiled. "Skye, you're an A-student and a star football player. You excel at basketball. You've become a good tennis player. You're a natural at sports." He faced his son. "Your mom and I are very proud of you." Harm placed his arm around Skye's shoulder. "You are your own man, and that's what matters."

"Yeah, well." He pulled away from his father. "There's also goofy old Aunt Helena who comes and goes like the wind. It's hard to explain a crazy relative."

"She's a free spirit."

"Yeah, well, I wish she was normal. It's like my family is trying to sabotage me."

"Skye. Is that really fair?"

"Maybe not, but it's the way I feel sometimes." His laugh was unsteady. "You know the weathered fence that borders the house? Mom tells the story about the day when the redwood posts were nailed together and set in cement and how you had been so proud of your work, that even now it makes her smile. Then grandpa adds that he had looked on that day because he knew the importance for a man to work his own land."

Harm felt his chest tighten but let his son continue.

"Well, those redwood posts look old and shabby. They need to come down, and a real fence should be put up. Then there's the stone house. It's so..." he paused looking for a word that would work but found none.

Harm looked at his son. "Why don't you invite friends over? Have a party? It's a great place for groups to gather together and talk. Lots of space."

"Ahh, dad," he sounded uncomfortable. "Groups don't *gather* anymore. We grab a pizza, talk, listen to music, and dance. *No one*," he overstated, "gathers." Stepping away, he shook his head. "Besides, the house and all the stuff inside is...you know, embarrassing."

"The stone house is embarrassing?"

"Yes." Skye offered a grin showing a mouth full of braces. "Plus it lists to the right."

"Hey, I've tried to fix that several times." Harm joked back, "There's only so much that can be done with a place that old."

"It's okay, dad. I know." Skye looked out to sea. "I'm sorry I said it was embarrassing."

"That would hurt your mom's feelings."

"I don't want to do that. And I'm sorry I said that about the fence, but, dad, it does look bad."

"I know." Harm smiled. "Maybe it's a project we can take on together?"

Skye looked toward the waterfall and mumbled, "Maybe."

"But you'd prefer..."

"A real house in Carmel, I guess." His eyes lit up. "Maybe a swimming pool? Not an ocean for a backyard. Heck, you can't even swim in the ocean. It's too choppy, got too many rocks and..." he paused in thought, "...an undertow that'll drag you out to sea."

"Well, son, we all have our own way of thinking, and you need to explore what you feel is right for you. Your mom and I aren't trying to force you to think like us, but we'd like you to consider some of what we say before you make your decisions."

"Sure, dad."

A throw away answer, Harm thought.

The two tall men watched the long stream of water fall from the cliffs onto the sand. He wanted to ask his son to think more about the bigger picture, what the future might hold, but how would he understand such a question at the age of sixteen? Or maybe it was the answers he'd get that he didn't want to hear. At least he'd be there for Melissa if Skye wasn't. It would be best to let his son go where life would take him, hoping eventually his heart would lead him back home.

****

By the time Skye entered college, it had become increasingly clear that even though Big Sur had always been a cherished part of his mother's history, and though his father had embraced it with love, it wasn't going to be in Skye's future.

Pete and Alice were experiencing some problems with Duane, and after several long discussions, both sets of parents agreed that it was time to let go of their children so they could make their own way in the world.

Skye pursued business with a self-confidence that bordered on arrogance, and his aggressive attitude surprised even his parents, while Duane went into pre-med with quiet determination, preferring the company of select friends who shared his interests.

Chicago, Illinois

After Jackson von Campe donated a new science lab to Georgia State, his granddaughter, Delaney Covington, graduated suma -cum laude.

She entered Tech World International, at the home office in Chicago, as a senior consultant where her father was president and CEO and her mother was vice president. Together they decided that a support staff would review their daughter's every move, as well as travel with her, preparing her for client meetings.

By the end of the first year, she was good as gold as long as someone guided her through complicated business decisions and allowed her to have the full satisfaction of personal achievement. She learned to place a look of great concern on her face and followed it with a smile that would charm and reassure a potential client while her team took the necessary notes used for planning the strategy. It all made for good press; the president's daughter, who was both beautiful and smart, was part of their winning team.

Unfortunately, her success with boyfriends was not as good. When she told them how to cut their hair and what to wear, they often moved on. The few who stuck it out didn't last long because Delaney had a way of being too critical, too often.

However, James Douglass looked like he would make it. Tall and good-looking, he held a degree in Business Management with a strong determination to get to the top. Having dinner one night with Delaney at her father's club, she insisted on ordering their food. James went along with it, but after that night, it became something she did whenever they were out.

He looked annoyed, "Please don't do that, Dee Dee. I would prefer to order my own food."

"Don't call me Dee Dee. I hate that name. It's pedestrian and beneath me. Besides, I thought you appreciated my efforts on selecting your food."

"Not so much. Okay?"

Taking a deep breath, she snapped the menu shut. "Okay. Order whatever you want. Just remember some foods give off a foul odor, and I don't like that."

James ground his teeth. This wasn't the life he wanted. Let someone else deal with her. He looked at the very pretty girl across the table from him and said, "Fine Delaney. You order for both of us."

She beamed. "Oh darling, I knew you'd see it my way."

That was their last date.

****

When Delaney complained to her mother, who was also her best friend, about not being able to keep a relationship alive, Terri Sue Ellen told her, "You're a superior child, darlin'. You are flawless, and it's difficult for men to grasp hold of that fact and then deal with it in an acceptable fashion." She sat in front of her dressing table, fluttered her hands, and thought fondly of her famous peach float wave as she took a sip of vodka. "Why, oh mah goodness... here we have you takin' *your* time, which, I point out, is a precious commodity, to give your boyfriends the advantage of personal guidance. Now that there is a gift we von Campe/Covington women share. It's our propensity toward intelligence that winds us up in trouble." Bringing her hand to her chest, she paused and exhaled. "Why, such a skill set can be an affliction."

Bending toward the dressing table, Terrie Sue Ellen tested the stickiness of the glue on her false eyelashes and returned her attention to her daughter's dilemma. "Ah understand so well what you're experiencin' because of mah own royal German background as well as mah responsibilities as honored Peach Queen . Why, the weight of the world rested on mah shoulders."

She touched her daughter's cheek gently and continued, "Honey, havin' those powerful accountabilities leads us to being super smart, and that scares men. Half to death. Yes, it does. But ah was lucky as your daddy could deal with it." *Of course, ah provided sex. As long as his male parts were happy, he was happy.*

She applied the eyelashes to her lid and looked at her reflection in the mirror. "You followin' this, Delaney Mae Anne? Ah don't want to be goin' too fast."

"I'm with you, mother."

"Excellent! The point is ah could out-think many of my dates." *Especially when they didn't have on their trousers 'cause men tend to think either with their big brain or their little brain. But that's a story for another day 'cause first off, you've got to get a fella before ah can share those words of wisdom.*

"Oh, now that ah reflect back...." She exhaled in exasperation as she looked at her empty glass. "All the boys needed so much help. It was truly hard to decide who needed it most." *But once a fellah was stiff and happy, he would be focused on what ah was doin', and ah was very good at what ah did, so that presented a perfect opportunity to whisper a little idea in his ear...when ah got up there.*

Ah remember learnin' early on that those ideas would stick 'cause, more than anything, boys like to be praised about what they have and proper timin' was everything.

She waved her hands as if trying to find the right words her daughter would understand. "See here, honey, a mother knows things. Ah'm sure you inherited my sharin', carin' nature, and you will have to learn to live with it." Facing her daughter, she smiled. "We will get into a more detailed discussion at another time when you have yourself a steady beau. You still understandin' what ah'm sayin?"

"Yes, mother."

"Good. Because ah don't want you to be feeling higgledy-piggledy about this subject matter. You see, someday the right man will pop up, and he'll be putty in your hands." *That is assumin' you know how to satisfy his animal-like desires.* She leveled a green-eyed blink at her daughter who blinked back. "Excellent. Ah shall consider our discussion complete." Turning to a Hermes scarf of blue and green silk, she held it toward her face. "What do you think of these colors?"

"They're okay, I guess."

"Oh, goodness me. Mah little girl is feelin' low. We need to open us a bottle of Cristal and think happy thoughts."

"Yes, mother."

"Outstandin'. Ah'll ring for mah maid."

Delaney let out a deep breath. "Being perfect is very difficult. But I shall rise to the occasion and carry on."

"Beautifully said." Her mother beamed. "Ah'm just so proud of you! Poo on those boys who couldn't appreciate your winnin' ways." There was a knock on the door, and Terri Sue Ellen called out, "Enter."

"Si, Mrs. Covington."

"Maria, finally! You need to learn to climb those steps more lively like. Sor'ta usin' the quick foot movements of your Mexican hat dance. Now, ah want you to think on that some."

Maria, who understood only certain words of English that focused around alcohol and food, nodded pleasantly as her employer continued to chatter.

"Meanwhile, fetch us some Roederer Cristal, and arrange it in a silver ice bucket. You might as well add some caviar and toast points with the proper Russian service. The kitchen staff will assist you. Hurry now. Mah daughter is a bit on the blue side, and ah need to perk her right up."

She faced Delaney with a sigh. "There's just no tellin' what she'll bring back." Gazing into space, she continued, "It's times like this ah so miss my Nellie. Daddy had a big ol' bell he'd ring whenever we needed her services. Ding dong and she'd come a'runnin'...or, as was the case in her later years, a'hobblin'. But the key word was come. In gratitude for her years of service, we paid to accommodate her in a home for old colored folk. Oh, she so wanted to stay on in her little room off the kitchen, but how could we keep a worn out old person in the big house? It wouldn't do." She sniffed loudly. "Let us pause for a moment in remembrance of her passin'." Mother and daughter looked toward the ceiling. "Bless her heart. It was a sad day. Darkies came from all over to send her to heaven. Of course, ah couldn't be there, but your granddaddy shared it with me."

"Yes, mother,"

"Now do tell darlin', what are your plans for the week-end?"

Chicago, Illinois
Robert and Evelyn Covington Residence

"I understand Delaney is having a problem with keeping a boyfriend?" Robert looked at his wife as he continued, "Charles told me about it."

Evelyn sighed, "Do you find that difficult to believe?"

Robert pursed his lips and looked away. "No."

"My understanding is that Terri Sue Ellen is counseling her daughter." Evelyn offered a weak smile. "Need I say more?"

Robert felt his shoulders droop and returned to his laptop.

Big Sur, California

As the years flew by, Skye and Duane drifted apart, and the families saw less of each other.

With Skye living away from home and enjoying his first taste of success as a consultant in the computer industry, Melissa and Harm, now in their late forties, discovered they had personal time for each other. They joked that it appeared in the spaces between their careers. By enjoying long talks and shared humor, they felt less hurt as they grew accustomed to the fact that their son was ignoring them.

"After all," they told each other. "A young man has to get out in the world to discover where he fits in." He'll be back was Harm's mantra, but Melissa questioned his undying faith in their son's return.

****

As a young couple, Harm and Melissa had enjoyed hiking in Big Sur.

Now that time was available once again, they started with morning walks and planned to work up to full day hikes.

Harm's only problem was a slight backache and nagging pain in his abdomen that started mid-way through a walk. They agreed that neither of them were quite as youthful as they remembered, and Melissa admitted to having cramps in her calves when they went up hills. Changing their agenda to less strenuous climbs, they promised that they would keep in mind a more challenging goal as their bodies adjusted to the demands of their new endeavors.

Pete and Alice joined them on their shorter walks and talked about Duane and the pride they felt in his devotion to his budding medical career.

Life seemed to be just about where it should until the evening Harm complained about a deep pain in his back. Melissa suggested he lay down while she finished preparing dinner. He'd admitted to feeling faint and nauseous as she helped him to get comfortable in their bedroom. *He's healthy as a horse. What could be wrong?*

A trickle of fear spiraled through her as they talked for a few minutes about the fish they had for lunch and wondered if that could be the cause of his problem. She decided to call the doctor.

"Stay put. I mean it." She looked at him and thought he was short of breath. "Really, Harm, don't get out of bed. I'll make that call and be right back. Does your chest hurt?"

"Nope."

"Your skin feels clammy."

"Sorry." His smile was tight.

"Left side of your body seem okay?

"Yup."

"One word answers are not a big help." She struck a belligerent pose with her arms crossed over her chest. "I'm very troubled. This is just so unlike you."

"I'll be fine." Weakly, he reached for her hand. "Don't get all upset. Okay?" He nodded. "Gon'na catch forty winks. It's all this exercise. It's done me in," he joked and closed his eyes.

She hurried toward the kitchen to make the call and turned off the stove while waiting for the doctor to call her back. She thought of phoning Pete and Alice to help her get Harm to the car because it seemed that he should be taken to the emergency room. Food poisoning could be serious.

A few minutes passed, and she wished they had put a phone jack in the bedroom. They'd been meaning to but just hadn't gotten around to it. Cell phones were not reliable on the coast so they had to count on the landlines. *Tomorrow*, she promised herself, *I will get that extension installed*. It was taking longer than usual for the return call so she walked down the hall to check on Harm.

He was lying as she'd left him except there was a stillness that had settled around him. When she couldn't revive him, she ran back to the kitchen and called the ambulance, but, deep inside, she knew he was gone.

All she could do was sit on the bed and hold his hand. She whispered, "It's motionlessness. Your hands are always moving, typing, telling a story, planting seeds, building something... always moving. Please don't leave me, Harm."

She stroked his face gently. It was calm, and his eyes were shut. She began to rock and felt her tears flow silently as she whispered words of love. She believed, in her heart, that he could hear them.

Later the doctor told her that Harm had suffered from a ruptured abdominal aortic aneurysm. No doubt, it had developed slowly over the years, and there had been no signs or symptoms. No one could have seen it coming.

Skye had been difficult to reach, but Alice remained with Melissa and helped her get through the first days until he arrived.

Day of the funeral
Big Sur, California

With all the mourners filling the stone house, it was difficult to remember everyone's name. Of course, Melissa knew them all but just couldn't think straight after the memorial service on the cliff. So many people had spoken good words that her heart ached for her husband. The stress she felt made it difficult to take a deep breath, and she was reminded of her first job at the McGregor Art Gallery when she felt pressured to do and say the right things. She'd dressed in black that day, too. But she'd met Harm, and her life had truly begun. Now it was over.

All she wanted was to be left alone so she could grieve quietly. The aromas of freshly baked pies and oven casseroles made her feel nauseous. The need to step outside was overwhelming. She stood at the screen door. It was what she and Harm had often done when a problem seemed insurmountable. She could hear his words in her mind. "Let's have a breath of ocean air." She smiled wearily, holding back her tears.

Suddenly Alice was at her side, guiding her out the back door where the view looked up to the highway and beyond to the soaring cliffs. The women sat together on the bench that Melissa's grandfather had carved.

Alice spoke slowly, "I'm so sorry. You know that Pete and I are here for you."

"I know." Melissa clasped her hands in her lap and nodded toward the glider. "I can't sit there. Harm and I always sat on the glider, and I just can't do it."

Alice reached over and gently pried one hand loose. She held it firmly in a warm embrace. "It's okay to feel that way. The bench is fine." They sat very still for several seconds.

Melissa whispered. "An aneurysm. One moment he was alive and happy, and we were making plans, and the next..." she felt the words catch in her throat, "he was gone. Just like that. Oh Alice, we are never ready for that."

"No. We're not."

"His soul is up there." Melissa indicated the grey sky that was swept with rain clouds. "He's watching over me. But what do I have left? The urn with his ashes was scattered over the bluff this morning. I have my memories, but that's not enough! I want to reach out and touch him." She slapped her hands across her knees in an angry gesture. "We belonged together. No matter what happened, we were there for each other. I want him here. Now!"

"Hold on to me, and cry it out. You have to make do with knowing that Harm..." Alice hugged Melissa, searching for the right words, "That he was called and had to leave. Fair or not. So cry it out and let life carry you wherever you're meant to go next."

"Skye had to return to his job today." Melissa's shoulders fell as she murmured, "His flight was right after the memorial service. That's why he left. He didn't talk to many people. He's been gone so long, I don't think he remembered all our friends." She took a breath. "I feel so alone. I'm independent but, oh, how I counted on Harm each day for so many little things." She wiped at her tears. "I hoped Skye would stay for a bit, help me sort through his father's closet, talk with me..." Her voice trailed off.

Alice thought of Skye's self-indulgent attitude at the visitation the previous evening. He'd spent most of his time checking his messages and making calls. Although he'd stood with his mother to receive the people who had come to pay their respects, he'd seemed rushed, almost rude.

Pete had hushed her by saying that everyone dealt with death in their own way and she shouldn't be judgmental, so she'd pushed it to the back of her mind as she held her friend's hand.

Melissa turned to her with tear-filled eyes. "How am I going to get through each day alone?"

"I'm not going to leave you."

Melissa smiled weakly through her tears. "You're my crutch?" she asked.

"I'm whatever you need."

"Right now I need to lay my head on Harm's chest. I need to smell his skin fresh from the shower. I need to tell him how much happiness he gave me. How much I loved him." Melissa stamped her foot. "We had so many plans!"

"It's okay to be angry, honey." She held Melissa and rocked with her as the tears fell. "Can you smell the moisture? Rain's coming. Let's go back inside."

"Yes. That's a good idea." She wiped at her face. "Besides, Harm's sister, Bev, came down from Washington and I need to spend some time with her." She looked into the greyness of the sky. "You know, Bev was at the art gallery when I met Harm." Blinking back more tears, she stood up. "He walked me home that night and we were never apart again...until now."

****

When the long day ended and the last mourner departed, Melissa turned to Alice. "It's been a sad day, filled with nostalgia." Melancholy touched her words, "I know you want to stay, but I need to be by myself tonight."

Alice looked worried. "You've been through so much."

Tears welled up, but Melissa breathed deeply, "Please give me this time."

"Very well, my friend." Alice hugged her. "I'll see you in the morning."

Melissa watched the car drive away, and she locked the door. She tried to pull her thoughts together. *I feel cheated, Harm. It wasn't fair for you to leave.*

The kitchen had been cleaned, but she mopped the counters anyhow, needing something to do. Finally she walked toward the front door and let her fingers trace across the beveled glass. *Now I know how Aunt Helena felt when the young man never came back from the war. Her heart was broken, but her life went on.*

She felt Harm's approval gently embrace her, but she also felt his question. "Where is our son? Why isn't he with you?"

Looking past the meadows toward the hills and cliffs above her house, she watched the rain twist within the flow of the wind and quietly answered Harm, "Skye is gone. He was called back to work."

With winter past, the spring lupine mixed gaily with California poppies, covering the hillsides. Even through the downpour, she could see the dark blue petals from her ceanothus bush scattering in slantwise patterns across the stony earth of her backyard. Each season produced its own life; such was nature's way. She'd learn to live again, but for now, she let the tears fill her eyes as she walked toward the bedroom.

Atlanta, Georgia

The funeral for Jackson Beauregard von Campe was impressive. His daughter was clearly grief stricken as she received mourners at the Grey Coat Funeral Parlor. She held a lace hankie to her eyes but refused to lift her black veil. Her tall, handsome husband stood by her side, and their lovely daughter flanked her mother.

Miss Sylvia Dickens, who had been Jackson's close friend for a number of years, lightly embraced Terri Sue Ellen. "I offer my sympathy. Your father was a good man, and he loved you above all else."

"Ah am wracked with grief."

"I'm sure you are. You were his princess."

"Thank you. Ah'm so happy you could be with daddy the last ten years. He enjoyed your visitin' with him so much. Yes, he did, Miss..."

Charles leaned over and whispered 'Dickens' in his wife's ear. Terri Sue Ellen propelled the woman along. "Ah thank you, Miss Dicky, for comin' today." There was a break in the line of mourners, and Terri Sue Ellen turned to her husband and daughter, sizzling with annoyance, "Ah declare! Did you see that tramp? Sleepin' around for years with mah daddy." Leaning over, she addressed her daughter, "Did you follow that Delaney Mae Anne?"

"Ahh, I think so, but..."

"Good! Note that as an example of poor white trash invadin' your granddaddy's life in his old age. It was his weakness for the flesh that took him down. Disgustin'."

Charles leaned in, talking softly to his daughter, "Doodle Bug, don't upset your mother."

Delaney looked distressed. "I thought Miss Dickens was his nurse."

"You make no mind what she said she was! Your momma knows what was goin' on. She was the jelly on his toast. Truth is that your poor old granddaddy was beddin' the hired help! It tarnished our good name." She sniffed in anger, "Why, her comin' here to pay her respects is revoltin' Ah ask you, what has happen' to the South? My Methodist upbringin' would have called this a wicked sacrilegious sin."

"Oh, mother! That's frightening!"

"It is!"

"I didn't know that you and granddaddy were members of a church."

"Of course we were! You can't live here and not be members of a church. Honestly, Delaney Mae Anne, you've got to learn to think before you speak." She paused dramatically and added, "We just never attended services due to the fact that they were held on the same day every week, and we had other commitments to attend to. However, my daddy was forever sending money for religious necessities like stained glass windows, padded pews, and all those flashy robes for the minister...why, the preacher looked like Liberace in Las Vegas. Daddy even donated a gleamin' white organ for the choir so they could sing out joyfully." Turning, she faced Charles, "Where's mah flask?"

"It's not here, sugar."

"The pressure." She signed loudly and clutched at Charles's sleeve for the benefit of those around her. Standing on her toes, she whispered in his ear, "Let's speed this up, some. Ah need a martini, and ah have me a tee off time in the mornin' at daddy's club. All this cryin' and grievin' is bad for my digestion, which throws off my ability to play good golf."

****

Sylvia left the funeral home, shaking her head. She was motioned over to a group of friends standing outside in the shade of an old magnolia tree.

Beatrice Lee asked, "How was daddy's princess?"

"She's something, that daughter of his," Sylvia replied. "She never visited once in the last few years when her daddy was so ill. He was a fine man, but his little princess is a self-centered bitch."

General comments and nods confirmed her thinking.

****

Inside the church, Terri Sue Ellen turned to the next mourner. Speaking slowly in a soft southern tone, she continued, "Thank you so much for comin'. Why, it means the world to me and mah family. Ah know my daddy is lookin' down on us from heaven, ever joyful in the turnout of family and friends who have seen fit to honor his royal memory."

****

After the catered cocktail hour at the personal residence of the von Campe's, Terri Sue Ellen sat at her daddy's big oak desk sipping a martini and eagerly signed the papers to list the property with Century Twenty One.

After all, her daddy was with her mamma now, and Chicago was her home. She wanted to return as soon as possible, but Charles had explained how it was vital for her to remain for the reading of the will, which seemed like a waste of time because most everything was hers, anyhow.

The elderly attorney and long-time family friend of the von Campe family, Sullivan Picket, adjusted the spectacles on his nose and glanced up at Jackson's daughter. She was still pretty but broad in the beam and self-centered as ever. His granddaughter was lovely as well, but didn't appear too bright. Charles, on the other hand, had done well with the money Jackson had given him and had proved to be a successful businessman, repaying every cent loaned to him.

The will detailed many aspects, and while Terri Sue Ellen dozed, Charles paid close attention.

Victoria, who was now in an assisted living facility, was financially cared for. Charles breathed a sigh of relief because having the responsibility of two women who enjoyed alcohol too much was not something he'd looked forward to.

All the servants were given sums of money and letters of recommendation while several charities were honored with donations. Everything else went to Jackson's princess.

Charles nudged his wife awake so she could hear the reading of her inheritance, which was lengthy. She continued to play the role of bereaved daughter right up until she learned that her father had added an amendment leaving a small sum of money to his companion and caregiver of ten years, Sylvia Dickens.

"Whatever for?" She whispered loudly to Charles, "That woman was a paid nurse who seduced mah daddy. Probably with all the physical activity she demanded from him, it was the cause of his early death."

"Sugar, your father was ninety-one."

"Makes no matter. Obviously daddy was senile." She blurted out, "We should protest the will."

"Shush." He gave his wife a warning look. "

"That hussy getting' a penny of my daddy's hard earned money is against my better principals."

"Be quiet." Charles placed his wife's head on his broad shoulder. He nodded at the lawyer. "Mr. Picket, give me a moment please." He looked around the room, addressing the people in his deep voice, "My wife is tormented with sorrow. Please excuse her." Charles mumbled in her ear, "You got everything, sugar. You don't want to protest the will."

"Forgive me." She smiled tearfully at the old lawyer. "Ah am undone with the glum reality of mah daddy's passin'. Amen. Carry on." Whispering in her husband's ear, she continued, "We should have someone check the silver to be sure none is missin'. Hired help like that will steal you blind unless they're watched, and ah want to sell it as a whole set. Ah'll get more for it that way."

When the reading was complete, coffee was served accompanied with tiny pecan buns in honor of her father's memory. Some small talk followed, but soon the guests departed, glad to be on their way.

Terri Sue Ellen fixed herself another martini and confirmed her tee off time for the following morning. After all, Atlanta could get real hot by noon.

Charles dealt with the family attorney. He polished off the final details of the will, put the elderly man in a car, and sent him home where his son, Clemet, waited.

****

"How'd it go dad?"

Sullivan put his attaché on the hall table as he'd done for fifty years. Taking a deep breath, he answered, "Jackson was one of my first clients, and we became good friends. However misguided he was as a father, he did try. His daughter is a putz and has a large ass for a woman who was once skinny. His granddaughter is self-centered like her mother and not very bright, and, Lord love his sister, Victoria; she's in a home for alcoholics where she belongs." He sighed heavily. "I'm glad that's over."

Sullivan patted his son's shoulder. "The law practice is officially all yours. I've fulfilled my promise to Jackson Beauregard von Campe, and now I'm completely retired. The new letter head will hold your name, son, Clemet Bernard Picket, Attorney At Law."

"I understand, Dad." Clemet watched as his father walked slowly into the library. "I'll join you for bourbon, and we'll toast the honor of the von Campe's."

Clem paused and allowed himself a moment of self-indulgence. *Terri Sue Ellen may have a large ass now, but I'll always have the memory of steamy nights with an aim-to-please girl in the front of my Chevy...all for the price of a cherry snow cone.* He couldn't help the grin that tipped up the corners of his mouth. *Ahh. Sweet youth!*

Sullivan looked up as his son entered the book-lined room. "I know about you and Terri Sue Ellen. The whole county knew."

Clem's face grew red with embarrassment. "I'm a changed man, dad. I'm a devoted husband and father. Lisa Louise showed me the light."

"For the love of God, I hope so."

Three Years Later
Big Sur, California

Three years after Harm passed, Alice Bailey had a fatal heart attack. Her husband was inconsolable. Duane had finished medical school, but he was busy with an internship, so Melissa talked with Pete for hours on end, offering friendship and understanding.

Skye was pursuing his career as well and hadn't been home since his father's funeral, so Melissa and Pete found support in each other. They reached out to people who had lost loved ones and tried to talk through their feelings. They joined a dinner club in Big Sur so they would go out more often.

****

Pete was the designated driver on the ride home from the Wharf Restaurant in Monterey. The other passengers had been dropped at their respective homes in Carmel and Big Sur, and Melissa was the last person in his car.

He walked her to the front door. "You know it's been almost two years we've been having dinner with these people. I've grown fond of them all. And I'm especially happy that next week it's Dave McLaren's turn to pick up folks. Good thing he lives close so he can get us." Pete smiled. "And I can have a glass of wine with dinner."

"Being the designated driver is difficult, but we all have to take a turn," Melissa replied. "There's comfort knowing a sober person is going to be at the wheel, but next week, we'll have to climb all the way back into those little seats in the rear of Dave's SUV because we're first on his list." She joked, "But that's good exercise for us."

"Well now, speaking of exercise..." Pete grinned. "I was thinking that maybe we should join a gym. Get some work-out time on the calendar."

"What do you mean 'we'?" Their banter had become comfortable over the last few months.

"Surely you wouldn't let me go alone on an escapade like that?" Pete looked shocked.

"Sure I would." Melissa smiled. "But whatever for?"

"Well, Duane said I was packin' on a few pounds."

"Oh, that's silly. You look fine to me, and I see you more than your son does."

"I'm in agreement." Pete nodded as he brushed his hand over his bald head. "I guess being a pediatrician is time-consuming, and I'm just glad that Duane makes it back here every so often."

"Well, that's better than Skye. He hasn't been home in years." She shrugged. "At least I get the occasional phone call."

Pete nodded, sensing her disappointment. "Say, I got an idea. How about we go to the movies instead of signing up for a gym membership?" His face curved into a smile. "I'm up for something exciting. Maybe a thriller? What do you say?"

Melissa laughed. "Sounds like a plan to me. You want some coffee before heading home?" She pushed hard to open the front door. Reaching inside, she flipped the switch, and the blackness of night disappeared. "Door sticks if we've got a lot of moisture in the air, but then you already know that."

"The whole of Big Sur knows that."

"Sure enough." She felt relaxed. "Come on in. I believe I have decaf, and it's even a dark roast." Dropping her purse on the table in the entry, she was suddenly aware of Pete's presence. It was a contented feeling, and she turned to find herself in his arms.

"Gosh, I'm sorry," he said. "I didn't mean to be so close behind you." But his blue eyes sparkled, and she laughed, kissing him lightly.

"Yes, you did." In flat-heeled shoes, she was slightly taller than him and lowered her head to look in his eyes.

"Maybe I might have." He kissed her back.

She wasn't aware how it happened, but it felt like fate had waved a magic wand, and their friendship turned a corner until he took a step back.

"We didn't do anything wrong, Pete."

He looked at her for a long second. "I know."

"My love for Harm ran deep, and it will never change. I know you loved Alice just as much, and no one ever can take their places."

He reached out for Melissa's hand. "Truth be told, Missy, I didn't want to take advantage of you when you're feeling blue."

"Oh, you mean Skye." She shrugged. "Like I said, I get a phone call now and then. Oh, sure, I wish it was different, but you can't change what it is unless that change comes from within. He has years ahead of him, and lots can happen." Her eyes searched Pete's face, and she spoke simply, "We all know that my son never shared my love of Big Sur. He needed to do what he liked best...offer up his own opinions." With lightness in her voice, she joked, "Some might call him bossy." She paused, and her tone turned brisk, "And I have to accept that."

"Yup, guess that's true enough and a good way to look at it." Pete spoke guardedly, "On the other hand, seems we have a life to live, too. We should add some excitement to our golden years."

"Yes. I know what you mean. I remember turning forty and thinking, well now, I'm old. That was silly." She laughed. "Then I passed fifty, and each day became a treasure, so overall, I figure I'm dealing with this event called aging in an okay way."

"You're a wise woman," he proclaimed with a wink.

She kidded back, "Now I know that sixty is somewhere out there, and I need to get a move on with my future plans. Add a little hustle to my life." A thoughtful expression settled across her face and she continued, "You know that Skye has no interest in returning home. He goes through girlfriends like water over a dam." She shook her head. "Oh, I'm not privy to his personal life, but I hear a girl's name now and again. Always a different one. No one pleases him for long." She wrinkled her forehead. "Or maybe he doesn't please them? Who knows if I'll ever have grand babies?"

Pete nodded, "You know how it is with Duane. No grandchildren coming my way either."

"Well, that means we have each other."

"But we can't be having any babies," he joked.

"Oh, Pete! You make me laugh. And that's a good thing."

"Now Missy, you know what the experts say. Sixty is the new fifty, and fifty is the new forty."

"Oh, who told you that?"

"Duane, and he's a doctor."

She studied the man in front of her. "Okay. I'll accept that." She smiled happily. "I'm willing to chop off ten years, if you are."

"We got us a plan." He winked, running his hand down her arm, where he let it linger. "You're my best friend, Missy."

"And you're mine, Peterson Bailey." She smiled, touching his face. "I want that never to change."

A wisp of reddish hair, now woven with a sprinkle of grey, trailed in front of her ear. He touched it with great care and released his breath, speaking softly, "I'm gon'na pass on the coffee for now, but why don't I come by around five tomorrow and pick you up? We'll have a date night. Get popcorn and sodas at the movies." He laughed. "Cost is no problem."

"Good to know you're financially secure," she teased back. "Now that I think about it, a movie would be nice." She didn't fidget. His kiss had felt good.

He didn't move too swiftly, as if he was still feeling his way. "Well, okay. I'll be back."

"Isn't that a line from a movie?"

"It's my line now."

She watched him leave and smiled at their mutual discomfort. *It's going to work* she thought, *because we care enough to be concerned if we're doing the right thing. Can't analyze it too carefully but we need to run it by our hearts...see where we come out.*

****

The next day Melissa pondered over what to wear for their date. Feeling silly that she was fussing with her clothes, she decided that Pete would be wearing jeans and she would do the same.

At five sharp, Pete knocked at the door, and she looked through the beveled glass to see a man in a navy sports coat with a red handkerchief in his breast pocket and an open collared white shirt.

She pulled the door open. "You're dressed up!"

"And Hello to you, too," he replied casually. "I'm taking a lady to the movies."

"But," she looked down at her Levi's, "people no longer get dressed up to go the movies."

"I'm trying to impress you."

"Give me ten minutes."

"Nope." He reached out to stop her, and they're eyes met. "You look mighty good in those jeans, Missy." He grinned. "Got yourself some real long legs."

"Oh, Pete, you're flirting with me."

"Am I?"

Her heart began to race.

He ran his hand across his head and looked up. "It's been a while. I hope I remember how to proceed. Seems like I'm supposed to bring an offering of my affection. So here." He pulled a pottery jar out of a paper sack. "I've mastered the wheel–throwing skills."

"Yes, you have," she replied with a raised eyebrow. "Seeing that you have the Peterson Bailey Big Sur Pottery School and students come from all over the United States to take your classes, I'd say you've done good work, and I'm honored to have an original piece." She grinned and asked, "Did you sign it?"

"Sure did."

"Well then, that's extra special."

He felt his cheeks blush and pushed the jar toward her. "This is for the entry table that your granddaddy carved. Open the top and see what's inside."

Carefully, Melissa lifted the jar's cover. "It's filled with petals." She spoke softly, "And they smell like roses."

"Yup. Picked 'em from Alice's rose bushes."

Melissa's words were filled with affection, "I remember the first time Alice brought roses to my mother's table. It was years ago on Thanksgiving. That's when we were both pregnant. My goodness," she spoke quietly. "We were in our early twenties. Well, Pete, I'm glad you tended her garden after she passed. It's lovely, and I always admired it. She had a real green thumb."

"That she did. Right from the get-go, Alice selected hearty roses, and all I have to do is pull a few weeds now and then and add some fertilizer in the spring."

Being slightly taller, she leaned forward and brushed her lips across his forehead. "I shall put this on the table you intended it for and enjoy the fragrance." Turning to place the pottery jar on the entry table, she nodded to herself. *We're moving to the next step, and it feels comfortable.*

He reached out to touch her hair. "You ready to go?"

"Well, Pete," she faced him as a serene feeling drifted through her body, "Truth is, I don't really like to go to the movies."

"That so?" He moved a step closer but didn't enter her space.

"Yes. That's so. Seats are not that comfortable, and the floor tends to be sticky."

"Those theater seats got nothin' on your swan sofa when it comes to cozy."

"They don't make em like that anymore." Her smile broadened, and she added, "Matchless quality."

Pete snapped his fingers. "I got it. You can tell me a story about your family's history?"

"I was thinkin' along the lines of why don't we sit out back in the glider." She made a small movement toward him and spoke softly, "You can tell me about sculpting and coil pots and clay impressions." She bent to whisper in his ear, "I've always had a hankerin' to learn more about designing pottery."

"I'm your man, Missy."

"You called me that before. Why?"

"Sounds right to my ears. Say..." Taking her hand, he led her toward the kitchen door. "Something I got to ask you. Do you like bald guys?"

She laughed, "I could."

"Well then!" he exclaimed happily. "I'd say that's a piece of good news for me."

He brushed the seat of the glider with his pocket handkerchief and indicated she should sit down first. "Moon is real pretty tonight." He sat next to her and draped an arm over the back of the wooden frame. It moved with a creak. "I can fix that," he stated confidently.

"Men have been fixing things round here since the beginning of time." She thought of Harm and smiled.

The ocean sputtered against the rocks far below the cliffs with a sound that was both hollow and happy. Which would she embrace? It was time to move on. She slid closer to Pete and put her head against his shoulder. "You smell good. Sort of like limes and basil."

He joked, "I bought some fancy cologne, and I think it's supposed to smell better than fruit and herbs."

"It has a fresh scent. I like it."

"That's the result I wanted."

She asked simply, "Will you kiss me again?"

The moon shone with silver light as Pete gathered Melissa in his arms.

****

Months later, they were living together, and it felt good—the way it was meant to be.

Chapter Six

Two Years later
Chicago, Illinois

"I believe I found the right man for the job." Charles Covington sat back in his leather chair and swiveled slowly so he was facing the ceiling-to-floor windows in his corner office. His eyes drifted across the Chicago skyline where sunshine played within the white clouds that floated against an endless blue sky.

"Good education. MBA in International Business. Ohio State." He smiled as he spoke to his wife, "He's thirty-four, Delaney's age, ambitious and desires power with a fast climb up the corporate ladder."

"Ah see." Terri Sue Ellen waited. Checking her image in the mirror, she leaned forward to study her jaw line. Smooth, no sagging skin there. Appearances meant everything, and she planned to keep hers in top shape. If only her rear end was smaller, she would be perfect.

Charles continued, "He wears designer suits and carries the appropriate accessories. He's an only child. His father was a journalist, now deceased, and his mother is a Big Sur artist with whom he has little contact." A preoccupied expression settled across his face. "I believe Forrest and Callie-Lynn Durous have one of her paintings in their North Carolina beach house. It's a sea-scape."

"Well, the Durous family has never been known for their good taste. Anyone can paint a picture of the ocean if they have the color blue. The only art ah remember seein' at their house was a black velvet paintin' of dogs wearing visors, smoking cigars and playin' cards."

"Yes. Well, sugar, that was a joke for Forrest's man cave. He'd get it out when his poker club met."

"You sure about that?" She stirred the olives in her martini. "Quite frankly, darlin', being an artist is similar to being unemployed." She grasped at her chest suddenly, "Good Lord! Don't tell me he has to send money home to his mother?"

"No. It seems she has a lot of property in Big Sur, so she's self-sufficient."

"How nice." She perked up. "Hotels and such?"

"No. Undeveloped."

"Really," her voice went up a notch in anticipation. "Well, ah must say that's an opportunity in the nest just a'waitin' to take flight."

"Don't set your hopes high. Not yet. I've learned that the California Coastal Commission has a no growth policy, and it'll be difficult to get around it... but I'll make a few calls."

"Oh now! Aren't you smart checkin' into things like that," she purred. "Why, he sounds just perfect for our Delaney. Can he be molded to fit our image?"

"Yes." Charles paused reflectively. "I believe this one can."

"And the land." She gazed steadily at the mirror. "What a lovely bonus."

Charles swung his chair around. "I'll work on the questions for the Big Sur property, and Delaney can talk to him about it when the timing is right." He chuckled. "But first they have to meet and connect and think it's all their idea." He paused in thought. "Manipulation can be a loving skill when property applied."

"So true, darlin'." She lifted her drink.

Leaning back in his chair, Charles smiled. "We'll be getting what we want, and so will he. I think he's going places, and we want to be there to guide our daughter in his direction." *Just like your daddy was there for you.*

"Ah'm getting' ahead of myself here, but ah'll bet our Delaney can even assist in selecting friends for our new employee." Terri Sue Ellen fluttered her hands. "Because ah'm sure he'll want to improve his position in life once he's datin' our little girl...you know, due to mah royal heritage and such. Plus it's always good to know whose influencin' his ideas. But, as you said, darlin', we can never, ever let on that we orchestrated this happy event."

"Absolutely not. It will be their decision to become a couple."

Terri Sue Ellen blinked several times. *Oh goodness. That's a stray chin hair.* Reaching for the tweezers, she continued, "Oh, perhaps our little girl can be a bit bossy at times, but that's just when people are not payin' attention to what she's tellin' them to do." *Ouch. Oh my lord, it's curly!* Looking at the black hair, she forced herself to focus on their conversation. "Ah feel that Delaney is a born leader."

Charles grunted in agreement, "She's been taught since she was a child that to be successful, you have to ring the bell, bring the deal home. Not just in business, but in life as well." He lit his cigar and added, "That includes relationships that bring money into Tech World International."

"You are such a good daddy, Chuck." She selected a coral lip pencil and continued, "It's high time our little girl had a boyfriend who was a keeper."

Charles snorted. "The other men she dated weren't good enough for her."

"No, they weren't! Not a one of them." *And there were so many.* Terri Sue Ellen leaned toward the mirror and applied a fine line of color to outline her lips. "Now maybe our Delaney didn't always get the best scholastic grades in college, but with the new science lab at Georgia State being such a lovely building...she did graduate with honors." She studied her lips and continued, "Suma cum laude just smacks of intelligence." She paused thoughtfully and added, "Much the way my college records do."

"Of course, sugar."

"Thank you, Chuck."

His heart skipped a beat as he thought of the hot, humid nights in Georgia. "You excite me when you say that."

"Ah know." She reached for her martini.

"Perhaps later we could..."

"Ah'll set out your silk shorts, and we'll see what comes up."

"Good!" He closed his eyes in anticipation and allowed himself a moment before he returned to the conversation. "I'll have my secretary schedule lunch tomorrow at the club. She can even send one of our impressive invitations over to his hotel room. After all, we'll be entertaining our newest employee...hopefully, our future son-in-law."

"Excellent idea, darlin'! Ah'll even move mah Thursday tee time for a wee bit earlier so that ah will not be rushed. After all, ah want to look my best, as well as be prompt as a pigeon."

Charles nodded as he surveyed the picture perfect sky. "I'll see you tonight, sugar. Why don't you have the cook prepare something elegant for dinner?"

"And ah'll open some Cristal and think up some fun things for us to do later. As ah recall, Big Daddy likes to..." she drew the word out for emphasis, "slide...from under his silk boxers and have himself a look around."

Charles caught his breath.

Sex is power, Chucky. Mah name isn't on the official company documents for nothin'. Smiling brightly, she added, "Oh, where are my manners? What is the young man's name?"

"Skye Topple."

Lake Michigan Commemorated Country Club
Chicago, Illinois

Thursday was windy and clear...a good Chicago day. Skye paid the taxi driver, adding a healthy tip. He exited the cab at the circular drive in front of the exclusive club. Taking in the crisp air as it flew across Lake Michigan, he felt secure about his new career at Tech World International. He'd made his decision based on his negotiations of a handsome employment contract as well as the company's impressive client list.

When a business wanted to improve profits, they contacted Charles Covington, and a team of high powered associates reviewed the work place, implementing new policies and procedures, often replacing employees with the newest in twenty-first century technology. It was a rough game, but when the revenues soared, the client was satisfied.

Skye was ready for the challenge. He looked once again at the elegant summons for lunch. The club name was imprinted with golden letters. He was impressed and carefully presented the embossed invitation to the door man.

Timeless and traditional mahogany framed the French doors that opened into the posh dining room at the Lake Michigan Commemorated Country Club. Creamy Irish linen dressed each table with elegance and a deep blue carpet muffled all sound. Staff in dark jackets and club neckties moved silently, bearing cocktails on leather-covered trays.

Yes! He thought, mentally giving himself a thumbs-up. *This is the life-style I've been waiting for.*

Oils of Riding to the Hunt were set in heavy gilded frames against grey silk wallpaper. Glass-enclosed cases with golf and tennis trophies paired agreeably with winning cups for sailing regattas. His eyes drank in the décor. Money was everywhere, and it felt good.

Charles Covington, aware of his height and power, stood as his newest employee was ushered to his table. The usual amenities followed, and Charles nodded toward the French doors. "There she is now...my sweet southern belle and Vice President of Tech World International." He made a show of standing again to hold the chair for a pear shaped woman who had swooshed dramatically into the room, smiling theatrically, and waving at imaginary friends.

Skye scrambled to his feet, hitting the table and splashing water across the cloth. He mopped at it self-consciously.

With a nod Charles replied, "Let it go. One of the waiters will attend to it. What's important is that a gentleman always seats his lady."

"Yes sir." Skye watched a plump woman navigate nimbly around numerous tables and servers, bearing a path toward them.

"Terri Sue Ellen," Charles called. Glancing at Skye, he spoke candidly, "My wife. Two names are good, but three names make a southern lady feel very important." He winked, and Skye waited a few seconds to see what his boss would say next. When Charles smiled at him, Skye wondered why. Was it because he had refrained from commenting on how many names it took to make a lady feel important? It had seemed to be a personal observation so he'd kept quiet, and it must have been the right thing to do.

He wasn't sure but felt that his MBA in International Business was only the beginning. The politics and nuances of Tech World International were going to be learned in the field. He thought of himself as a soldier ready for battle.

Charles turned toward the approaching lady whose long flowing pink Chanel blouse covered her ample bosom and expanding rear end.

"Oh, mah darlin'," she gushed as her hands waved at the air. "Mah golf game was absolutely atrocious. But hold on a minute." She blinked her green eyes at Skye as if she'd just seen him and settled her voice into a soft purr, "How do you do?"

Skye offered his hand as Charles introduced them.

"Ah am so very pleased to make your acquaintance." She drug out the sound of his name, "Skye."

"Let me assist you." Charles pushed her chair under the table as she bounced up and down to eliminate some of her weight.

"Why, Chuck has had nothing but praise for your resume. Ah am so delighted that you could join us for a bit of lunch before assumin' your new duties. It's such an honor to be sittin' among you boys. Why, ah'm all but flushed."

She fanned at her face, and her eyelashes bobbed up and down as she tossed a smile into the room looking for people to impress. "Being vice president is a weighty title, and ah do my best, but it's really Charles and Delaney who run Tech World International."

Speaking to the waitress, she continued, "Ah believe that ah'll have a martini with Stolichnaya Vodka Celebrated."

Skye thought a martini would be the right drink but waited to see what his boss was going to do. Charles didn't respond, so neither did he.

"Oh, you boys. Are y'all goin' let a lady drink alone?" She pouted and fluttered her wrist, letting her diamond bracelets cling together. "Ah so hate to consume alcohol without company. And y'all know that Stolichnaya Celebrated is filtered at sub-zero temperatures, making it a tad more expensive but..." she laughed, "ah'm worth it." Taking a moment to stroke her finger across her cheek, she let it rest on her smooth chin.

Skye nodded, waiting to see if more information was forthcoming. It was a habit he'd picked up from his mother years ago.

Terry Sue Ellen reached over abruptly, touching her husband's hand. "Ah will never win the women's tournament unless ah improve my swing." She slapped her palm on the table to emphasize her point causing Skye's head to jolt up. "More lessons. That's what mah daddy would have said."

"I heard that you finished second today," Charles replied calmly.

"Oh, but darlin', second is not first, and first is mah goal." She turned sharply to Skye. "Do you play golf? Good golf?"

"Well, Ms. Covington, I try, but your husband is a difficult man to best."

Terri Sue Ellen raised her index finger in a scolding manner. "Now Skye, don't you go callin' me Ms. Covington. Why, you'll make me feel like a little ol' lady." Her heart shaped mouth pouted into an 'O' and she released a tiny puff of air. "Ah insist you call me Terri Sue Ellen. Oh now." She waved her hands. "Ah suppose Chuck has already made a joke about my three names." She blinked her lashes coyly while sipping her drink.

Skye inclined his head but committed to nothing. He was a quick study.

"Why, even our daughter, Miss Delaney Mae Anne, has three names although she only uses her first name for business. She is such a smart girl. Isn't she, darlin'? Ah've no idea why she hasn't been snapped up by some brilliant man."

Charles beamed with pride. "Probably just waiting for the right one to come along."

"Why, our little Delaney followed in my footsteps. Ah come from the royal von Campe family of Germany although ah was born in Atlanta where ah graduated suma cum laude from Georgia State...as did Delaney."

"Congratulations," Skye intoned, thinking that had been a boat load of information and wondered if he should comment on the mention of royalty, but, after a moment, he decided to pass. "You must both be very proud of your daughter's accomplishments."

"Oh, indeed we are. And Chuck here," she reached over to brush his arm again with the well-designed move, "is a huge contributor to the college, same as mah dear departed daddy. Isn't that true, darlin'?"

"Well, sugar, we all try to do our part for higher education."

She sipped her martini. "It is divine. Won't you boys join me?"

The waitress appeared, and Charles nodded at Skye. "Can't let a lady drink alone."

"No sir. We can't do that."

Terri Sue Ellen looked at the waitress. "Ah'll just have me a tiny bowl of those luscious, very large, green olives with..." She arched her finger in the direction of her glass. "Another one of these Stolichnaya Celebrated martinis." Smiling brightly, she accepted the menu then handed it back. "Why, ah don't need me one of these. Ah know exactly what ah'll have."

The waitress remained poised for the order.

"One of those marvelous, organic, mixed spring green salads, and give me just a squeeze of lemon, if you please. Do spin those greens at least three times in bottled water and give them a light salt rinse and hold back on all the dressin'."

Skye detected a ghost of a smile on the waitress' face, as if she'd heard this all before.

"Gentlemen?"

Steak sandwiches were ordered, fries were added, and Terri Sue Ellen picked up the conversation where she'd left off. "Why, with my family's support, Georgia State lives on to triumph for another day. Jubilation, darlin'!" She faced Skye. "And what school did you graduate from?"

"Ohio State."

She awarded him a green-eyed blink. "Ah do remember now and with an impressive degree. Isn't that simply divine? And you've had executive positions with other corporations, and they've given you outstandin' recommendations." She touched his hand with a finger.

Conversation hummed for several minutes until the waitress arrived with the cocktails. Terri Sue Ellen held her glass high. "Shall we raise our glasses in a toast to our college days?"

"To the future," Charles added, and glasses clinked. Skye tried to imagine what college was like that long ago but had no success.

Using her napkin to daintily touch her lips, Terry Sue Ellen looked up at the waitress who was placing a salad in front of her. "You're such a tiny little thing, dear." She scanned the room for new comers then turned to Skye, leaning into his face. "Ah say this to her all the time 'cause offerin' encouragement and support to all the employees at the club is my responsibility." She pulled back and looked up. "Why, Lorraine here, and myself, well, truth be told, we're just like sisters. We've known each other for simply ever. Haven't we?" She smiled magnanimously.

"Yes, Mrs. Covington." The waitress placed generous sandwiches in front of the men. The aromas of seasonings and hickory-grilled steak filled the air.

"So she understands that ah have to watch every morsel ah eat or my hips would just expand into never-never land." Make-up creased the fine lines around her eyes.

Skye blinked, at a loss for words, as she continued, "Lorrain has worked herself up the ladder of success here at the club, and just look at her now. Head waitress! An exhilarating position!"

Skye glanced at Lorrain and saw that "Lana" was written on her nametag. He raised his eyebrows, and Lana narrowed her eyes. Pulling his attention back to Terri Sue Ellen, who was now touching his wrist, he shifted his thoughts to the flow of table conversation.

Charles glanced up. "Thank you, Lorraine. You may go now."

****

Lana walked toward the kitchen and was stopped by another waitress. "I see you got the Covington table."

"Well, Molly," she answered in a low voice, "soon as we saw them come in, we cut the cards, and I lost."

"My sympathy to you. I see they're interviewing yet another husband candidate for their unpleasant daughter. It reminds me of trying to satisfy a cat in heat."

"Yes, it's like trolling for a mate. Mr. and Mrs. We're-So-Important are pouring it all over him."

Molly smiled. "Has she covered the 'I come from a royal family, yet?'"

"Sure enough. She took care of that early on."

"So, how's this one doing?"

"Better than the others."

"Huh? He looked smarter than that. Have you been called to do the..."
Molly rolled her eyes. "French fry ceremony yet?"

"Soon." Lana paused. "Wait for it."

****

"Oh! Now just look at you with your scrumptious steak and buttered
bread and those golden French fries. No wonder ah play so much golf. It's
self-help to evade those extra pounds." Terri Sue Ellen allowed her fingers to
stoke across her neck in a theatrical gesture. "If only, ah could eat like that."

The restaurant manager approached the table. "It's always good to see
you Mr. and Mrs. Covington. You do brighten up the room. I trust everything
is to your liking?"

Charles looked up. "Everything is fine. But I have a request for our
waitress, if you would be so kind as to send her back to our table."

"Absolutely, sir. Right away."

"And there it is." Lana nodded. "Time for the sacrament to begin." She
reached for a plate and two forks with a sigh and walked back to the table.
"Mr. Covington, how can I be of assistance?"

"Could you bring a small plate for Mrs. Covington?"

Lana produced the plate as if by magic and placed it in front of Terri Sue Ellen.
"Would you like one, sugar?"

"Oh, my goodness." She sat back with a practiced expression of surprise.
"There, Skye, you can see my husband knows me so well. Why, ah've never
been able to hide my weakness for those deep fried potatoes."

She glanced up at the waitress. "Mah husband has insisted that ah indulge,
so if you would just put a fry or two on mah plate that would suffice. You see,
Lorraine, ah became addicted to these when ah lived in France for two weeks.
They're prepared in peanut oil across the pond."

Lana paused. "I did not know that."

"Well, of course you didn't. Ah'm here to share mah education with you
so you can repeat these knowledgeable tidbits when you serve food to other
club members. It makes you look more credible."

Skye caught a look of irritation cross Lana's face as she used two forks to transfer several French fries.

"I'll just play an extra nine holes tomorrow." As she slipped into her second martini, Skye wondered briefly about the number of calories in alcohol and olives but felt the thought idle and disappear.

She picked up her end of the conversation and flashed the room with another happy look, "Way back when, and ah do mean waaay back when, ah was Miss Georgia Peach at Fort Valley State University, and ah was just as tiny as Lorraine." She paused for the appropriate comment.

Skye glanced at his new boss for guidance, and Charles moved the conversation along. "Her college pageant days went on hold when her daddy insisted that she enter Georgia State, Atlanta, to pursue her educational program. And what a pity she left the world of beauty galas and balls behind, but, by doing so, some of the other young ladies were given a chance to win."

She placed two fingers over her lips to cover a tiny belch and continued, "Why, Chucky, aren't you the sweet one?"

Skye looked at the slightly tipsy, older woman across the table and felt he should say something. "I'm sure you were a perfect peach queen."

Charles nodded in agreement thinking of the various sexual positions his peach queen had introduced him to.

"Ah was." She touched Skye's arm. *Horseback ridin' gave me a good spread and a firm ass.* Facing both men, she buzzed with more words. "Ah remained lean and trim right up until my child bearing years, when my hips and my derriere developed individual lives."

Skye blinked.

Lana shut her eyes, offering a deep sigh. "Will there be anything else, sir?"

"We're fine for now." He signaled her to stop the flow of martinis and returned his attention to his wife. "You have a lovely figure, sugar."

"Why, aren't you precious? It was all worth it to have our little Delaney Mae Anne enter our lives."

"Having a daughter is a worthy event." Charles slapped Skye on the back. "Someday you'll know the feeling."

Terri Sue Ellen was floating in her own words, "Perhaps we'all could play golf one of these days."

Skye nodded, feeling confused by the quick change in conversation.

"Golf is my wife's passion."

She smiled, and her eyelashes flashed up and down, catching Skye's attention. Charles pointed toward his own eye and nodded at his wife.

"Well, ah do declare." She pushed her eyelashes back in place. "Thank you, darlin'." Skye breathed a sigh of relief as she continued, "Now do let me go back to where ah was." Taking another look around the room, she asked. "Where was that?"

"You were discussing Georgia State."

"Thank you, Skye..." She let his name stick like molasses on her tongue. "For payin' such astute attention. Allow me to take a sip and wet my whistle." She faced her husband. "This young man is indeed an asset to Tech World International."

Charles turned to his newest employee. "I'm glad you're part of my team. Ambitious, young, well turned out. Your first assignment will be in Finland, after the International VP briefs you."

"I look forward to the challenge, Mr. Covington."

"No more Mr. Covington. I prefer my executive staff call me..." he took a second to deepen his voice, "Chuck."

****

The luncheon ended on a high note leaving Skye feeling like he lived on top of the world. He was offered a suite in the stylish hotel that was next to the Tech World International building and, for a couple of weeks, took care of routine business. He was introduced to people at the company headquarters and, by the end of his second week, he was leaving for Helsinki.

Tech World International Headquarters
Chicago, Illinois

Standing in front of the impressive building, making a half-hearted attempt to hail a cab to the airport, Skye's mind was fully absorbed with congratulating himself on the many benefits and perks that came with his title of Senior Team Leader.

A chauffeur appeared suddenly at his side with the news that Ms. Covington was on her way to the airport and would share her limo with him. He smiled to himself. This was turning into another good day. However, it would be wise to wipe the grin off his face and humbly accept the ride from the president's wife.

Plus, if he was completely honest with himself, he could handle a lift to the airport and be quite charming at the same time. Surely this was multi-tasking at its best. He chuckled to himself about his own clever wit and tried to recall what Ms. Covington looked like.

She had sported long fake lashes that resembled an insect he couldn't quite identify, and she had an over-the-top southern accent. But maybe not? He hadn't had a lot of exposure to the South so he shouldn't be judgmental. On the plus side, she was hopelessly involved in golf, which was rapidly becoming his favorite new sport ever since her husband had emphasized that big business was done on the course.

Skye nodded at the chauffeur who placed his luggage in the trunk and then held the door open for him. He wondered absent-mindedly if he was supposed to tip him as he bent down to lower his tall frame into the rear seat.

Upon seeing a young woman searching through a briefcase of papers, he felt confused. This was definitely not Terri Sue Ellen Covington. He found himself staring at a beautiful lady who was wearing a Chanel Classic Black Wool Boucle Suit, accessorized with Signature Gold Buttons; his heart raced faster. She looked up to acknowledge his presence, and the spark he felt ignited to a full blaze. Her heart-shaped mouth wasn't outlined with a peach colored pencil, and she was much younger. He blinked as he looked into her jade green eyes.

She responded by introducing herself using only one name, Delaney, and she explained that her father had pointed him out as the new associate on board at Tech World International. The timbre of her voice held a commanding note, and he was impressed with her sense of power. She explained she'd returned a few days ago from an assignment in Paris and wanted to welcome him before he left for Finland. A ride to the airport seemed fitting.

Somewhere in the first few minutes of meeting her, it registered that she didn't share her mother's southern drawl, and he found that to be a pleasant discovery.

An open Hermes attaché briefcase sat on her lap. Nestled in the soft red leather interior was a copy of L'Officiel, a fashion magazine from France. Lowering the lid, she snapped the gold clasps in place and looked up, offering a friendly smile that showed perfect teeth. He was instantly grateful for the years he'd spent in braces.

His sandy colored hair, cut close to his head, held blonde streaks that were emphasized from two days of golf with her father. He radiated a healthy glow and smiled back.

His Vassili GM laptop bag that was usually slung across his shoulder had slipped off when he entered the limo. Its glacier colored leather strap sat on the seat next to her, and she recognized his choice of Louis Vuitton. She took in his Italian made Dolce and Gabbana "Martini" strip suit and open collar dress shirt.

You're mine. She ran a hand through her hair, and it fell perfectly into place.

After the initial surprise of meeting the boss' daughter, Skye met her stare evenly in spite of the fact that his heart thumped wildly against his chest. They both knew, at that moment, their paths were meant to cross.

Chapter Seven

A few months later...
Key West, Florida
Robert and Evelyn Covington Residence

Evelyn settled herself in a chaise lounge, under a colorful umbrella on the terrace of their new Key West home and smiled happily. "Florida is so nice in December."

"What you're trying to say is we don't have to spend Christmas with Terry Sue Ellen."

"Being eighty has its advantages. We're not expected to travel quite so much anymore. Besides, I do enjoy our son's company, and he can visit us anytime."

Robert reached for his iced tea. "But his wife doesn't like Florida."

"Such a pity."

For a few minutes, they watched the sailboats bob with the waves far out at sea. Evelyn broke the silence. "I really wonder what kind of young man Skye Topple resembles. What is his character like? Does he have a good value system? How is his moral judgment?" A frown settled across her face. "Clearly he can't have much taste if he's impressed with both mother and daughter."

Robert looked directly at his wife. "I think Charles has given him a pay incentive. He got the idea from Jackson Beauregard von Campe."

Pursing her lips in thought, she let the idea settle. "So you think he'll actually marry Delaney?"

"I'm guessing it all depends on the monetary amount." Robert shrugged. "Of course, there is the off chance that he fancies himself in love."

December
Chicago, Illinois

By Christmas, Skye and Delaney were an official item. Her parents invited him to spend the season with them at their Lake Shore house. Holiday parties in Chicago and sleigh rides north of the city combined with family dinners and festivities at the club. The whirl of activity left him breathless and more in love then he ever imagined.

On the one afternoon they spent at home, Terry Sue Ellen introduced him to their family tradition of telling holiday stories. They sat together in the formal living room admiring the professionally decorated tree that soared twelve feet toward the cathedral ceiling. Christmas ornaments shaped like plump cardinals with bright red plumage adorned the flocked white branches, and shimmering ribbons streamed graciously from the tree top to the floor.

"Ah so like ribbon. It's festive and personifies the season. Mah weddin' gown was festooned with satin ribbons...ya do remember my ribbons, Chuck." *And all the things we did with 'em.* "Ribbons make a celebration special. Isn't that so?"

"It is indeed, sugar."

Terri Sue Ellen leaned toward Skye. "See there. Those big golden balls..." she turned to wink at her husband and returned to Skye. "Ah asked the design company that did up the tree to add them to every branch. Ah love golden balls."

Skye looked at the massive white tree and nodded. "Very nice." The entire house seemed overdone and was kept too warm for his taste. but it pleased Delaney so, therefore, it pleased him.

Terri Sue Ellen was well into her martinis as she spoke "Now, Skye, this is the time we'all tell a tale about a family funny. So, to put y'all at ease, ah'll start. But first...." Her words rolled out merrily, "A tiny sip to keep out the winter's cold." She looked happily at the fresh flowers that were sprayed gold and silver and sat on tables in the living room. They appeared to be wilting in the heat. "Good Heavens! Someone had best water those. Call for Maria." She breathed loudly, smacking her lips. "Mah, this is a good martini."

Dabbing at the corner of her mouth with a delicately embroidered napkin, she continued, "My Nellie made these as a little weddin' gift for me. Ah so treasured her endeavor to create something pretty."

"Go on with your story, mother," Delaney urged as she snuggled closer to Skye. He felt warm wearing a red turtleneck sweater, but Delaney had picked it out for him saying that it was appropriate and fit the season.

"Why, ah remember, after ah gave birth to my precious Delaney Mae Anne and the nurse handed my flawless little bundle to me. It was a moment of perfect bondin' between mother and daughter. Then I looked at her real close and thought to myself, 'Oh my goodness! This baby's little face looks round as an Eskimo's. Could she really be mine? But it made no difference because ah loved her anyhow. Just the way she was."

Both parents laughed, and she continued, "You see, it's a family funny because after a couple of weeks..." She held up a finger to indicate a pause and raised her glass again. "Our precious baby looked picture-perfect. Why, she was just all peaches and cream. Weren't you darlin'?"

"Oh, mother!" Delaney flipped her hair and blinked charmingly at Skye. "Mother can exaggerate."

"You're beautiful now." Skye's eyes showed his love as they gazed at each other while hundreds of clear lights from the tree reflected in the winter windows of the elegant home. The fireplace burned brightly with artificial logs while electric candles nested in the windows.

Terri Sue Ellen winked boldly at her husband. "Why, we just knew we had us a winner." A smear of bright peach lipstick smudged across her front tooth drawing attention away from her brilliant holiday smile. Charles touched his teeth discretely, and his wife nodded.

"Thank you, darlin'." She let her eyes wander down the front of his trousers causing him to smile. "Fun times," she murmured as she wiped the delicate napkin across her tooth and dropped it on her hors d'oeuvres plate. "Maria will get that when she waters mah flowers. She's so good with these little things." Moistening her lips, she faced Charles. "We were talkin' about winners. Is that correct?"

He appeared lost in happy thoughts but made an effort to pull himself back to the conversation. "Yes. Winners." He cleared his throat and located his deep tones. "We got us another one right here." He slapped Skye on the back. "I have a toast to make. Raise your glasses. Here's to my daughter, Doodle Bug, and more winners and mothers and," he winked at his wife, "warm Georgia nights."

"Oh, Chucky. Aren't you romantic. Hold that thought." She screeched, "Maria! I detect a bit of a draft. Perchance the heat needs to be adjusted." Smiling, she turned back to her husband. "Servants require constant supervision. There, with that work out of the way, do go on."

"Here's to my wife and mother of my beautiful daughter."

As if a thunderbolt had hit him, Skye thought of his own mother. "Excuse me. I need to make a call."

Delaney looked surprised, and her heart-shaped mouth dropped open. "Whatever for? It's almost Christmas Eve."

"My mother is all alone, and I should call to wish her a Merry Christmas. With all the excitement here, it completely slipped my mind. I won't be very long." He pulled his cell phone from his pocket and turned around. "I'll just step outside for better reception." *And a breath of cold air. It must be ninety degrees in here.* He pulled at his turtleneck as he left the room.

"What a loving thing to do, Skye," Terri Sue Ellen called after him. "You are just the most devoted son. Such carin' ways."

Delaney sighed. "I'll ask Maria to freshen our drinks."

When they were alone, Charles and his wife exchanged smiling looks as she replied, "Mercy me. He almost forgot his own mother. Poor dear, all alone on Christmas Eve. It must be our entertainin' company, darlin', that threw him off."

"Like I said, sugar," Chuck smiled. "He's a keeper."

Big Sur, California

Melissa hung up the phone. The call from Skye had been brief but pleasant. While they'd talked, she'd watched the fog as it twirled softly through the Monterey Pines bringing a sensation of timelessness to the early evening. It had been five years since Skye had been home. When she asked if he remembered the holidays, he'd made an off-handed comment, and the call was over.

Oh well, she thought to herself. *I can't stand here and feel sorry for myself. Children move on, and that's a fact.* She reached for a potholder and thought of the brown aprons she and her mother had shared so long ago. *Even broadcloth doesn't last forever.*

The ocean thumped against the rocky shore carrying a vibration across the floors of the stone house.

Moving toward the oven, she smiled bravely, *I need to season the roast and wrap the last present. I have a life, too. Duane and Sandy will be here soon.* She paused and spoke in a quiet voice, "I really need to tell Skye about Pete."

"What ya say, Missy?" Pete walked into the kitchen.

"I was talking to myself. I said I need to tell Skye about us." She turned to face him. "And if he ever has a minute to talk to me, I'll get right on it. He should know that I have a very important person in my life and that we have moved in together."

"The proper time will come." He gathered her in his arms. "Meanwhile, Sandy called just before Skye and said they were about an hour away." He rubbed his hands together and smiled. "I recall that Duane always liked Christmas Eve best as a kid. Seems that Skye did, too."

"Skye enjoyed it once upon a time."

"Well, he lives a long way off now. I'm lucky that Duane's settled up in San Francisco. It makes a drive down here a good get-away, plus there's your cookin' and..." his eyes twinkled. "We got presents, decorations and a live pine tree sittin' in the living room just waiting to be lit up." He planted a kiss on Melissa's cheek and asked, "You decide where we're going to plant it when Christmas is over?"

"Right in the line with the other pines that my father planted. It can grow up to be a part of the trees in the wind break." She made a small gesture toward the outdoors and noted in a quiet voice, "Have itself a good life."

"Fair enough. But for tonight, it will be all shiny with tinsel and colored lights and decorated with family ornaments. It can't get any better than that, Missy."

"Yes, the old decorations bring back good memories." Looking toward the phone, she stared at it in a loss for words.

"You have more to say. Out with it."

She repeated uncertainly, "Skye couldn't talk long because he was busy with social activities and his new boss, so it was a quick Merry Christmas. Guess I should be comforted because he did send a poinsettia." She raised an eyebrow. "Did you see the card?"

"Yup. It's signed, 'Yours truly, Skylar."

"I know." Melissa smiled. "Even good secretaries make mistakes." Facing Pete, she continued, "I'm grateful for you and Duane and Sandy. We're a family."

He held her hands. "I know you miss your parents and Harm, just as I miss Alice and our folks. Holidays are meant to remember the good times, and we should take a moment to do that."

She sniffed and wiped at her eyes. "It's important to remember Aunt Helena, too. Oh, she wasn't always here in person, but she was always in my heart. And," she paused, "I knew I was in her heart, too."

He rubbed her knuckles gently with his thumb. "They're chapped. You cleaned and cooked too much getting ready for tonight. I'm going to get you some lotion, and I'll be doing all the dishes after dinner. Don't want to be seeing your hands in any more water." He reached for the beeswax salve and applied it gently. "Feel better?"

"Yes, it does." She looked into his eyes and spoke softly. "Thank you."

"You're most welcome, Missy."

They let the silence settle around them, each lost in thoughts from the past.

Pete cleared his throat and spoke, "I believe I only met your Aunt Helena the one time. Seems she'd just returned from Brazil, if I remember correctly. She was teaching Duane and Skye a native dance, and they were whooping and yelling to beat the band."

"Yup." Grinning, she replied, "Aunt Helena had lots of information to share."

"Was Skye fond of her?"

"Then, yes. As he got older..." she answered simply, "not so much."

"I see." He put his hands on her shoulders. "Why don't you sit down while I start the salad dicing'?"

"Good thing your boy's a doctor. Last time you cut up the salad fixings," she teased, "you nearly took off your finger."

Pete staggered back. "You have wounded me with the sharpness of your words."

"Oh, I have not!"

"Missy, let me remind you that it was a tiny nick. Barely a snafu in the choppin' process."

"It took three stitches."

"Only because Duane was being overly cautious."

She rolled her eyes and smiled. "Wait a bit on the salad. Sandy always likes to help out in the kitchen. Let's both sit for now. Shall we have a glass of wine before they arrive?"

Middle of February

Shortly after Valentine's Day, Skye called his mother to announce his engagement to Delaney Covington. Melissa had been delighted. She would have a daughter now as well as a son.

Chicago

Covington Home

Feeling that some advice was necessary, Terry Sue Ellen called Delaney into her sitting room. "You must fly on out to California and meet his mama to see if she measures up to our high moral standards. Ever since Skye shared that God awful story about his Mexican and Cherokee Indian heritage, ah've had me some doubts." She thumped her fingers impatiently on the dressing table. "Mah, how ah wish he would have put that information in his employment application."

"But, mother, that's discrimination."

"Oh, fiddle diddle! It's a matter of statin' the entire situation so there are no rude surprises. The real problem here is that his family could have a dark-tone in it. Did you follow what ah said, Delaney Mae Anne?"

"Ahh, no."

"That's alright. Your job is to go on out there and cast a wonderful impression. However, keep your eyes and ears open at all times because as a Mexican/Indian artist, his mother may have velvet paintins' sittin' around. Ah think the Durous family has one of them at their beach house, and good old Forrest, bless his heart, drags it out from time to time as some kind of joke."

"I can handle it, mother."

"Good! Listen carefully now 'cause you must be ever vigilant on this trip. If his mama tries to talk to you about art, well, you cut her off sharp-like by saying that you prefer the classics. If she tries to give you a paintin,' lose it in the airport. Do you understand?"

"Yes, mother."

****

Delaney checked her calendar and found a few days in March that would suit her schedule but forgot to tell Skye. When she was packing, she informed him of the trip, and he called his mother, giving her a twenty-four hour notice for their weekend visit.

Big Sur, California

"I'm sorry, Pete, that you can't be here, but I know that Duane has the weekend free from his practice. Sandy can use my ticket to the play, and you'll have a fine time. You can tell me all about dinner in San Francisco and give me a recap of the theater when you get home." Puzzled, she paused, "I really don't know what Skye was thinking not giving me a heads-up a little sooner but..."

"It's alright, Missy. You can share some quality time with your son and his special lady."

"I wanted him to know about our living arrangement. And I wanted to tell him you're not just my boyfriend but my dearest friend." *Or is Skye too absorbed in his new life to care?*

Pete's words were filled with affection as he held her close, "Ain't love grand!"

****

Skye's fiancée had never been in a family built home whose backyard was the Pacific Ocean. Delaney blinked at the majestic sea. "Oh my! That is bright."

Melissa sighed happily. "Sunshine is wonderful."

Delaney flapped her hands in the air, turning her head toward Skye. "Where are my dark glasses?"

He picked up her fuchsia colored Chanel purse and gave it to her. "My mother has always been into nature. It goes with her being a painter. You'll need to forgive her enthusiasm."

"Of course I will." Delaney smiled and plunged on, "I see you looking at my purse. It's iconic Chanel Classic styling with quilted lambskin leather. The gold tone hardware is rather edgy, don't you think?" Her green eyes blinked several times before she continued, " Oh, never mind. I can see I've gone over your head. Anywhoo," she leaned toward Skye. "It's important to instill who knows what early on." She faced Melissa and added, "We can now move into a different room where this light isn't so distracting."

Melissa felt her forehead wrinkling as she led the way toward the parlor. *She's a rude young woman.*

They moved in an orderly fashion until Delaney stopped abruptly causing Skye to back up. She extended her left hand. "Look here. This is my canary diamond engagement ring. Isn't it gorgeous?"

Melissa, determined to be polite, added, "Well, that is lovely." She faced her son. "You have very good taste."

"Oh. I selected it." Delaney wound her arm through Skye's possessively.

"Ladies, I must excuse myself and return some calls. My two favorite girls can get to know each other."

Delaney kissed both sides of his cheeks before he left. Then she faced Melissa. "You do know that I'm his most favorite? I mean, wouldn't it be silly if his mother was his first pick? So," she smiled brightly as she continued talking, "what room is this?"

"What did you say?"

"I asked you what room we're in?"

"Before that. Oh, never mind." Melissa swallowed her exasperation. "This is the parlor."

Skye called from down the hall, "Be careful of the sofa."

"What does that mean?" Delaney looked perplexed. "Oh, your son. He's such a kidder." She moved toward the swan sofa and sat down, sinking deeply into the seat cushions. "Oh my!" Placing her arm across the end of the sofa, she asked, "Swan necks?"

"Yes. My grandfather craved them for his bride as a wedding gift."

"Oh. I understand now." Delaney nodded vigorously as she spoke, pulling herself up. "My mother's family is from the South, too. Family gifts. You just have to keep some of them." She fanned at her face with her free hand. "And this is one really big thingamajig. You might want to consider disposal."

"What?"

"Goodness, I've overstepped a boundary."

"You have." Melissa felt riled, took a deep breath, blinked, and regained her composure. "The seats are rather deep so you need to wiggle around to find your place." She tried a tentative smile. "We joke about it."

"But this isn't funny."

"Oh, I wasn't laughing at you," she replied quickly and then smiled. "My Aunt Helena commissioned a disclaimer in calligraphy but, well..." she shrugged, "I didn't realize I'd need it."

Delaney spoke firmly, "All precautions should be taken to prevent accidents."

"Of course."

When Delaney seemed interested in an old map on the wall, Melissa asked, "Do you like history?"

"Sometimes." *It's so muddled with odds and ends and doodads and, well, junk. I've no idea how Skye lived like this?*

"I can share a story with you." Melissa paused. "If you like?"

"Ahh. Sure." Moving her hand in a nervous gesture, she picked at her Gucci slacks. "We'll have to do something until Skye gets back. Won't we, Mother Topple?"

"Who?" Melissa blinked.

Delaney cleared her throat and found her smile. "So, tell me a story." She leaned too far forward causing her shoes to make a thump on the floor as she settled herself on the stiff board at the sofa's edge.

Startled, Melissa pulled back. "Are you alright?"

Waving her hands in circles, Delaney replied, "I sure am."

Not knowing what to do, Melissa continued, "My story is about the map on the wall. When California became a state, Congress wasted no time in placing a hardship on the grant holders to map their lands." She indicated the yellowed paper within the glass. "The map is a part of Skye's inheritance." Stopping to see if she was boring the young woman, she realized it was actually difficult to be sure, so she risked another sentence. "It was necessary for the government to understand how much California had to offer the nation."

"Really?" Delaney smiled at the room in general.

Melissa nodded but felt a wave of annoyance pass through her. "Even though no one was overly concerned with the amount of coastal property, members of my family complied with the government's requirements. Let me close by showing you the map."

She stood to remove the framed drawing, and when she turned back, Delaney was no longer perched on the edge of the sofa but was sitting in the center of the seat. Melissa asked politely, "Is that better?"

"It is."

Silence ensued, so Melissa extended the map toward her guest. "The first maps were drawn up by my father's great-great grandfather McPhee. You're holding one of originals." She smiled and added, "It's a work of art in so much as it resembles a painting."

"Ahh, yes. Paintings and art." Smiling knowingly, Delaney replied, "I prefer the classics." *I'm really fortunate to be so smart and poised.*"

Realizing that Delaney's interest span for historic maps had reached its end, she fell silent. She shifted positions and noticed that Delaney wore a large watch. "That's quite practical."

"Oh my, no! It's not practical; it's very expensive. It's from the Quai de l'ile Collection: a modern expression in watchmaking by Vacheron Constantin."

"Well, in that case," Melissa sounded confused, "I guess I'm, umm, impressed."

"People are supposed to be mesmerized when I say Vacheron Constantin."

Melissa sat back in her chair, letting her arm rest on the end table. Her fingers dangled over the carved pocket, and she felt a rock in the bottom of the indention. From memory, she knew it was painted blue. *I gave this to my mother when I was a little girl, and she kept it. Would this woman keep a hand painted rock from a child?*

Chicago
Covington Home

"Book Club isn't the same without your daughter, Terri Sue Ellen. Her input is always insightful." Adeline grinned as she faced the other women. "Am I right, ladies?"

"Yes, indeed."

"Judicious judgement."

"Sharp-witted."

"Mah daughter does have an eagle-eye for things."

"She takes after you. Always knows what to say and do." Adeline finished her drink and put the glass on the table.

"Thank you so much. Here, let me pour a bit more for you. Oh, my goodness, it's empty. Maria, bring the Cristal! Honestly, that woman has to be told everything twice."

"Where is Delaney?"

"Vistin' California. Meeting Skye's mama and, no doubt, charmin' the socks off her. She's an artist, you know, so mah daughter studied-up on paintin' and such, so she could carry on an intelligent conversation."

The women exchanged looks.

Adeline asked, "Did anyone read this month's book selection?"

"No, dear."

"You know we're just here to gossip."

"And enjoy a flute of champagne."

"Where in California does his mother live?"

"As you know, it's a very long state, and she lives sor'ta in the middle. A'hm sure Delaney will be able to offer up a thorough accountin' when she gets back home."

Big Sur
Sone House

"My watch is 18K White Gold." Delaney leaned forward and dangled her wrist close to Melissa's face, forcing her to pull back. "Black alligator strap. This is the man's model, but I just adore it. Do you have any other questions or comments?"

"About...?"

Delaney pushed her wrist forward.

"Oh. It's, umm, very large."

"I'm worth it," she replied, offering a pretty smile. "My canary, that's what Skye and I call my diamond, which is also set in 18K White Gold. Yellow gold is for old people."

Melissa blinked abruptly. "Where do you get your information?"

"My mother. She's very knowledgeable." Delaney looked charitably at Melissa. "I can see it's good that I'm here, and none too soon. I'll bring you up to speed Mother Topple. I have to do that often. Now do you have any more stories?"

Bring me up to speed? Melissa paused and stared at Delaney. *She's a peculiar young lady.* With a sigh, she continued, "Let me see, I could share a story about an early business venture in Big Sur."

"Oh!" Delaney's emerald eyes showed interest. "I understand business."

Melissa breathed sharply through her nose and answered in a monotone, "Family members entered the tanbark industry in the 1870's. And shortly after, they branched into limestone, but the days of industrial operations had been on borrowed time in Big Sur."

"Huh?" Delaney shook her head causing her hair to flip right and left. "Are you talking about stones and dirt?"

"I am."

"How nice. Are you done? I'd like to move on to gold. It was discovered in California. I know that because mother and I were history minors, and we both graduated suma cum laude. Oh, you'll want to write that down so you can put it in the local paper when you announce my engagement. Goodness, I see the stress in your face. I'll provide you with the correct spelling of suma cum laude." Tilting her head, she smiled sweetly. "Don't be embarrassed, Mother Topple. I realize that artists aren't supposed to know how to spell Greek words."

"You mean Latin words?"

"Whatever. Back to the matter at hand When you announce my engagement, you'll want to mention my royal background and my mother's Peach Queen title...very prestigious in the South." Delaney leaned forward. "I believe we were discussing gold." Her face became animated. "Did your family have anything to do with that?"

Pausing to let her thoughts catch-up to the change in topics, Melissa shook her head. "Gold was discovered near Alder Creek around 1880, and it led to the Big Sur Gold Rush."

"Ohh! A real gold rush. Now you have my undivided attention."

"Well, I don't like to dampen your spirit, but it wasn't as big as the gold rush in Sutter Creek or Sonora, and in fifteen years, the gold was gone."

"Gone?" She looked dismayed. "Where did it go?"

"It was mined."

"Someone took all of it?"

Melissa felt her eyebrows shoot up and looked closely at her guest. *Suma cum laude is a big stretch. here...a really big stretch.*

"People can be so disappointing. Delaney frowned. "What else was your family involved with?"

Melissa took a deep breath and continued slowly, "My ancestors raised cattle, then sheep and goats, but they learned quickly that the rugged beauty of Big Sur was not accommodating to livestock."

"You were farmers? I had no idea. That's troubling."

"Why?" Melissa gestured with her hands. *Stop that! You're picking up her bad habits.* "Are you sure you're comfortable there? We have chairs."

"I'm not a quitter."

Melissa leaned forward to check the hall, but her son was nowhere to be seen. She turned back to Delaney and pushed the conversation valiantly forward, "The redwood canyons came next in my family history. Relatives invested in a steamer line to move the lumber from the mouth of the Little Sur River."

"Are you talking about boats? " Delaney's green eyes glowed with delight. "Daddy has a cabin cruiser on Lake Michigan. It's very big, and sometimes I sit in the captain's chair, but we have staff to drive it."

Melissa paused; the hope of a close relationship with her son's fiancée was all but gone. Clearing her throat, she continued tiredly, "It was a steamer." When disappointment pulled at Delaney's face, Melissa barked, "Yes, that's a boat!"

"I'm glad to hear it!" Delaney sat forward and stared at her shoes. "They're Banjo Spiked Cap-toe Booties by Christian Louboutin. See the red lacquered sole?" She held her foot up, and the lovely smile reappeared. "Now let's go back to the family boats."

"No. They were not family boats! Look, it's important to understand that the rocky shores were treacherous to ships. By 1889, my relatives had begun work, with other early pioneers, to build the Point Sur Lighthouse." Melissa released an irate sigh that sailed over Delaney's head. "I've really gone on too long. I'm boring you." She felt a headache forming.

"Do you have a bathroom?"

Melissa massaged her temples. "Of course."

"Is it outside?"

"No!"

"Well, that's good to know. When I visit someone for the first time, I have to ask about the facilities." Her forehead wrinkled as she went on, "Did Skye inherit this lighthouse? He should bring something to the table besides the land." Her tone turned weary, "It's difficult grasping onto all this knowledge in just one day. Therefore, you should back up and recite the full story of the lighthouse. It would help me to assimilate the facts."

Ahh, and there it is: a throbbing over my left eye. "Many people contributed to the idea and construction of the lighthouse."

"Oh, that's better. Now I see where you're coming from." Some of the tiredness left her voice to be replaced with a steely tone. "It was a joint venture."

Melissa felt herself laboring on, "Kerosene lamps penetrated the dark nights to protect the ships that passed along the rocky coast." *And I'm done.* She sat back in the chair feeling mentally drained.

With her feet firmly on the floor, Delaney spoke, "I'm getting the hang of this sofa. I can do anything once I study it."

Skye entered the parlor. "My God. I thought I heard..." He rammed the words together, "...the-golden-beacon-lighthouse-story." He sounded embarrassed. "Please don't tell me she was talking about family history."

Delaney closed her eyes hopelessly and nodded. "She was."

He struck a belligerent pose. "And did she get to the part where in 1907 new laws required the official recording of maps for the larger land grants so they could be subdivided for future sales?" He continued speaking too fast, "Her family had declined selling their land so their grant remained intact, and its beauty is undisturbed to this day?"

"No. She did not," Delaney replied, bestowing Melissa with her signature smile. "But I'm sure we were heading in that direction."

Skye nodded and looked at his mother. "And that about covers it, so we're done here."

Melissa raised an eyebrow at her son's sarcastic tone but found that the flexing of her forehead muscles aggravated the pounding over her eye.

Skye offered his hand to Delaney who gratefully accepted his help.

"It's a challenging place to sit." She placed her free hand on the corner of the sofa and pushed up. "It sags."

"Yes. I'm quite familiar with that. It's okay. Save yourself for the important things."

"Oh please!" Melissa sighed grimly.

"If you'll excuse me, Mother Topple, I'll freshen my make-up now and join you in a few minutes." Pausing, she looked at Skye. "Which way do I go? She said it was inside the house."

"What?" He looked confused. "The bathroom?"

"Yes."

"Of course it's inside. I'll show you."

Within minutes, he was back. "Why was Delaney perplexed about the bathroom?"

"I have no idea. Perhaps she's muddled in general. Now what did she call me?"

"Mother Topple is a term of endearment."

"I don't like it."

"Delaney is really trying, mother."

"Yes. I agree. She's very trying. And who told her she came from German royalty?"

Ignoring her comment, Skye headed toward the door. He paused, looking at his mom in her jeans and flannel shirt. "You know, you could change clothes and come with us."

His eyes glanced around the room taking in the tall cabinets that held old books, pottery, photos and mismatched items. Bouquets of flowers, both dried and fresh sat in nooks, and old lace was tossed across table tops, each piece of fabric having a story attached to it. He knew his mother considered this to be ageless, but in his eyes, it was just messy.

He faced her. "And you'll keep in mind our engagement party, won't you? You could fly into Chicago, and I'll put you up in a hotel for the weekend. I could even have a company limo pick you up at the airport. You've never been in a limo so that would be a new experience for you. Fun, right? The long and the short of it is that it will be a brief trip, and I can't spend much time with you." Attempting a smile, he continued, "But maybe someone could take you shopping in Chicago for, you know, some nice clothes."

She stared at him feeling both hurt and irritated but didn't comment.

He shifted his weight from one foot to the other. "So." He cleared his throat. "As for lunch, we've selected an Asian restaurant in Carmel that had excellent reviews online." He remained close to the door, waiting for Delaney. "We would wait while you put on something else and fixed your hair."

"I am not Mother Topple."

"Please! Delaney will hear you."

Chapter Eight

Melissa watched as the car disappeared up the drive and thought of waving good-bye but knew they wouldn't be looking back. She realized she was angry because she'd allowed Skye to be rude to her. *Shame on me for not speaking up!*

As she heated leftovers, she watched the sky fill with fast moving clouds, the color of coal. The western side of the wrap-around porch glistened with fog and waited for the rain. *I wish Pete was here. I need a friend.*

She poured a glass of wine and let her thoughts surface. *Skye is insensitive, but I don't want to argue with him. It's his first visit in five years, and I want to remember it with happiness.* She sighed. *But the real truth is...I'm not happy. Mother Topple, my ass!*

****

The next morning, standing in the kitchen with the pleasant smells of fresh coffee permeating the air, Melissa tried again, suggesting a plan for the day. "Skye, why not take Delaney for a hike?"

She turned to her future daughter-in-law who was wearing cropped leather Fendi pants and a crewneck sweater with shimmering threads and colorful jewels. The little voice inside her head told her to stop talking, but instead, she smiled warmly at Delaney. "We have some breathtaking trails in Big Sur. I could pack some apples and sandwiches for you to take along." Turning to her son, she added, "You remember how you enjoyed hiking and camping when you were earning your Eagle Scout Merit Badge?"

"Your what?" Delaney's head jerked up. "I've never heard about any kind of badge like that, so it's probably not significant. Right?"

"It was important to Skye at the time."

"Mother, not now."

"Really? Not now?" Melissa felt her hostility grow quickly and muttered, "You could both take a hike."

"Ah, mom." Skye drew a deep breath ignoring the sarcasm of her words. "Delaney isn't into hiking, and neither of us do sack lunches."

Melissa grumbled as she poured fragrant smelling coffee into a mug. Checking her temper, she turned to Delaney. "Are you sure you won't have some?"

"I only do herbal teas."

"I can get you some chamomile."

"Nooo. I only do herbal teas if I know what the herbs are."

Melissa paused and shook her head hopelessly. "Skye, do you want a cup?"

"I don't like coffee breath on Skye." Silence filed the kitchen until Delaney asked, "Why are there porthole sized windows in here? I thought they belonged on boats."

"Yet, here they are. In my kitchen, facing the ocean, so I can look out of them."

"Mother!" Skye spoke sharply. "I believe we were discussing hiking."

"Oh, now Skye, it isn't that I don't like hiking." Delaney bobbed her head, and her hair obediently swirled around her shoulders. "I'm sure your mother could find me some old boots and a used sweatshirt. She must have lots of them." She fluttered her eyelashes in his direction.

Without thinking, Skye checked to be sure the glue was holding. He recognized it as a bad habit he'd developed after his first lunch with Terri Sue Ellen.

"I know with your historic heritage and your big land grant..." She winked at Melissa who felt her forehead scrunch. "Oh my! Don't do that. Wrinkles call out for cosmetic care, and I'm just not talking about my wedding where, of course, you'll want to look your very best, but I'm speaking about the rest of your life. Why, my goodness, Mother Topple, even old women who have been exposed to the outdoor elements, without proper skin care, still want to look good, and, in your case, artfully applied make-up will be your best friend."

"What did you say?"

Delaney blinked and asked, "Where was I?"

Another flash of her mother jumped across Skye's mind, and he added, "Land. You were talking about land."

"Oh yes." Delaney ran her fingers through her hair giving it time to gracefully reassemble. Catching Melissa's attention, she replied, "It's in the cut, Mother Topple. I'll introduce you to Mr. Freddy. He's a little toad but knows his way around a scissors."

"Ahh. I'll certainly look forward to that meeting, but as to Mother Topple..."

"Good. I'm glad you like it. We should all have special names for each other."

"I'm working on a special name for you."

"Mother!"

"Nice to see you're on board with my program." Delaney added with a smile, "I'll look forward to hearing your choice. Meanwhile, I believe I was discussing walking your land."

"You were."

Delaney exchanged another look with Skye. "As you know, darling, I hail from an old family, same as you. It's just that my family isn't full of Mexicans or cast-offs from Scotland or Indian warriors. But, be that as it may." Her hands flew around, and she finished her thought, "We can't change our heritage now, can we?"

Skye snuck a glance at his mother who looked seriously displeased and, with a quiver, closed her eyes.

"I've attended socially correct eastern prep schools, and the University of Georgia, plus I have a southern plantation background, which is highly regarded in today's world. My mother personally researched that fact."

"How?" Melissa asked sharply.

"Why, on the Internet, of course. And my heritage also involves my royal background...which I spoke of yesterday. Hopefully, you took some notes."

Melissa shook her head, clearly frustrated, and Skye stepped in quickly. "I think we can move along."

"It's alright, Skye. Your mother has never met anyone of noble bearing before, and she's impressed with me. She recognizes her shortcomings and wants to learn from me. You know how I've helped others." Melissa's mouth dropped open as Delaney continued, "So, what exactly do you call it here in Big Sur? Acreage? A spread?" She raised her hand in a superior manner. "Never mind. Time for the details later. You do understand what I've said, Mother Topple? Sometimes it's hard to know because you're not saying much today."

"I, I..."

"What you call hiking, my family called walking one's property, and it was important to my relatives." Pausing in thought, she added, "Well, perhaps not as important to my mother because her family was from the South, and it's very warm there, so the servants do most of the walking. But we must keep in mind that mother now plays a lot of golf, and that's similar to hiking."

Melissa asked, "May I back up for a moment?"

"Of course." Delaney murmured graciously, "Did I go to fast for you?"

"You must of," she replied caustically. "Allow me to digress. I don't like the term Mother Topple."

"Mom, don't be mean!"

"Oh now, we're doing just fine." Delaney patted his arm affectionately. "Your mom needs some time to adjust to me. Let me revisit our prior conversation, and I'll go slower. I could walk your land, if it was absolutely necessary, but under no circumstances..." She wiggled her fingers and shook her head. "...would I do a bag of lunch." Smiling sweetly at Skye, she reached for his hand.

He nodded his head in agreement, and Delaney looked back at Melissa. "Anywhoo, thank you so much for the offer of sack sandwiches, but that is a pass. Perhaps you could change into...well, change out of those clothes and we'd be happy to take you out to brunch?"

"That's a great idea, Doodle Bug. Why don't you tell my mom how you got such a cute name. Show her your Vacheron Constantin. It has a retrograde annual calendar. Mom likes stuff like that. Don't you, mom?"

"No." Melissa smiled faintly. "Not really."

"I'll be right back, Delaney. You gon'na be okay?"

"Of course I am," she responded brightly. "Your mom and I are going to have girl-talk time. I do that often with my mother."

Melissa felt her brows fold in and wondered vaguely if another headache was forming. With Skye out of the room, she asked abruptly. "How *did* you get the name of Doodle Bug?"

"Oh, Skye is so cute when he calls me that. My father bestowed it on me when I was just a little girl because I was cute as a bug in a rug."

Melissa let that image wander around in her head for several seconds. "I think the adage is snug as a bug in a rug."

"Oh well, you know when a person ages, things can get mixed up. I won't hold it against you. Now what was I saying? Oh yes, I was going to expound on the only child topic. Well, you can see that right from the start, Skye and I had a lot in common. Being only children was just the beginning. Our taste in accessories...oh! Perfect from day one! We were meant to be." She offered a beautiful smile. "Gosh, I didn't realize that the nights are so damp here and the mornings filled with that dreary grey fog. It's difficult to enjoy this weather."

"It's the coastal mist. It can sock us in."

Delaney looked befuddled. "What does that mean?"

"You see, the mist usually doesn't cross the ridge line."

"What line? Where are you going with this?"

"The mist stays on the coast; only the interior land remains warmer."

"Oh, why didn't you just say that in the first place?" She shook her finger in Melissa's general direction. "Although, I'm not so sure about this warm weather you speak of."

Melissa found her annoyance growing and spoke slowly, "Our mornings and evenings are not warm because we're not inland." She pointed toward the Pacific and emphasized each word. "We live next to the ocean, so we're on the coast."

"Oh, I guess you can't change that. It's a pity, really, that you didn't build farther away from the water." She reached out gingerly to touch Melissa's hand. "So nice having this talk with you. Now I must dash off and freshen before we depart for Carmel. Skye showed me the indoor facilities, and they're quite nice."

Melissa opened her mouth to reply, but realized she would be speaking to Delaney's back.

****

The next day, after they left, Melissa enjoyed a cup of coffee and thought about her son's fiancée. Delaney certainly didn't eat much and had left lots of wet towels in the bathroom for someone else to pick up. And, oh yes, she enjoyed hearing herself talk, even if she didn't make sense.

Unfortunately, the long awaited 'catch up' talk with Skye that she had looked forward to never took place. It was apparent that his fiancée required a good deal of his time.

Plus, she was still called Mother Topple: an annoying situation that had to change.

The Queen's Salon
Lake Michigan Commemorated country Club

Delaney belted her spa robe and settled next to her mother in the Quiet Room where soft blue light bathed the walls. "I selected the coconut rub with a sugar exfoliation."

Terri Sue Ellen nodded. "Excellent choice!"

"Well," Delaney whispered loudly, "I've got to relax after being forced to endure that horrid weekend in Big Sur, in a drafty stone house, with Mother Topple.

"Of course, I told Skye that it was a lovely event, but I had to reinforce that his mother carries no weight in the big picture."

"So true. How did he take it?"

"He shook his head in the affirmative."

"He's such a smart boy." She patted her daughter's hand. "It's good that you're back home. My heart went out to you. I believe with his mother's

Cherokee Indian background, there were probably wigwams sittin' about...did you spot any?

Delany looked blank. "What color are they?"

"Dark, ah imagine. They're usually made from the skin of a bear."

"I didn't see any bears."

"Well, that's good. Here, have some cucumber water."

"Thank you, mother."

"Ah'll just pour a little for me while ah'm at it. Tell me, did Mother Topple like your choice of names?"

"New concepts are difficult for her to accept. When I introduced the subject, she was void of comment, and I could tell that she had difficulty keeping up with my rapid thought process. One minute she was chattering away about boats and gold and sacks of hiking sandwiches, and the next, it was as if the cat got her tongue." She paused thoughtfully. "Not that they have a cat."

"Ah understand." Terri Sue Ellen looked at her daughter kindly and smiled at the fish swimming peacefully in the tank of clear water. "Do not tax yourself, Delaney. It will lead to wrinkles and then on to cosmetic details." She shuddered. "We must remain on the alert and never allow creases to scatter about our faces. So let us continue with the report. Did Skye's mother show you her velvet art? Were they displayed on the walls and such?"

"No. But I wasn't looking."

"Oh, honey, even you would have noticed black velvet paintin's of dogs playin' poker."

"She had dirty maps on the wall and, I think, bedspreads."

"Good Lord!"

"And she dresses in flannel fabric."

"Why, that's just sinful!"

"She wears her hair in a long braid. It's going to be an enormous responsibility to correctly groom her for my wedding." Holding her head high, Delaney pressed on, "Her idea of a good time is sitting in a rocking chair on the front porch looking at the ocean. I don't believe she holds any club memberships or dines out." She shuddered with a new thought. "Oh! Perhaps she's mentally challenged. Many artists are a bit off."

"So true. But there is wealth involved here. As mah daddy explained it to me, money doesn't just talk; it shouts from mountain tops, and there are lots of mountains in Big Sur. Ah believe they are the southernmost Canadian Rockies"

"I didn't see them."

"Listen to your mamma now, Delaney Mae Anne. You can't be givin' a thorough report unless you're makin' observations. Fact is you're goin' have to be more attentive when you're travelin'."

"I'll make note of that."

"Very good idea."

"I do realize that the Mexican Land Grant is worth a fortune, but Skye's family has coveted it for years with the idea of preserving it for mankind." Delaney scoffed. "I'll tell you what mankind wants.'

"Oh honey, ah know the answer to that."

"They want hotels and golf courses, fine restaurants and spas."

"Yes, that too." *And lots of sex. If ah'd of known that keepin' Chucky happy required so much time on mah knees, ah would have bought me a little pillow long ago.*

"And I know that daddy is looking into the possibilities of developing Skye's Big Sur property." She sighed heavily. "The burden of being so smart weighs heavily on me. But never fear, I will rise to the occasion."

"Yes, darlin', ah know you will. Just like the little soldier you are."

"Mother!" Delaney gasped, "I am a general, not a soldier."

"Ah stand corrected. But, honey, we must remember to keep our voices hushed in the Quiet Room." Terri Sue Ellen removed a small flask from the pocket in her spa robe, unscrewed the top, and added the contents to her water. "Although my beauty pageant days are behind me and my early years are but a shimmering shadow..." She paused to study her bottom lip in the reflection of the fish tank. "Ah'm thinking of making my lips a bit puffier."

Throwing her hands up, she added, "How quickly youth flies away."

"I think you still look young and fresh."

"Well, thank you. Aren't you simply precious?" She nodded happily. "Holdin' beautiful thoughts, such as the one you just had, well, that's the true key to success." Smiling introspectively, she added, "A shapely bottom and big breasts are also wondrous assets. Let me see, what else is there...oh yes, you must have a gorgeous smile. Carry a toothpick at all times so if food gets stuck in your teeth, you can get right on it. What have ah left out?" She stared thoughtfully into the tranquil space. "Ah remember now! Do show a sincere caring for others. Now tell your mama the truth, honey." She leaned closer. "Does Skye make you tingle downstairs?"

"Where?"

She inclined her head. "Down there."

"I don't follow."

"In your private area, Delaney! Do you twitter when you think of him?"

"Oh!" Delaney gasped.

"What size shoe does he wear? Ah ask because his feet appear average."

"Umm, I don't know."

"Ah always used it as a gage, but it's of no matter as long as he's gifted."

"Of course, mother." Delaney blushed

Ah'm hopin', for your sake, that it's true because boys with little parts require you to continuously tell them how joyful they make you feel. With any luck, that is not the circumstance here. "We can count ourselves fortunate that he has an intelligent look that says he'd only marry a smart woman." She patted her daughter's hand. "That's very good for your image, Delaney." *And if he is really as sharp as your daddy says, we need to move this weddin' along quickly. Skye can only go off to foreign countries so many times. Eventually he has to come home and be with you. Let it be a married you.*

A woman wearing a white uniform slipped into the Quiet Room and spoke softly. "Ms. Covington. Coconut oil with a sugar exfoliation."

"Oh! That's me!" Delaney exclaimed. "Mother, I've got to dash.

Two weeks later, Nineteenth Floor of The Overlook Condos
Lake Shore Drive, Chicago, Illinois

"You will not believe this!" Delaney's cultured voice held anger. "Estelle, my hired help, is pregnant! How could she do that to me? Honestly, mother, I'm so upset!"

"There, there," Terri Sue Ellen replied, counting on her sugar-sweet tones to sooth her irate daughter.

"I don't understand what Estelle was thinking. She knows when I'm home, I count on her to vacuum and dust, to fix my meals and run my errands." Delaney's mouth puckered with annoyance as she brushed carelessly at her tailored Versace skirt. "When I'm on the road, I head the team of Tech World International Consultants." Her hands stabbed the air to make a point. "My job is to go in first, make the big impression. I let my co-workers put it together just like I let Estelle put together all the little things on the home front. I'm the valuable member of the team. I ring the big bell, and I bring the project home. You know all the catch phrases, mother."

"Yes, darlin', ah do." Terri Sue Ellen glanced out the bedroom window of her daughter's condo. Nineteen floors below Chicago sparkled with flickering threads of light as cars sped along the many lanes of highway heading for numerous destinations. The full moon peeked through a break in the clouds and painted Lake Michigan with a silver glow.

Delaney joined her mother at the window, paying no attention to the breathtaking view. "I'm really trying to put myself in a better frame of mind because I know that daddy made a lot of spectacular preparations at the country club for tonight's announcement of my engagement." She turned her attention to the built-in jewelry tray next to her bedroom mirror. "What do you think of the Tahitian black pearl necklace and the matching earrings? I want to look fabulous."

"And you will, darlin'. Let me see." Her mother licked her finger and folded over a corner on the page she'd been reading in Golf Digest. "Oh honey, they would be lovely, but the cream pearls will bring out the rose in your cheeks."

Delaney held both up to her face. "You are correct."

"Ah am, as usual. Now continue tellin' me about your household help situation."

"It's out of control."

"Ah'm on pins and needles."

"I know Estelle can't help herself." She faced the shorter, overweight woman who reluctantly lifted the magazine off her lap and placed it on the bedside table. "It's in her cultural background to produce children. I am not an insensitive person, just super busy because so many employees count on my intelligence to guide them through their day."

"So true, darlin'. Estelle is just a hired helper and should be seen and not heard. We, as an aristocratic people, know that everyone has to have staff. Ah'm sure mah daddy's highborn relatives in Germany had dozens of helpers in their castles." Pausing, she frowned into space. "Unfortunately, there was a fallin' out with the families so we'll never know for sure how many people they employed. It's a pity to have lost such historic facts. But ah do remember our happy southern ways and the beloved black face of mah Nellie. Such a dear." She lifted her martini and took a sip. She touched her eyelashes. "The right one feels loose."

"Let me see." Delaney leaned over. "No, they're both perfect. Your new adhesive is a wonder."

"You are my baby girl, through and through. Sharp as a crack and cutting as a whippet. No one can pull anything over on you."

Pushing her fingers through her hair, Delaney let it fall around her shoulders and studied the results. "It's nice, isn't it?"

"Oh, honey, it's lovely. My Aunt Victoria always said that cream rises to the top. A moment to reflect on dear Victoria, please." She bowed her head and reached over to the table as she flipped a page of her magazine.

Delaney glanced over her shoulder. "Are we done, Mother?"

"Yes." For a pear shaped woman with a heavy derriere, she turned in a graceful circle. Delaney stood next to her in front of the mirror, and Terri Sue Ellen nodded. "You are dazzlin'. That little troll, Mr. Freddy, has given you the perfect hair-cut." She leaned into the mirror to study her own profile. "This is significant, Delaney Mae Anne, so listen up. We must remember to treat him kindly because he will play an important backstage part at your weddin'."

Delaney puckered her lip and released a popping noise, "Oh, mother, do you think Mr. Freddy is gay?"

"Yes, ah do. But we must keep an open mind. Not everyone comes from good breedin'. If they did, where on Earth would we find our staff? Your second cousin Thomas." She paused in thought. "That would be on your daddy's side, of course. Well, let me tell you, that man just whittles off your daddy's good nature. However, ah bring him up only because he has that same feminine swish as Mr. Freddy. But we never talk about it. We refer to him as artistic. But...honey...we all know." She dismissed the subject and faced her daughter. "We were talking about hired help."

"Yes, of course." Delaney threw up her hands "Well, yesterday, when Estelle was out of sorts, with this, this...pregnancy! I had to take the elevator down to the lobby and walk two blocks to the cleaners to pick up my clothes. Do you know what that meant?" She spun toward her mother. Her emerald eyes narrowed in anger. "I was doing Estelle's work!"

"Well." Terri Sue Ellen scooped the olive from her drink and sucked out the pimento. "Don't that beat all. Shame on her for shunnin' her tasks." The olive disappeared in her mouth, and she talked around it, "What on earth was she doin' that she couldn't hop to it for ya?"

Delaney's voice quivered, "She was throwing up!"

"Oh my!" Her mother pulled back, making a face. "That's just nasty."

"The smell of furniture polish made her nauseous. Did you ever hear of such silliness?"

"Heavens, no!"

"Of course, I was extremely inconvenienced." Delaney crossed her arms over her Italian cashmere sweater. "I shared my feelings with Estelle. Both about her derelict duties and about not keeping me informed as to the delivery option extended by the dry cleaners."

"Good for you, darlin'. We von Campe/Covington women are mighty vigorous when it comes to expressin' ourselves. As ah see it, the pregnant Estelle can work until she swells up like a whale. Then ah will send Maria over to assist you. It's her daughter who is with child so she can do double duty durin' this inconsiderate period that they have thrust upon us." Terri Sue Ellen smiled knowingly. "Ah imagine that Estelle will be back to work promptly after she gives birth."

"How long did you need to recover, mother?"

"Oh, honey, our constitutions are very different from the maids. Why, it took me months to recover, but that won't be the case with Estelle because she needs the money that we pay her, and we only pay her if she's workin'." She faced her daughter and blinked. "That's mah policy. No one gets a free ticket."

"As always, mother, your ability to pull the facts together is brilliant."

"Yes, indeed."

"I'm so glad that you're here to advise me."

"Kindly note this as an example of showin' a sincere carin' for others. We must allow them both to keep their jobs." She gave Delaney two air kisses. "Now, we'll move forward with our agenda, which means you cannot be havin' yourself a case of the "angry-nerves" over incidentals."

"Thank you, mother, for pointing that out." Delaney stretched her tall, slender frame to her full height of five-feet-eight inches. "After all, I'm the one in charge, and I'm the one who graduated suma cum laude."

"Oh, how mah heart flutters when ah hear you speakin' Greek like that."

"Mother, are you sure that's Greek?"

"Absolutely. Ah was the history major, and ah studied these events in great detail." Her smile broadened as she continued. "Thanks to your grandpa and his generous donations to university buildings, we both graduated suma cum laude just like other marvelous Greek women of the ages...such as Nefertiti. Now, many people do not know this as it's been down played, but Nefertiti was the very first suma cum laudean. It's the truth. Ah researched it. Ms. Nefertiti was a senior princess in Athens and resided at a very impressive cathedral. Why, the white columns of her front doors stretched all the way to the sky. You do know that our southern plantations were patterned after that very idea."

"If you so say, mother."

"Ah do. Now back to the immediate circumstances. Why, it's not every day mah daughter gets engaged." *And it was a long time comin' for you so we must snag this boy, now!* The Chicago skyline reflected in the mirror as Terri Sue Ellen continued. "This evening is all about us, our wishes, and our happiness. Your daddy and Skye are but accessories."

"Has it always been like that?"

"Of course, it has, honey...throughout weddin' history, it's always been about the bride and her mama so we must agree that you have to be ever so perky tonight. And do remember to give your daddy some sugar 'cause he's footin' the bill for this inspirin' event" She glanced at the mirror and smiled. "You do look fabulous as a couple, both tall and slim with your heads held high, lookin' like you're important people."

And we don't want to change any of that. So, if his private parts are not adequate, but ah'm hopin' they are, for your sake, well, just give 'em big names like Boomer and Blaster. It'll make him proud of what he's got. She looked at her daughter who was staring out the window and sighed. *Oh mah. Ah can see ah'll need to have this talk with her soon.*

Looking over her shoulder, Terrie Sue Ellen gasped, "Will ya just look at mah bottom! Ah swear it is larger than it was this mornin'."

Delaney turned to face the mirror. "Mother, that's not so. Your Vera Wang evening suit is absolutely delicious."

"You are mah joy...you do me proud." Holding Delaney's hand, she raised it gracefully toward the light. "A brilliant canary diamond shouts prosperity and fine taste. Flash it in a most sophisticated manner." Smiling patiently, she handed her daughter a tissue. "Your lipstick is a bit off. Do re-apply."

Within minutes, mother and daughter walked arm-in-arm into the warm living room where the electric fireplace sent up wavering flames of orange and red.

****

Charles had insisted that he and Skye step outside on the terrace by telling his future son-in-law that a man looked important holding a Cuban cigar. Skye had agreed even though he didn't like the taste of tobacco. He watched as Charles dipped the end of his cigar into his glass of scotch and smiled pleasantly. Skye followed suit, but the taste of the cigar didn't improve. *It's alright,* he told himself. *I can get through this.*

When they heard the women, Charles nodded, and they moved back inside, leaving behind the backdrop of towering sky scrapers. The distant glow of the wharf's lights along Lake Michigan resembled fallen stars, but no one noticed their sparkle as Charles latched the terrace doors.

Skye ran his fingers through his expensive haircut. He didn't like the style, but Delaney had assured him it was perfect.

When he moved toward her, she frowned. "I was beginning to think you and daddy were going to stay on the terrace all night with those smelly old cigars."

"Not a chance when I have you waiting here." He smiled happily, embracing her. The smoke that clung to his designer suit overpowered the crisp scent of his aftershave.

"Now Doodle Bug," Charles began affectionately. "Having a glass of ninety-year-old scotch is a father's entitlement when celebrating a grand event. We were toasting your future and the fine wedding that's to come. Not to mention the promotion that I have in mind for my soon-to-be son-in-law." He clapped Skye on the back. "You made a damn good choice when you fell in love with my daughter!"

"Oh, daddy. It was fate—not choice." Delaney put a hand on her hip and felt her voice take on an edge, "How many times must I tell you that?"

Charles bent forward and brushed her cheek with a quick kiss. "I know that fate is a good word for what happened between you two young people."

"Well, oh mah goodness, ah declare, as the mother of the bride, ah'm feelin' left out." Terry Sue Ellen offered a pretty pout and fluttered her lashes.

Immediately, Charles kissed his wife, and Skye responded by giving her a hug.

Delaney gushed, "Oh, mother, I just love you so much! The four of us are such a happy family."

Skye felt an image of his mother fill his mind, but he pushed it aside. *She really wouldn't have been comfortable here.*

"That's better." Terry Sue Ellen laughed. Pointing toward Skye, her emerald and diamond watch caught the lamp light and sparkled wildly. "Skye, darlin', would ya call for the car so we can be on our way to the club? Chuck, honey, will you get my fur? It's a big ol' windy night out there in Chicago-land." *Here ah am, still tellin' the boys what needs doin'.* She smiled lovingly into space. "Ah do so miss the warm, soft evenings of my childhood in Atlanta." *And my youthful escapades at the outdoor movies before the responsibilities of life poured themselves upon me.* She spoke pleasantly to her daughter. "Remember when you enter the club, lightly touch Skye's arm. It says he's mine with an elegant gesture." Over her shoulder she called out, "Skye, honey, will ya turn off the fireplace, please." Facing her daughter, she added, "He is such a dear boy." *And we all feel so blessed that he's actually goin' marry you.*

Stone House
Big Sur, California
Same night

Melissa sat on the back porch capturing a moment of private indulgence. She listened to the ocean as it splashed below her house. Experience told her that the whitecaps would twirl within the rock-strewn cliffs until every drop of water was welcomed back to the sea. *It's a dance,* she contemplated, *with partners who know each other's moves and always end in a loving embrace.*

The deep purple evening boasted a sky that was jam-packed with stars. The kitchen door opened, and a streak of light appeared. Pete carried a tray of hot coffee.

"I can smell the brandy." She chuckled knowingly.

"As was my intention."

"Well, stand there for a minute and let me turn on the lantern to guide your way." She lit a match and adjusted the flame. "Presto! You know, Pete, we don't want to be falling down and hauling each other into Monterey to visit the hospital." She added a droll smile, "Especially at our age."

"Fifty-six is not old," he joked and put the tray on the redwood table. "You know we've got a porch light, and it works just fine."

"This is so much better. Dreamy and romantic. Besides," her smile broadened when she looked at him, "this reminds me of how great-great-grandmother Lillian must have felt when she performed."

"Is she the spicy one who sang in saloons?"

"Yup. And those saloons had lanterns. I like to think of it as the first form of filtered lighting." She added humorously, "Makes a gal look youthful even when she's not."

"Must have worked for your great-great-grandmother. Didn't she marry a gunslinger?"

"She did not!" Melissa pulled back, looking offended. "She married a banker. And you've heard the story enough times to know that."

"Banker. Gunslinger," he quipped. "What's the difference?"

"Respectability." She knew when Pete was teasing her. "Gunslingers shot people first...then robbed them." She added dryly, "Bankers just took their money."

"Well, maybe I should be making notes so I can keep all these women straight." He continued a running banter. "There's always your Aunt Helena? Wasn't she..." he wisecracked, "something?"

"Oh Pete, you're just trying to get a rise out of me."

"Am not."

"You are so!" She slapped her leg and laughed amiability. "You know my dad's sister was a free spirit."

"I only met her the one time when she was instructing Duane and Skye to dance like cannibals waiting for a supper of missionaries."

"She did no such thing!"

He winked. "I got you to chuckle."

"Oh Pete!" Her eyes settled on his face with a look of amusement. "Aunt Helena was a lady ahead of her time. She traveled to the hot spots of the world and always found a way to do something good...before celebrities made it popular." Smiling to herself, she added, "You know she was very tall, and I was pushing five feet nine inches as a gangly kid, so I was self-conscious about my height. She made me feel better...like it was normal to tower over my friends."

"I always liked tall girls." Shifting toward her, he kissed her cheek. "My being on the shorter side never held me back."

"So I noticed," she joked and let her mind drift back in time. "Aunt Helena passed shortly after my dad. When she came back to Big Sur for his funeral, she left her will with me. Harm and I had a private service for her, right here. Did I tell you that her body was sent home from Mongolia?"

"I didn't realize she died in a foreign country."

"She probably wouldn't have had it any other way."

"Whatever was she doing there?"

"Helping to establish care centers for homeless children, I believe. It was difficult to keep up with her." An easy silence filled the space between them, and she added softly, "You don't have to distract me, you know." She faced Pete, releasing a deep breath. "I really don't mind not being in Chicago at Skye's engagement party. Let's just say Delaney Covington is not the type of person I'd pick for a friend."

"Is that polite for saying you don't like her?"

"She's all caught up in herself. Could be I just feel sorry for her going through life like that. She wasn't well informed, and her values were misaligned. Did I mention she was difficult to follow in a conversation?"

"How so?"

She lowered her head and looked sideways up at him. "She didn't make sense."

"Oh my. That's really too bad, Missy. Your son's signing up for a lifetime with her."

"Yes. I know." She stood and appeared to float through the ground fog as it nestled into swirls across the floorboards. Stopping at the redwood flower boxes, she gazed down on tiny leaves that had pushed themselves up from the damp earth. "This is nature's art—the giving of life each spring. I remember how eager Skye was to see the seeds emerge."

"Children grow up. New thoughts replace old ones."

"I understand." She continued talking in a voice that was delicate with emotion. "The seedlings remain my private keepsake of past hours. Aunt Helena told me that one only needed to look to see good memories." She rolled her shoulders and inhaled. "She was right. Got lots of smart women in my family."

"That you do."

She smiled pensively knowing she would have to make a pact between her heart and emotions when it came to the relationship with her son and the woman he loved. Walking back to Pete, she leaned over and looked at the drinks. "You put extra whipped cream on these. Pete, you are my hero."

"Being a whipped cream hero is a big responsibility, but I got us covered. Hold on while I get the rest of my super hero equipment."

Pete reappeared a few minutes later carrying two red and purple plaid blankets. "They're wool. That coastal fog has your feet all swallowed up in a mist. Here," he held out a blanket. "Got'ta keep my lady warm. Just in case you didn't know...that's real hero talk."

She leaned into the weathered cushions that padded the glider. "Being that thoughtful will get you far."

"You don't say?" He sat down next to her. "How far?" She snuggled closer to him, and he tossed the blanket across their laps. "Truth is, Missy, it's mighty cold out here." He put his arm around her protectively. "April is a brisk month this year."

"That it is," she answered simply, leaning forward to place her drink on the table. "But not nearly as cold as Chicago in April. I hear tell the spring can be gentle as a lamb, or the wind coming off Lake Michigan can be fierce like a tiger."

"You don't say."

"That's what I hear."

"You're really okay with not being there?" His face showed lines of concern as he pulled back to look at her.

"I am." She shrugged and then nuzzled her head into his shoulder. "Oh, what the heck? I might as well admit it. I'm sad."

"Missy, I'm sorry."

"Don't be. Skye's invitation to attend his engagement party was half-hearted and coolly delivered." She pushed her long braid over her shoulder. "My son expects me to be there for the wedding but has a concern that my exterior manifestation will not be correctly presented."

"Huh?"

"I said I have to look good for the wedding."

"You always look good. Is he going to be concerned about my exterior manifestation, too?"

"Oh yes." She laughed, reaching for his hand. "Once Skye knows about our relationship, you'll be on the guest list and wearing a tuxedo." She scoffed. "Or, at least, I think that's the way it will happen."

Giving the glider a nudge, he added, "Maybe we should give some more thought to this important shindig that's about to enter our lives."

"Not much more to say, really."

Her laughter echoed in the night air causing Pete to ask, "What's so funny?"

"Well, take a look." Raising her legs above the ground fog, she glanced at her feet clad in yellow socks imprinted with colorful pansies. Turquoise suede Birkenstocks rested on her toes. "I guess I'm gon'na have to shape up some."

"I find your feet to be colorful. It's almost a pity to tuck them under a blanket."

"Oh, Pete, you're a smooth talker!"

Reaching over to the small redwood table, he picked up her coffee drink. His blue eyes reflected both love and good humor as he handed it to her. Wrapping the second blanket securely around their shoulders, he chuckled, "I got'ta tell ya, Missy, I'm rather looking forward to meeting Delaney Covington and her affluent parents. You say she thinks she's an aristocratic, huh?"

"Skye said her mother told her that."

"Well, this meeting could be a real rib-tickling event."

She laughed heartily. "I can't say I found Delaney to have a good sense of humor. She appeared to have an attention deficient problem when she was here." Licking the whipped cream from her upper lip, she murmured with pleasure, "Oh my. That's very good."

"Huh? ADD, you say. Well, if we're gon'na help the young lady focus, next time she visits, we'll need us a plan."

"And what would that be?"

"I'll pick interesting yet simple subjects to discuss, and I'll talk real slow. That way she can follow the conversation with ease."

"Yeah." She spoke tongue-in-cheek. "That'll do it."

"Are you being negative?"

"No. I don't believe I am."

"Let's hope you won't have to eat your words on that one," he replied dryly.

She gave him a straight-faced look. "Oh, I don't think that's going to happen."

Chapter Nine

A few weeks later
Big Sur, California

The pine-scented hills of Big Sur were sheltered in the warmth of a May afternoon. Even though the rocky bluffs had been captured within a seductive morning mist, by afternoon, the fog had vanished like a wood sprite, melting into a mix of clouds and sunshine, each vying for space in the endless blue of the California sky. The weather continued to shift directions as it released unseasonably heated temperatures followed by dark clouds that spiked the air with the taste of rain.

Pete had left early that morning for Walnut Creek where he was the guest speaker at a pottery convention. Melissa declined the invitation to join him and stayed home to finish a water color for a client. By mid-day, she was ready for a break and stood at the door, looking at the swirling mist through the beveled glass. She gave a hard push and moved outside.

Settling herself in the rocking chair, she watched as honeybees battled the stiff breeze in a final attempt to gather pollen before flying back to the safety of their hive. Blue and lavender flower petals twirled within the roll of the wind as the afternoon moved quietly into the wet dusk of the day. In moments like this, she allowed herself to drift back in time.

I wonder how Harm would have replied to Skye's suggestion to sell the land? She released her question into the wind, remembering the many storms they had shared as a family, sheltered by the stone house.

Annoyed by the scattered cards she had been dealt, she rested her head in the palm of her hand and wondered if Skye would ever embrace his family's inheritance with care. Listening to the rhythm of noise created by the rainstorm, she shook her head. *I'm whistling in the wind on that hope.*

Her thoughts centered around her son's engagement to the boss's daughter. *Could this be a part of his plan for future success? No*, she shook her head, *absolutely not. Besides, it isn't good to second guess his choices. It's like inviting an uncomfortable question to haunt my life forever.*

The wet drops made a soft plop as they hit the porch roof, and the old trumpet vine wobbled in song, dropping bright orange flowers on the floorboards. Grannie June had always said that the sounds within a storm bore memories of the past.

Shaking her head, she let the freshness of the downpour envelope her with old musings. The long ago sadness of her miscarriage wrapped around her as she turned the faded pads over on the chair seat and sat on the dry surface

I remember how I wanted to roll up in a ball and have the world go away. Even when the doctor told us there would be no more children, Harm held me through all my heartache. Damp air flowed across her face. She felt its moisture like forgotten tears. *When I was released from the hospital, Aunt Helena called from Tibet. She told me how she'd felt my sorrow. After pouring out my sadness to her, she said that I must mourn my daughter until I accepted my loss, and then my life would go on. Believe in the future, Child. Those were her words.*

Thunder rolled far out at sea. Raindrops bounced in the puddles like coins being tossed in a fountain. *Do they hold happy wishes?* She pushed her toes against the planking of the floor causing her rocker to sway gently. She could make out the sounds of cars as their tires splashed past on Highway One, high above her home. *I feel like a secret,* she mused quietly. *No one knows I'm here.*

She turned her head to look at the freshly tilled earth. *My ollalieberries will like this weather.* But, try as she might to think of her garden, her feelings remained scattered.

Aunt Helena's words whispered in the wind "Rationalize...then set a course of action."

Alright! She slapped her knee to emphasize a decision. *I will accept it.*

Raising her eyes, she pursed her lips. *Besides, what choice do I have? I can hope that Skye will show me the same courtesy when I tell him about Pete.*

Cold rain continued to swirl thru the cypress trees. She watched as the storm blew itself out to sea.

Melissa heard the insistent sound of the phone ringing and pushed herself out of the rocker. Once more, she turned to inhale the earthy scent of the day before going back inside.

The redwood trim had expanded in the rain, and she had to force the door shut firmly behind her. Walking down the hall, her shoes made squishing sounds. She kicked them off as she entered the warmth of her kitchen and moved toward the wall-mounted phone.

Skye's voice boomed happily across the wires. He was calling from Spain, where he had finished a series of client meetings in Madrid and was now looking forward to flying home. His conversation was filled with humor as he related his attempt to order lunch with his limited grasp of the language.

He telephones when Delaney isn't with him. And he's usually cheerful. Her forehead wrinkled with concern.

After the call ended, Melissa paused to look through the porthole-sized windows. When she saw the enormous rainbow, her breath caught in her throat. Moving toward the screen door, she went outside to look at the wide iridescent rings that stretched across the hills that lay behind her. They arched over her home and dropped into the ocean, creating a watery shimmer of pastel light. She smiled, quietly thanking the elements for the pleasing gift.

As her eyes traveled to the distant horizon, she noticed that dark grey clouds continued to gather. *Another storm is brewing, perhaps far out at sea.* The thought stayed with her as she watched the rainbow until the colors faded into the sky. A weighty feeling of life changing events surrounded her, and she released the air in her lungs slowly, allowing the strength of the moment to find its place in her being.

****

A sound sleeper, Melissa couldn't describe what made her wake up. When Pete was gone, she missed his closeness, but this feeling was different and left her agitated. Abandoning her warm bed, she got up to check the windows where a lively breeze ruffled the lower tier of the cottage curtains. The rainstorm had left the air as fresh as the day it had been born. She inhaled deeply before nestling back into the feather mattress. Her eyes followed the ornate curly cues along the corner poles on her bed, and she noticed the sheer fabric in the canopy sway with a puff of wind.

When the faint clatter of knocking could be heard, she turned her head against the pillow. *No one would be at the front door at this hour. It's my imagination.* Changing positions, she rolled over and tried not to think about sounds that lingered in the darkness. The knocking came again, and reluctantly, she donned her favored thread-bare slippers and flopped her way down the hall.

Suddenly the voice of reason shouted at her, warning of an intruder. Her heart picked up its pace as she hurried back to the bedroom. She opened the top drawer in the nightstand and removed a gun. Fear settled itself in icy fingers along her back as her breathing increased. *How stupid to have this gun and not know where the bullets are. What's the matter with me?*

Her frustrations were mounting by the minute until she heard a faint cry. It was an echo carried by the wind for her ears alone, and the sound weakened her knees. Stealthily, she approached the front door, clutching the empty gun in her right hand. Without turning on the lights, she peeked through the beveled glass and saw a basket next to her rocking chair. The movement within caught her by surprise, and she placed the gun on the entry table. Gasping slightly, she pulled hard to open the door and stepped into the starry night.

The baby lay nested in pink blankets. Disposable diapers and baby formula had been placed in a box. Melissa stared in disbelief at the infant who waved tiny arms and began to cry. Bending over, she touched the baby's warm face and within seconds had the basket and the box collected and placed on the floor inside her house.

Sensing a movement, she turned quickly to see a figure running up the drive. She pushed the heavy door shut with both hands then gathered the baby in her arms and carried her down the hall.

She heard the sound of a car engine starting from the top of the drive.

As lights blazed in her kitchen, she rocked the infant, murmuring soft words. The child's big, brown eyes studied her face with clarity as if her purpose had been fulfilled. Not until the baby had finished a bottle and was tucked in her old iron bed did she return to the basket. It was then she found the note. Carrying it back to her bedroom where she had left her reading glasses, she clicked the switch on the table lamp three times so its brightest light appeared. She slipped the paper from the envelope and settled the glasses on her nose.

It began, "Dear Mrs. Topple." Melissa blinked twice at seeing her name.

"I'm writing on behalf of Nathalie LaVeron, my dear friend and the mother of this baby. We shared an apartment in San Francisco, and Nathalie confided in me that she was your son's girlfriend before he moved to Tech World International and stopped taking her calls. He never knew he had a child.

"My friend was tragically killed in an auto accident. I've enclosed the newspaper coverage and a copy of her will naming you as the legal guardian of her baby.

"I know that Nathalie had no family so I am appealing to your compassion to do what's right. If I give this child to the authorities, she will go into the system and be lost forever. I apologize for not seeing you in person, but I couldn't risk you saying no.

"My career is taking me to London, and I had to reach a decision about Monique. I pray you will care for your granddaughter.

"Please know that Nathalie's heart overflowed with love for her child, and I ask that you share this with Monique when the time is right.

"Her Birth Certificate is enclosed. You will see that it names your son as the father."

Melissa was dimly aware that her mouth had slipped open as she read the letter a second time and realized that her granddaughter was almost six-months-old. Running her fingers through her long hair, she glanced back at the sandy-haired child The baby's hands were curled into tiny fists as she slept blissfully. *Many babies have fair hair. But her eyes are brown, like mine. Like Skye's.*

Standing at the bedroom window, she let the silkiness of the vast night sky gather around her. She had very few answers, but she knew one thing for certain: life had just changed paths.

O'Hara International Airport
Chicago, Illinois

The plane landed with the usual bump as its wheels touched the runway. Given clearance to a gate, the jumbo jet lumbered toward the main terminal.

Skye flexed his shoulders as he waited patiently for the smiling flight attendant to bring him his trench coat. The First Class passengers deplaned quickly, and he allowed his long limbs a well-needed stretch.

It had been a rough three weeks of business meetings during the day and long nights spent reviewing statistics that would modify his programs to meet the company's needs. It was too bad that many employees would lose their jobs, but production strategy was his area of expertise.

For what it was worth, he could have been anywhere for all he had seen of Madrid. Some elaborate late night dinners at restaurants with his clients, followed by nights of room service, had added a few pounds to his lean frame. His well-tailored suits had stood up better than he had. But the important things had been taken care of. The transnational program was in place, its operations fine-tuned, and Tech World International had another victory.

He smiled to himself. Now that he was home, he could look forward to playing tennis and getting in eighteen holes at the club. His mind turned to his fiancé. *Damn, I should have thought of her first*, he chastised himself. *Some of my best decisions took place after we met.*

He'd stopped communicating with most of his friends in Big Sur because Delaney had exciting people in her life who were cultured and well-traveled and enjoyed prominent careers. His friends clearly didn't measure up to her standards. She preferred that they socialize entirely within her circle where she was most comfortable. Besides, no one knew as much about climbing the social ladder as Delaney, and he wanted to be with her on the top step, living the good life.

Her sparkling green eyes flashed like magic in his thoughts as he cleared Customs and walked briskly toward the Tech World International driver.

"Welcome home, Mr. Topple."

"Thanks, Brady. It's good to be back. Did you pick up the roses for me?"

"Yes sir. They're in the car."

A feeling of relief swept over him as he acknowledged that Delaney's idea of having efficient staff was necessary in his busy life.

His phone rang softly from inside his suit coat, and within minutes, he was discussing an alternative approach to next week's meeting. When the call was complete, Brady indicated that he had taken the luggage and that the car would be brought around. Skye removed his trench coat, and the chauffer reached for it. "Allow me, sir."

He walked into the sticky night air where taxies and shuttles vied for curb space. Spring had come while he was gone. People swarmed around him with too many bags, their tempers short. Pollution clouded the sky, and trashcans overflowed. A stroller cut him off, and he stopped short to let the young woman pass. He took a deep breath, inhaling the odious fumes of the city and wondered vaguely if a small child could become ill from the repulsive smells.

Within ten minutes, Brady was back and got out to open the door. They pulled into the flow of traffic as Skye leaned comfortably into the leather seat of the Mercedes limo. It was good to be home where he could read the street signs and understand every word of what was said. Of course, most people spoke English in Madrid, but it still bothered him that he'd never mastered a foreign language. It was on his list of accomplishments yet to achieve.

While watching the assault of headlights on the highway, the men exchanged mild pleasantries before Brady devoted his full attention to the road.

Skye reached inside the refrigerator and removed a bottle of sparkling mineral water. Charles Covington kept all his cars stocked with wine, champagne, and spirits, but only when Delaney was in the car did he indulge in the other choices. It was their little secret: a tribute to their first meeting, when they'd shared a bottle of Roederer Cristal champagne.

Months later, Delaney had told him that when she first saw him get in the limo, he'd reminded her of a Greek god and that's why she'd stared at him for so long. When they had announced their engagement, she decided to make Greece the first stop on their honeymoon.

Skye uncrossed his legs and stretched them out as he watched the flow of humanity cruise along the toll road in an orderly fashion. This was where he wanted to be. The world of business represented a battleground of decisions, where finesse ruled and the payoffs were in gold.

He opened the bottle of water. *So maybe I do get some preferential treatment. But what the heck, I'm about to be the president's son-in-law, so everyone might as well get used to it. I haven't done anything wrong. I work harder than most people. I excel in what I do and bring big money to the company. I'm content with my life's choices, and I deserve my....* He smiled to himself. *My affluent remunerations.*

Delaney slipped back into his thoughts as he looked at the twelve perfect white roses on the seat next to him. Her parents were thrilled with their relationship, ecstatic really. He couldn't remember having seen many people so overjoyed. Life was good, right on schedule.

Nineteenth Floor of The Overlook Condos
Lake Shore Drive
Chicago, Illinois

Traffic was moderate, and Brady was a seasoned driver. Within two hours of landing, Skye was at the condo he shared with Delaney on the nineteenth floor of The Overlook, one of the most exclusive high-rises in Chicago.

Maria took the white roses to the kitchen where she cut the stems. Delaney supplied a Brunelleschi vase and asked that the flowers be placed on the Tuscan end table, a treasured piece of furniture that her mother had purchased at an estate auction.

Unwanted thoughts of another table slid into Skye's mind...one his grandfather had carved as a wedding present for his parents. It was another piece of mismatched furniture that occupied his childhood home. A chipped vase was usually holding tall and short wild flowers, softly scented, all different colors and shapes, a collection from his mother's garden. None of them were as perfect as the long stemmed roses that were Delaney's favorite.

"How I missed you!" She hugged him again, very lightly. "Happy Birthday, darling! Maria has prepared a simple fare for dinner, organic baby green salad, a medley of al dente vegetables, and sole with lemon and capers that I will serve personally." She waved a hand in the air, leading him toward the dining room. "The table is set, and candles wait to be lighted."

She turned to the housekeeper, who wore a maid's uniform of navy blue with a white collar. A starched apron covered her heavy stomach.

"Now, Maria, I know I mustn't keep you too long. Mother is waiting for you to return so you must scurry along. I do hope your daughter is doing well, and please tell her that I so enjoyed the pictures of her little baby boy, Juan or Pedro or whoever. Here are the photos. Put them in your pocket. He is absolutely precious."

Maria nodded at Delaney, not understanding all the words but getting the general meaning as her employer kept talking. "When do you think Estella can return to work? I know this is difficult for you to rush back and forth between my parents' house and my condo, what with the traffic and all." She hurried the maid toward the door and patted her once on the shoulder. "Don't take the bus again. It's difficult for mother to send someone to fetch you."

Maria opened the hall closet to get her sweater.

"Oh, Maria, no, no! You mustn't put your sweater in *that* closet. It's for my good coats. Keep your wrap with you and put it in the laundry room. Now here is the money for cab fare. Mother will deduct it from your pay check."

"Si, Miss Delaney."

"Good. Then off you go."

When the door shut, Delaney faced Skye, clearly exasperated. "She has no idea how inconvenient my life has been with her daughter having that baby! Honestly, these people just don't think of anyone other than themselves! The last few weeks that Estella was working, she was such a whiner. This hurt, that hurt, her feet were puffy, and when she bent over to dust, oh my

God! It was not a pretty sight You know they breed like rabbits?" She shivered and added, " Oh, darling, I didn't mean to insult your Mexican heritage."

Yet you did. He let the thought go as she flipped her wrists and took a deep breath.

"Enough. I promised myself I wouldn't get upset, again." Looking radiant in her Versace pinstripe jacket and leather trousers, she tossed her hair behind her ear and touched the roses. "They're beautiful."

"I'm sorry you've had a few bad weeks." She smiled seductively as Skye gently caressed her face. He inhaled a sweet-woodsy scent, "Mmm. That's nice. Did I tell you how gorgeous you are?"

"Only once." She stopped abruptly. "Some days I think my face is too round. It's that old Eskimo story mother tells. It troubles me."

He replied patiently, "You're perfect."

She continued to look at her reflection in the Hepplewhite mirror. "I think I'll talk to her about it. But for now...on to other things." Running her fingers along the floral garland of the oval mirror, she continued, "I adore the beaded trim and the gilt and garnish of tradition. Mother was right. The mirror is perfect here."

He admired the expensive mirror but found it too fussy for his taste. Then again, no one had asked his opinion, but in reality, it was so much nicer than the yellowed mirror that had been hauled across the prairie in a covered wagon and that now hung on a wall in his childhood home. He narrowed his eyes in an attempt to filter out the old memory. Turning his focus back to Delaney, he nodded approvingly at her image.

She shook her hair letting the golden highlights dance in the muted glow from the chandelier. "Do you like, darling? I know my hair or, as Mr. Freddy calls it, flawless chestnut, is a beautiful shade, but he said that blonde highlights would bring out the hidden joys of my natural color. Oh, it cost a lot but..."

"You're worth it," Skye added with a smile. *She really believes that.* He took a deep breath. *And so do I.*

"Mother said that Mr. Freddy's prices have escalated and he's only taking selected people." She smiled smugly and added, "Being from German royalty, me and mother add dignity to his upper-class client list." Placing a freshly manicured nail against her lip, she tapped gently. "We think Mr. Freddy is gay, but so what? It's rather popular right now. Besides, Mr. Freddy is always expanding his services. After his last trip to the orient, he brought back exotic scents. Today when mother told him that I reminded her of the Greek Princess Nefertiti, he dashed into his private room where he created an original fragrance for me. It's based on ancient Asian sandalwood from Sri Lanka ...two hundred dollars an ounce, but he said that it would help balance my mind and spirit and gift me with intelligence. Alas, he didn't quite have the perfect scent for mother worked out, but he assured us he was all over it."

Skye sucked on his bottom lip. "I thought Nefertiti was Egyptian."

"No, she was Greek. Really, Skye, you know that mother was a history scholar."

"Greek antiquities?"

She hesitated. "Of course. Along with the Civil War."

Skye took a deep breath and decided not to argue. He lit the candles. "Mr. Freddy is gay, huh?"

"He's also pudgy and mousy and prattles on endlessly about boring subjects. You're, well..." she moistened her lips. "More focused on me." Her voice now held a sweet musical quality, "I've missed you, dreadfully. Mother and I talked about it. I believe that I tingle and twitter for you."

His forehead wrinkled.

"Don't worry. It was just girl talk. But she did let a secret slip...she's getting you a pair of shoes, probably from Giuseppe Zanotti; they're father's favorites. I imagine it's a birthday present, so do act surprised."

"Okay." His fingers moved in a lazy manner as he caressed Delaney's face causing her to frown.

"You're sure it isn't too round?"

"Absolutely."

"Oh, Skye, you're so good for me." She kissed the air around his cheeks and pulled away. "Your hair appointment is for tomorrow with Judy, and I've given her full instructions on what you want."

Skye's brown eyes reflected his concern. *I need to remember she's a take charge type of woman and that's what I've always wanted.* He smiled and replied, "I couldn't do it without you, Delaney. You've got all the bases covered." *And I will work on appreciating that.*

"We're a team, darling." Moving toward a table, she picked up a frosted Cernuschi dish. "There, you see that?" She held it toward him, clearly irritated. "I told Maria to use a Q-tip when she cleaned the etched flowers on the rim of this bowl. But, of course, she didn't." She glanced at Skye, "You wouldn't know the Mexican word for Q-Tip, would you?"

"No."

'My point being that good help is difficult to find."

Skye had heard this before, and he knew it was best to nod in agreement, as her mood would pass quicker.

After a reflective moment, she lost interest in the bowl and continued, "Isn't it wonderful that we have such influential families? Which brings me to my next point. We should think of pinning your mother down on a current value for the Big Sur land. Which she probably won't know, but father's lawyers can handle those details." Smiling, she melted into Skye's arms. "Very soon, darling, we'll own the world. Oh, did I say Happy Birthday?"

"You did."

"Good. I've so much on my mind, I wanted to be sure. I've made the most delightful plans for our celebration...Wisconsin inns, quiet restaurants, antiquing and..."

Skye thought that watching a game, drinking a beer, and sitting around in sloppy clothes would be a great way to spend his birthday, but Delaney smiled devilishly as she finished her thought, "Whatever else we may find to enjoy. Does that sound divine?"

"Sure does."

"Did I mention that I've selected your wardrobe? Maria pressed the shirts, and they're color-coordinated with my ensemble. Oh, not so we'll look like twins, but we will look great together."

"You think of all the details. Thank you, Delaney."

Her lips sought his neck with small kisses as she murmured, "My happiness is you, Skye."

His voice was husky. "I've missed you."

The oven bell jarred them apart. "Damn!" Reluctantly, she backed away. "My amorous behavior got the better of me." Laughing impishly, her green eyes narrowed. "Well, there you have it. I'm such a tart." She ran her hands down her body in a suggestive manner. "Just shame all over me. I started too soon, didn't I?"

"I love that side of you. Spontaneous and free."

"We still have our candlelight dinner and..." She let her eyes trail toward the ice bucket.

"Roederer Cristal champagne?" He smiled. *She does have all the bases covered.*

"Of course, darling." She fluttered her lashes playfully.

They were in place, and he felt himself relax.

The champagne bubbles sparkled brightly as they raised their glasses. Delaney spoke, "To us. To my wedding."

Delaney whirled out of his arms in a dramatic move and stepped back, using her hand to fan at her face, "You bring out the heat in me, Skye. Or should I say the devil?"

"I hope both," he replied suggestively.

"I'm told that my southern relatives always instructed their kitchen staff to prepare the master's favorite food before starting anything else. They believed that the way to a man's heart was through his stomach." She blinked innocently, "Do you think that's true?"

"Times have changed. Feel free to explore other avenues on the way to my heart."

"Is that so?" She slipped out of her jacket and slowly undid a pearl button on her silk blouse. "Oh, I almost forgot." Her smile faded and she added, "Your mother called today. She wanted something. I believe there was..." she struck a thinking pose. "Oh, I remember now. There was urgency to her tone." Moving toward the kitchen, her narrow hips swayed suggestively. "Perhaps we should eat first. We'll need our strength." She smiled seductively, "Did you notice that my trousers are leather only in the front? The back is form fitting jersey."

"Yes. I was quite aware of that." Skye raised his champagne flute. "To your..."

The kitchen door swung shut behind her, and he remembered she hadn't finished the message. "What did my mother want?"

Her voice was muffled, "Oh yes. That." She poked her head out. "Well, your mother sounded, I guess, worried. But I don't know that much about her. We only had a short time of girl bonding, and that didn't go as well as I had planned." She drew a shudder. "Pity I didn't get to see her art. Such a disappointment."

"She sells most of it."

"I had no idea there was such a big market for that style of painting. There's no accounting for taste." Skye looked puzzled as Delaney raised her face toward the chandelier, letting the soft glow highlight her features. "Your mother said you're to call and I quote, 'As soon as you're home.' It was rather demanding. Which, I considered over the top, as she lives a laid back life style." Delaney rolled her eyes and frowned. "With all that stuff just sitting around...and those bedspreads on the walls...uck!"

"They're heirloom quilts."

"Whatever." She shook her head. "She really doesn't do anything. I mean, come on, what's a little painting on velvet now and then?"

Skye frowned. "I'm not following you."

"Of course you're not, darling. I get it." Flipping the hair out of her face, she continued, "Do you think you could talk to her about cutting off her long braid?" Her forehead wrinkled, and she paused to take a calming breath. "Does your mother still have that monstrosity of a swan sofa?"

"I'm sure she does."

"Really?" she asked surprised. "I just assumed she'd get rid of it after I almost hurt myself sitting on it. Well, as soon as we inherit the house, we'll take care of that problem. It's dangerous and it could have sand fleas. Ohh." She shivered. "It gives me goose bumps to think that I actually tried to embrace it...for your mother's sake, of course."

She paused, letting a new idea surface. "On the other hand, do you think it could be worth something?" Her hands fluttered, "Maybe we'll leave it, and when we run tours through the house, and I think we'll be successful with that because the house does have historic value, we might fluff off that ugly sofa as a bit of original art. We'll need to rope it off so no one sits on it and falls over. We wouldn't want to be sued.

"Perhaps we could put up a few pieces of your mother's velvet art. After all, that's what she's known for, and they would help to hide the blemishes in those old stone walls."

Skye's face held a perplexed expression. "My mother is a well-known artist, and her expertise is water color seascapes featuring a focal point of color."

"I realize that." She added patiently, "*On* black velvet. Let's move along. All those gardens will have to be cemented over so there's space for tourists to park their cars."

"Delaney, you do remember me telling you that my grandmother was also a celebrated artist? She was famous for her oil paintings of flowers and birds."

Pausing, she looked him in the eye. "I promise not to tell."

He wondered about her sense of humor but let it ride. After all, some of her plans had merit, so he nodded as she turned back to the kitchen.

Joking, she pushed open the swinging door. "A woman's work is just never done. However, after we eat, the night is ours. Maria will be back when she's done at my parent's house. I suggested she take a few hours off between jobs. Maybe stop at a fast food place and get something to eat. Mother always says that it's important to have a sincere caring for others. Plus if Maria gets here late, she can also do the guest bathrooms so they're sparkling in the morning."

Skye nodded as she carried a pitcher of iced water, floating with oranges and limes, to the table. "I had to tell Maria to put freshly cut fruit in the bottom of the pitcher, than add water and ice and more fruit on top of the ice. Honestly, Skye, sometimes I feel that I have to do it all!

"But before you call your mother..." She placed the pitcher on a silver plate and stepped back. Her voice turned brisk. "Let me cover a more important agenda. Father called earlier and said the job in Spain had gone very well." She raised her fingers in air quotes and repeated, "Very well! They liked your presentation and your style. Now doesn't that make you happy!" She blew him a kiss. "Off you go to make your call. Don't be long, darling. Dinner waits and so do I."

Skye settled his tall frame into the linen cushions of the overstuffed chair. Terri Sue Ellen's designer had selected their furniture, and he accredited the lavender and Limon-cello color scheme that permeated the living room as being stylish and correct, even if it wouldn't have been his first choice. But the artificial red geraniums in deep orange pots that Teri Sue Ellen had personally added, after the decorator finished the job, still struck him as being a bit off.

Pushing the phone's button that would connect him with Big Sur two thousand miles away, he let the colors of the room fade away.

Melissa answered her telephone on the second ring and got right to the point. "Did you know a woman named Nathalie LaVeron?"

"Yes," Skye squinted as he tried to remember his life before Tech World International. It was only a year and a half ago, but it paled to what he had now.

Nathalie was the French girl he'd dated. His mind slipped back in time. She had dark hair and gorgeous good looks, a dazzling smile and delightful accent. As he remembered, she'd put him first, even buttering his morning bagel for him. *I liked that about her. She was also witty and strong willed, had a small apartment in San Francisco and was an advertising executive...a good one. Lots of potential for future earnings.* His face turned stern. *No past girlfriends are ever to be mentioned. It's a Delaney rule that I must obey to the letter.*

"So, mom, I haven't kept in touch with many old friends. Once Delaney entered my life..." he joked, "well, let's say, she's all consuming." He added quickly, "In a delightful way." There was a heavy pause on the other end of the phone so he felt the need to continue. "I knew Nathalie LaVeron. Why?" He watched the city lights dance at his feet and felt powerful in his nineteenth floor condo.

Melissa spoke sharply, "Did you love her? No, wait. Did you have sex with her?"

"Now, Mom, that's rather personal. I'd never ask you that question. Ahh, not that you'd do anything like that, of course!" Smiling to himself, he continued, "Actually, now that I think about it, I would consider any relationship that you had, not that you'd have a relationship, but it would be your business."

"Yes or no, Skye."

He sighed wondering again where this was headed. "Yes, we had sex. No, we were not in love." A tiny flicker of concern slipped down his back. "Why are you asking me this?"

"Because Nathalie LaVeron was killed in an automobile accident a month ago." Melissa lowered her eyes to the large drawer she'd carefully padded with pillows and covered with a towel. The baby wiggled comfortably and returned her stare.

"And..." Skye felt confused. "Look. I don't mean to sound callous, Mom, but let's face it; people die every day." There was an awkward pause. "So, that's too bad. She, umm," he searched for a correct response, "she had a bright future."

A feeling of sorrow swept over Melissa as she listened to his uncaring words. "Nathalie LaVeron gave birth to your daughter, and the baby was left by my kitchen door two nights ago."

Deep silence suddenly crammed the air, and Skye felt a corner of his world chunk off and tumble into a deep abyss.

Melissa wondered if the phone had been cut off. "Are you there?"

His voice had lost its robust tone. "How do you know this? Where is the baby, now?"

"I know because of a letter and a birth certificate. The baby, her name is Monique, is here with me."

"Mother, listen to me. You've got to contact..." He paused, wondering who he should tell her to call. He realized that his heart had struck up a painful rhythm. *Not good*, he thought. *Not good at all! I'm on overload. Got'ta take a deep breath. Okay, that's better.* "Ah, we've got to contact...someone. That's step one."

His mother's voice was clipped, "Perhaps I could start with Child Welfare."

"Sound idea, mom."

"Really? And then should I try the police?"

"Yeah, sure." She was working with him. That was a good sign.

"Maybe Social Services?"

"Well, I don't know." Skye paused. "Ahh, that might call too much attention to this...let's call it a situation. Okay?"

"Okay. A situation." Melissa felt her anger rising. "So is there anyone else you can think of that I should call? The fire department? The sheriff? A neighbor?"

Doubt crept into his mind. "Don't do that."

"What should I tell all these people? That you had an illegitimate child and you don't want her? That her mother died and you don't care?" Her psyche whipped out unspoken thoughts. *Should I also tell them that your daughter needs love and a home and a father? And you need to step up and take some responsibility.*

"I can't deal with this now!" Skye's mind was spinning. "You can't possibly think that I want a baby in my life. What's the matter with you? I'm getting married in three months to the woman that I love!" He placed his feet flat on the floor jarring his legs. The swan sofa slipped into his mind, and he angrily pushed it away.

Melissa took a deep breath. "How do you plan to tell Delaney about this baby?"

"I'll handle it." He'd need to take the bull by the horns on this one. "Right now Delaney and I have a full weekend planned to celebrate my birthday."

"Your birthday isn't for two weeks yet."

"This is a convenient time for Delaney."

Melissa was astounded by his statement. "Well...I so hope you and Delaney will enjoy yourselves at her suitability. Meanwhile, your daughter and I will continue to get to know each other."

"Ohh." Skye groaned, "That can't be good."

The baby's face clouded over, and she began to fuss. She pushed her chubby arms into the air and wanted to be held

Skye froze. "Oh my God! What's that sound?"

"Why don't I feed my granddaughter now and you can call me after you've had a chance to think about this."

Granddaughter? Absolutely not! The phone line went dead, yet Skye continued to hold the receiver to his ear. *This isn't happening to me.*

Chapter Ten

Delaney brought the salads out. "Thought I'd toss them in the kitchen. Plating is so much nicer than having to deal with it at the table. Less messy, you know? Anywhoo, after dinner we'll get..." She glanced toward Skye. "What's the matter? You look so pale. Is your mother all right?" Delaney clutched at her throat. "Is she going to die? Soon?" She moved swiftly to his side. "That would be awful just before my wedding." Her hand covered her heart. "How sad for you. Would we have to change the date?"

"She's fine." He held Delaney at arm's length. "But I'm not. There seems to be a problem."

"What kind of problem? We can work together to solve anything. Both mother and father feel that way."

He attempted to regain his focus. "Yes, they're right. We can solve anything."

"So what is it?" She ran her fingers lightly across his face.

Taking a deep breath, he looked at her and was still for a moment before he replied, "It seems that I have a daughter."

"What!" Delaney melted into the lavender and Limon-colored sofa. "You have a what?" A frown line etched her forehead. Skye knew that was a very bad sign.

He needed to remain centered. "I have a baby but, but..."

"A baby?" Color drained from her face. "How can you have a baby?" Her hands shook. "Don't even think it, Skye! I'm not taking in some other woman's child."

"Of course not! I would never want that child to be with us. No, Doodle Bug, never think that." Sudden astonishment flooded over him. "But what a brave woman you are to have entertained that thought." He looked deep into her eyes. "You go beyond valiant."

Delaney looked surprised. She paused, taking a moment to evaluate the situation. "Yes, of course." She sniffled, "Thank you, darling."

It was best to be direct. "Nathalie LaVeron was the girl I dated before we met. She was pregnant and never told me."

"That French advertising tramp! I remember her."

Suddenly the crisp white shirt he had changed into on the plane felt old and wrinkled.

Delaney sprang up. "She called you at Tech World International a couple of times, and I helped you avoid taking her calls. Some of them I never told you about because she was such an imposition in my life!"

"Yes, and now she's dead, killed in an auto accident, and my mother has the baby."

The words hissed from Delaney's lips, "Your mother!"

Skye nodded and then rushed on, "DNA would establish if she is really mine. A fact we should know. Don't you think?" He glanced at his finance for reassurance.

"Why?" The shock of reality caused her voice to assume a sharp edge. "Who cares?" She felt suspended in time. "How old is this baby?"

"I don't know. I didn't ask. Maybe I should have?" He sounded confused and reached for her hand.

Her eyes were wide. "Adoption. Yes! This child can't be very old. That's the way this should be played out." She faced him. "You have to convince your mother to give that baby up. She can't keep it." Panic filled her voice, and she released his hand. "Besides, that, that baby..." she shuddered, "...would always be there for me to see! I couldn't bear that."

Skye took a deep breath and pinched his nose with his thumb and forefinger. He opened his mouth to answer, but Delaney cut him off, "Oh God, eventually this baby would know you're the father. Then what?" Her voice ended in a wail, "What about the children I would have? What would you say to them? Daddy had a little *faux pas* with a French quiche and made a *bebe*?" She glared at him. "How could you do this to me?" Her face was flushed with anger as she began to pace, narrowly missing the pot of red geraniums.

Tears streamed down her cheeks. Skye reached for her, but she pushed him away. "Don't touch me!" Her voice rose higher, "Didn't you use protection?" She waved her arms in the air. "Everyone uses protection."

"Calm down, Delaney."

"Never tell an excited woman to calm down," she screeched. "What's the matter with you?"

He wanted to stay strong, but terror circled his heart. "Here," he handed her a linen napkin. "Wipe your face. You'll feel better."

"No, I won't!" She swatted at the napkin and wailed loudly, "Didn't you use protection?"

"Yes, of course I did. And she was on the pill."

Delaney slowly turned toward him. "Maybe it's not yours? I know...maybe she had sex with lots of other men?" She sniffed noisily. "French people are promiscuous, and they drink lots of wine so they don't remember things. I'll bet she forgot to take the pill and decided to blame you."

"DNA can tell us if it's my child. Here, sit next to me." He attempted to duplicate a tone of voice that soothed upset clients, but the sound came out shaky, "Let's talk this through."

They perched nervously on the edge of the sofa, and she let him hold her hand. He had no idea what he wanted to say so they sat in silence with Delaney waiting for him to begin. "Yes, Skye. Go on, darling." She squeezed his fingers.

He felt the sun lines around his eyes etch themselves deeper into his face. Clearing his throat, he spoke wearily, "It seems that the lovely weekend we planned is not going to happen." Even to himself his voice sounded far away, "I'll get a flight tomorrow and see what I can do about damage control. It will only take a couple of days, and I'll be home. We can celebrate my birthday closer to the real day."

"No! This works better. I have it on my calendar for now." She threw herself against the back cushion. "Oh God! Who cares about a birthday? My wedding is three months away." She focused on Skye, and he could see a small pulse beat wildly along her temple. "Mother and I have planned my wedding forever. My dress has pearls and rhinestones and platinum thread."

She sat up straighter and glared at him. "With a five-foot train. The attention is to be focused on me! No rumors of ill begotten children will tarnish my day."

He reached for her, and she slapped his hand away. "Stop that! Every essential principal that I hold dear is at risk." Her voice rose to a shrill whine, "You've sabotaged me by having an illegitimate child with that French bitch!"

"That's not so, and you know it! I would never do anything to jeopardize our relationship." He paused, thinking that hadn't come out as planned.

Her hand gripped at the linen fabric of the sofa. "Oh God! This is so inconvenient. What do I tell my bridesmaids?" Her voice dropped to a desperate whisper, "They're planning a shower for me next month. I've already selected an Oscar de la Renta lace embroidered day dress. We're all flying to New York to celebrate. Everyone has planned their ensembles." She focused a wild-eyed stare at Skye. "What about all the other parties and the showers? And the gifts we've registered for? All the pay back, from all the people, we've given wedding gifts to." She bellowed, "Those people owe us!"

She jumped up and looked down at him. "I had nine fittings for my designer gown. Did you think they were easy? No!" Her voice became a piercing squeal, "Maintaining my weight, never gaining an ounce. What about that? I want to feel embraced in my wedding dress. I deserve all the glamour of my day!"

Skye's mind was whirling. He knew she wanted reassurance, but all he could do was reinforce that they had to remain strong as a couple. It was the wrong approach, and her fears increased to cover more aspects of the wedding ranging from formal announcements to personal tastings of wedding cakes to their four-week honeymoon.

The champagne warmed to room temperature, and the food grew cold as Skye, feeling beat up and tired, repacked his suitcase while Delaney ignored him and called her mother.

When Maria arrived, she cleaned the bathroom and cleared away the uneaten food. Delaney wasn't speaking to Skye, and he didn't blame her. If an ugly truth had materialized about Delaney, he would have been equally as upset. Well, maybe not quite as upset, but he would have wanted an explanation and wanted it mighty damn fast.

Big Sur, California
Next day

After the pottery convention, Pete drove into San Francisco to spend time with his son and Sandy. He got caught up in traffic so it was mid-day before he arrived back in Big Sur.

Melissa watched his truck come down the drive. The afternoon sun ricocheted off the bright blue fender creating a brilliant flash. Squinting her eyes, she shifted Monique to her other arm. She'd avoided telling Pete about the baby over the phone because she wanted to do it in person. They'd talked instead about the unusual rain that had plummeted Big Sur, filling the creeks and nourishing her gardens. But now that he was home, he might as well see Monique straight off.

Her eyes filled with love as she watched Pete reach into the back seat and pull out a bouquet of yellow daffodils. She noticed that he wore a pair of new wrap-around sunglasses. His favorite baseball cap, embroidered with the letter "P," shielded his balding head. With his free hand, he pulled the brim lower as he walked toward the front porch. He yanked hard on the beveled glass door and muttered, "Got'ta fix that one of these days."

He stepped inside, and Melissa whispered, "Surprise." The baby slept blissfully in her arms.

He looked inquisitive when he smiled. "What's that you got there?"

"Oh Pete!" She looked toward the flowers and flushed. "Those for me?"

He nodded and gently separated the blanket from the infant. Monique opened sleepy eyes and squinted at him with a put out expression at his intrusion. He placed the daffodils on the table and turned his attention back to the baby. "She ours?" Playfulness danced in his blue eyes as he lowered his sunglasses. "Might be you should have asked me first. This is not as simple as getting a kitten."

"Stop now!" She thanked him for the flowers with a smile and placed the baby in his arms. "I'll put these in water." Monique started to babble sleepily then spotted his baseball cap and reached for it. Melissa turned. "Her name's Monique."

"Pretty name." Pete cradled the infant tenderly but raised his eyebrows when he saw the gun on the entry table. "Did you shoot someone?"

"Couldn't find the bullets or I might have."

"Well now, you don't say?" He waited, and when nothing else was said, he asked, "You got more to add to that?"

Melissa sighed. "I heard a noise and got the gun and, well, there was no one there but the baby. She seemed innocent enough so I put the gun on the table. Quite honestly, I forgot about it."

Pete nodded his head and asked, "She arrive with the rain?"

"Yes."

"Seems you forgot to mention that."

"It was by design."

"Was there a big hullabaloo? A trumpet blast and lots of people?"

"Dropped on the doorstep, so to speak." Melissa grinned.

His mouth opened wide with astonishment. "You've been a busy woman, Missy. Heck, I was only gone a few days. What happened here?"

Her fingertips stroked the baby's silken hair. "She's Skye's daughter."

"You don't say?" Pete looked over the top rim of his dark glasses. "Didn't know Skye had a child."

"Neither did he."

"Didn't know Delaney Covington was pregnant?"

"She wasn't."

He took a step back and chuckled. "You've had yourself an eye-opening weekend. Makes my pottery convention just pale away in comparison." He winked and added, "Say, for real, should we get us a little one like this to nurture and adore?"

"Oh, now. Stop it!"

Grinning, he removed the wrap-around sunglasses. "Duane gave 'em to me. Said it would cut down on the glare from the sun and the ocean."

Melissa's eyes were flecked with whiskey colored highlights that sparkled in good humor. "Makes you look like a senior spy."

"Does it now?" He perked up. "Well then, it's a double celebration."

"How's that?"

"You being with a child. Me being a spy." He grinned. "Seems statistics for those facts actually happening are off the charts." He picked up the gun. "We should put this away somewhere safe."

They walked down the hall and into the kitchen. "How about I put the pistol right here for now?" He laid it on the counter and turned to Melissa. "This calls for some wine."

She ran a finger under the baby's chin. "What about the baby?"

"Heck no, she can't have no wine." Pete laughed. "Melissa Topple, don't you remember anything about babies?"

"Oh Pete! You're impossible. I mean should I drink a glass of wine? You know," she cleared her throat, "what if the baby needs something? Should both of us drink at the same time?"

Pete looked concerned. "You plan on falling down in a drunken stupor?"

"Of course not!"

"Well then." Removing his baseball hat, he tossed it on the counter next to the gun. "Long as you're not nursing... you aren't nursing the baby, are you?"

She rolled her eyes in exasperation.

"I'm gon'na take that as a no." He moved toward the door that led to the pantry. "So as I see it, long as you're not nursing and you are planning on behavin' yourself..." He looked over his shoulder and smiled. "I'd say you can have a glass of wine." Turning around, he winked, "There. That decision's been made. Wish they were all so easy." He touched Monique's nose. "Has a real inquisitive look. Does she get around yet?"

"I'd say it won't be long before she starts creeping and crawling."

Chicago, Illinois
Covington Home

Moisture beaded the outside of the martini glass as Terry Sue Ellen paced in a circle around her sitting room. "You've got to get out to Big Sur and fix this. Right now! You hear me, Delaney Mae Anne? A baby! Ah declare, this is just the most undesirable occurrence ah have ever heard of."

"Yes, mother." She clasped her hands together on her lap.

"All southern women stand by their men through thick and thin. Just look at the leaders of our country and note carefully the magnitude of sacrifices those women have made." Her scarf had come undone and dangled around her neck. She pulled it off and let it fall to the floor as she faced her daughter. "You do know that your presence is mandatory in Skye's life at this tricky time? He is in need of your words of wisdom."

"Yes, mother."

"Well then, ah am all but tongue-tied. If you know all that, just why are you sittin' here when the most important social event of the year is a hangin' in the balance?" She spun quickly, and vodka splashed out of her glass. "This pickle of a predicament calls for you to spin Skye's head around his neck a couple of times so it gets cleaned out. Whatever is the matter with your senses?"

Delaney looked up. "I thought I'd come home for support and think about the situation. Put a list of how to handle this in my laptop, print it out, and study it. Make revisions, enter more data..."

"Ah can't believe what ah'm hearin'!" Her mother released an exasperated noise and continued, "It's a good thing you talked to me first 'cause you thinkin' that you can make lists and study on them...well, that's not an option. Check off that idea right now! Go on, get it done."

"I, umm, don't have an actual list."

"Ah was speakin' of the list that goes on within your head. Cancel it!" She finished the martini and bent down to look her daughter in the eyes. "You don't have the luxury of takin' time out to meditate over this quandary. Skye understands your personality and loves you in spite of your idiosyncrasies." She stood up and called, "Maria! Where is that woman? Ah am parched."

"Mother, I would like..."

"We don't have time to discuss your likes, Delaney Mae Anne. Action is what's needed to fix this ugly outbreak of sinful rumor." She raised her arms like a crossing guard. "Now you listen to your mamma; a groom is necessary for our well-planned weddin' to flow smoothly. So you get yourself goin'. Lickidey split." She turned to the door. "What is takin' her so long? Maria!"

"All right, mother." Delaney stood with a groan and straightened her shoulders. "I'll go home and pack immediately."

"Excellent idea. Oh honey, ah don't care what anyone says, you are a smart girl! You call me, soon as you get Skye alone. And you stay away from his mother's studio or wherever she works. Ah don't want you bringin' any of that velvet art home with you. You do understand what you're supposed to say to Skye, right?"

"I think so."

"Not good enough. Here's a writin' tablet. Make notes. He works for your daddy, and your suggestion is that he get some derservin' family to adopt that baby. And you be sure to say deservin' 'cause it shows your caring' nature."

"Yes. I've got that." She handed the pen back.

"No! You keep it for other notations you'll be needin' to make."

"I'll review what to say on the plane."

"Maria! Ah need me a bell. Maria!"

The door opened, and the maid appeared out of breath. "Si, Mrs. Covington."

"Get my daughter a cab. She's goin' home. Bless her heart. And freshin' my martini."

Key West, Florida
Robert and Evelyn Covington Residence

Evelyn held her husband's hand as they walked along the sandy beach. "Do I understand that we don't have to fly to Chicago for a wedding?"

"According to Charles, he hopes they can patch it up. There aren't that many prospects out there."

"I recognize that."

Pedro Cruz greeted them at their terrace door and offered assistance to Evelyn, then Charles, as they removed their shoes and washed the sand off their feet. He provided them with towels and dry sandals.

When they were seated comfortable on their sun porch, Robert took a deep breath. "Terry Sue Ellen thought it was best for Delaney to fly to Big Sur and offer to help."

Evelyn opened her eyes wide. "That's not right. The only thing worse would be if Terry Sue Ellen went out there."

"I agree." Robert nodded at Pedro. "Bring some iced tea, please. Perhaps a little fruit, too."

They sat for a few minutes in silence, listening to the sounds of the lazy afternoon. Evelyn turned to her husband, "If there's a baby involved, tell me who is going to rear the child?"

Pedro placed a frosty pitcher of tea and two crystal glasses next to Robert "Our son has his attorneys looking into adoption but..." Robert frowned. "Skye's mother and her boyfriend want to keep the baby."

"And you say they are unmarried Big Sur hippies who live in some type of stone dwelling that's located behind a wigwam?" Evelyn shook her head.

"Yes, that's what Terri Sue Ellen claims."

"You know she's not all together."

He poured two iced teas and handed one to his wife.

"No, thank you. I need something stronger."

Robert smiled. "Perhaps some fruit? Maybe a sherry?"

"No. Scotch." Evelyn returned his smile. "No ice."

Big Sur, California

Pete opened the door to the wine closet. "Looks like we'll have to baby-proof the house. Maybe put a latch on this. What do you think? It's a very popular thing young folk's do now days. Duane gives his patients a list of what to lock away. Bet we could get us a copy." He winked. "We got connections with the doctor."

"That's a good thing because we'll no doubt need help. When Skye used to touch things he shouldn't, I just told him 'no,' but I don't think that applies anymore."

"You think babies have changed?"

"No." She smiled complacently. "But the parents have."

"Yup. That's for sure. I remember Alice and I used to tell Duane "stop it," and he turned out alright. But I agree with you; it's different now."

Turning back to the wine closet, he continued, "Why don't I get us a nice light Pinot Grigio. How about one with some soft peach and melon flavors? Maybe a pear aroma on the nose and a crisp apple finish to even it out? Unless you'd rather have the thrill of a new discovery?" He glanced up with a grin. "Or maybe you've had enough thrills for a while?"

She smiled back. "Just pick one, and let's get on with it. I was about to put Monique down for a nap, so give me a minute." Moving toward the drawer, she bent over and tucked the baby between the pillows. "She had a bottle just before you got home, so she's sleepy."

Watching them both with a worried expression, he sensed that acting too concerned was not the right move so he elected to focus on finding a bottle of wine.

Melissa asked, "You lookin' to get the one that's just right for my story?"

"I almost have it," he teased, to lighten the moment. "Hold on."

"Well, Pete, that wine course that we took doesn't have any pairings for the tale I'm about to tell you."

"You know, Missy, in the two years we've been living together, our life has been, for the most part, a smooth pool of water." His eyes narrowed mischievously, "Something tells me you're about to toss in some pebbles."

****

Melissa's story came out in bits and pieces. Pete listened to every word, nodding at some comments, frowning at others.

When she was done, she sat back, letting a peaceful silence fill the kitchen. From the open window, she watched yellow and black bumblebees dance among her brightly colored spring pansies. Their soft buzzing added a feeling of serenity to her garden. She spoke quietly, "All the details of daily life are beautiful. Have a look."

"Yup, I'll give you that, Missy."

He smiled at the sleeping baby then studied the padded drawer. "That's quite a bed for the little one." He took a sip of wine. "You do it yourself?"

She teased, "I was successful with my first attempt." As she twirled the stem of her glass, she added, "I've always said that need facilitates creation."

"Been like that throughout history." He bobbed his head several times. "What'cha gon'na call it?"

She watched a butterfly as its white wings fluttered gracefully, carrying it in creative circles among the flowers. "A name should indicate the product. Don't you think?"

He nodded as he watched the same butterfly.

"I'm calling it Bed Drawer."

"Names don't come no more descriptive than that. It does you proud." Bending down, he kissed her head. "I'll bet you fed the little one, but not yourself. Let me take the Pinot away and open a Merlot. Cheese and crackers be okay?"

"Monique came with a box of Cheerios."

"Is that so?" Halfway to the cupboard, he turned around. "Did you want the Cheerios?"

"Oh, Pete! Of course not."

"Thought it best that I should double check. Now that I'm living with two women, it seems I'll need to sharpen up some." He grinned at Melissa, and they both turned their heads as the sounds of another car coming down the drive diverted their attention. "Judging from that noise, I'd say you got yourself a visitor." He moved toward the window and asked, "Who do you know drives a Ford Taurus?"

"No one." She squinted into the bright sunshine, and Pete pushed his wrap-around glasses toward her. "Put these on. You're gon'na get yourself wrinkles, and you won't be my trophy woman anymore."

"Stop now!" She teased back. "You know a woman's got to be fifteen years younger to be a trophy. You quit playing around and straighten up. We got company."

The rental car stopped next to Pete's truck. Skye got out and stretched slowly. Now that he was here, he wasn't in such a hurry to face his mother.

The flight had been bumpy, and he'd been put in economy, the only seat available on such short notice. He still felt cramped because there had been very little room for his long legs. He'd forgotten coach seats barley reclined, and now his back ached, as well.

He had purchased a box lunch on board, and it had proved unfit to eat. In exasperation, he'd asked the flight attendant, a woman who looked old enough to be retired, if she would feed the contents of the box to her family. She'd said no and then went on to the next passenger who had a question.

He'd wondered, *How do people travel like this?*

The only wine offered had a screw cap, and that was unacceptable so now his stomach hurt from a combination of tension and too many beers. *The last time I flew cattle car was years ago. When Tech World International gets their Gulfstream G4, I'll be flying private...as it should be.*

From the beginning of his relationship with Delaney, he'd enjoyed the benefits of her extravagant lifestyle. Some co-workers said she was standoffish and manipulative, but they were just jealous. He saw her as possessing astute abilities. He liked that her parents could make important decisions quickly and efficiently. Well, maybe more her father than her mother, but they were a team just like he and Delaney were a team. He admired her aloofness and had to admit he even found it sexy. With an audible sigh, he returned his thoughts to his current problem.

Facing his family's home, he let his eyes see all its peculiarities. *So much can be done with this land instead of leaving an old stone house on it. Good Lord, electricity didn't even arrive in Big Sur until the 1950's!*

As a child, he'd heard the stories about the first homes the early settlers had built. *Well,* he thought, *big friking deal.* His temper flared. It was high time to bring the property into the twenty-first century, and he was the man who could do it. He nodded confidentially to himself while trying to ignore the scent of Monterey pines that floated across the edges of the ocean air. It was a homecoming he hadn't expected and didn't want.

As he approached the front door, he noted that sunshine and shade sprinkled the newly planted flower beds. His mother's rocker rested on the porch, where a fresh coat of stain had been applied to the wooden floor. Warm thoughts of his father perched on a ladder, painting the overhang, filled his mind. *I wanted to help, so dad gave me a brush, and I swirled paint on a board.* He smiled. *I made a mess. How old was I? Six or so? Mom offered me a Popsicle in exchange for the paint.*

Melissa watched her son walk wearily across the porch. She pulled hard on the knob to open the door. "Welcome home, Skye."

He frowned as he nodded at the beveled glass in its redwood frame. "You've had some rain." He hugged his mother thinking that her shoulders seemed smaller than the last time he had embraced her. That had only been a couple months ago. Before that, he hadn't been to the stone house in...what was it, a few years? He felt sorry about his neglect but told himself that at least he called when he had time, and he did send Godiva Chocolates on her birthday. Well, he didn't do that personally; someone on his staff did it for him, but he was the one who'd supplied the correct date. Truth was that he barely had enough time for Delaney and her many needs.

Melissa pulled the wrap-around glasses down on her nose so that she could study her son's face. There were fine lines around his eyes making him appear tired. She kept her voice light, "You could have called. I would have picked you up."

"Mom, don't worry. San Francisco is three hours away. It was just as easy for me to rent a car." He noticed her hair was flecked with silver threads. *Was the grey in her hair when I brought Delaney here?*

Pete was slicing cheese when Skye walked into the kitchen. Skye stopped to stare at the stranger, then looked over his shoulder to where his mother stood. "Who's he?"

"You remember Pete."

Skye looked closer at the short balding man. "Peterson Bailey? The potter?"

"Nice to see you again, Skye." Pete wiped the cheese from his hand before extending it. "Why, your mom's been telling me great things about you."

Skye spotted the gun and exclaimed, "What's that?"

"It's a gun," Melissa replied calmly. "We were just about to have some cheese and crackers to go with our wine. Would you like a glass?"

"Why do you have a gun?"

"For protection."

"From what?"

"Bad people."

"Where are the bad people?"

"There are no bad people." Melissa smiled. "Because I have a gun."

Skye's eyebrows knit together. "Guns are dangerous."

"Yes, they are. But as long as it's out, I'm going to oil it and find the bullets. Seems I've misplaced them." She paused in thought. "I've looked everywhere."

"It isn't loaded?" Skye asked bewildered

"Not if I can't find the bullets." His mother smiled again. "Would you like to join us for a glass of wine?"

Skye pushed the gun toward the back of the counter and repeated himself, "Guns are dangerous, mom." He sucked on his bottom lip and added, "You shouldn't have one."

Tawny flecks sparkled in her brown eyes as she watched her son search the counters for the bottle of wine. He'd want to see the label, know the price, and check any tasting notes. *Sometimes he crosses the fine line between curious and nosey.* Moving in front of the bottle, she successfully blocked his view. *And he can be quite bossy. But of course, I am mad at him so I may be a bit sensitive.*

Handing the sunglasses to Pete, she commented, "They do block the glare."

Skye added, "Cool shades...but usually, they're worn outside." He looked at his watch, and in turn, he nodded at her glass. "You know that it's only three o'clock."

Also opinionated, she remembered quickly and felt her shoulders stiffen. "Somewhere in the world that's cocktail hour. Yes or no to the wine?"

"Sure." He turned to reach for a glass and looked over her shoulder. "Is this a blind tasting?"

She teased, "Here on the coastline of Big Sur we know what we're drinking."

He gave the kitchen a quick look. "Got a new stove?"

"Yes. Two years ago." Melissa let her eyes drop to his wrist. "Is that a new watch?"

"Oh yeah." His voice filled with pride, "It's a pre-wedding present from Delaney." Holding it out for his mother to see, he smiled. "A Rolex."

"Yes. I can see that from here." She took a sip of wine, "Even without my glasses."

"It's a Cosmograph Daytona with a Tachymeter engraved bezel."

Pete looked up, raising his eyebrows at Melissa, and she replied patiently, "He means it's an important watch."

"Got it. A fine-looking timepiece."

Smiling sweetly, she added, "It's certainly big."

"It's 18K yellow gold and stainless steel. It's my sports watch. Not my dress watch."

"Goodness me. You and Delaney have detailed taste in accessories, but I thought yellow gold was for old people."

"Huh?" Skye looked baffled. "Delaney feels the same way."

"I believe it's a nugget of information from her mother."

"Well, yes, that's probably true. She's online a lot doing...ahh, research," he added limply. "The important thing to remember is that a watch does make a statement. Says something about the person. So..." He raised his glass. "Salute."

"To your watch," Pete added with a grin.

The merlot was generously flavored. Ripe plum fruit lingered with a nuance of oak. Skye inhaled the aroma and commented, "I detect a hint of black pepper. Adds complexity. This is a good wine, appealing and lush." He wondered if they knew what he was talking about and asked casually, "Was it a gift?"

"We picked it out ourselves." His mother swirled the wine and inhaled the bouquet. "I get lusciously ripe black-cherry in the nose." She sipped. "Mmm. Silky in the mouth." She turned toward Pete. "What about you?"

He sniffed and sipped. "Nicely structured. Some cocoa and espresso notes interwoven." Setting his glass down, he resumed slicing the cheese. "It's a good Merlot. Got a fine balance of cherry and chocolate." Pausing, he looked at Skye. "There is a touch of herb. Good call on the black pepper."

"Huh?" Skye felt as if a joke had just been played on him, one he didn't fully understand.

"Australia and New Zealand are doing some outstanding wines." Pete continued, "Why your mom and me have been thinking about taking a little trip down under."

"Really?" Skye looked at Pete in surprise. "You mean sign up for a trip with other older people from the area?"

"Nope." Pete placed the plate of cheese on the table. "Just us."

"Just you?" Skye blinked. "That's a long way to go...just the two of you...alone, at your age."

"Really? At our age." Melissa smiled.

"You know what I mean, mom."

"Actually, I don't. However, let me assure you that we wouldn't be alone if we were together."

He pulled out his long-suffering tone. "This is not a joking matter. You do know that those are two different countries you're talking about? Right?"

Looking at Pete, she rolled her eyes then focused her attention on her son. "Yes. We do know that Australia and New Zealand are different countries. Was that a concern?"

"Well." He laughed nervously. "Many arrangements have to be made. Flights, reservations, hotels, tours..." He puckered his lips in thought. "Tickets. Yes, you'll need lots of tickets. And passports. Let's see..." he added in a patronizing tone, "you might require a Visa and, well..." He sighed hopelessly. "You've never really traveled before. This could be overwhelming for you."

Melissa asked, "Does this go back to your comment about our age?"

"It could."

"Nonsense." She waved him off. "No time like the present to start new things. I think if we put our minds to it, we'd do just fine."

"Yup." Pete nodded. "We could make plane reservations on the computer. It's an amazing machine."

"Machine?" Skye blinked.

"Yup. We call our computer the "machine. We spend so much time with it, we gave it a real nice name. Why, we can see what rooms look like and what they cost. We can even read opinions from people who have been there, and we can book our lodgings with just a click here and there. We pop some corn, settle in, and have us a fine night's entertainment."

"What's the name?"

"Zippy."

Melissa added, "Visas can be done online, too."

Pete continued, "I hear you can also check-in for a flight sittin' in your own living room. Is there merit in that rumor, Skye?" He was about to answer when Pete added, "Why shoot, we might even rent us a car and drive on the wrong side of the road."

"It isn't as easy as you think." Skye let his breath out and focused on his mother. "I'm not comfortable with you doing it."

"I wasn't comfortable with you starting a gardening service when you were fourteen, but I encouraged your endeavor."

"And I made a mess out of it."

"That you did."

"And...and, well, that's my point!" Without meaning to, his eyes traveled to the drawer and the sleeping baby. He blinked and quickly looked away.

Melissa nodded at Pete. "Do you have any reassurances you want to give to my son?"

"I'll take good care of your mother." He smiled broadly. "I won't let her drink too much."

"Pete! Stop that."

"Well, I mean it, Missy. I'll be watching out for you the whole time. Unless I'm drivin' on the wrong side of the road in which case, because I'm old, I'll need to focus on just my driving."

She grinned. "Now that we've got the details of our trip under control, that's one less thing for us seniors to worry about."

"Takes a load off my mind." Pete looked at Skye. "You a little more relaxed with the idea now that we've discussed it some?"

Touching her son's arm, Melissa directed him toward a kitchen chair that was covered in a print of brightly colored poppies. He paused as a remembrance from a simpler life dusted across his memory. Sunshine and blue skies combined with gentle waves as his mother tossed a large red and orange ball toward him. He chased it across the white sand at the beach in Carmel. Blinking the thought away, he brought himself back to the reality of the day.

His mother was talking to him, "Here, Skye, sit down. I assume this visit is about Monique?"

"Who? Oh yeah!" He laughed nervously. "That's a gim'me."

Looking at Pete, he asked, "Do you think I could have some..." He made quotations marks in the air with his fingers. "Retreat space with my mother?"

Pete looked at Melissa with a muddled expression. She glanced toward the ceiling, breathed deeply, and closed her eyes. "He uses words oddly at times. I think this could be a business phrase asking for privacy."

"Sure enough. I understand." Pete wiped his hands a second time. "Must be like medical terms. Our boys are all grown up now. Got their own language." He placed a sampling of goat cheese next to Skye. "Try it with a water cracker. Your mom enjoys the mold-ripened cheese. Tells me it's rich on the palate." He nudged the plate closer. "We took a cheese sampling class in Carmel."

Melissa smiled at her son. "It was on the heels of the wine course we took at Monterey Peninsula College."

"Your mom, she did real good at both. Changes, new ideas, lots of learning going on here."

Skye blinked as Pete picked up the drawer with the sleeping baby. "We'll just take us a little nap, but before we drift off, I'll fire up Zippy. See what he's got to say about Australia and New Zealand. I'll let you know what we discover, Missy."

Skye's neck stretched forward as he watched Pete walk down the hall. He turned back to his mother. "Why does he call you that?" A puzzled look settled across his face. "I don't like that name." He shook his head. "Is he staying here? For a reason...you know, like his house is being remodeled?"

"No." Melissa leveled her eyes at Skye. "Pete lives here."

"No, he doesn't." Skye pointed out the window. "He always lived down the road." Pausing in thought, he added, "About two miles."

"Not anymore." She sipped her wine, waiting for him to catch up to what she'd said. *Not exactly as I'd planned it but...* She shrugged and pushed the cheese plate toward him. "It's very good."

"The only cheese you ever had in the house was Velveeta and, oh yeah, something else that was gooey and came in a jar." He felt confused. "If you don't mind, let's get back to Pete for a moment." His voice took on a pompous tone, "Exactly why is he here?"

"For sex."

"Oh, mom!" He grimaced. "That's disgusting!"

"Then stop asking me stupid questions. Pete is my significant other."

"No, he isn't." Skye's voice held a note of disbelief. "You don't have a significant other."

"Yes, I do."

His tone changed to righteous outrage, "How could you do that?"

"Do what?" Her whiskey tinted eyes looked into her son's brown eyes, and she noted that the deep golden shading was the same as Monique's.

"You know what." He puffed up, and his voice was higher pitched then he was comfortable with when he spoke, "Live with a man? That's what!"

Her eyebrows rose up. "You lived with several girls."

"That's different." He spat out the words.

"How so?"

"It just is!" He fidgeted. "What does Pete's son...what's his name, Dewy?"

"Duane."

"Yeah, Duane. Well, what the hell does he say about this, this, arrangement?"

"He's good with it."

"Yeah. I imagine he would be," Skye answered sarcastically and continued. "So what has he done with his life? Throw pots with his dad?"

"Duane's a doctor."

"What?" He sneered, "The nerdy kid from high school, who couldn't get a date for the prom, is a damn doctor?"

"A pediatrician in San Francisco."

"Bullshit! How do you know that?"

"Duane drives down for dinner and a visit when he can get away from his practice, and, oh yes, did I mention, I live with his father so I'm aware of what goes on in their family."

"Parents can exaggerate the accomplishments of their children."

"Are you referring to Delaney's parents?"

"I most certainly am not!" Skye sucked in air quickly. "For God's sake, you're my mother, and you can't do things like live with a man. That's it. This discussion is over!"

She frowned. "What did you say?"

"I said we're done discussing this subject."

"Oh, I'm sorry. Did you make a rule that I missed?"

"I'm going to ignore that remark." His look turned contemptuous. "You've embarrassed me! And you've embarrassed Delaney! And her parents! And, and..." He tossed his hands in the air, "they don't even know it yet."

Melissa reached out and brought his hands down. "Don't pick up her bad habits."

"What?"

Placing her chin in her palm, she waited.

Skye muttered, "When she gets excited, she moves her hands. It's no biggie."

She let the quiet built between them.

When he finally spoke, his voice was flat, defeated, "You're really living with a man? Is he paying his fair share of the bills? I hope he's not sponging off you."

"You're out of line, and whatever our arrangement is, it's been going on for two years."

"Two years!"

"Yes, I would have told you if you ever had time to listen."

"So," he scoffed, "this is my fault."

"No and it's none of your business either."

"If he's in my family home, it is my concern."

"You don't give a damn about your family home."

"It has value, and I care about that. I don't want to see someone free load off of you."

Her tone turned icy. She placed both hands flat on the table. "You're rude."

"Rude?" Skye sat back, "Me, rude? I come home and find out that my mother is living with a man, and I don't know anything about it, and you tell me that I'm rude?"

"Yes. 'Who's he?' is rude. Talking down to him is rude. And asking him to leave the kitchen is rude." Her face turned angry. "Especially rude when he's caring for your daughter. Now would you like to discuss *that* subject?"

His voice squeaked, "Don't say daughter! Don't even think it." He paused to take a deep breath. "Look, I'm sorry. I don't mean to sound so unreasonable, but I've had a really bad twenty-four hours. And Delaney, oh God." He shook his head several times in denial. "She's had an even more dramatic experience."

"Heaven knows we wouldn't want to upset the bride-to-be. She's so delicate." Sitting back in her chair, Melissa willed her temper to cool as she studied her son's face, "So Delaney..." Her forehead wrinkled in puzzlement "Well, I'm not sure. How is she taking all this?"

Leaning forward in an effort to make his mother understand, he pressed on, "She's affected on a very personal level." His hands waved again at the air. "I don't even want to go there. Right now, she's not speaking to me. The baby thing could ruin her wedding day."

"*Her* wedding?" Melissa snapped, "Is she doing this alone? Somehow I think not!" Her eyes narrowed. "I believe what you mean to say is "our" wedding because it does take a groom to be there for the bride, unless she can use a Ken doll to stand in for you."

Skye looked bewildered. "What's that supposed to mean?"

She rolled her eyes and leaned forward. "Let's see now." Her voice held its sharp edge, "If you're there." She pointed to the floor as if assigning positions. "And she's here. Oh my, do let me think on that for a moment." Snapping her fingers, she replied, "I believe I've got it figured out. By golly, there *are* two people involved. That would make it an "our" wedding. Correct?"

"No, mother, you don't understand...it is Delaney's wedding. And, of course, it's Terry Sue Ellen's wedding; she's her mother. Did I mention that she was a peach queen?"

"Seems that I've heard that...several times, yet somehow I remain not impressed."

"Well it's a family thing. Don't let it worry you."

"Oh, I won't."

"That's good." Skye felt slightly embarrassed but plunged on, "Since Delaney's conception, her mother has been planning her wedding. There will be two supreme rulers that day, the bride and the bride's mother. So the subject is closed, and the final word is the baby has to go."

"Do you hear yourself?"

Worry lines etched his face as his eyes deepened in anger. His voice was edging higher again, and he made a conscious effort to lower it. "The things that are important to me...well, they do not include this child." He moved forward. "I want you to give it up. Give it back!"

"And who should I give 'it' back to, Skye? Her mother died in a car accident. Have you no feelings?"

"I'm telling you my feelings!" He shouted, "You aren't listening to me. Get that baby out of your life! The sooner, the better." He tried to control his anger and switched to his business voice, "It's for your own good, mother. So you don't become attached. Surely you understand that?"

"Don't try to manipulate me. I don't like it," Melissa shot back. "And for your information, I *am* attached. She's my granddaughter." She crossed her arms over her chest. "Her mother, who loved her very much, is deceased, and she only has us." Looking into his eyes, she continued, "Can you show some compassion?"

"My life is on the line here!" Pushing the chair back, he stood up and began pacing. "Everything, I've ever wanted is within my reach. The career opportunities of a lifetime, money, power, the woman of my dreams." He slapped his hand against his chest. "My happiness."

"You put your happiness in an interesting order. It was last, and both money and power came before the woman of your dreams."

"That's crap! They're all one and the same."

"No." She felt sad. "They are not."

"Don't mess with my thinking." Taking another breath, he paused. "I'm not about to let a little mistake screw-up my life. "You never understood, did you?"

She sat back looking puzzled.

"I always lived in your shadow or dad's shadow. Everyone expected me to be a great artist or a newsworthy writer. I was neither, but now I'm successful on my own. No one is taking that away from me!"

"We did not ask you to follow in our footsteps." She looked bewildered. "We encouraged you to explore the world. You're angry about things that never happened. We suggested you consider Big Sur in your plans for your future, but we never insisted. We wanted you to be your own person."

"And I am." He looked wounded. "I didn't have your skills, and I never wanted to work for an environmental company to save the world. Nor did I want to manage a restaurant or a hotel. Those were Big Sur jobs. I wanted success away from here, in the real business world, and that's what I have." She tried to speak, but his rage surfaced again. "Now you come along and try to mess with my triumphs all because of this child. You want to steal what I have and force me back here!"

"That's not true! Until a few days ago I never knew there was a baby." Melissa stood up, infuriated by her son's accusations. "*You* made this child. *You* bear the responsibility for her! Like it or not!"

Pete reappeared in the kitchen, holding a fussy baby, "I've changed her, but she's hungry again. Did you say she came with Cheerios?"

"Yes," Melissa stood up, stiff with fury. "I also have a box of rice cereal that can be mixed with her formula and some jars of strained fruit. Here, let me show you."

"A well-equipped young lady, she is." Pete turned to Skye, "Sorry to interrupt your "retreat space" with your mom, but I'm out'ta practice. Too bad Duane isn't around." He smiled. "You remember my son, Duane? You guys did that poison oak fort together. When was that?"

"A long time ago. Okay." Skye's voice had a raw edge.

"Well, Duane now..."

"I know. You claim he's a pediatrician."

Melissa shook her head. "He's cross referencing Delaney achievements based on what her parents say she did."

"Is that so?" Pete looked mildly confused.

Melissa added, "I'll go into detail later."

"I'll look forward to that discussion, Missy."

Skye glared at his mother. "Delaney has many accomplishments."

"Name one."

"I don't want to have this conversation with you."

"Then behave yourself and mind your manners." She began to mix cereal and formula. "Your 'little mistake' is hungry. 'Would you like to feed her?"

"Of course not!" He stumbled against a kitchen chair then set it right. "Don't be ridiculous."

"Shall we let her starve?" Melissa opened her eyes wide.

Moving further away from the infant, Skye's voice filled with irritation, "Don't do this, mom. Not to you...not to me."

To offset the anger in the room, Melissa spoke softly to the baby as she moved toward the refrigerator, "Your daddy is grumpy right now, Monique, so grandma will give you something to eat."

"You're not a grandmother!"

"Yes, I am."

"And you've given it a name."

"No. She arrived with a name. Her mother gave it to her. Monique LaVerone Topple."

"It can't get any worse," he groaned.

She looked at her son with a raised eyebrow.

Within minutes after eating, Monique was nursing contentedly on her bottle, her large brown eyes fixed squarely on Skye. He cautiously moved closer to peer into her face. Milk bubbles appeared from the corners of her mouth, causing him to frown distastefully. "Ugh!"

"Skye!" Melissa gave him a warning look.

"What a mess." He turned angrily to Pete and continued, "Tomorrow is DNA day for me and that baby. As soon as I know if this is my kid, then the correct action will be taken. Help my mother to accept it." With an effort, he shook his head and added, "Please help her to accept the situation."

Pete tried not to notice Skye's acid tone. "Need help with your bags?" He reached for his baseball cap and pulled it on.

Skye hit the palm of his hand against his forehead. "Aren't you people listening?"

"Heard every word." Pete nodded toward the car. "Got any bags?" He turned to Melissa. "Missy, you seen my sunglasses?"

Skye exploded, "Why are you calling my mother that name?"

"She likes it."

"No! She does *not* like it."

"Actually, I do." Melissa smiled at Pete. "Your wrap-arounds are by the cutting board. Could you hand me that towel?" She burped Monique then wiped her chin. "How's grandma's girl?" The baby cooed and looked at Skye. Laughing, Melissa leaned sideways and attempted to joke with her tense son, "House lists to the right, if you remember?"

Skye felt like he was caught in a twilight zone. "I know that, and I never found it funny. Nor do I find the damn door that swells up with moisture every time it rains to be funny either. You should move to a real house and enjoy some comfort as you age."

Melissa's smile disappeared. "Are you trying to be hurtful?"

"No. I'm trying to be practical." Turning to Pete, he answered, "I don't need help with my bag. I only brought one change of clothes for an overnight and then I'm out of here."

Melissa shrugged. "Oh, I wouldn't be so sure about that. These things can take time."

He jabbed his finger in the direction of the baby and felt himself puff up with self-importance. "Pete, talk to my mom about that, that..."

Melissa straightened her back. Her words came out clipped, "Skye Harmon Topple, you are a very smart young man. You hold an MBA in International Business. You have a prestigious job, and people respect your opinion. Therefore, I will only have to say this once." She paused, letting her voice turn ice cold. "Do not call this child 'it' or 'that.' Her name is Monique." Two red spots highlighted her cheeks. "Do you understand what I have just said?"

He moistened his lips to speak, but the words caught in his throat. Had he just been sharply reprimanded? No one spoke to him like that. What was wrong with her? If he wasn't mistaken, he was also the brunt of their "wine and cheese" humor earlier in the day.

Chapter Eleven

Chicago, Illinois
Tech World International Headquarters

"Office of Charles Covington."

"This is Mrs. Covington. Connect me immediately."

The receptionist rolled her eyes and pushed a button. "It's your wife, sir."

Charles, who had been avoiding the turmoil at home, picked up his private line with a sigh. "Hello, sugar."

"Leave work! We got us some talkin' to do. Our daughter is at her condo packin' for a visit to the badlands of Big Sur, and we need us a plan. Pronto-like. As in the tick of a second. "While we're a'gabbin' away here, ah have instructed mah maid to get out our luggage. Are ya followin' me on this?"

"I have a few business commitments to deal with first and..."

"Oh no, you don't! Chucky, you get your ass home right now."

Big Sur, California

That long day finally ended, and Skye retired early with his laptop and cell phone as bed mates. He had to admit that supper was very good. His mother prepared pasta with shrimp, and he'd eaten more then he should have. The wine was also excellent, but he was sure that had been just a lucky guess on their part. Classes or no classes, what could they know about selecting a truly fine wine?

He tried Delaney several times but only got her answering service. Tomorrow was another day, and it would be better.

While doing the supper dishes, Melissa and Pete discussed the idea of getting some extra help with the chores around the house. Pete had a pottery student, Angie Walters, a quiet, responsible young woman he'd gotten to know personally. They talked often, and he liked her strength of character and moral values. She'd also impressed him with her skill at making a series of pinch pots and was quickly moving toward surface texturing. Melissa suggested they offer Angie the use of the back bedroom and a small salary in exchange for her help until they could decide how to handle the new turn their lives had taken.

Skye, on the other hand, was another matter and needed to be dealt with on several levels, ranging from his selfish behavior to duty and commitment. Melissa thought they should act as normal as possible and let Skye find his own feelings for his daughter. She also admitted that the long ago plan her and Harm had come up with for their son to discover the beauty of Big Sur on his own had not gone well.

"Oh, Pete." She shook her head miserably. "It's not just the baby that has Skye upset. He told me that when he was growing up people asked him if he could write like his dad or paint like his mother." She dried her hands on the dishtowel and began to pace wearily. "I gave him crayons and paint, and he fooled around like all kids, but he didn't seem that interested so I didn't push it. He excelled at sports, and we applauded his ability." She sat down and wiped at her eyes. "We let him go his own way. When he wanted to major in business, we supported the idea." She continued to cry, and Pete handed her tissues. "Now he thinks I'm trying to destroy the future he's built at Tech World International."

"Don't worry, Missy. He's got his thoughts out in the open, and he'll be able to deal with his situation in a better light."

Resting her head on his shoulder, she spoke softly, "He's so angry. I never knew he felt that way." They sat quietly for several minutes while she gathered her thoughts. "I feel like I failed him."

"Now, Missy, truth is that parents are only responsible for a part of what their children become. The rest is up to them. They make their own decisions as they move through life. You didn't fail as a mother. You were loving and compassionate, and Harm was a damn good father." Pete held her hand and continued, "Duane didn't like pottery. He chose the medical profession. Skye chose business. You gave him encouragement to discover new horizons."

She sniffed loudly. "Okay. Now that he's aired it, maybe his disposition will improve." Her tone held a hopeful note, "Let's hope that he wants to learn more about Monique. I think that's the first step."

He understood her frustration, and because he didn't have a better solution, he agreed with her.

She took a deep breath. "I'm sorry about Skye's lack of courtesy and his self-absorbed attitude."

"Missy, don't worry."

"He was very rude to you, Pete. There was no call for that."

"We'll deal with it. There's a lot at stake here for your boy."

Chicago, Illinois
Covington Home

The chauffer dropped Charles in front of his house where his wife was waiting. "We can't dilly-dally none, Chucky. We need to buck-up and get on out there to fix this."

He took a deep breath and pulled at his tie as he walked through the front door. "Steady, sugar. The plane has to land first, and the executives have to be transferred to commercial flights. Our Gulfstream doesn't arrive until next year so we're dealing with a Lear that needs to refuel and change pilots." He made a concentrated effort to be supportive as he moved closer to his wife. "Try to pull strength from your southern upbringing."

"Hog wash!" Her makeup was smeared from tears. "You do know there are not that many young men who want to marry our little girl and, therefore, we have us a problem."

"Now, sugar, there are no problems, only opportunities waiting for a solution."

"Bullshit!"

Charles lowered his head and nodded sadly. "We'll be there tomorrow and get to the bottom of this situation."

"You can bet your boots on that, Chucky. Ah didn't just pull this husband challenge out'ta mah hat; it's been brewing for years. We finally had us a solution and now, boom!" Her fist punched at the air. "He's got mystery babies." She backed up and gasped, "Ah feel so deceived."

"There, there, sugar."

Maria," she shouted. "Where's mah martini?" Turning back to Charles, she continued, "Ah'm startin' to pack right now. Have someone on your staff call Pebble Beach and book us in. Have that secretary of yours get me a tee time...and a massage. Ah am frazzled out of mah mind with the shambles this debacle has created by upsettin' mah weddin plans." Her husband stared at her, and she added righteously, "And so is our little girl."

Big Sur, California
Stone House

When the kitchen chores were done, Melissa and Pete moved into the parlor. Her tone was sarcastic, "It was so kind of Skye to offer to assist us with the dishes."

"Now, Missy, he just wanted to get away and think." Pete sat next to her. "It never occurred to him to pitch in and help after dinner."

"Oh, I'm aware of that!"

Monique made waking sounds, and Pete reached into the Drawer Bed while Melissa spread a blanket on the floor. The baby offered a lively evening's entertainment for her grandmother by pushing up on her knees and hands until she toppled over while reaching for a rattle. Pete declared her to be a young lady who knew what she wanted and watched the love spread across Melissa's face.

Skye stayed in his room, and that seemed like a good plan for everyone. The jet lag from Spain had combined with his flight to California, and he'd fallen into a dreamless sleep.

When Monique finished her last bottle, she'd burped loudly and dozed off. Melissa placed her back in the drawer and gratefully climbed into the old iron bed, wiggling comfortably into the feathers of the mattress. She and Pete were exhausted from the pressures of the day and quickly fell asleep, but she woke after thirty minutes and began to pace the bedroom floor in bare feet.

Leaving the soft wool of the Flokati rugs, she moved into the hall. Walking quietly across braided mats that had been woven by many women who'd passed from this world, she thought, *I have a granddaughter whose feet will touch this floor when she learns to walk. Maybe? If she's still here.*

Her eyes traveled to the collection of quilts that adorned the walls, and she thought of other lost ancestors whose work was still displayed with pride. *So much to show this child. Will she care? Will she be allowed to stay?*

Her thoughts turned to Nathalie LaVeron, and she spoke softly as if in prayer, "I promise you I will fight for the tiny baby that you brought into this world. She is truly loved. My home is simple. I have no swimming pools in my back yard or elegant rooms in my house; no Persian carpets lie on the floors; no priceless masterpiece hangs on my wall. No hotels or restaurants are perched on my land. I honor the essence of family and friends, their stories and lives. Tragedies and joys linger in every room. I will share this with your daughter, my granddaughter. Even if I have to do battle with my son. And I promise you, Nathalie, that I will tell her how much you loved her."

Melissa returned to bed but tossed and turned long into the night while thoughts of losing her granddaughter filled her mind with anguish. She knew that Skye was being demanding and bad-tempered but realized that the biggest problem was yet to arrive. Delaney Covington would not let a situation that affected her future go unattended.

Big Sur, California
Stone House

Early the next morning, Pete left for his studio where he knew several students would be working with his senior assistants on hand-glazing assignments. He bet that Angie Walters would be among them.

Within a couple of hours, he was back home, accompanied by a quiet girl who had a purple streak in her spiked hair and proudly wore a nose ring.

Melissa sat in the glider on the back porch and studied the young student who appeared both confident and eager to please. Angie had brought an old brocaded valise that held her clothing and personal sundries. She had deposited it on the first step by the olallieberry vines when she shook hands.

A satchel from a different century, carried by a young woman who reminds me of a flower child of the sixties. Of course, there are some twenty-first century updates. Melissa looked carefully at Angie's spiked hair. It was a cross between plum and lavender shades. She felt herself smile. *It's actually quite pretty.*

Angie's clothes settled around her in soft folds of swinging fabric. The long colorful skirt and peasant blouse suited her youthful body. A cheerful red shawl draped across her slender shoulders. "I love babies," she said with a pleasant smile. "I was working on a full-sized pitcher, my first, when Mr. Bailey arrived. After he explained what he needed, we went back to my roommate's apartment so I could pack for a few days to stay with you." She held out her hands in a comical gesture. "I washed up really good, and I changed clothes."

Melissa replied with a smile, "I like your shawl. It's a happy color."

"Thank you, Mrs. Topple. I think a shawl adds a graceful touch to any ensemble." Bending over the drawer, Angie reached out to caress Monique's cheek. "She's very lovely. All soft and sweet."

"She's my first grandchild."

The infant's inquisitive eyes studied the sun-kissed dew that clung to the honeysuckle vine. Melissa had planted it the same year Skye was born. She'd clipped and cultivated so many cuttings she could no longer tell the old from the new so, in her mind, it was still Skye's honeysuckle. Now she could share it with his daughter.

Loving thoughts surged through her as she recalled how tenderly Harm had held his son. Skye was welcomed with love into the world while this innocent baby was lost somewhere in life's shuffle. Like it or not, the decision that Skye came to would change his life forever.

Even though she had been named legal guardian of Monique, she wondered if a court would rule against a father's wishes. So many questions. She hoped Skye had inherited his father's courage and sense of what was right, and she hoped he would apply those virtues to his daughter's future.

Pete smiled at the tenderness of the moment, wondering how often Harm Topple shared space with him in Melissa's thoughts. His own Alice was often on his mind, and it had been five years, last March, that she'd passed away. It was only natural after so many years of being together they would still think of their spouses with love and compassion.

Chicago, Illinois
Morning at the Covington Home

"Ah want mah first grandchild to be mine! Not from some fling that mah son-in-law had with a French hooker." Terri Sue Ellen tossed clothes on the bed while Maria patiently picked them up, folded them, and arranged them between dress bags and suitcases.

"Did you hear me, Chucky?"

"Of course, I heard you, sugar. You need to calm down."

"An outstandin' idea." Holding a bottle of vodka, she took a swallow and wiped at her chin.

"Get her a glass, Maria."

"Darlin', don't bother mah maid. She's busy packin'." Turning to her husband, she pulled him out of the room. "Our daughter caught a red-eye flight and is landin' right now in San Francisco to fix this outrageous predicament. Mah point being that she's headin out to visit the trailer folks in the holler without us."

"They live in a historic stone house, and she going to Big Sur, not a holler."

"Everyone knows that anything past San Francisco is a hippy holler that extends all the way down to where civilization starts again...Hollywood. This is just flat ass bad timin', Chucky, that we are not by our daughter's side."

"Now, sugar we're doing our best."

"Oh no, we're not. We can do better! You do realize that if this engagement falls apart Delaney may want to come home to live with us."

"You don't know that for sure."

"Oh yes, ah do! She will be very, very unhappy. Probably cryin' a lot."

Charles looked up at the ceiling then down at his feet.

"Look at me, Chucky! Right now. Don't be starin' around. Our little girl will be poutin' a bunch, and she will be all around this house, all the time, grimacin' and peevish and, no doubt, unreasonable. Bless her heart. Am ah getting' through to you?" She held the vodka out and nodded at it.

"You are." Wearily, Charles accepted the bottle.

Big Sur, California
Stone House

Pete's smile faded slightly when he noticed Skye was behind him. He called to Melissa, "I'll be out in a bit."

"Ah, excuse me." Skye looked upset. "A moment of your time, please." He took a step back. "In here, if we could."

A small oil canvas showcasing orange poppies flowing from a blue vase stood out among the unique pottery that graced the kitchen shelves. The frame was made of sticks tied together with twine. Skye stared at it, remembering how secretly he worked on his project so that he could surprise his mother and grandmother for Mothers' Day. He'd only been nine years old, and it had never occurred to him to make two frames. After all, they were both artists. When his mother accepted his gift, she'd placed his grandmother's painting in it and assured him he'd done a good job. He could still feel how he'd puffed up with pride. *My god, she kept it,* he thought. *How silly is that?*

Pete followed him back into the kitchen, letting the door shut behind him. Smiling, he said patiently, "You picked a good time for a visit. Not too damp. Plus the weather's going to be unseasonably warm." He wanted to support Melissa's idea to keep things normal so he assumed a positive note. "Nothing like a burst of late spring sunshine to brighten up a day." Inclining his head toward the back porch, where Melissa sat with Monique and Angie, he smiled. "Isn't that a pretty scene?"

"It is not a pretty scene!" Skye blinked rapidly. "No. No. Not, not a pretty scene at all."

"What's on your mind?" Pete asked calmly.

Skye's neck stretched to an unusual angle as he stared outside. "Who is that crazy looking person with the spiked hair and the..." He blinked several times and focused on Angie. "The thing in her nose?"

"One of my pottery students."

"Well, I should have known that!" Rolling his eyes, he smacked his hand against his forehead. "Get her out of here. We don't need any strangers involved in this scandal."

"What scandal? I hired my pottery student to help your mother."

"Help her do what?" His voice raised a notch, "For the love of God, that girl has purple hair, and she's dressed like a, a..." Looking back at Angie, he jerked nervously, "A gypsy. Damn it! This can't be happening to me!" Leaning closer to Pete, he confided, "You know I had chest pains when I found out about this baby."

"That can't be good. You'd best settle down some. Try taking a deep breath. Here," he said, "do it with me. Inhale; go deep." Pete sucked in air as Skye inhaled through flared nostrils. "Better, right? Now blow out." He released the air through his mouth in a rush. "Go on, try another breath. Several of 'em."

Skye felt his temper flare. *This is more crap!* He shook his head, "No. I am not better because of deep breathing. That's just some dumb ass Zen stuff that people do in Big Sur." He began to pace and ran his fingers through his hair. "Well, maybe, I'm some better." Throwing his hands in the air, he continued, "I don't know how I feel."

"Well," Pete scratched his head. "What say we head on out and meet your daughter's baby sitter? Why, if her purple hair has got you all twisted up, maybe you could discuss it with her...in person? Nice like."

"What? I don't want to talk to her!" He nodded sharply several times to himself. "I want her gone."

Pete filled two coffee mugs and asked, "Why?"

"I don't like people who look like that."

With his elbow, Pete pushed the screen door open. "Say, Skye, got my hands full. Could you get me those wraparounds? Right over there on the table. Just hook em' over my coffee mug. Thanks." He moved toward the porch.

"Wait! Wait, don't do that." Skye pushed in front of him blocking his exit. "We need to have a meeting, discuss this right now."

"I like meetings." Pete spoke in a level voice. "Thanks for holding the door. Why don't you get yourself some coffee and we'll have that get-together outside?"

"No! In here." Skye stepped back indicating the kitchen using both hands. "The meeting should be in here."

Pete moved easily through the door. "Would you mind bringing that basket of apple cinnamon rolls? All meetings should have refreshments." He inhaled the pleasant aroma of warm spices and grinned. "Your mom baked those fresh this morning."

Frustrated, Skye spun around to face the kitchen. He disliked the smell of cinnamon; it reminded him of airports and cheap food. He struck a belligerent pose and looked outside. *There they are...all sitting around like a big, happy family. This is nuts!* He massaged his temples. *No one out there understands a damn thing. I've got to call Delaney.*

The mouthwatering aroma from Melissa's cinnamon buns drifted through the screen door. Pete, needing a moment to recover from his conversation with Skye, paused to look toward the raised wooden planters in the back yard. The vegetable garden would produce a good crop this year. He turned his attention toward the ocean where a breeze crowned the waves with mist, and whitecaps lapped farther out at sea. The moment was cleansing.

Looking at the trailing olallieberry vines, he noted that they clung hardily to their trellis. They had a short growing season but they were a coveted treat, and the pies and jam Melissa made were worth every berry he picked.

Following the vines back to the porch, he stepped nimbly over Angie's valise. Melissa placed Monique in the drawer. She reached up and unhooked Pete's sunglasses from the mug as he handed her the coffee.

"I took it on a garden tour to cool it off some."

"That you did. It's the perfect temperature." She looked toward the screen door. "Is Skye going to join us?"

"I suspect so. He's getting ready to head up the meeting."

"What meeting?"

"The meeting he's about to chair."

"Peterson Bailey, what are you talking about?"

"We're about to have an important get-together to discuss the issues."

Melissa raised her hand and waved at the air. "Oh pooh. We are not."

Pete grinned. "Truth is I left him looking at the coffee pot."

"Well, that's better." She bobbed her head in a positive manner. "I can understand that. He always had an interest in electrical things."

Pete nodded toward the raised planters. "We can't go running off to Australia or New Zealand till we harvest them vegetables, and they're not all planted yet. Looks like it's still a way off for the summer tomatoes. They'll need lots of hot afternoon sunshine." He handed the second coffee to Angie.

"Thanks, Mr. Bailey."

"You're most welcome. And you can call me Pete."

"And me Melissa."

He turned to her and chuckled. "Guess we'll just have to wait on our big trip, huh?"

"Well, as I think on it..." she shrugged her shoulders, "Maybe next year is better. It seems it would be best to go in our spring 'cause it would be fall down under and we could see them harvest the grapes."

"Aren't you the smart one?"

"I am." She grinned at Pete. "Coffee's fragrant and strong. Thank you. You want to sit down?"

He adjusted his sunglasses as he joined her on the glider. "You think we were too rough on your boy yesterday?"

"I was just about to start chastising myself." Gazing up at the pale blue sky, she smiled. "But then I decided that you can't wallow in yesterday's mistakes. Mind now, I'm not saying we made a mistake." She gently slapped her knees. "Why, here it is, a brand-new day! And, as a special surprise, according to you," she looked at Pete and raised her eyebrow. "My son is going to conduct an important meeting right here on my porch. Do I get to guess what it's going to be about?"

"He has a fine education, Missy."

"Indeed he does. So I guess we'll just have to wait and see how he uses it."

Key West, Florida
Robert and Evelyn Covington Residence

"They're both flying out to California." Robert pinched the bridge of his nose."

"Did you tell him that was a bad decision?" His wife studied her cards.

"They want to help."

"You mean Terri Sue Ellen thinks she can help."

"Yes."

"You do know that she has limited ability?"

"Of course." He adjusted his glasses and added, "Charles thinks she's drinking too much."

"She is." Evelyn looked out to sea and laid down her hand. "Gin."

Chicago, Illinois
Covington Home

Terri Sue Ellen paced by the front door waiting for the car to take her to the airport while Maria added a pair of boots to her suitcase.

"No! No boots. Ah'm goin' to the land of sunshine. Wait." She stopped short, stumbling over her feet. "Ah will be in a remote area some of the time. Put'em in. Where's mah driver? Ah've got to get to the airport." She flapped her hands at the maid. "Is mah husband still in the bedroom? Lordy be, packin' for this trip to the outback is not all that difficult."

Climbing the stairs in a wobbly fashion, she called over her shoulder, "Maria, get me a bowl of olives and put 'em in a fancy glass filled with vodka. Put some plastic wrap over the top and hold it down with a rubber band. Make it a to-go. Ah've got to be prepared for any situation that ah may run up against."

She paused and looked down at her maid. "My future son-in-law is of Mexican and Cherokee Indian heritage. You can relate to that so pay close attention to what ah'm about to say. His mother is an artist who paints on velvet." Her mouth turned down. "Naturally that would be more to your likin' than mine. She might try to give me one... sort of like a peace offerin' for her no account son siring a baby with trash from some honky-tonk. If I have to bring it home to hold this weddin' together, you can have it. Think of it as an early Christmas present. Did you get all that, Maria?"

"Si, Mrs. Covington."

Big Sur, California
Stone House

Melissa pushed the glider with her foot and settled into a soft swing. Leaning back, she turned toward Angie. "It's gon'na be a real warm day." Smiling, she spoke to Pete, "We were getting acquainted. Angie tells me you teach a fine pottery class. Got good technique." She leaned over and kissed his cheek." "Of course, I already knew that."

Angie grinned and bent over Monique. She was rewarded with a soft cooing sound. "She's precious. Listen to her sing."

Skye called from inside, "A little help here." The irritability in his tone pierced the air like razor-edged darts. He held a coffee mug and the basket of warm pastries.

Angie jumped up to hold the door for him.

He walked through without comment and placed the basket on a small redwood table, then turned to look at the young girl. Distaste showed in his face. "Who are you?"

"Don't be rude, Skye." Melissa's tone took on an edge, "We talked about that yesterday. Apologize to Angie, please."

"Hi." She faced Skye with an open stare and offered a bashful smile. "Your daughter is beautiful."

"You have a nose ring, and it's disgusting."

Angie opened her eyes wider. "You're no prize yourself. I just opened a door for you, and the polite comment is thank you, not who are you?"

"That's it!" Skye rose up to his full height and towered over her.

She looked up. "You're a bully!"

He snapped his fingers at her. "You're fired."

"I think not," Melissa replied calmly. She smiled at Pete. "You need more room. It's a big glider. Let me move over."

"Now Missy, I'm fine."

"Stop calling her that! Her name is Melissa. This Missy name sounds like...." He raised both hands in exasperation. "It's not right."

His mother smiled indulgently. "Skye, you understand how people give loving nicknames to others? Didn't Delaney's father give her a cute name when she was a child?"

"It's not the same."

"Of course, it is."

A wry smile tugged at the corners of Pete's mouth. "Sure glad we got that settled. Otherwise I'd have to re-do my thinking process and come up with something else to call you."

"Nah. That won't be necessary." She turned to her son. "I see you're having coffee today." Looking toward Pete, she continued, "Delaney doesn't like coffee breath, so he can't drink it when he's with her."

"You don't say."

Melissa nodded and they rocked peacefully.

Skye, visibly upset, stood to one side. He stared at Angie who ignored him and smiled at Monique.

Chicago, Illinois
Covington Home

"You'll need to be calm when we get there, sugar. No theatrics or Delaney will go to pieces." Charles closed his suitcase and looked carefully at his wife.

"Don't you worry yourself about me, Chucky, ah can handle it. You just dump those executives off the Lear and get me on board. What we got here is a shameful abomination that requires mah good breedin' and delicate touch." She swayed on her high heels as Maria entered the room with the chauffer.

Brady nodded. "The car is ready, Mr. Covington."

Terri Sue Ellen interrupted, "Maria, you remember what ah told you."

"Si." She nodded pleasantly as Charles looked confused.

"Mah maid has pledged to take any oddities ah may be forced to bring home. She will dispose of them as we have discussed. Employee to employer. The end." She leaned toward her husband. "Shortly after our daughter met Skye, ah pulled up all this velvet paintin' craze on the internet and saw a lot of Mexicans and Indians swirling bright colors all around in buckets and swishing them onto velvet backgrounds. His mother was one of 'em. Ah'm tellin' ya Chucky, it's a good thing Skye has pale skin and resembles his father."

"We've no idea what his mother looks like."

"Makes no difference. Look at Maria. They're all short and squatty. Now let's saddle up and ride." She removed her shoes and handed them to Charles. "Hang on to these for me. Ah got'ta navigate the stairs." She wobbled unsteadily out of the bedroom while the chauffer collected the remaining bags.

"Hold the hand rail, sugar." He turned to Maria. "Is there black coffee in the limo?"

"Si, Mr. Covington."

Half way down the steps, Terri sue Ellen shouted, "Fire up the jet, Chucky, we got us a trip to take."

Chapter Twelve

Big Sur California
Stone House

Melissa looked up toward the rolling hills that climbed the far side of the highway. "Time glides across the tree tops in a measured breath. Isn't that so?" She spread her hands trying to convey the meaning of her words.

Angie answered, "It speaks to my heart."

"So it does." Melissa turned her face toward the blue Pacific that was her backyard. "Sor'ta time washed with memories." She smiled at her son. "What do you think, Skye?"

"This is unbelievable. A load of crap." He paced the floorboards looking unkempt in his rumpled clothes. "Are you both nuts? I'm telling you that we have a situation here. It needs to be dealt with now. You can't run a business like this, ignoring the facts...and you damn well can't run your life this way."

Pete reached for Melissa's hand remembering their agreement to act normal. "Boy's got a point, Missy. As this is going to be Skye's meeting, we'd best let him conduct it to his likin'."

Melissa faced her son. "Carry on. I'm sure we'll all learn something."

He moved closer to the old glider in an attempt to force himself to center stage. "I hope you understand fully what I'm about to say." Clearing his throat, he stood straight. "I'm taking matters into my own hands."

Melissa sighed. "Being that pushy doesn't become you."

He bent his head lower so that he spoke directly to his mother, "I will have the proper department notified this afternoon and that, that..." He looked toward Monique and pointed ominously. "That baby will be gone!"

"When DNA testing proves she is your child, what should we do then?" Melissa continued to look calmly at her son. "And while this is being determined, where will she go?"

"Away. That's where!" He stood back and turned to glare at Angie. "And so will this, this...gypsy with her purple hair and loathsome nose piercing."

Angie looked close to tears as she stared back at him. "You're hurtful, and you're a grumpy person."

Melissa spoke quickly to avoid the oncoming scene, "Angie, why don't you take Monique inside? Just leave her bed here and spread out the blanket that's on the back of the sofa."

"Okay." She sniffed and tried to smile. "It's a very pretty sofa. I like swans."

Skye groaned but was cut short by his mother's stare.

"You'll see that Monique can sort of plop herself up on her hands and rock a bit...that is right up until she falls over." She smiled with pride at everyone. "I think my granddaughter is quite advanced and will be sliding around on her tummy in no time. Go on now, Angie. I'll be in shortly." She faced Skye. "Soon as I have a word with my son."

Angie picked up Monique, and Melissa reached into her arms. "Look at this, Pete." She tickled the baby under her chin. "I get the biggest smile ever, and it's complete with lots of babbles. Same as Skye when he was this age."

Monique gurgled with pleasure and waved her tiny arms. Skye felt a twinge of compassion but pushed it far away.

"Now that's just precious!" Melissa dropped kisses on the baby's forehead and gently covered Monique's face so the sun wasn't in her eyes.

"Skye, come have a look at your daughter."

He straightened, looking disgusted. "No thank you, mother. I'm done here."

"Oh, I think not," she replied, then nodded at Angie. "Go ahead and take Monique inside." She waited until Angie was gone before she spoke, "It appears you are having another one of your malicious moods. I'm tired of them." Looking directly into her son's eyes, she clipped her words, "Fix your attitude and be civil to all the people in my house."

He pushed his lips together and made a face. "I'm going to my room, where I have calls to make."

She replied curtly, "A good place for you to think. Be sure to apologize to Angie when you pass."

He paused at the screen door. "Mother, that person has got to go. She'll tell others what you have here." He started to push the door and turned back. "Didn't it ever occur to either one of you that she could be a runaway or a criminal?"

"No." Melissa and Pete exchanged a bewildered look. "Can't say it did."

"She's got a nose ring, for god's sake. She's probably dirty."

"No, she washed up and changed clothes before Pete brought her over here."

"Unbelievable!" He replied sarcastically and allowed the door to slam shut behind him.

Minutes passed, and the silence was broken by Pete's whisper, "Did you just send your thirty-four year old son to his room, Missy?"

"I did. He was about as offensive as he could be." She nodded, breathing hard with anger. "The air is nicer out here with his nasty attitude removed."

"Your boy is confused."

"Yes, he is." She punched at the glider pillow with annoyance. "And he's being mean-spirited." Taking a deep breath, she whispered, "I'm so scared, Pete." They rocked quietly as she regained her composure. "Layers of my life sweep over my heart every day. This layer should be good, filled with love and rejoicing." Leaning toward him, she reached for his hand. "The wonder of a baby makes a body rediscover the magic of life."

He raised her hand to his lips. "That it does."

The late morning air was sweet as honey, and Melissa's gaze settled on the May hills thickly dotted with wild flowers. "Once I saw a picture of a Viennese ballroom after the dance. The floor was covered with confetti like my hills are covered with flowers. Each summer my hillside blossoms like a burst of music." She looked beseechingly at Pete. "I so want to share that with my granddaughter."

"And you should."

Melissa nodded, but she was far from being reassured.

Chicago, Illinois
Airport

"Have some coffee." Charles pushed a cup toward his wife.

"No! Gim'me me mah vodka."

He handed the cup to the flight attendant who took it away. "Please put on your seat belt, sugar."

She fumbled with the buckle and asked, "Don't you wonder what our future son-in-law is doin' right now as we dance a jig tryin' to fix his mistake?"

"Knowing Skye, I'd say he's working on the problem the same as we are."

"Hell's bells! Nobody is tryin' as hard as us!" She gave her husband a long green-eyed blink. "We'd best get us down to the holler before too much is said and done."

"It's Big Sur, not a holler."

"Whatever."

Big Sur, California
Stone House

Skye couldn't get reception on his cell and walked around the house hoping for a signal. Pausing in the dining room, he noticed that nothing had changed. Oddly shaped chairs sat around the long table where many family gatherings had taken place. *Gatherings,* he thought. *That was one of my father's words.* He continued to stare. *This is where I learned the art of conversation.*

In the center of the table, a cut glass bowl from Ireland held fresh red apples and sat alongside leather bound books of poetry. Pencil cup holders and paper for writing down ideas, were pushed to one side.

I did my homework there. My mother always joked that if I had an earthshaking idea I should use the parchment paper to record it. The multipurpose paper was for shopping lists. I liked that concept, even though I don't remember having many earthshaking ideas. Not like my dad's.

Glancing toward the desk in the corner of the parlor, he noticed a computer screen and keyboard. Next to it was a slim line tower and speakers. *So, that's Zippy. What a stupid name. Old system, but a step in the right direction.* He moved closer. *This is where they plan to book the trip they're talking about.* His forehead wrinkled. *What's with this travel? My mother's never been anyplace so why would she want to go now?*

Turning around, he saw Angie who sat on the floor playing with the baby. She glanced up, and he felt the need to say something, "I'm sorry that I don't like you, or your appearance, or your clothes."

"Ditto."

He was taken back by her response. "Well...all right then. I'll be outside." He walked down the inside hall thinking she had no idea how important he was at Tech World International. He turned back to set her straight but saw she wasn't looking at him.

Still holding his now cold coffee, he retraced his steps to the kitchen and decided to try talking to his mother using a different approach. Moving toward the screen door, he pushed it open. "I'm sorry, mom. I was rude, and I apologized to her."

"Who did you apologize to?"

"Her. The gypsy. What's-her-name."

"What is her name, Skye?"

He spread his hands. "Okay, I get it." He took a deep breath before responding, "Her name, mom, is Angie. Is that better?"

"Much."

"Good. May I come out and join you?"

She nodded, and Skye stepped onto the back porch. He inquired politely, "How's it going?"

"Well," Pete mused, "I predict those ollalieberries will be bright and shiny and have more intense flavor than the blackberries. But you already know that... growing up here. "

"Ahh." Skye looked blank. "Sure."

"And if we get those tomatoes planted and the sun shines, they'll color right up and be showy as rubies." Pete took off his baseball cap and set it on the table. "Yes sir, you can eat 'em like an apple straight from the tree."

Skye studied Pete's baseball cap while thinking of a correct response to such an outlandish statement. Determined to be well mannered, he cleared his throat and continued, "Well, nice to know that...about the garden crop." He motioned toward Pete's cap that sat on the table. "What does the 'P' stand for?"

"Potter. Pete the potter. Your Mom had the 'P' embroidered on the hat for me. Say, if you like it, next time the carnival comes through, she might win one for you."

Melissa gave Pete a strange look.

Skye blinked. "That would be...something special to have." No one spoke, so he searched for more words, "Ahh, a carnival cap."

Pete broke the silence with his enthusiastic reply, "Money in the bank on that! Why, your mom's got a mean right arm. She can take a baseball and knock those stuffed dolls right out of the tent." Pete laughed at his own joke.

Skye sucked on his bottom lip. "I had no idea carnivals came through Big Sur."

"Oh, they don't. We have to travel some."

Skye's eyes went to the drawer by his mother's side, "What's that?"

"That's Monique's bed."

"It looks like one of the old drawers where you kept the winter clothes."

Raising an eyebrow, she smiled at her son. "It used to hold your daddy's long johns."

"Oh." He took a breath to regroup his thoughts. "Why does she sleep in a drawer?"

"Because it was available on short notice. I call it 'Drawer Bed'." Melissa joked, "Here in Big Sur country, we make do with what we have on hand. You remember the time you and Duane got poison oak from building that fort? And we started treating it with hand-made calamine lotion. Looking back, I believe I should have used more Rose Kaolin clay...it draws out toxins, if you remember. Anyhow, in proportion to the zinc oxide power and..."

"Stop, mom. It didn't work."

She shrugged and continued, "Sometimes you need more help, and it's important to know when that happens so you can take the next step." Pausing, she looked at her son. "Give it some thought."

The air felt heavy with silence, and Skye made another attempt to sip his cold coffee but knew the acidity would grind away at his stomach so he set it down next to Pete's cap. Realizing that the conversation had taken an uncomfortable turn, he added, "Okay. I'm gon'na take a shower now."

Backing toward the screen door, he turned to enter the hallway and bumped against the table that his great grandfather had carved. Water splashed out of the vase that held the last of the spring daffodils and beaded into clear balls on the newly oiled wood.

He thought about all the times he'd run into that table as a child and never once had his mother raised her voice to him. *Well, maybe once or twice? But usually she just shook her head at my clumsiness and mopped up the mess.* He hit his forehead with the heel of his hand, a gesture he was growing all too familiar with. *That's it! That's what being a parent is all about... some kind of super understanding about kids.* He congratulated himself for recognizing the truth. *I seem to be the only person in this house who knows that I don't have what it takes to be a dad.* He stopped to let that thought digest. *Granted it could be a flaw in my personality, but it quickly will self-correct when Delaney has my children.*

On the way to his old bedroom, the thought struck him that there was an easy way between his mom and Pete. Simple gestures like holding hands meant something to them. They didn't have a clue what went on in the real world. *It's like that story my mother used to tell about Big Sur being a beautiful make-believe place until the highway came through. It was a state of mind. It wasn't real. Big Sur will be commercialized, and Delaney and I will lead the pack.*

As he passed the window, he glanced at the wild flower garden. Tall lacy leaves of yarrow waved in the breeze, tiny white flowers grew in clusters, and wild looking snapdragons mixed with California Poppies. *What a mess,* he thought. *Without some direction, nature would take over.*

He paused, listening to the sounds of the ocean. He associated it with his mother's long recitations of family lore that put him to sleep at night. *Well, perhaps, as a small child, I wanted to hear about my distant relatives, in all their glory, but that has no place in my life now.*

The smells of spring trailed through the open window, carried on the late morning breeze. Honeysuckle spread itself over the rock retaining wall, the fragrant white blossoms turning a soft yellow. He found himself looking up toward the ridgeline where the windbreak of Monterey pines grew on the southwestern end of the property. He nodded in their direction, thanking them for the protection. *What the hell is wrong with me? That nodding thing was just something I picked up from my mother. Trees don't understand thoughts.*

Sounds of traffic pushed its way into his memory, and a vision of long stemmed white roses on the Tuscan hall table filled his mind. He wondered if the petals had opened to full bloom and if they had a sweet, pleasant aroma. Hopefully, not too much scent as Delaney was sensitive to smells. He wondered how she'd been talked into wearing the sandalwood. It was strong, almost overpowering.

He thought of Delaney's tearstained face. *I want to make her happy, and we deserve the lifestyle we've built together.* He shrugged. *Actually, I sort of walked into it, but I'm very supportive of her ideas.*

Pete returned with Monique when Melissa went to the kitchen to refill their coffee. She carried the mugs out and placed them in the cup holders that Pete had carved in the wide arms of the old glider. Sitting down, she gave it a gentle push with her foot while Pete cuddled the baby.

"She's a sweet little girl. Pretty, too. Looks like her grandma." He winked at Melissa. "Thought I'd give Angie time to unpack her overnight case and settle in. She's in the little room at the end of the hall."

"I'm going to bet that Skye settled in his old bedroom, which I plan to turn into my office slash studio."

"He did." Pete took an exaggerated deep breath. "For now, all seems right with the world." Looking down at Melissa's long legs, he commented, "Those shapely limbs of yours could send us swinging smack into the center of the ocean. I'm not sayin' that would be a bad thing, if it was just the two of us adults here, but you can see that I've got your granddaughter."

She scolded him lightly, "Don't you try to change the subject we were discussing earlier. Let us return to the letter "P" that is embroidered on your cap.

You know that letter stands for "old fart" as in the name you've given to yourself." She raised an eyebrow as she looked at him. "I had the responsibility to select only one letter, and I went with an 'F' as it was most descriptive."

"I must have forgotten that." He attempted to look chastised. "Slip-ups can happen at my age."

"Uh-huh. Church Circle is where I got your cap. Adeline Becker did the embroidery, and she wasn't wearing her glasses so the "F" got mixed up and it came out a 'P'."

He replied somberly, "May she rest in peace."

"She's not dead! Stop your spoofing." Her brows knit together sharply. "We both know it's a perfectly good cap and no reason to disregard it for the lack of a correct letter."

"Well, Missy, I just cleaned up the story some for your boy."

"What?"

"I didn't want him to think his mother had taken up cussin'."

"Cussing! What do you mean?"

"Old fart is cussin'."

"Oh, for heaven's sake." Pushing playfully at his shoulder, she shook her head. "It is not. And we haven't gone to a carnival in many a year. Last one was in Monterey at the fairgrounds, and we passed on it because the year before we got dizzy on the Ferris Wheel."

He smiled pleasantly and tickled Monique under her chin.

"Don't go wakin' her up just yet." She waggled her finger at him. "We're not done with our discussion. Pete?" She raised her chin as he peered over his sunglasses. "Were you trying to distract me by foolin' with my son in his time of trouble?"

"Boy's way too serious, Missy. He's got to loosen up. Learn to go with the flow of things."

Monique cooed as if in agreement, drawing a smile from Melissa. The baby wiggled and grabbed for her feet.

Pete stretched out his finger and she held on, "Reminds me of Duane at that age. Guess they all do this finger grabbing, but it sure is nice when it happens. Makes me feel protective."

"You big softie." She kissed the top of his bald head.

Reaching down to stroke the baby's face, Melissa blew her kisses and looked up. "She's a sweet-natured child. And her brown eyes already beam with curiosity."

The sounds of a car startled them. Pete looked toward the direction of the drive. "Way too late for morning callers and too early for afternoon tea." Putting a hand to his ear, he listened again and frowned. "Car is definitely in your drive, Missy. Did you put up a sign to take in boarders?"

"Oh, Pete."

"Why, I hear tell they come and go at all hours." He teased, "Awful. Just awful." He settled Monique back in the drawer. "Shall I see who's disturbing our daily meditation?"

"Go on with you." She waved him toward the door and looked down at the baby. Her eyes were sleepy, and Melissa marveled how easily she could drift off, no matter how much turmoil surrounded her.

Pete was back within seconds, a puzzled look on his face. "It's another of them Ford cars. Seriously, you expectin' company?"

"Do I look like I'm having company? Sittin' here in my old robe with my hair not even braided?"

"That's right. I forgot. When you're socializing, you're sitting on the front porch."

"Oh Pete, stop now with your playing ways. You just go tell whoever is outside that we're not buying anything."

Minutes passed with no sounds, until Pete reappeared with a curious look on his face. "It's a city girl."

"Oh Lord!" Melissa jumped up, knocking the porch swing into a veering motion. She quickly looked down at Monique sleeping soundly in the drawer. "Thank heavens I didn't disturb her."

"Don't get all riled up." Pete raised his arms in defense. "The driver appears to be looking in the mirror getting herself fixed up before she starts down the walk."

"Is it Delaney?" Her hand flew to her chest. "Tall, pretty, wearing something expensive?"

Pete shrugged. "Can't say. She was still sitting in the car brushing her hair when I came back inside." He chucked the baby under her chin and was rewarded with a sleepy gurgle, "You think it's time I fetched Skye?"

"Quick as you can, unless you plan to be doing the entertaining."

He looked mildly put out. "I like to think I'm always entertainin'."

Quickly running her fingers through her hair, she shooed him toward the door. On his second step, he turned around. "Shall I bring you a brush?"

"Yes, please. And take off those dark glasses. You'll scare her."

His eyes widened. "She frail?"

"Of course not!" Melissa chuckled, "Mostly just skinny."

Delaney used the driver's mirror to add lip-gloss. She fumbled in her Chanel bag for the glass ampoule of sandalwood. A drop behind each ear was all she needed. *How dare that flight attendant wrinkle her nose as if my sandalwood was offensive. She had no idea what I paid for it!* Flipping her hair, she narrowed her eyes. *Plus I was in an economy seat so she didn't treat me with the respect I would have had if I was in First.*

She stepped carefully out of the rental car and brushed at her clothes. Her stripped Gucci suit was a sharply cut fashion statement in spite of its wrinkles. Thinking back over the events of the day, she felt herself tighten with annoyance. Having been to the stone house just once, she'd had only a minimal idea of what to take. Correct attire was so very important that she'd lost time while selecting her ensembles. To add to her stress, she'd had to pack her own suitcase because Estelle was still on maternity leave and Maria was working at her parent's house. Her life was riddled with frustrations.

She'd missed the Red Eye at O'Hara by ten minutes due to difficulties in getting a cab. The airlines had put her on another plane that sat on the runway for two hours while the engine was checked repeatedly. She'd raised havoc with airlines personnel who'd listened to her because of her Premier Status, and she'd been placed on the first flight closer to her destination. Sitting in an uncomfortable seat in Economy. Plus, she had consumed too many cokes, and now the effects of the caffeine left her jittery.

When she'd spotted the house suspended on the cliff above the boiling ocean, she reaffirmed her opinion; it was a dreadful sight and probably not even safe to inhabit.

As she walked down the path leading to the front door, the ocean breeze ruffled her hair, and she offered a word of thanks to Mr. Freddy for the wonderful style he'd created. *Oh, to be back in Chicago among the civilized!*

However, she was in charge of her self-esteem, and that served her well as she walked with determination up the steps to the wrap-around front porch. She swept past the planters and the old rocking chair and knocked loudly on the beveled glass door. It was her power statement, and she was ready to face the problem at hand.

A short man with a shiny bald head and inquisitive blue eyes pulled hard to open the door. "How do? You must be Delaney."

She jumped back. "How do you know that?"

"Missy told me."

"Oh. Very well. In that case, are the Topples at home?"

"Sure." Pete helped her through the front door and held her hand toward the light. "Say, that's quite a sparkler, you got there."

"It's mine." Her eyes widened as she pulled her hand back. She felt short of breath. "It's my engagement ring."

"Yup. I know that. You want to sit down and take the load off?"

She stared at him for several beats, feeling herself losing the coveted position of dominance. "Are you a Topple?"

"No, Ma'am. I'm a Bailey."

Skye flew down the hall, still stuffing his long arms into a red velour bathrobe. He hugged Delaney. Her scent was overpowering, but still, she felt good in his arms.

Pete rocked on his feet for a couple of seconds before speaking, "That's a real nice ring you gave your girlfriend."

"She's not my girlfriend!" Skye bellowed, "She's my finance! What is it with correct terms that you don't understand?" He sneered at Pete, "You,

you..." He was still glaring as his mother pushed open the kitchen door.

"I was out back but thought I heard company." She greeted her future daughter-in-law with an awkward hug. Pink fuzz from her robe stuck to Delaney's dark Gucci jacket. "Oh my. I'm so sorry. It's an old robe." She was tempted to brush the fuzz balls off Delaney's lapels but thought better of the idea and nodded at her son. "What are you upset about this time?"

"I'm not upset!"

"Good." Ignoring him, she turned back to her future daughter-in-law. "Skye's wearing my new robe." She gave Pete a nudge forward. "This is Peterson Bailey, my dear friend."

Pete opened his arms to hug the young woman who appeared overwhelmed by the gesture.

Skye yanked hard to open the front door and hurried Delaney onto the front porch where she looked over her shoulder at the people inside until Skye turned her toward himself.

Several seconds passed before Pete spoke. "She's a thin one, sor'ta like a reed." He squinted as he continued to stare through the beveled glass. "Dark blue is not her best color. Makes her look washed out."

Melissa tilted her head sideways. "Pete, are you making a fashion statement?"

"Nope." He smiled faintly. "I'm judging it as a potter. I know a little something about color." He turned to Melissa. "You think she was impressed by me?"

"What! Why would she be impressed by you?"

"Heck Missy, here it is early afternoon and you and your son are flying around in bathrobes. Shoot, I'm the only one in the house who's dressed." He laughed good-naturally. "You gon'na offer her coffee?"

"Like I said yesterday, she doesn't drink it and is opposed to anyone who does."

"Seems rather overbearing on her part."

"She can saturate a day with her ideas. Besides, I think Skye will take her out for breakfast."

He laughed, "Not while he's wearing red velour he won't. Say, didn't I give that to you for your birthday?"

"And it's my favorite, though velour is more of a cold morning wrap, and today's clearly going to be very warm. Besides," she nodded toward her son, "you can plainly see that Skye needs the robe."

"It must have been hanging close to your shower. Seems he was in quite a hurry to get out here." Pete rubbed his head. "Guess he didn't realize that I could open a door and greet his lady love." Rocking on his heels, he continued, "You'll notice that I spoke slowly to her because of her attention deficit problem."

Melissa grinned broadly. "That was kindly of you."

Pete was lost in thought while he watched the back of Delaney's head as she ran her hands through her hair several times.

Standing behind him, Melissa looked over his shoulder. "We're being a couple of old busy bodies staring at them like this."

"We are indeed," he agreed pleasantly.

Skye's head swung up and down approving of whatever Delaney was telling him.

Melissa squinted at Pete. "Do you think he looks happy to see her or struck dumb?"

"I'd say a little of both."

Skye raised his arms to enfold Delaney but quickly dropped them as he pulled the robe closed.

"Oh!" Pete smiled. "If he'd of remembered the tie for the waist he wouldn't be havin' that problem." He turned and chuckled. "I've got to say that red's a nice color on the boy."

"Always has been." She thought for a moment. "Blue's good, too."

They continued to watch the animated discussion until Pete asked cheerfully, "Where you think he'll take her for food?"

"Well, she doesn't eat eggs."

"She got somethin' against chickens?"

"Not that I know of." She paused in thought and then continued, "As I remember, bacon never touches her lips either."

"She don't care much for hogs, huh?"

"The time she came for a visit, she brought her own blend of granola."

He looked suspiciously at Melissa. "You're spoofing me."

"Nope." She kissed his forehead. "I'm going to step into the bedroom now and put on some jeans and my red checked shirt. As long as I'm preparing for the day, I think I'll go ahead and braid my hair."

"Good in my book." He turned his attention back to the activity taking place on the other side of the door.

When Skye and Delaney entered the house, Pete spoke first, "Say, how about we all go to the kitchen and have us a cup of coffee?"

"Nooo."

"Okay," he replied gently. "You don't have to get upset."

"She not upset!" Skye added hotly.

Pete nodded patiently and faced Delaney. "Missy went on down the hall to freshen up."

Skye threw his arms up in exasperation. "He calls her Missy. God knows why." He grabbed quickly at the robe. "Sorry."

When Delaney offered a sluggish smile of understanding, he gave the front door a push and added, "You're sure you'll be alright? You don't have to leave the entry." Facing Pete, he held the robe closed. "This is De-la-ney. Okay?"

"What's that?" Pete grinned and put his hand on his ear. "Say again?"

"De-la-ney."

"Okay. I got it now."

Skye hurried down the hall, calling over his shoulder, "I'll be quick. I promise."

Pete picked up the conversation. "And when Missy gets here, she'll be fully dressed. Just like you. Well..." He thought again and replied, "Not exactly like you. She won't be in business attire. However, she will be braided. Sure you don't want to step into the kitchen? Sit a bit?"

"Nooo." She shook her head, letting her head swing from side to side.

Pete rocked on his heels wondering if he could create a similar pattern that would intertwine around a clay pot.

Melissa hurried down the hall and stopped next to him. "You look like you're in deep thought."

"That I am." He nodded solemnly.

Raising her eyebrows, she gave him a questionable look then turned toward her guest. "It's good to see you again, Delaney." She paused when there was no forthcoming comment, adding dryly, "And so soon."

"People enjoy my company."

Melissa whispered, "Did you hear what she said?"

"Yup."

She shook her head. "I'm going to try again." Facing Delaney, she asked, "Would you like to wait in the parlor for Skye?"

"No, Missy! Don't ask her that. It seems to set her off."

"Off?"

"Yup." Pete rocked back on his heels. "Off."

Standing in the entry, Melissa looked puzzled. "Would you like some orange juice? It's freshly squeezed."

"It wouldn't agree with me. I've had no food due to airports and planes, annoyances and delays."

"That presented the inability to feed yourself?"

"It sure did."

Pete spoke slowly, "Say. I've got the perfect solution to your hungry tummy. How about a freshly baked cinnamon roll?"

"Sweets are not part of my nutritional program."

"Is that so?" He winked at Melissa and turned back to their guest. "How about some cereal?" He leaned over and lowered his voice, "See there, Missy, I brought the subject around to where she's comfortable."

"Cereal?" Delaney looked surprised. "Oh, no thank you." She moistened her lips and continued, "I have a private brand of granola that's made for me. It's expensive, but I'm worth it."

"Come again?"

"Ahh, it's specially formulated for my dietary needs based on my metabolism and nutritional requirements achieved through scientific testing, to assure me of a healthy start in the morning."

Melissa folded her arms. "You just wanted to hear her say that."

"Yup." Pete nodded.

"I can text you both some names for people in your area who do this type of study."

"Missy, do we text?"

"We don't."

Delaney blinked several times. "I, ahh, don't know anyone who doesn't text."

"You do now," Pete joked as he slipped his arm around Melissa.

Delaney took a step back, and her hip touched the entry table. She turned and noticed the daffodils in the chipped vase. "Spring flowers."

"They're from Pete. He's such a romantic."

She turned on her perfect smile. "Romance at your age."

"Did she imply we were old? Because that's the second time in twenty-four hours we've been told that, and I don't feel old."

Changing the subject, Melissa asked, "Shall we go to the kitchen where we can sit down? There's no need to stand here."

"But," Pete added emphatically, "Delaney favors the entry."

She flipped her hair, and Pete watched with interest as it settled neatly around her shoulders. Nodding, he commented, "It's interesting how that works."

"It is." Melissa searched for more words, "Has sort of a swing to it."

"All that whirling would look good on a narrow vessel." His fingers moved through the air. "Like this. A surge of motion in clay."

"Clay doesn't move."

"It does when I work with it."

Delaney had little interest in the dialogue between the bald man and her future mother-in-law. She turned away and let her eyes wander around the entry. "That old table seems to list a bit. Is this the part of the house that slid to one side?"

"That's the north end. It's very old but, Skye's father installed heavy support beams with the help of friends and neighbors so the problem was almost corrected. We talked about the lighthouse last time you were here and how people got together to build it."

"Oh. I remember. Like a work crew on the highway. They usually come from penitentiaries." Stopping abruptly, she frowned. "Not that that happened here, of course. You employed friends...not convicts. Well, maybe some convicts. Didn't they settle in this area?"

"They did not!" Melissa felt her temper flare.

"We know all our neighbors, even the shady ones." Pete chuckled. "Probably same as you know yours."

"Oh, my no! We live in the city and don't pry into each other's lives."

Pete looked perplexed and faced Melissa with a scowl. "She's a hard one to follow. I'll try a different approach." He spotted Delaney's watch and opened his mouth, but Melissa shook her head implying he shouldn't comment. "I was just going to be complimentary," he whispered.

"Don't go near the ring either."

"I already did." He continued in an undertone, "I told her it was flashy."

Melissa groaned, "Did she tell you the canary story?"

"She did not. You know I like a good story."

Delaney paid little attention to their quiet conversation and let her fingers run through the beads of water that remained on the entry table. "Wet."

"Oh that." Melissa wiped at the water with a corner of her shirt. "Skye used to run into that table often when he was a boy." She laughed. "Guess some things never change."

Searching Delaney's emerald eyes, she found them filled with uncertainty and something else that might be fear. Her heart went out to the younger woman, and she reached for her hands.

Delaney pulled them back but quickly extended them, adding a nervous giggle. "I didn't know you were going to pull at me."

"I'm sorry. I didn't mean to startle you." She smiled warmly and added, "My father gave Harm and me that table as a wedding present." Her voiced filled with pride, "He carved it himself. See here," she placed Delaney's hand on the table and traced her fingers over the initials that were notched along the side and added, "You can feel the love."

Delaney gingerly moved the French tip of a well-manicured nail across the carving. "Oh yes." she replied nervously. "There it is."

Melissa added shyly, "One day I'd hoped to pass this on to Skye...and his bride. This might be the right time."

"Oh," Delaney's voice squeaked with mounting tension. "My. Oh my." The idea of the table in her living room left her feeling short of breath. "That would be a very..." She moistened her lips and continued, "Well, certainly, a very special, special...item." Feeling the need to sit down, she nervously looked around. The parlor yawned in front of her. She saw the sofa and caught her breath.

Glancing down the hall in hopes of seeing Skye, she realized she'd have to handle this on her own. "You should never part with that table. No, we couldn't ask you to and...we wouldn't—because it's a family treasure." With an effort, she leaned over to warily touch the old wood and felt perspiration break out above her upper lip. Knowing she was at a loss for words, she ended flatly with, "A family treasure that should never, never leave the family."

Melissa answered briskly, "My son is my family."

"I knew that." Delaney, feeling out of breath, realized she'd made the wrong comment and changed the subject. "I see you still have a braid."

"I do." Melissa fought to reply evenly.

"And it is..." Delaney's voice was barely a whisper, "...another treasure." She took a second to moisten her lips and wondered if she should excuse herself and wait in her car for Skye, but the baby's cry interrupted her thoughts, and she jumped. "What's that sound?"

Angie rushed down the hall. "I'll get her. I'm unpacked and settled in." She glanced at Delaney. "Hello."

"Another Topple?"

"No. Angie is a student of Pete's."

"Pete is a professor?"

"He's a Master Potter and well known as an instructor of pottery techniques."

Delaney raised both hands, palms out. "Isn't that nice?" Lowering her hands, she released her breath and faced him. "Was the crying sound the..."

Pete filled in her missing word, "Baby?"

"Yes, the baby." Her eyes darted around the hall. "Is she white?"

"And pink. Pretty little thing."

"White?" Melissa repeated uncertainly.

"Yes. White as in Caucasian." Delaney reached out to touch her hand briefly. "It's okay. I know about the darker side of your family. Mother told me that was the reason for your passion about velvet paintings. It's ethnic. You can't help it."

Melissa looked blank.

"It's difficult to keep Mexicans and Cherokee Indians a secret. Skye told me early in our relationship about your historically shaded past. You should know that my parents are very broad minded about blended families, and they support many charities that clothe and feed the less fortunate."

"Well, alright then." Melissa took a breath. "Isn't that good to know?" Facing Pete, she frowned. "She's a wealth of information, but I've no idea what she's talking about."

"Let me try again. I think short questions are best." He turned back to Delaney. "The baby is a cutie. Want to see her?"

"Oh no!" Her hands flew up.

Pete ducked to avoid the waving gesture and continued calmly, "All little girls are pink and white."

"I don't know that much about the subject, but maybe French babies..." Delaney pondered. "...are prone to a rash?"

"What?"

"Can't help ya, Missy." Pete lowered his voice, "I'm floundering around, too."

Raising her eyebrow, she added, "Even with your short questions."

Skye arrived in time to stop further discussion. He was dressed in the clothes he'd flown in and looked none too fresh.

"Well, off we go, Delaney." Steering her toward the door, he turned to his mother. "We'll catch up with you later."

"Good bye, Mother Topple."

"Don't call me that!" Melissa looked surprised by her outburst.

Pete's eyebrows elevated. "Mother Topple?"

"Oh, now. I'll work on another name if you like." Delaney smiled. "But really, Mother Topple has a ring to it. I like the way it comes out of my mouth."

"Let's be off." Skye indicated the door. "This way."

Delaney's emerald-colored eyes raked over the stone walls as she turned to go.

"Wait." Melissa studied the young woman's face. "Your eyes are a lovely shade of green. It's a color I'd like to capture in a painting."

"Really? Can you paint green on black velvet?"

"What *are* you talking about?"

"Another subject for another day." She fluttered her eyelashes, and Skye observed the blinking action closely as she continued, "Many people comment on the shade of my eyes. The ability to pose comes naturally. Mother, being a peach queen, that's a coveted title in the South and requires grace and dignity. Well, those social skills never leave you. When mother received her crown, she generously gave each loser a rose and a peach as souvenirs of her big day because they had the honor of serving in her court. I grew up on that story. That kind of caring has been passed on to me."

"I'm left speechless." Melissa turned to look at Pete. "What do you think?"

"Sure enough. I see peach queen written all over her." He squinted at Delaney as she smoothed her jacket.

"I believe you wanted to see my eyes in natural light?"

"Yes. I do. They're the soft misty green that occurs just prior to a wave crashing against the shore." Melissa gazed steadily at her future daughter-in-law. "The moment the sun shines through, it leaves an iridescent emerald glow for a split second. When it breaks, it's gone forever."

Skye sucked in his breath. "Thank you, mom, and now we're out of here." He propelled his fiancée toward the door. "Going for breakfast. We'll be back later."

Melissa moved down the hall. "I'm getting Monique."

Skye grabbed the doorknob and pulled hard. "Come on, darling. Outside." He grumbled over his shoulder, "Someone should fix this damn door. It's a menace."

"Got some tools in the back," Pete replied cheerfully. "You want, we could take it apart tomorrow."

"I don't think so! Haven't you done enough to screw with my life?"

Delaney ignored his outburst and asked, "Was that a compliment? That thing your mother said about my eyes?"

"Yes." Skye wandered but responded positively, "Of course, it was. She's an artist. They say things differently."

Melissa returned holding Monique, who babbled contentedly as she grabbed at her grandma's braid. Pete gave them each a kiss as Melissa untangled the baby's fingers and looked at Pete with a half grin. "I had no idea you kept tools out back to fix that door."

"I didn't know you were interested in painting green things." He bestowed a long look on her.

She shrugged. "They completely gone?"

"Yup. Out looking for food. Guess there wasn't anything here they could handle."

"Apparently there's something in the kitchen because Angie has offered to fix us French toast."

He made a zoom sound and let his fingers dance around Monique's tummy. The baby squealed with laughter as he turned to Melissa. "Say, you're not about to part with that table from your daddy, are you?"

Her smile broadened when she looked at the old table. "Not now that I know how "special, special" it is." A thoughtful look highlighted her face and she added, "The table should never leave the family. You heard her say that."

Chapter Thirteen

Big Sur, California
Highway One

The car's interior was hot as they started up the drive. Skye immediately adjusted the temperature knowing that Delaney disliked being either too warm or too cold but, to his dismay, no cool air blew out. *Ah shit! It's not working.*

Delaney watched the stone house disappear into the cliffs. "Oh, my God," she murmured. Her speech pattern changed to a series of rapid sentences. "Did you see that odd looking girl with the flowing clothes? They hung all over her body. Does she live there?" Before he could answer, she continued, "There was something in her nose. I think it was a ring." Her neck snapped sharply to the left so that she faced Skye. "That can't be sanitary." Alarm filled her eyes. "You didn't touch her, did you?"

"Of course not!"

"Please tell me she won't be coming to my wedding. Good Lord, her hair stands up in points! And it's purple." Her words changed to a soft whimper, "Oh, I don't think even Mr. Freddy could fix that."

"Don't worry. She won't be at the wedding. She's hired help."

"Umm." Delaney paused before replying, "She didn't look Mexican. Does she clean the house? I ask because she doesn't do a very good job. Mother and I excel at pointing out faults and making corrections. I suppose as long as I'm here, I could talk to her."

"No, no! She's not a housekeeper. Hopefully, she isn't any kind of a keeper. She's more a..." His thoughts continued to slide around. "Let's call her a Pottery Nanny."

She asked befuddled, "Is that something native to the area?"

"She's a first."

"Really? Because it's difficult to believe that your mother is on the cutting edge of anything."

"Oh, but she is. You, ahh, need to be around her more to pick up on that."

"Very well. I'll watch closely. Now, what responsibilities does a, a, a Pottery Nanny have?"

"Really, Doodle Bug, do you care? We have more important items to discuss."

"Who hired her?"

He dropped his head in exasperation. "My mother and Pete. It's complicated." He reached for her hand. "They hired a pottery student to be a nanny for the baby."

"Well..." Her mind shifted gears. "Thank God that baby is white. Mother told me to look at it and be sure."

He raised his eyebrows. "What did you say?"

"Oh, you know what I mean. It's actually a relief to know that you can produce Caucasian babies."

He sighed, "Did you actually think differently?"

She ran her fingers through the left side of her hair letting it fall behind her ear. "That Pete person said it was a white baby but had some kind of a rash, so I didn't want to get close. A girl can't be too careful in today's world. You may not know this, but mother researched it so I have the facts; babies can have serious germs and major skin defects that adults have no immunity to." She waved her hand indicating that the subject was closed.

"As soon I get cell reception I'll call my parents with the good news. You know that mother's golf game is really off due to her heightened concern about you." She watched Skye's reaction to be sure the poisoned dart had hit home.

She fingered the narrow lapels on her Gucci blazer. "Let's move on. Your mother and Pete seem capable enough to handle a baby for a few days. Do you think they need a Pottery Nanny at this time?"

"It would appear so."

"Nooo!" Delaney clung to his arm. "That's not right! I want our lives to be back in place! Is that too much to ask?"

"Of course not, Doodle Bug."

"I don't like people with purple hair. Neither do you." Her words came out snappish, "We don't want strange people walking into our world. Do we? No, of course not. We want my friends around us at all times. I've selected them for reasons. Just who is Pete the Potter? Note what I say, Skye." She shook her finger at him. "We don't have the whole truth about him."

There was no easy way to say it, so he sucked in a mouthful of air and spoke rapidly, "He's my mom's live-in, but that doesn't concern us."

Delaney slowly sank back into the seat. "Live-in what?"

He felt himself flinch and replied weakly, "Boyfriend."

"She has a boyfriend? Your mother has a boyfriend?" She shook her head and her finger at the same time, emphasizing each word, "No, no, no! I won't have that!"

Skye recognized her anger building like invisible waves of energy and pulled away.

"Well, what else can these people do to me to ruin my life?" She snorted loudly, "Your mother and a man, a potter for God's sake, living together, right under your nose, with my wedding date just three months away?" She covered her mouth and gasped, "Oh my God! What do we tell people?"

"It will be alright, Delaney. We'll work on it."

"This is an example of your mother keeping the facts from you." Exasperation filled her tone. "I am enraged that I wasn't informed of this situation earlier. This is the same as the dry cleaner and the delivery service."

Skye looked baffled. "I didn't follow that."

"Never mind. You weren't there. I had to bear it alone." Sagging back against the seat, she continued to rub the side of her head. "I'm getting very warm. Please adjust the air conditioner."

He turned the dial for the non-existent cool air, hoping for a miracle.

"I want our life to be just the way I had it planned, and I want you to want the same thing." Sweat beaded across her forehead, and she wiped at it with the back of her hand.

"I do want the same things."

She faced him and wailed, "My mother wants us to be happy. I've no idea what your mother is thinking."

"She's thinking whatever you want her to think."

"Good! I'm glad you had the wedding talk with her." Skye looked puzzled but made no comment as Delaney continued, "That's the way it should be. I'm the bride, and my way rules." She pointed at the air conditioning vents. "You know I'm delicate and need to maintain my correct temperature."

He made a show of turning the vents and pushing buttons as she nervously pulled out a brush from her Chanel purse and began to tug it through her hair. "My scalp is sweating, and my make-up is running. Even Mr. Freddy's Sri Lanka Sandalwood doesn't smell right." She stopped all movement and stared, "What's wrong with that air conditioner?"

Skye held his hand in front of the blower. "Damn it! It isn't working." His fist thumped the steering wheel. "This is unacceptable!"

"Can't you fix it?" she bellowed.

"I'm not a mechanic," he shouted back, regretting his raised voice immediately.

She began to cry, and he pulled off the road into a scenic outlook. "I'm sorry, Doodle Bug. I shouldn't have gotten angry. Look, this is an unseasonably warm day. Lower your window and take off your jacket."

She sniffled. "It's Gucci."

"I know. You look beautiful wearing it."

"I'm worth it."

"Yes, you are." He comforted her. "We'll go someplace nice tonight. In Carmel."

"I'd like that. It's just so wild and uncivilized here while Carmel is awash with delightful eating establishments and fashionable dress boutiques." Making a small gesture with two fingers toward Skye, she frowned. "Do you have something else that you can wear? You're a shade wrinkled."

He thought of his hastily packed overnight bag and decided that a little white lie was in order. "I'll find something." Gently he put his arms around her and whispered in her ear, "We both need a hug. I love you so much, Delaney."

"Please don't blow in my ear. It's too warm."

"Of course. I'm sorry." He pulled back and continued, "Your being here means everything to me."

"Oh look!" she exclaimed as she fished the cell phone out of her purse. "I have reception! I'm going to call mother right now with the news about the pale skinned baby."

Within minutes, Delaney's was connected to the Lear.

"Oh, mother, I have an excellent report! Skye produced a white child." She listened for a moment and replied, "The Navy stripped Gucci. I agree. It shouts power." There was a pause. "Of course, his mother was impressed." She faced Skye. "Your mother was impressed by my appearance. Right? And by the fact that I flew so far to be by your side in your time of need? Again, correct?"

He opened his mouth to respond, but she returned to her phone conversation.

"Right now I'm sitting on the side of the road. Yes, of course, in a car. No, mother. I haven't done any hiking. When will you be here?" She looked sideways and smiled at Skye. "Mother and father will be landing in Monterey shortly."

"What?"

"Yes, mother, salads are the main stay of life. We must both keep fit for our big day. Are you leaning toward that glamorous champagne silk by Vera Wang or the bold crème taffeta by Christian Lacroix?" Delaney listened carefully to the answer. "Oh, mother! No!"

Worry etched Skye's voice, "What's the matter?"

"Mother thinks she may need a plus size." She spoke emotionally into the phone, "That's not so. Your bottom isn't big!" More silence followed before she reached for his hand. "We send our love and can hardly wait to see you. Bye-bye, mother."

"I had no idea that your parents were coming to Big Sur!" His exasperation was lost on Delaney.

"Well, Skye." She took on a snippy attitude. "My parents are here to help, and once they arrive, we'll get to the bottom of this baby debacle before it does both mother and me in."

With the windows open, fresh ocean air swept through the car, dissipating the heat. Skye took a deep breath and tried to regain his composure.

Following her mother's suggestion, Delaney attempted to put her arms around his chest. His shirt was damp, but she worked through the unpleasant feeling and cuddled closer.

Skye stroked her back, hoping to reduce the tension that had frozen her muscles into knots. "Better?"

A few tears fell, and control returned to her voice, "We need to think of this like," her voice developed a steel note, "like a business problem."

While Delaney continued to talk, Skye watched the sapphire blue ocean as it sparkled brightly in the spring day. Fragments of his boyhood adventures in the Big Sur hills brushed against a corner of his mind. He realized how often he'd tried to release that part of himself, only to have it return when he least expected it.

Delaney's voice seemed far away. "Are you listening to me?" She tugged on his arm. "We need to treat all the facts as separate items, working toward the center of the issue which is..." She locked eyes with him. "What's best for our wedding."

"Our wedding?" He sounded surprised. "You don't often refer to it as 'our' wedding."

"No, silly, because weddings are really all about the girls. Men look the same in a tuxedo, but all women wear a dress that's created just for them. It's our shinning day. Don't you agree?"

"Sure. But most brides dress in the same color, white."

"Mine is designer white." He sucked on his bottom lip as she continued, "A dashing groom rounds out the day and," she added playfully, "and I have the perfect one."

He grinned. "Yeah, I guess that's true."

"So we're back on track." She blinked rapidly and asked, "What's the main goal when two people deal with a problem? Optimum results, right? We've got a constricted time frame. You do understand that."

"Yeah." He massaged the tight muscles in his neck.

A few seconds passed, and the sharpness of her voice pierced the silence. "Now let's take this situation apart. I'll start with number one." She held up her thumb. "That child has to disappear. Number two," her index finger joined her thumb in a salute. "We need to get back to Chicago. Number three," her middle finger shot up forcing Skye to lean back. "We need "our" time. Just the two of us to recover from this catastrophic misfortune."

Reaching out, he gently pushed her fingers away from his face and curled them into his hand. Her engagement ring sparkled brightly in the sunshine, and he realized, with a start, the large bonus check from Tech World International had arrived just in time to buy the Canary diamond. Was that calculated? He shook his head to clear away the direction his mind was taking.

"There are no feelings involved for this baby." She pushed belligerently for an answer, "Am I right?" Something about hearing her words was offensive, and he looked irritated, causing her to laugh nervously. "Because you know I don't like to be wrong."

"I'm not comfortable with the method you're applying."

Her voice squeaked, "What do you mean?"

"Look, Delaney. Let's find somewhere to eat and think."

"You don't feel that my direct approach is best?" Rebuffed by his lack of enthusiasm, she felt anger settle jaggedly across her mind. Even though her voice had grown cold, she sensed a rising panic creep toward her heart. It was time to change the subject. "I want the windows up. I hate all that wind blowing around me."

Skye muttered, "It's going to warm up real fast."

"I don't care!" She sat back against the itchy fabric seat of the Ford Taurus. Crossing her arms over her chest, she thought if she had only one wish at this moment, it would be for the comfort of the Cuoio-colored leather seats in her Mercedes. And, of course, air conditioning. That went without saying.

Covington Lear Jet

"How much longer? Mah patience is wearin' thin." Terri Sue Ellen was staring at her elevated feet. "They're puffy from bein' in this small plane. Ah'm goin' need me bigger shoes."

She pushed the call button, and Ruth, the company flight attendant, got up and walked two seats down the plane. "Yes, Mrs. Covington?"

"What size are your shoes?"

"Seven."

"Too small. Get me some peanuts, and freshen mah cocktail."

Charles sighed. "Perhaps you should be a little nicer to her."

"Bullshit. How much farther?"

"We're close."

"That's first-rate news 'cause we got'ta be all over this like a mouse slidin' on snot."

Ignoring her comment, he asked, "How was Delaney when you spoke to her?"

"She was fine and handlin' her humiliation with focused care. Ah'm just so proud of our little girl."

Big Sur, California
Highway One

After eating, driving, and talking, Delaney pointed out that the food at the local restaurant was overcooked and greasy and that the rented Taurus was unworthy of her presence. Skye wisely agreed on both points.

As they headed back to the stone house, she became car sick from the twisting road. It was clear she had no appreciation for the most beautiful stretch of highway in California.

"My headache is back," she snapped.

"I have one of my own."

They agreed to lower the windows, and the hot afternoon air swished around the car's interior, blowing up dirt and dust from the carpet.

She sat stiffly, her hands clasped in her lap. "It's the worst day of my life."

"Look, I'm sorry the food didn't agree with you."

"I'm talking about the dirt in this car! We've already covered the horrible food." She snapped back, "Stay on point, Skye."

Attempting to lighten the mood, he tried a humorous approach, "Well, I'll admit my little problem isn't a subject covered in Tech World International's training manual. Maybe my, ah, situation requires a refresher course in problem solving."

"You don't need more education, Skye." She cut off his words with icy tones, "You need to forget you're dealing with a family member, and you need to be more assertive."

He felt admonished and remained silent as she continued to criticize him, "To be successful you have to be glaringly clear with your demands!" Throwing her hands up, she scowled at him in annoyance. "You already know that words like 'please' and 'thank you' are signs of weakness and never to be used, especially with people like..." she spat out the words, "your mother! She'll do you in with kindness and there's no recovering from that. Are you following me?"

Skye frowned. "Not exactly."

Pushing her hands irritably through her hair, she realized it felt limp, and she hated Big Sur even more. "Anyone who stands in your way has to be eliminated. Where's your drive to win this?" Sneaking a glance at him, she changed her direction, trying out a softer pitch, "How we influence this situation will be very helpful to your mother so she can deal in a better light with the problem you created."

Her words left an uncomfortable silence in the car, but Skye reached across the scratchy seat, resting his hand lightly on her knee. "It will be easier to think about what to do if you let it rest a bit."

"Stop touching me! It's hot."

Covington Lear jet
Approaching Monterey Airport

"Showin' her lovin' nature." Terri Sue Ellen popped a peanut and sighed happily, "Those are the words ah'd use to describe our little girl. She's doin' us proud."

Charles watched out the window as the plane began its descent. "That's good."

"Good? Why, that's fab-ulous! Skye needs to focus entirely on our daughter, not his mother and that damn baby. His type of wishy-washy thinkin' isn't worth spit." She sipped her martini and set the glass down with a slap that splashed vodka across the table. "Thank God Delaney got the facts straight and that little boy is white."

"I thought it was a baby girl."

"Who cares?"

The flight attendant appeared. "I'll need to collect your glass now, Mrs. Covington."

"Hog Wash! This is my private plane. Find something else to do."

"Sugar, put on your seatbelt."

Big Sur, California
Highway One
Scenic Pull Off

Sensing she'd been too critical, Delaney whimpered, "Oh, Skye," "I'm in shambles."

He felt obliged to stop the car and hold her again. His eyes roamed the green hillsides that rolled downward to the rocky cliffs. He knew the ocean would sweep across the pebbly beach far below. Gently pushing Delaney away, he cupped her chin. "Look around you. It's so peaceful, not like the turmoil we're feeling inside."

Tears glistened in her emerald eyes as she glanced at the terrain of Big Sur and continued to sniffle. "It reminds me of the green velvet jewelry box Daddy gave me when I was a little girl. Inside was my first pearl bracelet—all creamy and delicate." She wiped at her nose and pointed toward the hills, "Those white flowers that look like silky pom-poms...they remind me of the color of the pearls."

Skye nodded, thinking of the expressions that danced across his mother's face as she painted the ocean against a soft spring landscape. "They're from the aster family." His voice was flat, reciting a lesson from memory, "The flowers are actually yellow, but they're hidden by the long white petals. The wind catches them and they blow away." For a split second, all he desired was to hear the laugher of his youth. "They're called Blow Wives."

"An interesting name."

"Yes." His response was automatic. He knew he'd fallen in love with a sophisticated lady, by choice, and didn't want changes in his adult world.

With her tears under control again, she sighed heavily, "We had so much going, and now I feel that we're losing it." She stopped Skye from talking by raising her hand. "You're not stepping up to the plate. Work with me, Skye. We have a future—a glorious bejeweled future!"

"Yes" His mouth felt dry. "A great future together."

Monterey, California
Airport

The private jet taxied to the terminal. Charles breathed a sigh of relief when Terri Sue Ellen surrendered her drink.

"Are we finally here? Thank goodness! Now ah can deal in person with this hodgepodge calamity that ah have been sucked into. Call for the car. Ah want to visit this stone castle as quickly as possible."

"It's a house," Charles replied patiently.

"Whatever. Bring my bottle of Stolichnaya Celebrated. I can't imagine that a family living in a stone shed would have anything decent to drink." She brushed peanut shells off her blouse. "Lookee here, mah fingers are all salty. Someone get me a tidy-up."

"I'll be driving us, so you can't approach the counter with me to rent the car. Your breath is..."

Ruth arrived with a warm towel, and Terri Sue Ellen wiped her hands then faced her husband. "Now help me up."

"Are you alright, sugar?" He pulled hard, and she popped out of the seat, dropping the towel as she tottered down the aisle. Glancing at her feet, he held her arm and asked, "Aren't you going to put your shoes on?"

"Of course, ah am! Do you think ah was born in a barn?" She pulled loose. "Call the flight worker to shove mah feet into 'em."

Ruth appeared and bent over while Terry Sue Ellen sat down and pushed. "See there. Fit as a fiddle. Thank you so much, Lorraine." She nodded at the young woman who looked up at her.

"My name is Ruth."

"Well then, you'd best print it out and stick it on your uniform. And while you're thinkin' about doing that, pick up the dirty towel ah left and see to it that it's laundered." Raising her wrist in a dramatic gesture, she placed it on her forehead. "Oh! What a burden ah bear...always tellin' others how best to do their jobs. Where was ah? Oh yes. Ah think ah'll wait in a chair inside the airport and coordinate my thoughts. Ah'm tellin' ya, Chucky, all this waddlin' around a surprise baby has made a jumble of mah life. And do note, ah am a finely organized person."

She opened her crocodile handbag. "You there, Lorraine, put the rest of the peanuts in mah Hermes purse. Be careful 'cause it's expensive. Chuck, help me down the steps and be so kind as to point me in the direction of where ah'm goin'."

Highway One
Scenic Pull Off

Delaney cleared her throat. "Mother had an idea, which I think we should address. This, this, baby." She waved her hand dismissively. "It needs to be adopted and remain close to your mom." He was about to speak, but she stopped him. "Follow this, darling. If we let that happen, it would be good because when we have our children, your mom wouldn't be quite so involved." She waved at the air again. "Because she would have another child to think about. That would mean that our children could have the full advantage of my parents, and we both know they are brilliant and loving people."

"We've discussed it," he replied, feeling uneasy.

"Exactly! Instead of trying to alternate holidays back here with your mother and then back East with my parents..." She shook her head vehemently. "What an inconvenience that would be! Am I correct, darling?"

He looked at her pensively, and she rushed on. "We could enjoy all the holidays in Chicago with my parents. You know that's the way it should be. For instance, who has a more lovely Christmas party than father's club? It rings in the season with the correct amount of elegant joy. The lavish party for children and their nannies is performed perfectly. Everyone is given a gift; clowns and balloons abound with Christmas cheer, and fireworks go off. It's a delightful festivity."

"That's their Fourth of July party."

"Whatever. All children's parties are the same except for the pony rides...no one at the club wants pooping ponies to tarnish the December jamboree." She sat up straighter. "My point is that I'm the only child, and I couldn't imagine spending time away from my family's traditional galas that are focused on kindness for everyone."

He looked straight ahead thinking, *I'm an only child, too, but it's been years since I spent a holiday with my mom.*

Delaney took his silence for agreement and picked up her cue, "Of course, we wouldn't forget about your mother. Oh, no. Never." She found a concerned look and placed it on her face. "That would be cruel. We are not cruel people."

She closed her eyes, lost in thought, and Skye appreciated the silence until she snapped her fingers. "I've got it. We could add a gift certificate for someplace where your mother shops, you know, like Wal-Mart. I could ask Estelle or Maria to look into it. Adding that to the poinsettia that you already send her would bump her present up to the next level. She'd be so happy."

He felt his annoyance worsen as she plotted against his mother, but, on the other hand, she had many good points, even if her way of presenting them was unpleasant.

"Skye." She pulled annoyingly on his arm. "Are you paying attention?"

"I'm thinking about your plan."

She sat back and fanned at her face. The musty scent of old sandalwood emanated from her body, and Skye opened his window all the way.

"As I was about to say...we would continually extend an invitation to your mother to visit us." She winked. "Knowing the outcome, of course. We have to know the end results before we make a suggestion; otherwise how can we control the game?"

He remembered that his mother had talked about Australia and New

Zealand. If she was willing to travel that far, a trip to Chicago would work out, but his instinct told him to keep that to himself.

Delaney felt a victory within reach. "By keeping an open invitation for your mom to come to Chicago..." her voice purred.

He nodded automatically, realizing he did that a lot around her.

"We could tell our friends it was your mother's choice not to see her grandchildren. Everyone would think the error was in her court, not ours. They would see her as a browbeating grandmother who demanded to have the grandchildren brought to her remote house in Big Sur."

He continued to stare at the ocean while she picked at her blouse. A new idea formed, and she moved ahead. "We could arrange to come out here to see your mother when it was convenient." Her clipped words finished her thoughts, "Not often, of course."

Fumbling in her bag, she picked up her brush. "Ah, there it is." She laughed nervously. "You know that brushing my hair soothes me. Right, Skye. You know that?"

His tone filled with exasperation, "Yes. I know that."

After running the brush through her hair several times, she glanced up and saw his anger. "Oh!" She quickly backpedaled, "Above all else, your mother would be happy. Of course, we'll look at getting her into assistant living as soon as we can take over the house. It can't be that many years away. I hope she doesn't put up a fight, as I only have her best interests at heart." She searched for lip gloss and continued, "Missy, and I actually had a two way conversation today. It was about furniture. Yes, a table." She nodded. "I think we've grown closer. Isn't that nice?"

Annoyed, Skye shook his head. "Her name is Melissa."

"Oh." Delaney applied gloss across her lips with a precise motion and checked the mirror in her compact. "Speaking of mothers, what's important to realize is that my mother needs her golf time every day so she can win the First Place trophy for daddy's club. That hasn't happened because, as you know, she's been helping us." Skye felt himself stiffen, but she wasn't through. "They don't give those awards to just anyone. You have to earn them; the same way I earned my Junior Tennis Cup."

He let her words sink in and wondered what the going price was for a name to be engraved on a trophy at the Lake Michigan Commemorated Country Club.

She dumped the gloss back in her purse and faced him. "Are my lips perfect?"

"Yes." Skye felt strange but realized that some of the guilt he'd had a few days ago was dissipating. "I suppose a local adoption could work." He spoke with concern, "We'd want to find a good family."

"Of course. Hopefully, someone who's at least a high school graduate, maybe has some trade school experience. Or even another artist would do in a pinch. If you work your charm..." she batted her eyelashes and, without thinking, Skye checked to see if they were in place. She continued, "Your mother would definitely agree because you're so good at manipulating people. "Oh, goodness me." She wiggled her fingers and continued, "I know what folks say, but the truth is that tweaking the thought process in others is not bad. That's why we have all the toys and..." She shrugged and omitted a puff of air. "They don't."

A part of him knew she was being brutally honest, but he also recognized the nastiness of her words.

"We both know daddy used to think I was the best maneuvering agent, but now he looks toward you to deploy that direct action." Her face was shining with a smug glow. "Therefore, the adoption idea should come from you." She clutched at her chest. "Heaven forbid that I interfered on such an important issue." Rolling her eyes, she added, "Even though it's my life on the line here." She waved her hands to emphasize her point, and Skye wished she'd stop fluttering.

Unaware of his annoyance, she glanced out the window of the parked car and felt a triumph smile forming.

Big Sur, California
Inside the Covington's rental car

"Stop the car, Chucky. Ah have to tinkle. It's all that water Lorraine gave me on the plane."

Charles felt his temper flare but held it in. He answered patiently, "We just passed a gas station."

"Ah didn't have to tinkle then. Ah do now." She reached into the bag on her lap. "Here, have a peanut."

He shook his head. "I don't think there's another gas station before we get there."

"Then stop the car and go back. Honestly, do ah have to do all the thinkin'? See here, Chucky, we're headin' into wilderness country, and ah'm not about to drop my undies and pee on a rock. That's just disgustin'. Turn this car around speedy-fast."

Highway One
Scenic Pull Off

The side of the road, just beyond Delaney's shoulder, was overgrown with bright orange poppies. Skye watched them sway peacefully in the breeze until a persistent voice penetrated his thoughts, "So adoption it is."

Letting the scenario run through his mind, he replied, "I could get my mom to go along with it, if I do it right. I might have to stay here for a while." He wiped his forehead with the back of his hand. It came away wet, and he dried it against his damp shirt.

She bowed her head. "That wasn't what I wanted to hear you say."

"It will take time, Delaney." He reached for her hand.

"No! Your hand is all sweaty." She pulled away and instantly regretted her decision. Reaching toward him, she gave his fingers a tiny squeeze. Her body ached with anger as she thought of him staying in Big Sur, solving a problem that should never have happened. The silence between them grew awkward. "I'm hot and tired," she snapped.

"Me, too." He smiled wearily. "Let's go home and take a nap. The hills of Big Sur create a peaceful feeling. You'll see."

"As if that's a solution," she grumbled as the car bumped off the side of the road and back onto the highway.

Highway One
Inside the Covington's rental car

"There. You see a potty break barely takes a minute."

Charles pulled back onto the highway. "Why did you remove your boots from the suitcase?"

"Because ah'll need them in this isolated area to which we are headed if ah'm goin' do any hikin'."

"Hiking?"

"When our daughter came for a visit, Skye's mother tried to sway her into hikin' through a remote area. Fortunately, Delaney is not as athletic as ah am."

"I don't think that Big Sur is that remote."

"Well, ah do. Listen up now. This meetin' we're about to have with a Mexican Cherokee woman who has herself a big ol' braid a'hangin' down her back and sports a hippie attitude is something ah want in mah past. Let's get-r-done, Chucky, and be on down the road before she tries to overcharge us for one of her paintins'. Besides, if truth be known, the only velvet art I've ever coveted was a portrait of Elvis."

"Sugar, are you sure she paints on fabric? I thought she did seascapes."

"She does! Ah saw her on-line. The computer does not lie. She paints ocean water on black velvet and uses simply buckets of blue paint...unless she's paintin' card playin' dogs." She crossed her arms. "This is so inconvenient for me."

Charles focused on the road, his misgivings growing fresh. "Why do you think she's Cherokee?"

"Ah told you that! Why don't you listen up? Here now, ah'll say it again. Some relative was mixed up with a horse tradin' ring of wild Apache's in Idaho."

"I thought Skye told us it was the son of a tribal historian from a Cherokee village."

Terry Sue Ellen sipped from her paper cup of vodka. "Ah wish ah had me an olive."

"We should have our facts correct, sugar."

"Then I'd best give you a heads up on Indian culture. They're not big on bathin', other than in creeks and streams. Don't worry yourself none." She waved a hand in his direction and added, "Ah'll just hold a scented hankie over my nose, and you can breathe through your mouth. Why, just the likes of his mama in mah family is draggin' me under." Kicking off her shoes, she tugged on her winter boots. "Now ah'm ready to meet the tribe. Honestly," she looked at her feet, "the things ah do for my little girl."

Chapter Fourteen

Big Sur, California
Stone House

The stone house was cool compared to the shimmering waves of heat that rolled around the gravel driveway where a shiny black Mercedes sedan was parked.

"Hurry up, Missy. This awards dinner is to honor your work. And we don't want to be late." Pete looked dapper in a tuxedo as he stood in front of the old mirror and adjusted his bow tie. He called down the hall, "The car has arrived to whisk us away to the world of Spanish Bay where we'll be treated as royalty."

Melissa was an elegant vision in simple black as she walked toward him. "Oh. You mean we'll be treated like Delaney's German relatives." She smiled. "Won't that be nice?"

Stylish black heels added to her height. A ruby crusted choker hugged her neck, and her hair was twisted into a sophisticated French knot. Her pencil slim gown flared around her knees, skimming the floor with fluid movement as she approached.

He took her arm and smiled up at her. "You are a tall, beautiful sight. A woman wearing red lipstick always turns me on."

"You're a man of many well thought out words." She leaned over to lightly kiss him.

Smoky eye shadow caressed her lids, and Pete smiled, "Pretty eyes. Like the colors in whiskey...shades of gold and brown."

"You look mighty good in a tux, Pete. Seems it brings out the fancy words in you."

His blue eyes sparkled. "We'll need to do this more often."

Sheer color highlighted her cheeks as she nodded. "I have given a list of numbers and a page overflowing with instructions to Angie."

"Me too." Pete smiled. "I had Zippy coordinate with the printer, and Angie now has duplicate lists, just in case she should misplace one of them."

"Well then." She laughed. "We're covered."

Pete held a bottle of champagne. "As the Arts Guild has provided a driver and a car, I'm taking a bottle of champagne for us to enjoy."

****

The driver of the Mercedes sedan had maneuvered a sharp turn in the driveway and now stood outside the car, holding the door for his passengers.

Fifteen minutes later, as Skye pulled in the driveway, Delaney was still talking in an overbearing voice. "My parents will be staying at Pebble Beach, but of course, I'll forgo that luxury and stay with you."

Skye shook his head. He knew his mother would want a heads-up on company, especially the Covingtons, but he'd been unable to reach her.

Angie greeted them at the front door and explained about the awards dinner where his mother was the guest of honor.

Funny, he blinked, *she didn't mention it to me.*

Angie added that Monique was sleeping and asked them to be quiet.

Delaney put her hands on her hips and faced Skye. "What nerve! How dare a common Pottery Nanny speak to us like that." Her phone rang. As she dug in her purse, she whispered to Skye, "You need to do something about her arrogance. She's forgotten her place. Hello. Oh, daddy! Where are you?"

Angie gave Skye a passing glance. It held sympathy, if he wasn't mistaken, and that seemed wrong.

With the sun moving toward the western sky, the interior of the house was filling with golden rays, leaving only the corners of the rooms bedded in dreamy color. Skye felt the stillness of the moment until Delaney's voice splintered his thoughts.

"Guess what! They're almost here and very anxious to meet your mother."

She looked behind him. "Where did the Pottery Nanny go? I was about to have a sharp talk with her."

"I'll handle it." He wished Delaney would stop talking.

"Very well. I'm going to put on a different blouse...I suppose it would be too much to ask her to press it for me."

He narrowed his eyes as he looked at her." Don't do that."

"Well, oh my, aren't you touchy and for no reason at all." As she walked down the hall, she called over her shoulder, "I'll freshen up and be right back. You should change clothes, too."

"Yeah." He only had the casual slacks and shirt he'd worn the day before, but they were in no better shape than what he had on. He was more concerned about the strange feeling in the pit of his stomach when he thought about the forthcoming visit from the Covingtons.

Big Sur, California
Arrival of the Covington's
At the Stone house

The Covingtons stood on the front porch, next to the rocking chair, and Terri Sue Ellen whispered, "That's where she sits and daydreams." Charles attempted to quiet his wife, but she waved him off and continued to mutter loudly in his ear. "Ah'll bet she smokes herself a peace pipe. Indians do that. You know what ah'm sayin', Chucky?"

"Not now, sugar!"

Skye's smile was forced as he opened the door and air kisses were exchanged. He explained that his mother was not at home, hoping that they might decide to come back at another time, but Delaney urged her parents inside.

"Mother, what do you have on your feet?"

"Boots, for hikin'."

"But they're snow boots." Growing distressed, Delaney faced Skye. "Is this something else I wasn't told about? Is there snow in the Big Sur Rocky Mountains?"

"What?" He shook his head and closed his eyes. "No snow, no mountains."

"Ah'm wearin' em for the squaw. If she wants to hike, ah am prepared."

Skye looked perplexed. "What's she talking about?"

"Mother is very advanced, and we don't always understand everything she says."

Touching a stone wall, Terri Sue Ellen exclaimed, "Oh, mah lord! What is this? Ah don't believe ah've ever seen anything like it. Chuck, honey, what do you think?"

He took the vodka bottle from her and smiled at Skye. "It's been a long couple of days. Perhaps we could all sit down."

"It doesn't have germs growing on it, does it? Dirt walls are not clean walls."

"Stone walls," Skye added as he led them into the house. "They're stone walls."

From her hidden spot in the kitchen, Angie peeked through the door at the group gathering in the parlor. Monique was asleep in the Drawer Bed, and Angie turned it to face her as if defending the baby from intruders. What would Mr. Pete want her to do? Be polite for sure.

She pushed the door open and stepped forward, moving in the direction of the dining room. Clearing her throat, she got their attention and asked if she could get them something to eat.

"Oh, honey, what a nice idea." Tipping to one side, Terri Sue Ellen slid toward the sofa.

"No, mother! Not there. Over here...this chair."

"Come sit next to me, Delaney Mae Anne. Ah've been meaning to ask you...since you've been exposed to this habitat down here, you've never peed on a rock, have you?"

"Never!"

"Excellent!" Terry Sue Ellen dropped heavily into the chair.

Realizing she had to assume control, Delaney faced Angie. "Do bring us some hors d'oeuvres. Perhaps quail eggs with Danish smoked ham and add a chardonnay mustard. A bottle of Cristal."

"Ahhh." Angie backed into the kitchen. She shook her head. *That's not going to happen.*

She found left-over French toast, so she cut it into triangles and put it on a dinner plate. Adding potato chips to fill the void, she shook her head and put a bowl of applesauce in the center of the dish. Frowning, she studied the cuisine she'd put together.

She could hear Terri Sue Ellen voice from the parlor. "Where's mah bottle?"

"Right here, sugar. I was going to get some ice and a glass."

"Oh now, ah don't want to be a bother. Just gim'me the bottle, Chucky."

Charles turned to Skye. "Ice? Glasses?"

"Of course. Let me do that." He jumped up and hurried into the kitchen where he hissed at Angie, "Where the hell are glasses and ice?"

"Here." Angie shoved the plate of food toward him. "Take this dish out, and I'll get the ice."

Skye eyed the hors d'oeuvres with worry. Some of them looked sticky, and his trepidations increased as Angie hurried him toward the door.

Taking a deep breath, he left the kitchen and moved toward a table in the parlor where he put the food down. "Something to eat?" he asked hesitantly.

Angie followed with glasses and napkins then quickly exited the room.

"Mah, doesn't that look good. Is this a dip?" Terri Sue Ellen reached for the fried toast and used the spoon to put applesauce over it. "Why mah little crippled Nellie, bless her heart, used to fix something like this. It's been a long time since ah've had such a feast. Sort of soft and sweet. Here, Chucky, try this." She pushed the toast into his mouth and moved toward the chips. "Chew darlin'. Isn't that tasty?" Reaching over, she took the vodka bottle from him. "Oh now, ah don't need me any ice. Ah'm fine. Thank you so much for your concern."

Charles swallowed the sticky food. "Do you have any scotch?"

"Umm." Skye cleared this throat. "There's some tequila. I'll get it."

"She has tequila 'cause that's what Mexican's drink. Ah know mah facts."

Skye returned with a bottle and explained that his mother was the guest of honor at a dinner party.

Wiping her hands on a napkin, Terri Sue Ellen added, "Mexican themed dinner parties and Cherokee celebrations have become very popular events. We support all minorities. Don't we, Chucky?" Turning toward Skye, she blinked several times. "Ah don't see any of your mama's paintins' sittin' around."

"She sells most of them. But there..." Skye indicated a framed watercolor that hung on the wall. The flaming colors of the sunset glowed in the late afternoon light. "That is one that she kept. It's a good example of her burst of brilliance technique."

"Where? Ah don't see anything."

A silence ensued, but no one asked questions so Skye let the subject drop.

Charles poured tequila in a glass and moved toward the sofa, but his daughter stopped him by waving her arms. "No, daddy!"

"Doodle Bug, you've got to unwind some. You sound very tense. Perhaps you're overwrought, like your mother." He glanced at his wife licking syrup from her fingers and winced. Turning toward Skye, he continued, "Nice of you to invite us over."

"Right. Of course. You're here and it's...nice." Skye sucked in air. "My pleasure. Really."

"Don't be stand offish, Chucky," Terri Sue Ellen called from her chair as she bent over the food. "Have another bite."

"I'll pass, sugar." He sat on the sofa and fell backward but didn't spill his drink.

Delaney stared at the hors d'oeuvres with misgivings as her mother reached for more toast..

Angie, knowing that Mr. Pete would want a full report, continued to observe everyone from a safe distance by opening the kitchen door just a crack.

Big Sur, California
Stone House
Later that evening

When Melissa and Pete arrived home, the lights were on and a car was parked in her drive.

"Another Mercedes?" Pete asked. "Sort of makes you wonder, doesn't it?"

"Indeed, it does! Been lots of comings and goings lately." She smiled as their driver opened the door and assisted her in getting out. He handed her the award. "It's very impressive, Mrs. Topple. Congratulations, again."

"Thank you. I'm very pleased that I was selected to be so honored." She turned to Pete, pointing at the second car and commented, "Yes, that is a fancy rental."

"Yup, you can get 'em at the Monterey airport. See the Hertz plate?"

Her forehead wrinkled. "Could Skye be having company?

Pete took her arm. "Shall we see? Oh, and do allow me to help you with that statue. Is it heavy? Ten, maybe fifteen pounds."

"Oh Pete, stop now!"

"Looks like an Academy Award to me."

"They weight eight and one half pounds." She held out an attractive free form shape attached to a marble base. "This is not a gold-plated knight standing on a roll of film."

"Well, look right there." Pete pointed towards the statue. "It's a sword."

"No, it's a paint brush. And you know that."

"I'd be honored to hang on to it for you. You just tell me where you want it once we get inside."

"Here." She laughed. "You've been wanting to hold it all night."

"That I have."

****

Melissa stopped short in her parlor, staring in confusion at the sight of sleeping people.

Skye woke first and wondered who the sophisticated woman was in the black dress. She was tall and looked vaguely familiar. He squinted at the image. "Mom?" He asked flabbergasted. "Is that you?"

Melissa wiggled her nose at the smell of alcohol wafting through the room. Pete moved next to her and placed the statue on a table. "I gave the driver a good tip and sent him on his way." He blinked. "Are those people drunk?"

"I think so." She looked at her son. "Friends of yours?"

Delaney blinked the sleep from her eyes. "Wake up mother! Someone is here."

"Ahh, this is Delaney's mother and father." Skye paused to look at them and smiled weakly. "They've come for a visit."

Delaney moved next to Skye. "Who is that person in black?"

"My mother."

"Nooo."

Melissa took in the people with a sweep of her eyes. "Who are they, Skye?"

Pete added, "He introduced them as The Covingtons. Come for a visit."

"I heard my son say that."

"Then why did you ask a second time?"

"Because I wanted to hear him say it again. Slower, clearer, and with an explanation attached."

Charles rolled off the sofa and stood up. He brushed at his wrinkled clothes and held out his hand. "Charles Covington." He covered his belch by turning to the side. "It's so nice to meet you." Lowering his voice, he continued, "Friends and family call me Chuck."

"We've come about your son impregnating the French whore." Terri Sue Ellen bounced off the chair too fast and stumbled over her snow boots. She grabbed at her husband's arm for balance. "What a terrible situation this is. Simply appallin'. Where is the little black boy?"

"Sit down, sugar." Charles gently pushed her back on the chair.

"Oh, that's right. The baby isn't black." She titled her head. "Mercy, aren't we all glad about that." Smiling at the room in general, she added, "In any event, do be rest assured, ah'm here to help fix this." She lifted her foot and pointed. "Right after we take that ceremonial hike."

"What did she say?" Melissa's brows knit together.

Pete shrugged. "I don't know."

He turned to introduce himself to Charles. They shook hands, and Charles replied, "My daughter tells me the baby is going to need a home, and I'm willing to get my attorneys involved immediately to solve this awkward state of affairs."

Pete rubbed his bald head and smiled. "That may not be the best approach to take." He paused and added in a deeper tone, "Chuck."

Melissa stepped forward. "The baby is *my* granddaughter and her name is Monique. There's no awkward *state of affairs* here."

"See here." Terri Sue Ellen squinted at Melissa. "You are not dressed for a hike." She pointed at her daughter. "You said she was a Big Sur hippie and had herself a long braid. Now, honey, ah expected to see me a Cherokee woman."

"She is! And she does. This is just some kind of mean joke." Delaney turned toward her mother and whispered passionately, "She doesn't really look like that."

"Ah want to go the Pebble Beach right now. Skye, call for the car and turn off the fireplace. Someone get me mah coat."

Skye looked uncomfortable as Terri Sue Ellen stumbled toward the kitchen. Charles caught her arm and turned her around.

"Thank you so much, Chucky. It's clear as a bell that ah've been thrown off kilter with the weariness of mah frustration." She hissed, " How do we get out of here?"

Nodding at Melissa, she continued, "Ah have enjoyed our meetin', Patricia. However, we can't stay any longer. Ah'm so sorry that ah can't accept one of your velvet masterpieces, but ah just don't have another wall." She bumped into the entry table. "No! Don't try to change mah mind. We must be off." She shook hands limply, and Melissa pulled back, rubbing her palm.

"Why is she sticky?"

"Ah, mom...I can explain."

When Charles tried to open the front door, Terri Sue Ellen whispered to her daughter, "You stay here and fix this misfortunate flop-up." She listed toward her husband, murmuring, "Where is mah bottle? Go get it. Honestly, Chucky, why must ah always be tellin' everyone what to do? It's a drainin' task, it is."

Waving her hands wildly at Melissa, Terrie Sue Ellen added, "Good bye, again. If you ever paint Elvis, ah'll have me a look. Meanwhile, ah'll call, and we'll make plans to do lunch." Leaning into Melissa's face, she added, "That's the way white people entertain. It's a custom ah hope you'll pick up on."

Melissa pulled away and wiped her hand. "It's syrup." She faced Skye. "She has syrup on her hand."

"I know." He hung his head.

"Why is she wearing winter boots?"

"So she can hike."

Melissa looked long and hard at her son. "I'm going to bed."

Big Sur, California
Stone House
Next day

Skye woke early and apologized to his mother about the Covingtons' surprise visit.

Angie told Pete and Melissa about serving French toast, and they smiled about the events that had taken place, calling it a memorable evening.

Skye prepared a breakfast tray for Delaney who was still recovering from yesterday's events. After he explained that his fiancé was going to sleep in, he carried the tray to his bedroom. His mother, Pete, and Angie breathed a sigh of relief.

By mid-morning the first aromas of a roast were beginning to waft through the air. Skye knew that Sunday lunch would be served in the middle of the afternoon. A surge of family memories surfaced. When he was a boy, it had been fun to see who would arrive for the meal and what food they would bring to add to the feast.

"Is everything all right?" Melissa asked as she finished rinsing vegetables and reached for the dishtowel to dry her hands.

"Sure. I'm, ahh, walking around and, you know, thinking."

Instinctively, she reached up to push the hair from his face, a gesture she'd used since his earliest memory.

"It's a little long right now." He'd pulled back from her touch.

"Not to worry." She felt his rejection and added softly, "I'm sure you'll get it trimmed." Her face looked sad and she returned to chopping carrots.

"It's a good idea for Delaney to sleep in. Last night was well..." she shrugged her shoulders and attempted a smile. "Uncomfortable might be a word we could use. But I'm sure we'll all laugh about it at some point in time."

Skye noticed the sunlight as it skipped throughout the kitchen, settling on walls and counter tops in abstract patterns. His mother looked up, and he saw that her whiskey colored eyes held golden dots, the same as his, the same as Monique's.

"Do you remember what your dad always said about rest being the best tonic for a man's soul, spirit, and character?"

"Yeah. I know." He looked toward the hall. *I also remember dad saying a man needed to step up and take responsibility for his actions.* "Well, I've got to go. She's in the bedroom alone...waiting for me."

"I'm sure that you and Delaney have lots to discuss." Turning toward the oven, she asked, "Roast okay for a late Sunday lunch?"

"Good." Skye moved down the hall then stopped and looked back, "It always was my favorite. Are you doing the braised potatoes and veggies with it?"

"Sure am. I was just about to add them to the roasting pan."

"Ahh, you're not having a boatload of people come over, are you?"

Reaching for an oven mitt, she answered quietly, "There aren't that many relatives left."

He'd never thought about it like that and was lost for a reply.

"Oh, where are my manners? I didn't see any luggage for Delaney yesterday. Would she like to borrow one of my summer nightgowns? Fresh from the laundry."

"Ahh...no"

"I could press it."

Giving Delaney a previously used white cotton nightgown was not a chance he felt like taking. "That's okay, mom. She's got an overnight case from yesterday and a bigger suitcase in the car." His eyes scanned the room briefly, and he wondered where the baby was but realized it didn't matter.

Skye carried Delaney's suitcase into his room, where she was standing ramrod straight. "What is this?" Her tone was filled with icy disdain.

"What?" His good feeling disappeared.

She pointed in the direction of his bed. "This unmade, messed up, slept in..." Her voice rose higher with each word, "Is that where I spent last night? And look at you, wearing the same wrinkled clothes from yesterday. You've gone downhill fast, Skye."

He felt a flicker of anger but held it in check. "Delaney, listen to me. We slept in the bed last night, and with all the excitement of your parents' visit and our late morning, it didn't get made. And my clothes didn't get washed...or ironed." He joked, "This isn't a hotel."

"No," she snapped. "It would be on the condemned list."

"Oh, I don't think so," his tone turned cool.

Delaney's green eyes squeezed shut when she realized she'd done it again. This morning when her mother had called, she'd warned her about pushing Skye too far.

"Keep your man on the hot seat, darlin'. Make him feel his guilt, but don't drive him into an angry state. Your daddy and ah will play eighteen holes here and then we'll be flyin' home—so many important meetin's to attend, ah know you understand. We believe you can handle this situation. Be tough, but forgivin'."

She faced Skye. "I'm sorry. I was being bitchy." Tears trickled down her face. "And I'm sorry about mother and father and their surprise visit." Reaching for his hand, her voice softened, "Here, let me make the bed."

She began to pull at the sheets, but Skye stopped her. "We'll both do it."

Pebble Beach
Same Day

The Pebble Beach greens curved around the ocean, highlighting the one celebrity yacht nested quietly in the cove. Fairways gripped the cliffs, dotted with splashes of sunshine that whisked through Cypress trees. The golf course resembled green velvet, and a light breeze welcomed another perfect day.

Having been distracted throughout their golf game by the events of the night before, the Covingtons turned in shameful scores. They left their rented

Mercedes for Hertz to pick up, and while waiting for a limo to carry them back to the airport, they'd agreed to Bloody Marys at the Terrace Lounge overlooking the 18th hole.

"Let the golf go, sugar." Chuck pulled his chair closer to the table where a drink waited for him. "You're much better than the game you just played. I know it, and so do you."

"That's true, and ah will not fret about it anymore." She ate a handful of salty bar snacks and took a satisfying swig from her glass. "Mostly because we have other issues to talk about."

He felt himself cringe inwardly but kept a calm exterior.

"Ah don't know if you understand the full impact of the situation from mah point of view." She smiled sweetly. "In three months we're goin' to have us a prestigious weddin' for three hundred guests at one of Chicago's most sought after event mansions."

Picking up the celery stick, she bit off a piece and washed it down with another swallow, leaving a trace of tomato juice on her upper lip. "Allow me to highlight what I've worked so hard to achieve."

Charles raised a finger to his lip, and she snapped, "I've got it!" Using her napkin, she wiped her mouth before she continued, "Kindly allow me to finish mah thoughts before you start a pointin' at your face. Now, as ah was sayin', more than a hundred years ago, a wealthy beer monger..." She leaned toward Charles with a thoughtful expression. "Ah have upgraded him to beer executive because of the huge prices that are being charged to rent his old house. What he did was create a home of eighteen thousand square feet. It's callin' to modern brides is a seventy-five foot ceilin' with a glass dome that sheds natural light on an open staircase."

Reaching for more bar mix, she popped some in her mouth. "The staircase winds... " She used her hands to create swirls in the air. A spray of salty orange seasoning flew off her fingers. "Ever so gracefully down to a colossal foyer where weddin' guests will gather to watch our precious daughter float from above." Speaking sharply, she emphasized each word, "It is the only location worthy of her weddin'. Ah have personally assured her of that. Do you have any questions thus far?"

She sipped her Bloody Mary and snorted to herself as she thought of Skye's only request...that the wedding not be in the summer months as wearing a tux in the heat and humidity of a Chicago day was unbearable. The mansion only had one opening, and that was in August. Skye's request hadn't received a blink of consideration. This wedding wasn't about his feelings.

She scooted sideways so she was closer to her husband and continued speaking in low tones, "Expensive hors d'oeuvres will be prepared by mah favorite French chef, and to show mah considerate and caring nature, ah have assigned one waiter to watch Skye's mama so that she stays on the outskirts of the party and does not mingle. He is to feed her something called pigs-in-a-blanket so she'll feel right at home. For the important guests, ah have arranged other venues including stylish martini bars that offer the best in vodka and gin while Cristal champagne will be served by well-dressed waiters. Ah know they will be well-dressed because ah have personally selected their uniforms. That is how involved ah am, Chucky."

He nodded crossly as she sat back and took a deep breath. "Ah will continue. All of the guests will be in formal attire, as ah requested on the invitation. Chicago's finest photography studio has been hired, and they will capture the affluent event to utmost perfection."

Charles signaled the waitress, indicating two more drinks. "I know what's at stake, Terri Sue Ellen," he replied prickly. "I also know the course of events as I have seen the quotes and paid all the bills." His tone turned hostile, "Let me tell you what happens next...sugar." The word hung in the air while he took a deep breath.

"You can use that tone on others, Chucky, but you don't scare me none. Mah name is on the official paperwork."

He was growing tired of her attitude, but she was right, and there was little he could do. He forced a smile and continued, "Following the ceremony and a correctly placed reception line, a seven course dinner..."

He was interrupted. "A luxurious seven course dinner paired with the finest Napa wines will be presented. Now that ah have added clarity to your statement, please, do go on."

He faced her with an irritated look. "The next day, we'll host a formal brunch at the Signature Room on the 95th Floor of the John Hancock Center."

"Yes, darlin', that's for the guests who weren't invited to the main event. After all," she waved her hands in the air. "With the caterers, servers, the maids, and Mr. Freddy, plus his staff of hair dressers and makeup artists, there's just so much room at the mansion, and no one wants to crowd the bride or her mother. No sir, you do not want that to happen!" Leaning in, she grabbed another handful of bar snacks. "These are lackin' in peanuts. Get me another bowl."

Charles looked at her but didn't respond.

"Very well. Ah'll do it myself. Waitress," she roared, causing heads to turn.

A young lady appeared instantly.

"Thank you so much for being prompt. This is..." she pushed the bowl toward the girl. "Inadequate. It is in need of roasted, salted, Virginia peanuts. Take this away and bring me another."

Her tone dripped with sarcasm as she faced her husband, "Where was ah? Oh yes, ah was sayin, the overflow guests will be presented with a reception line at the Signature Room, so they can offer their good wishes to the weddin' couple. Do you think you can pick it up from here? Ah haven't gone too fast for you, have ah?"

Charles took a generous swallow of the fresh drink and continued, "Delaney and Skye will have a few hours to rest and freshen themselves before being chauffeured to the barbeque dinner at my club."

"The posh barbequed dinner, darlin.'" She dislodged a piece of pretzel from her tooth with a fingernail.

He flinched. "It will be done correctly."

"You bet it will," she added in a voice of southern steel. "And to show what lovely people we are, we will encourage everyone to relax and unwind at your club from the unforgettable whirl of events our daughter's wedddin' created."

He glanced at the ocean, dancing in the breeze, and turned to his wife who was eating the other celery stick.

"Ah will wind up our discussion." She looked at him over her drink. "Darlin', to pull this off, it is mandatory, absolutely, without question mandatory... that we have us a groom."

"Then you need to let our daughter work this out." He added crotchety, "Our presence seemed to annoy his mother last night, and we need everyone on our side right now."

"Who can figure out that mother? Why would a Mexican Cherokee woman be all dolled up, a'comin' home late at night with a short, bald, white man?"

"Let it go, Terri Sue Ellen."

"It's probably disgustin', anyhow, and mah refined upbringin' would be thrown into a shudder of devastation."

Charles grimaced as he looked at her while she picked through the new bowl of bar snacks.

"These are still wrong. This is some kind of Chinese snack with green peas. Just lookee here." She pushed the bowl toward him. "Ah declare! Didn't ah clearly say salted peanuts? What is the matter with hired help these days?"

Attempting to keep her calm, he whispered in her ear, "We have peanuts in the plane, sugar."

"Excellent! Ah will just take this foreign food with me." She put a napkin in her Hermes purse and emptied the bowl of snacks. "Ah can mix it properly once we're in the air."

With no comment from Charles, she looked out at the people playing golf. "Where's my limo, Chucky? I travel in style."

Chapter Fifteen

Big Sur, California
Stone House

As Skye and Delaney stretched out on the bed, a fresh breeze bathed the room with the scent of honeysuckle and pine. She sniffed. "I hope I'm not allergic to that. There are so many unpleasant smells here."

"Shush," he whispered. "It's only fresh air." *That's not offensive,* he wanted to add but kept his words to himself.

Delaney shifted to her side. She sounded frightened when she spoke, "Do you think that man...ahh, Pete" She pressed her lips together. "Will he be at the wedding? I mean, good heavens, we can't say he's your mother's live-in." She gasped, "Being a potter is like being unemployed. He could never sit with my family! At least your mother sells some of her paintings to validate a living, but pottery...ugh."

Skye felt drained and realized his words were edged with annoyance, "Bailey's Big Sur Pottery School is well-known." He found it difficult to believe he was actually defending Pete. "People come from across the United States to study his methods."

"No one I know," she replied sharply. "But my family isn't into earthenware." She sat up straight in bed, feeling tension fill her body. "Oh, Skye, how would we dress him?"

"You do remember seeing him in a tuxedo last night?"

"He'd need to wear the proper tux...the one I select. You'll also have to tell him not to smile and talk to people he doesn't know. And, and definitely, not to hug people he doesn't know! He did that to me, and it was so out of line. Fortunately, I'm confident and carry an air of sophistication so I'm able to handle difficult situations. As mother always says, because of our position in life, we must remember to be courteous to all." She sneezed. "Oh. I *am* allergic. Close that." Reaching for the box of Kleenex, she blew her nose as Skye got up to lower the window.

He returned to bed, yawned, and stretched, looking forward to a nap. But in a minute, Delaney sprang up.

"Your mother's French knot from last night was too severe. She needs hair that's short and fluffy, or maybe curly, yes, curly would be better." She looked beseechingly at Skye. "Tell me I'm right."

Nodding wearily, he tried to imagine his mother with short hair, but no vision appeared. He tried curly hair, but still nothing happened.

"Good! I told you we're developing a real bond. I think I'll call her mom. She'd like that, right? I mean Mother Topple annoys her. "

"Let's give it a little time before you call her mom."

"Too much, too soon?" Delaney felt depleted but needed to go on. "I'll ask the designer of my wedding gown to dress her." She took a deep breath. "I'm sure it will be her first experience with color coordination and..."

"She's an artist," Skye interrupted sharply. "She understands color."

"Well, she doesn't grasp what is appropriate footwear. I mean, other than last night when she had on heels, she wears those turquoise Birkenstocks. I truly wouldn't want our children exposed to her without my supervision. You can understand that?"

"Shush, Doodle Bug. Let it go for now. We'll talk later." Skye kissed her forehead.

She fell asleep quickly, but Skye remained awake. His thoughts simmered, and he left the bed to stand at the window. Opening it, he felt a warm breeze carry the sounds of bee's wings through the screens. The scent of honeysuckle was light and fragrant. He glanced at Delaney who slept blissfully on, unaware of any allergic reaction to the fragrance of the spring day. His eyes traveled up to the Monterey pines. It would be a good summer. He knew that intuitively and quickly pushed the thought away. Big Sur was not his home. The baby slipped into his thoughts, but he had no problem with the child being put up for adoption.

On to the next problem. Other than his mother and Pete living together, he didn't completely understand Pete's impact on his future. What could be said about a man who earned his living as a potter and was perpetually happy?

What seemed to disturb him now was Delaney's attitude toward his family. It was as though they weren't capable of proper behavior or dressing themselves correctly. Last night his mother had looked elegant in a floor length black gown, and Delaney seemed to be having a problem with that. He sighed heavily. Women were difficult to understand.

From somewhere deep inside, he remembered holidays, birthdays, and picnics as a child and wondered why he'd never been self-conscious about his family before. Spontaneous laughter and mismatched dishes had been a part of his life, along with odd furniture and storytelling.

Though Delaney's approach was cool and detached, the wedding was, after all, her big day. She and her mother had even offered suggestions of what colors would be best for the guests to wear if they were to be photographed with the wedding party. He remembered the numerous discussions he'd overheard about how much "show time" the bridesmaids, who had spent a fortune on their dresses, would be allowed to have. It was finally decided they could scatter rose petals as they descended the stairs.

Then a dramatic silence would fill the air, and a crescendo of music would alert everyone that something of great importance was about to happen. Eyes would rise up when Delaney appeared at the top of the stairs. She would dazzle the guests in a frothy cloud of pure white as she claimed her day in the beer baron's house.

He had agreed with all the plans, so why was he upset now? Another question he needed to answer, but he realized that the results were the same. It didn't matter how Delaney reached her conclusions; she was spot-on with her thinking. He lay back down and within minutes was dozing.

The cries of an unhappy baby filled the house, jolting Skye and Delaney awake. Her body was frozen in place as she listened to the disturbing sounds that were a direct threat to her future. The fear of failure constricted her throat, making it hard to swallow.

Taking a deep breath, she detected the smells of roasting meat that had drifted into the bedroom. She hated red meat. *Haven't they done enough to me?* She kept her eyes shut hoping the noise would disappear.

Skye stood up, but not knowing what to do, sat back down. Delaney felt the bed bounce, and she swung her legs over the side, mumbling, "My head is splitting. Can you make that crying sound go away?"

"It's a baby. You can't turn them on and off." Looking at her sideways, he spoke impatiently, "Perhaps showing some compassion would make you feel better."

She sucked in air and held her breath, trying to stop another bout of her own crying. The aromas from the kitchen filled her nostrils, making her want to gag. Her mother's words rang through her head.

Be brave, and stay firm, Delaney Mae Anne. He is a smart boy and will see it your way. After all, he does work for your daddy.

Delaney realized wretchedly that those words no longer applied as she rocked gently in place. Tears stung her eyes. "I'm really sorry." She felt her heart breaking. Skye watched sadly as she wiped at her nose and slowly folded into her knees. "Already, I miss you." She spoke dully, "You won't let me help."

"That's not so." A clear thought surfaced, and his words grew in strength, "You're doing your part. Now I need to do mine."

"I'm losing us," she sobbed.

He offered a tissue then put his arm around her, helping her to straighten up. "It's going to be all right."

Her words echoed with heartache, "No. I don't think so." She raised her head, using her fingers to push away the tears. "Not really."

The baby's cries picked up again, and she cringed. "I can't cope with this. It makes me very nervous." She looked into Skye's eyes while fighting for control. He waited, respecting her silence. When she spoke, her words came out flat, "My wedding day has been gravely affected."

He held her close, feeling the same loss. "Please don't cry." His chest muscles squeezed painfully around his heart when he realized a decision had been made, but he hadn't called the shots.

She untangled herself from his embrace and stood awkwardly on her own. "I'd better go back to Chicago." Her face was puffy and red; her shoulders bent forward, and mascara stains left black smudges under her eyes.

He felt clumsy as he stood next to her. "Please wait." Putting his hands on her shoulders, he felt her stiffen. "Give it until morning. Mom's fixing a late lunch. After that, we'll take a walk."

She sniffed the air. "It's a roast, isn't it?" Raising her face up, she searched his eyes, allowing him time to think. With nothing forthcoming, she spoke wearily, "You know I don't eat red meat."

With a sigh, he nodded, taking her back in his arms.

"Even the smells of meat cooking make me very nauseous." She moaned, "It's right up there with coffee breath."

"It's alright, Doodle Bug. I'll take you somewhere else."

After a heavy silence, she murmured, "Why can't we fix this?"

He held her tightly, feeling her shiver. "I'll need to stay and work on the adoption angle. It's better if I do it alone."

"Do you belong here, Skye?" Her face was buried in his shoulder—her fear so real she could taste it. Minutes ticked by.

His mind spun, and he knew that his life would change if he made the wrong decision, but still, the words came out. "I need to step back and catch my breath." He whispered in her ear, "That baby is my responsibility. I have to find it a home."

She pulled away, anger loading the tone of her voice, "What about us? That's a responsibility, too!"

"Yes." He felt his lifestyle split apart and replied weakly, "I know."

"Well, what are you going to do about that?" Her voice raised, and panic raked her words, "What's really your main concern?" The moment was fragile, and the sounds of the day became muted as she continued to wait for the words she wanted to hear.

"Oh, Delaney." Gently, he reached for her hand. There was no return squeeze. Another chunk of his world fell away. "I don't know what to do about us until I solve the problem of finding a home for the baby." His gaze locked with hers. "Do you understand?"

She spoke flatly as she moved toward the bathroom, "While I bathe, would you call the airline? It's too late to join mother and daddy on the Lear." She faced Skye, her eyes narrowed with resentment. "I think we can agree that my wedding day may not take place as planned. I realize you'll need to stay, but I've got to leave."

She used the tub while he washed in the sink then dressed in yesterday's clothes. Leaving the bedroom, he went in search of his mother.

Pete was bouncing Monique gently on his knee as she squealed with joy. "She's a born horse woman, Missy. Gon'na have to get her a pony, soon as she can walk."

"And where are you going to keep this pony?" Melissa asked happily as she opened the oven door. Mouthwatering aromas of herbs mixed with beef roasting in red wine flowed into the room. "Smells pretty good. Think I'll call Skye and Delaney."

"No, mom." Skye appeared in the doorway, looking both disheveled and upset. "Delaney wants to go to the airport now. She's still very upset."

"What?" Pete's smile faded. "And miss your mom's roast? No one leaves when your mom's doing a roast." He lifted Monique off his knee and placed her in the crook of his arm.

"Yeah. Well." Skye sighed. "I'm sorry."

Monique gurgled happily. She wiggled a tiny hand in Skye's direction. "See that?" Pete announced with pride. "She wants to hold your finger."

Skye backed up. "No."

Melissa questioned, "That's it. Just no?"

"I've got a lot to think about and she's..." he pointed at Monique, "She's the main problem."

He watched the disappointment settle over his mother's face. His words were clipped, "I'll be back late tonight."

Monique clapped her hands and babbled as Skye checked the time on his Rolex and walked down the hall.

"It's his loss, Missy." Pete put Monique over his shoulder and gathered Melissa into his free arm. "I've got my two girls right here. And a fine afternoon planned with a meal fit for a king."

"Oh Pete." She blinked at her tears. "I'm not really hurt...just disappointed. But," she pulled away so she could look at him. "I'm coming to understand that may be a way of life when my son and his bride-to-be are around." Straightening up, she smiled woefully. "Let's call Angie for late lunch. She's a delightful girl, and I enjoy her company."

Inside the Covington Jet

The plane had reached its cruising altitude quickly. A blue sky and almost no wind offered excellent conditions for the flight back to Chicago.

"Allow me to point out that we are without any works of art as ah was smart enough to avoid the subject with Sykes's mama." Terri Sue Ellen settled back in the soft cushioned seat of the Lear with a sigh. "Do you know that a ceremonial gift exchange signifies bonding two tribes together?"

Charles offered an abstract nod as she continued, "Instead you will note that ah introduced our custom of bondin' by doin' lunch. It's the way of our people, the Pilgrims."

She buzzed for the flight attendant. "Ah want a salad and a sparklin' water and a martini. Did you get that?" Ruth nodded patiently. "And mah husband will have the same. Ah am watchin' every ounce. Isn't that so, Chuck?"

He paid no attention to her, so she squinted at the young woman and asked, "Who are you, again?"

"Ruth."

"So, Ruth, did you get the French fries from MacDonald's that ah requested?"

"Yes, Mrs. Covington."

"Excellent. Put them in the microwave now. They are for mah husband. He wants them soggy and salty, and while ah'm waitin', ah'll have me a glass of champagne. Oh yes, mah husband would want you to put a couple of fries on a plate for me. See to it." She leaned over, clearly exasperated and stared at Charles across the aisle, "So here ah am, doin' all the talkin' for both of us... again!"

He nodded and tried to concentrate on his papers while she continued to eat and drink for the first ninety minutes of the flight.

Finally she buzzed for Ruth. "Bring me two pillows, the feather ones and a light weight blanket." She held out her champagne flute. "Ah have run out of vodka. Here, fill this up with Cristal and bring me some peanuts. Did you put hand lotion in the bathroom? Mah hands must remain soft and attractive, as ah have lots of work ah do with my hands."

She swiveled her seat so that she faced her husband. "Excuse me, Chuck." Her voice was harsh enough for him to jerk his head up. "Are you goin' finish your martini?"

"No. I need to work."

"Good! You, Ruth, put his drink in my flute. No need to waste good vodka. You can have the left over champagne. No! Wait. Don't you be tryin' to trick me." She narrowed her eyes. "You're on duty. You can't be drinkin' none. That's a violation of airline code."

Ruth stood still with her hands behind her back and smiled wearily.

Terri Sue Ellen shoved her crocodile handbag toward her. "Get these foreign bar snacks out of mah Hermes bag. Be sure you pick out all them nasty lookin' green peas and throw 'em away. Mix what's left with mah Virginia peanuts and put 'em all in a baggie next to mah half full bottle of champagne."

"Yes, Mrs. Covington."

"Don't you be sneakin' any, now."

After thirty minutes, Terri Sue Ellen reclined her seat and dozed off. Chuck sighed with relief. What a pair they made. Her name on the corporate papers made her a force to reckon with even though his own family money had put them on top of the world.

He studied his self-indulgent wife and watched as her mouth fell open and a loud snort shattered the silence. He disliked admitting it, but his mother had been right; Terri Sue Ellen's southern charm had worn thin.

San Francisco Airport
Domestic Terminal

The three hour drive to the San Francisco airport was filled with torment as Delaney's speech pattern become a moan of ongoing complaints that covered her anguish. Skye's head throbbed with each problem she discussed.

He entered the rental car return lane and realized, with a start, that he was returning her rental. His car, with the broken air conditioner, was still sitting in his mother's driveway, and he had no way home.

To complicate matters further, his credit cards were in his wallet on the bedroom dresser. When he told Delaney that he only had a small amount of cash in his pocket, she was without sympathy and insisted that he turn the rental car around and drop her directly at the departure curb.

After placing her bags at her feet, he bent to kiss her goodbye, but she stopped him and turned to summon a luggage handler. She'd glanced with disgust at the car and walked toward the revolving glass doors that led into the airport.

For the first time in many years, he felt truly alone. Going into an automatic mood, he dropped her rental car and checked the airport transportation. A bus left the following morning and could drop him in Salinas, within forty minutes of Big Sur. He had enough cash to buy a one way ticket and some fast food for his dinner.

Or he could rent another car? *Ah, hell, no I can't. Not without my driver's license, which is in my wallet. Why didn't I keep Delaney's car? Oh yeah, then I'd have two cars to return. Wait. I could have returned one at the Monterey Airport. I'm not thinking.* He bought the bus ticket and settled in for the long wait.

Feeling like a fifteen-year-old boy who'd done something wrong, he called his mother to let her know his new timeframe. She listened carefully to his explanation and sensed that his life was in chaos. It was almost nine pm, and Pete would leave now to pick him up. Skye objected firmly but was too tired to continue the fight.

He'd trudged back to the counter where he'd purchased the bus ticket. While standing in front of the woman who had sold it to him, he realized how bad he looked. He shifted his weight from one foot to the other. *Without Maria or Estella, who's going to do my laundry?* He hung his head in shame. *Dumb ass question. My life is out of control.*

Staring at the "No Refund" sign, he told the ticket agent his mother was sending a friend to pick him up and he needed his money back so he could eat. Because he'd paid with cash, she made an exception and offered him a sympathetic look. *She thinks I'm a just another loser.*

He pocketed the money and took the escalator upstairs. He couldn't go to the First Class lounge because he had no ID but, more importantly, he didn't want anyone to see him. He got a hamburger from McDonalds and found his way to an airport bar.

Sitting at a small table away from most people, he was steeped in depression and fearful they might ask him to leave due to his disheveled appearance. Fortunately, the waitress was too busy to care, so he ordered a beer. Her nametag said Lorraine, and he felt the dark humor of fate engulf him. Quickly, he ate his food from the greasy paper bag he kept hidden in his lap. He drank the beer too fast, and his head began to feel thick as he entered a nap mode. He left some money on the table and went back outside.

Leaving the cement interior of the airport behind, he walked into the cool San Francisco night. By waking up his thoughts, they returned like angry wasps buzzing around his head. What should he have done differently? The answer came back, everything and nothing.

As he lumbered along the dirty pavement, he lost track of time so he was late getting back to the designated area where he was supposed to meet Pete. He had seen the bright blue truck circle twice. It was apparent he couldn't do anything right. Luckily it was midnight, so the traffic was light, and he easily spotted the truck when it came around again.

Pete grinned, "Good to see you, Skye! I was getting worried, but the third time's the charm." He reached across the seat and pushed the door open. "You doin' alright?"

"Yeah. I'm good." He climbed in, feeling like a fool. "I apologize. It's my fault. I was walking and..." He shook his head. "I have no excuse."

"Not to worry. You're here now, and I can deliver you safely back to your mom."

"Let me pay for gas. I've got cash back from the bus ticket. It's the least I can do." He apologized again. "I wasn't thinking. I would have rented another car, but my license is at mom's." His voice sounded lost, "I could have done...something. I'm sorry you had to make this drive." *Damn!* He took in a sharp breath. *That's the third time I've apologized, and now I'm in a weakened position.* He stared out the window. *But even so, there are still people who care enough about me to not leave me stranded at the airport.*

Driving back to the Stone House

Traffic wove a straightforward pattern on the highway as the airport disappeared behind them. The truck bounced along while a country song spilled out of the radio. Pete pulled the brim of his baseball cap low. "This music okay with you?"

"Yeah."

"What do you listen to back in Chicago?"

"Jazz, mostly."

"That so." Pete signaled to change lanes.

"Delaney likes jazz." Skye settled his shoulders against the seat. "But country is fine. I remember being sixteen and going to a barn dance in Salinas. The music had my feet twitching to a two-step, but I didn't have the courage to ask the girls to dance. Duane did though." He looked at Pete. "Duane was a good line dancer. Knew all the fancy footwork."

Pete smiled with the memory. "Ought'a be. His mother taught him. She knew all the dances. Me, I'm kinda lucky to keep up with the two-step and not fall over my feet."

"Delaney and I are taking ballroom lessons for the wedding." He stopped abruptly, realizing that the wedding was on hold. He lowered his head, and the silence made him uncomfortable. "So, you got cruise control?"

"Yup."

"How's the truck do on miles?"

"Can't say as if I've paid it much mind. Okay, I guess."

"Good...that's good."

"Duane's car, now it's a sporty lookin' vehicle. Sor'ta bright and shiny like a freshly polished plum, but a real bugger for gas."

"Toyota does a lot of those bright colors on cars. But I thought they were pretty good on mileage. Guess some sports cars can still suck it up, huh?" Skye found himself running out of comments but made another attempt at being sociable, "Mom still have her old Chevy?"

"That she does, but talks about trading it in."

"On what?" He looked surprised.

"Couple of ones she's been lookin' at. Don't know which direction she'll take. She's still in the talkin' stage, hasn't reached the doin' part yet." Pete tuned the radio to get rid of the static. "I think she favors a fast little number."

"My mom?" Skye's voice held an element of awe.

"Yup." Pete gave him an affirmative nod. "Told me somethin' low and sleek."

He appeared at a loss for a reply and mumbled, "I was out of the loop on that one." Massaging his neck, he willed his mind to go blank. With the windows cracked, the night air felt good. He thought of his father and his old truck and the many trips they'd made into town with the windows down.

He felt his eyelids grow heavy. He drifted off realizing that his mother's boyfriend, who was another old person and shouldn't be driving late at night, had picked him up and was about to drive a total of six hours just to get him back home. The woman at the bus counter had been right when she looked at him like he was a loser. And, on that thought, he fell asleep.

Big Sur, California
Stone House

It was three thirty in the morning when Pete pulled into the driveway of the stone house. Skye woke to songs of frogs and the chirping of crickets that burst musically from unknown places. The ocean splashed on the rocks below, and he knew from memory that the water would leave a whirl of pearly gray liquid in the moonlight. His heart recognized that he was home. *Where'd that thought come from?* He shook his head in denial as he breathed in the salt air.

He thanked Pete for picking him up and apologized again. When his mind reminded him of his softened position, he pushed the thought aside and pulled hard to open the front door. He followed Pete into the house and said goodnight.

Walking to his bedroom, he considered showering first but instead fell into his rumpled bed, letting the blankness of sleep overwhelm him.

Pete tiptoed into the master bedroom. "You awake, Missy?"

"Of course." She turned on the small lamp that shed a rosy glow across the end table. "Was it a good ride home?"

He sat down and pulled off his cap. Running his fingers over the brim, he said, "Your boy's got some thinkin' to do. It's a tough one. It is. Lost his girl and, I'm gon'na bet, his job, all in one day."

"Yes," she agreed. "Life's got a way of throwing you a curve when you least expect it." She glanced toward the sleeping baby in the drawer and felt a wave of love. "Some curves are very good; others..." she shrugged, thinking of her son's loss. "Others, not so much."

Pete nodded as he headed toward the bathroom, walking slowly. "Gon'na get me a shower and sleep till noon. Be good if Skye did the same."

Big Sur, California
Next Morning

Skye slept late, but upon rising, he used the old tub in his room and took a bath then stripped his bed. He washed his sheets and put the clothes he had worn yesterday in a pile for the next load. He appeared for lunch wearing the slacks and shirt he'd flown in, figuring they were slightly cleaner and minimally less offensive.

Lunch was left-over roast beef and braised potatoes. His taste buds savored the appetizing flavors, and he helped himself to more carrots and another slice of meat.

He watched his mother bathe the baby in an enamel pan in the kitchen sink. It looked like the same pan his Grandma Lillian had used years ago for the holiday turkey. The baby splashed, seeming to enjoy the water.

"Oh, good Lord, Monique, Grammy is as wet as you!" His mother looked flushed with happiness. "Skye hold on to her for a moment while I get some more towels."

"I don't think so." He felt no pull as a father. "She looks wet and ahh, slippery."

Tossing him a look over her shoulder, she replied, "My, aren't you observant. That college education was worth every penny." She laughed. "Of course, she's both wet and slippery. Now come over here while I get the towels."

Pushing his chair back reluctantly, he approached the sink. The baby splashed, and he moved back cautiously. "She's doing stuff."

"Yes, she is." Melissa shook her head in amusement. "Now hold on to her so she doesn't slide."

He looked the sink over carefully and asked, "Where would she slide to?"

"Oh, Skye! She's a baby and could slide under the water."

He mumbled in the direction of his mother's back, "I knew that."

Glancing at Monique, he adopted a cavalier attitude. *How hard can this be? She's a little person and doesn't know shit.* "So, hey. How you doin'?" He put his cool hands under her warm arms, and she looked up at him in amazement. "Yeah, well. Let me explain that I'm sorry about the cold hands, but it's no biggie. Let's identify the problem, shall we?" He smiled confidently.

She looked at him with big brown eyes and the beginning of a pout.

"Ya, well. Don't give me a bad look. You're a little warm. And that's on you." He began to feel uneasy. "Listen, go ahead and splash some more. Go on, I saw you do it."

With his mother gone from the room, he was alone with his daughter. This was not a moment he wanted, and apparently, neither did she. When Monique realized her grandmother was missing, her face screwed up, and her eyes showed distress at the strange person holding her.

"Hey, don't cry!" His voice caught in his throat. "Really, please don't do that. Let's try this." He bounced her in the water. "Look. Babies like to jump around. I read that on Google. It's a fact." Water splashed out of the pan. "People know what they're talking about online."

He realized his voice was too loud but couldn't seem to lower it, "Hey, how about some toys...maybe a balloon? You want a red one? I always liked red balloons best."

Monique let out a shrill cry and began to flap her short arms sending him into a panic. He snatched her out of the warm bath water and held her at arm's length. The cold air against her wet body added to her discomfort. She continued to wail and started to kick at the air.

"What's the matter?" His apprehension turned to fear as Monique's cry rose in volume. "Stop that! I mean it. Do you want me to call my mom?" Not knowing what to do, he placed the baby against his shoulder and hollered, "Mom, hurry! Something's wrong with her."

Monique stiffened her body at the sound of his distressed voice, and her sobs turned earsplitting.

"She's having a seizure," he yelled in the direction of the hall. "It's escalating out of control!" His own heart raced in horror. "Where does it hurt? Talk to me!" He bellowed louder, "Mom, for the love of what's holy, get out here!" He panicked and found himself turning in circles. "I'm coming to you. Get ready for us."

Melissa found him jumping from foot to foot when she ran into the kitchen. She dropped the fresh towels on the counter and turned to her son. "Give me my granddaughter, and stop your spinning."

Monique settled quickly in her grandma's arms, putting her head on Melissa's shoulder. She stared sideways at Skye and hiccupped a couple of times.

"I've never seen anything like it." His eyes were large with shock. "She started crying when you left the room. She wouldn't tell me what was wrong." Taking gulps of air, he continued, "I couldn't fix it."

Monique popped a thump in her mouth.

"I should probably take my blood pressure. It must be off the charts." He looked around the kitchen. "Do you have a BP kit?"

Chapter Sixteen

Chicago, Illinois
Covington Residence

"Our poor little girl is besmirched by the shame of her false engagement." Terri Sue Ellen set her drink on the Louis XV dressing table and took a moment to admire the fanciful patterns of carved tortoiseshells. "But she is not as shattered as ah am. Kindly note that as fact."

Sniffing delicately, she raised a hankie to her eyes and using her free hand traced over the painted gold leaf before she continued, "Ah do believe Delaney will, eventually, go back to her condo, but right now she wants to come home to recover from the deceit she experienced with that ugly-minded employee who worked directly for you."

Letting out her breath she lifted her martini, watched her husband's reaction, and sipped. "We must, as her lovin' parents, do what is best for her in her time of dire need." Using the toothpick, she pierced an olive and slowly sucked out the pimento. "Are you followin' me on this? 'Cause ah've been thinkin' maybe you should send her off on an assignment so she can experience something other than her sufferin'."

"Yes, sugar." Chuck wanted a cigar and wished he was at his club. "That might be a fine idea."

"Tell me darlin', can we sue him for the mortification he inflicted upon us...both on a personal and business nature? And, of course, don't let us forget, there is Delaney's heartbreak. In her case, men are not a dime a dozen. Poor thing."

"I don't believe so."

"How about the weddin' costs like her gown, the caterers, the mansion, food...need ah go on?"

"I'll look into it."

"You do that, Chucky, and look into it real careful like." She stood up abruptly. "Ah need to play me some golf. It'll reduce my trauma level." She finished her drink and looked at Charles. "You should play golf with me 'cause we need to put up a united front while we manufacture us a damn good story. With mah havin' said that, let me finish by addin' that Skye's sexual comportment has been his undoin'. Just what do you think that deadbeat dad is up to now?"

"It's Skye's nature to keep a cool head. I'm guessing that he'll be in control of everything around him." With a sigh, Charles picked up the phone. "I'll call for a tee time."

Big Sur, California
Stone House

"I think I had a panic attack." Skye sounded breathless.

"Oh, you did not." Melissa shook her head as Skye took his pulse. "Monique was crying because she was suddenly cold and scared. She's fine, and so are you. Now come over here and help me." She placed the baby back in the water.

Monique, happy to be with her grandmother, raised her chubby arms and hit the warm water, splashing in all directions.

Skye backed up and pointed. "She doesn't like me."

"Act your age, and come here." Melissa nodded toward the yellow rubber duck. "Hand her that."

Monique watched Skye's every move as he picked up the toy and pushed it toward her. She reached for it and offered him a toothless grin.

"Now let go of it, Skye."

"Huh?"

"I said let go of the toy."

He looked closer at the baby. "You could have had a big red balloon. It would have made a statement. Said something about you." He turned to his mother. "You should know that I offered her a red balloon, but she didn't want it."

"Where's a balloon?"

"I would have bought one. I have the money."

Melissa let her eyes roll. "You think she understood you?"

"Well, I guess not," he grumbled. "She started to scream."

"She's a baby!" Nodding toward the table, his mother pointed with her head. "Get me that towel. Now."

"I don't want to hold her again. This has wiped me out."

"Open it." She picked Monique up and tucked the fluffy towel around her granddaughter. Shaking her head with disbelief, she walked down the hall, calling back to her son, "You can open your eyes now."

Bundled over his mom's shoulder, the baby looked at him, and in the briefest of moments, he felt as if he was looking into the eyes of Nathalie LaVeron.

He sat down with a thump. "Oh my God," he whispered. "I'm such a screw-up with our baby. I'm so sorry. I had no idea you were pregnant. I never meant for this to happen. That baby is ours, but I can't keep it." He put his head in his hands and felt himself rock back and forth. "I don't know how to handle this."

****

Before his mother returned, he got up, tossed the sheets in the dryer and put his offensive clothes in the washer.

Opening the screen door, he moved into the flower-scented morning where he tried to listen to the sounds of the day with his heart, as his father had often suggested. The warm sunshine lulled him toward forgetfulness; however, he wasn't accepting of its gift. He needed to face today and the responsibilities it carried. The truth was that part of him was relieved Delaney was back in Chicago; the rest of him felt guilty for having that reaction.

Not finding the peace he sought, he wandered back through the garden, annoyed with his life. All he wanted were some black and white answers with no guilt attached.

When Skye entered the kitchen, Pete was scraping off the lunch dishes.

Skye blinked as a scene flashed through his mind of his mother and father washing plates. He'd been about five years old and insisted on helping. He thought about the small step stool that he'd stood on as they offered him a cup to dry. The dish towel was blue with yellow stripes, and he'd used just the one, even though it was wet. It occurred to him that his parents probably had to dry some of the dishes a second time before they could put them away; yet they'd let him believe he was doing a great job, and his young pride had soared.

It was obvious that the role of a parent was confusing and complicated, and he definitely didn't want such an awesome responsibility in his life.

After all, he had Delaney's needs to focus on, and that was stressful enough...or maybe he didn't have Delaney in his life. He allowed himself to experience the impact, but all he got was a queasy stomach.

Pete begin to wash plates as Merle Haggard sang about drinkin' and cheatin' and old dogs while Skye dried the dishes thoroughly, as if making amends for his youth.

"What was all the ruckus earlier?" Pete asked.

Skye replied wearily, "The baby hates me."

"You don't say. What'd ya do to her?"

"I don't know." He reached for another towel. "I haven't done anything right around females for the last several days."

"You want to talk about it?"

"Nope. I want to forget about it."

"Think you can do that?"

"Probably not."

Before the pans were started, Pete stopped and wiped his hands. "Your mom leaves the pots for me. My wife used to do the same thing. Why, your dad and I used to discuss how we had own way of doin' em' so that they sparkled. It involved some Big Sur sand we'd carry up from time to time and keep in a bucket out in the garage. Don't go tellin' your mom, now." He looked closely at Skye. "Say, you want a snifter of brandy?"

"Huh?"

Pete half joked, "This attention deficient problem seems to be wide spread." He adapted a slower pattern of speech, "I said, 'Do you want a snifter of brandy?'"

"Ahh. It's pretty early, but yeah. Sure." He thought about his Cuban cigars and his enamel humidor back at the nineteenth floor condo he shared with Delaney. One word stuck in his mind...gone.

Key West, Florida
Robert and Evelyn Covington Residence

You say the visit was tainted?" Evelyn sounded annoyed. "What exactly does that mean, Robert?"

"No one told the young man's mother to expect company." He smiled half-heartedly and continued, "It seems that Terri Sue Ellen had too much to drink. Delaney had her facts confused, and our son put his foot in his mouth."

"Is that all?"

Robert cleared his throat. "There was probably more, but that's all Chuck shared with me."

"I see." Evelyn shook her head and focused on her crossword puzzle. "I need a seven letter word that means showing lack of good judgement."

Robert reached for her hand. "Can it be hyphenated?"

Chicago, Illinois
Lake Michigan Commemorated Country Club

"Ah've been doin' a passel of contemplatin', Chucky, and it's a fact that our family name has been sullied. But, on the other hand, do ya think you could stick this weddin' back together if you threaten Skye with something criminal? Don't hold back on your thinkin' process now. Let'er rip."

"Don't think so, sugar."

Terri Sue Ellen clutched her neck in a dramatic move. "Personally, it should be noted that mah health could be plagued with problems because of Skye's unholy pleasures and the falsifications he's made to our daughter." She looked sharply at Charles. "Now that there has got itself a price tag, doesn't it?"

Smiling brightly, she waved at the golf cart that pulled up behind them. "Hello there!"

Turning back, she whispered, "Delaney is afflicted, too." Making a slot machine pull with her right hand, she added, "Double the money. Am ah right, Chucky?"

Returning her attention to the golfers, she continued, "Why now, how y'all doin'? We're just dilly dallying a bit. Enjoyin' the lovely weather. Y'all go ahead and play on through."

With a sharp glance, she looked at her husband, who was lighting a cigar. Well?" she demanded.

"As I see it, it's up to Delaney and Skye." He puffed and watched the smoke float into the air. "She can be difficult at times. We both know that. Whereas, Skye is well-liked by everyone. That's a point in his favor. He may not be so willing to come back into our family when he gets support from his mother and her friends."

Big Sur, California
Stone House

Angie, wearing a bright blue dress that flowed to her ankles, stomped into the kitchen. Holding Monique, she stood in front of Skye, clearly annoyed. "Why did you make her cry?"

"Are you talking to me?" He looked startled as she continued to glare at him. Clearing his throat, he took a moment and then defended his position, "I did not make her cry!"

"Yes, you did." She handed the baby to Pete and turned back to face him. Placing her hands on her hips, she snapped, "I would have been here in a New York second if I had thought you were going to do something mean."

"I was helping my mother!"

"Oh no, you weren't. You made Monique unhappy and probably hurt her feelings."

"I did not! She's a baby and doesn't have feelings...yet."

The kitchen grew very quiet as Angie stared at Skye. "What did you say?"

He looked for support, but Pete frowned and shook his head. "Might be you used the wrong choice of words."

"Okay." Skye swallowed hard, feeling the pressure build. "Here's what went down. The baby had some kind of a fit. And she wanted..." He was at a loss for a moment. "That yellow duck thing." He pointed. "Over there."

"Why didn't you give it to her?"

"I did! And I offered her a red balloon."

"Red is an angry color."

"It is not!"

"Yes, it is! You're the perfect example. I've been here only a few days, and you've been angry the whole time."

Skye wrinkled his forehead adding weakly, "Red is a cheerful color."

Giving him a scornful look, she scooped Monique back into her arms. Kissing the baby's forehead, she continued, "Your daddy is very sorry he took your toy."

"I didn't take her toy!"

Disregarding Skye, Angie opened the refrigerator. "It's time for her bottle. After that, me and your mom are going shopping." She beamed. "Melissa said we need to get her some girl clothes." She smiled down at her army surplus boots. "I love shopping. I picked these out all by myself. They are really way cool!"

"No, they're not cool." Skye let out a sigh. "They look big and ugly on your feet."

Pete cleared this throat. "Not a good direction to take. Lots of my students wear boots like that." Angie looked at him, and he continued amiably, "They are fine boots." Looking toward her feet, he ended with, "Good color."

"Thank you, Mr. Pete. As an artist, I appreciate your comments."

She faced Skye with an aloof stare. Monique was watching everyone with curiosity as Angie spoke to her, "My goodness, little one, your daddy is so old, he doesn't even know what cool people wear." The baby cooed and grinned. Angie turned slowly to face Skye. "Your baby girl is so cheerful, it's difficult to believe that you had anything to do with making her."

"Excuse me!" He sounded exasperated. "Exactly what is that supposed to mean?"

Looking at him, she scoffed, "Move. You're in front of the microwave, and you're holding up the show."

He stepped to the side and looked at Pete. "She's doing it again. You saw her. I didn't deserve that."

"Is she pickin' on ya?"

"Yes!"

Putting the formula inside the microwave, she adjusted the setting to low. "Let's warm this bottle for a few seconds so you can finish it off and get started on a wee nap." She glanced at Skye dismissively. "Bet you don't know how to do that, Mr. Businessman."

He rose up to his full six-foot-four height and towered over Angie. "I've had just about enough of your comments."

"Okay. You fix her bottle, smarty pants."

"I will not!"

"That's 'cause you don't know how."

The microwave beeped, and she took the bottle out. "Oh, don't ask me if I've had any lunch. I'm sure you enjoyed the roast beef and vegetables." She drew in a breath and let it out slowly. "My goodness, you're just so thoughtful."

He slumped into a chair, feeling as if he'd been bested again and not sure how it'd happened. He asked flatly, "Have you had lunch?"

"Yes, I have." Her boots made a clunking noise as she moved across the floor.

He felt numb. He wasn't old. Was he?

Pete added more brandy to Skye's snifter. "Here's to good times!"

"What?"

"You need to focus on listening to what folks are saying to you. Why, this attention problem..." Pete made a tisk-tisk sound and smiled kindly. "If you try, you can probably overcome it with work. I'm sure everyone will be patient with you." Having warmed the brandy in a saucepan, he inhaled the richness of its pleasing fragrance. "Skye, I said to good times!" He held his glass up to toast, and Skye touched his snifter to the glass while Pete continued, "Now I'm going to start the pans. You want to get in on this?" He kept up a running conversation, "Angie is working out just fine. She's a big help to your mom. Loves the little one!"

"Angie is rude," Skye responded in a tired voice.

"Only to you."

"Yeah. Well, it's good for her that I'm willing to overlook it."

Nodding cheerfully, Pete added, "That's a wise decision."

The brandy loosened Skye's tongue, and he found himself talking a mile a minute about nothing and everything, until eventually he paused for breath long enough to learn that Pete's son was in a loving relationship with a surgical nurse at the hospital. However, Pete hesitantly admitted that having grandchildren of his own was not going to be a reality due to some vague medical reason.

A star burst over Skye's head. He didn't want to push it, but there was no time like the present. If Pete's son was seriously involved with a woman, a door had opened and he meant to step through it. "Have they ever thought of adopting?" His voice took on a note of eagerness. "You know if your son and..."

Pete supplied the name, "Sandy."

"If Duane and Sandy were willing to adopt, mom would still be able to see the baby. She'd be like a grandmother, you know? And you could be a grandfather." He paused in mid-thought and studied the sponge. "Yeah, that would be about right." Smiling nervously, he plunged on, "You both seem to get on well with, you know," he made a vague hand signal, "the little girl."

He started cleaning the stove and felt the idea grow as he rubbed the surface exuberantly. "Besides, there are lots of single parents in today's world. No one has to be married to adopt." He looked up to find Pete watching him closely. "I'd be willing to sign whatever papers are necessary to make it happen. So what kind of doctor is he?" Turning his head, Skye looked under the hood, "Greasy. Don't tell Mom. I'll get it tomorrow."

Pete nodded as he rinsed the sink. "It'll be our secret."

Skye smacked the side of his head with his palm. "Oh yeah. That's right. Mom told me Duane was a pediatrician. Normally I'm on top of this stuff, but the last few days I've seen a lot of trauma, pulling me in all directions." He thought he was talking too much but couldn't stop himself. "But, hey, that's really great...being a doctor is quite an achievement!" He forced himself to slow down with a solemn declaration, "He'd make a fine father, and she's a nurse, huh? Great parent material there. Am I right?"

Pete rubbed his bald head and continued to watch Skye dismantle the burners. He cleared his throat, "When your mom does that, she puts on a pair of gloves. You want some?"

"No. This is fine," he answered distractedly. "These should be soaked." He carried the burners to the sink and filled it with hot soapy water. "I'll finish them later. Then I'll get under that hood."

Pete looked through the window into the sunny day for a long time, lost in his own thoughts while Skye continued to talk.

"She's a cute baby. I mean she doesn't have teeth yet, so it's hard to say if she'll have a good smile." He paused as if remembering something important. "Nathalie had a gorgeous smile and beautiful teeth. Me..." He shrugged his shoulders, adding, "I wasn't so lucky, but they got straightened out. See?" He curled his lips up.

"What 'cha doing there, Skye?" Uncomfortably, Pete shifted backward.

"Showing you my teeth. Like I said, they're good now." He thought for a moment and sucked in air. "Truth is that I had braces as a kid."

Melissa entered the kitchen. "Why are you showing Pete your teeth?"

"I wanted him to know they're straight."

She smiled in Pete's direction. "Did you want to see that?"

"Nope. This is really about Monique's teeth."

Melissa smiled patiently, "She's drooling a bit but doesn't have teeth, yet."

"She will." Pete nodded as if that ended the discussion.

Staring at both men, Melissa paused. "Yes, that's the usual course of things." She moved toward the sink and saw the sponge in Skye's hand. "Goodness me. My, it shines in here."

"It was the least I could do. I should'a stepped up to help dry dishes, but I was distracted." He gave her a quick hug, "Thanks again for fixing the roast. I can't remember the last time I tasted anything that good."

She laughed. "Monique is down for a quick nap before Angie and I take off for our shopping trip."

"You just remember, Missy, that little one, why, she's growing like a weed. What fits her today won't fit her tomorrow." Pete nodded solemnly. "Besides, we have to be saving money for her first pony."

Skye interjected, "Possibly you'll want to look into an insurance policy that covers orthodontist bills."

Melissa looked perplexed. "Why are you saying that?"

"Could happen, mom."

"I'm more concerned about the pony and where we'd keep it."

Pete scoffed, "Oh Missy, ponies live outside. We'd build it a little shed and a fine corral."

"Who's going to care for this animal?"

"Maybe Skye, when he comes for a visit." Pete beamed. " See here, he could muck out the stall then feed the pony an apple."

"Ahh, no. Don't think so, guys." Skye shook his head.. "Probably not me. Animals are a big responsibility. You two would have to work out the details. Like post a list of chores on the refrigerator or something."

"Thank you, son, for the valuable input."

Pete patted her arm. "I'm confident we could handle it."

Laughing, she gave Skye a hug and noticed his shoulders were less tight. "You know we're kidding with you."

"I can never tell."

Skye excused himself to make some calls, and when he was out of hearing, Melissa turned to Pete with a question, "Why are my burners in the sink?"

"They're soakin'.'"

"Peterson Bailey, I can see that." She placed her hands on her hips. "What I'm askin' is why?"

He studied the soapy water for a minute then faced her with a happy grin. "I got some more news for you; tomorrow your stove hood gets cleaned."

"What for?"

"It's a secret."

"What are you talking about?"

"With you twisting my arm, like this, I'm gon'na have to betray a confidence. Do you really want me to do that?"

She raised an eyebrow and waited.

"Okay. Your son says it's got grease."

"It does not!"

Pete smiled. "Would you care to join me in a coffee and brandy?"

"It's the middle of the day!"

"So it is." He peeked in her direction, offering one of his exaggerated winks.

"I heard parts of your conversation with Skye." A stray curl had sprung loose from her braid, and she pushed it behind her ear. "It's getting grey and has a mind-set all its own. Hair will do that, you know."

Looking at her with a silly grin, he decided to pass on his comment. Instead, he poured the coffee, adding brandy and cream. "Wan'na sit on the glider for a while?"

Once settled, she asked again, "What were you boys discussing?"

"Mostly it was Skye's conversation." Pete reached over and twirled her curl around his finger.

"Stop that." Melissa pushed at his hand playfully and turned somber eyes in his direction. "You didn't tell Skye about Duane and Sandy?"

"I did. I said they were a couple."

"When were you going to add a little more than that?"

"Well now, Missy, I wasn't." She raised both eyebrows, and Pete continued, "I feel that an open mind and a gracious spirit are needed for acceptance. Your boy's not there yet, but..." he looked at her wisely. "Hold yourself a good thought now; he's getting' closer."

"You know, Pete, I'm real mad at him." She tapped her foot. "He should be taking responsibility for this little baby...for the life that he helped to create." Her voice rose, "It's not like him to try to duck out. He wasn't raised that way." Pete nodded as she continued, "Maybe I'm remiss. I could be straight-forward and tell Skye what I'm thinking."

"Nah. Boy doesn't need to know what you're thinkin'. He needs to figure out what he's thinkin'."

She gave the glider a gentle push. "At least he's talking now."

Pete's head bobbed up and down. "He's doin' a good job of that."

A light breeze from the ocean infused the air with freshness. They sipped their coffee drinks in silence until she spoke, "Problem isn't his alone. I'm a party in this situation, and I want to have a say."

Pete reached over and kissed her cheek. "I know that, Missy. But this may be a time when the less you say is best."

She wrinkled her forehead and frowned. "Are you asking me to suppress my parental knowledge?"

"I am." He faced her, tracing the angle of her chin with his finger. "Think you can do it?"

"Don't know. That's a big request."

Pete cleared his throat, "You know, Missy, I heard something in Skye's words today that I hadn't heard before."

"What's that?"

"He expressed concern for someone other than himself."

Melissa smiled to herself, and the glider shifted to one side as she slid over. "Skye's been away from home for a long time, both physically and in his heart." Resting her head on Pete's shoulder, she spoke softly, "One step at a time. It's all a mother can ask." A tiny squeak slipped from the overhead chains holding the glider to the ceiling boards of the porch. She asked, "You think that needs some oil?"

"Could be, but it sounds like a tomorrow job."

"No." Her words were gentle. "Let it go. It's a comfortable sound." She rose slowly. "I have an important engagement and must excuse myself." Beaming with joy she turned in the doorway. "I'm going clothes shopping for my granddaughter!" She called down the hall, "Angie, are you ready? You get to drive." Looking back at Pete, she added with a smile, "That's 'cause I've been drinking in the middle of the day. Shameless. Why, what's to become of a grandmother who does that?"

Pete winked. "I've got some ideas."

Big Sur, California
Stone House
Later that day

The shopping trip was a huge success, and Melissa and Angie carried in bags filled with dresses, toys, baby food, disposable diapers, and one helium filled balloon on a string.

"Our first stop was for a car seat." Angie showed Pete how it fit in the back and strapped into the seat belt. "It's way cool." She tramped back into the house as he turned to Melissa.

"Seems like you girls had a fine time."

"We did, and look what else I got." She pulled a pair of wraparound glasses out of a bag. "Got these at the drug store. Now we're matching. Plus, take a look at these. Angie found the tiniest sunglasses for Monique. They're pink, and they're shaped like stars. Isn't that adorable?"

"We can all wear 'em together when we take in the sunshine." He nodded at the balloon. "Babies like bright colors."

"Oh. It's for Skye. He always favored red balloons." Melissa smiled. "Apparently more than I knew." She motioned Pete to the side of the car and spoke in a low voice, "Angie bought Monique a pair of boots. They're similar to hers, not army surplus, but green and clunky. According to the clerk, if you take your six month old hiking, you want your baby to have proper footwear."

"But she can't walk yet."

Melissa looked at him with a grin. "Immaterial."

When they entered the kitchen, Angie held out a bag. "See what I found." Reaching in, she held up a white pinafore with the words 'Grandma's Angel' embroidered across the bodice. "This is just perfect for Monique. Is she awake? Can I put it on her?"

"Yup. And yup. Plus after I fed her applesauce, she was a mess so I gave her another bath. Now she's fresh as a daisy."

Big Sur, California
Stone House
That Evening

Skye invited Pete outside. The evening was pleasant and dark with only a few clouds. A sprinkle of stars fluttered overhead as the noisy sea splashed against the rocks. The men sat for a few minutes in silence.

Pete opened the conversation, "Say, it was nice of you to give your balloon to Monique."

"I owed her a red one."

He scratched his head. "How come?"

"To stop her from crying."

"Must have worked. She's quiet as a church mouse now."

"You should have heard her this morning. She gave me a panic attack." He shook his head. "Scared the hell out of me."

"Your daughter's got a good set of lungs." Pete nodded happily and continued, "Probably means she's got good teeth."

"Really?"

"Nah."

****

As the clouds passed, the dome of the heavens opened, and Skye spotted the Big Dipper. "It's made up of seven stars." He let his mind wander back to when he was a boy. "The last star in the handle of the dipper is called Polaris. It's the North Star, and if you follow it..." His finger traced a path across the glowing light. "See, there's another star called Cassiopeia. That's actually a constellation, and it represents a queen of great beauty who lived in a mythological Greek land."

Pete followed the trail of stars as Skye continued, "Cassiopeia was married to King Cepheus, and they had a daughter named Princess Andromeda. But Cassiopeia, the mom, was not so nice. She was stuck on herself... puffed up with her good looks." He paused in mid-thought while Pete waited.

"Well, don't stop there. You've got my interest. Seems story telling runs in your family," Pete said.

"It's been a long time since I looked at the stars." Skye settled back, his head tilted up. "Cassiopeia claimed she was prettier than the Nereids." He smiled and added, "They were gorgeous sea nymphs."

"You don't say?"

"On a scale of one to ten, they were off the charts. Anyhow, Cassiopeia's attitude didn't go over so good because Neptune, who was fond of his sea nymphs, got mad and sent a sea monster, Cetus, to destroy Cassiopeia's land. But she had a way out. She and the king had to sacrifice their daughter to save their kingdom." He paused, again.

Pete urged him on, "So what happened next?"

"Well, Cassiopeia had Andromeda tied to a rock, but just before the sea monster got her, she was saved by Perseus." Skye looked at Pete. "That's the equivalent of a tall, dark, handsome stranger."

"I figured that out."

"The one who was punished was Cassiopeia. Neptune chained her to her throne then tossed her in the sky. She spends half of her time hanging upside down." Skye took another deep breath. "The end."

"Shoot. That's some story. You pick that skill up from your mom?"

"Must have."

Pete waved at a soft blanket of light falling across the darkness. "I think that's the Milky Way."

"It has Cygnus, a northern constellation lying on the plane of the Milky Way. Cygnus is Greek for swan." Skye stretched his legs out in front of him. "It's more recognizable in summer because it has an asterism known as the Northern Cross." He added quietly, "My dad taught me that stuff. We used to sit out here for hours and talk."

"Harm had a good soul." Pete nodded. "He was a loyal friend and a person you could count on."

The men grew silent allowing their personal memories to share the night.

Chapter Seventeen

Chicago, Illinois
Covington Residence
Same night

Delaney sobbed in her mother's arms, lamenting the loss of her wedding, her scandalous personal embarrassment, and her love for Skye, in that order, while Terri Sue Ellen offered tissues and wished her daughter would stop carrying on so much. It had become tedious listening to her wailings. Besides, her tee time had been moved to seven am, and she needed a good night's sleep.

"Enough now. Shush. Daddy is sending you off to your favorite city for a bit of work, and you'll need to move forward as a true von Campe/Covington woman." Waving air, she looked at her daughter. "Oh honey, do leave this dreary problem behind you. Ah know that's what you want. Head held high, some fabulous new clothes..." *And a romance with a French escort to take your mind off your situation. It will set you straight! That's the God's truth.*

She smiled patiently thinking about a hole in one.

Charles patted his daughter in a clumsy fashion. "There, there, Doodle Bug. It will all work out."

She wailed plaintively, "How could he choose that baby and his mother over me? That's like putting me last!"

Terri Sue Ellen pushed Delaney toward her father. "You have a turn with her frettin'. It's gettin' late, but as this seems to be ongoin,' ah will freshen our drinks mah self. Ah've been noticin' that Maria has been short-pourin' in mah glass. Plus, there's no callin' for anyone other than us to witness the outpourin' of misery inflicted by that thoughtless cur that you hired."

"So much for family support," he murmured.

"Don't you go gettin' crusty-like with me, Chucky!" She shot back as she walked out of the room.

Charles held his daughter and felt the time had come to suggest she might employ a less aggressive approach to relationships. Still it galled him to realize that his future son-in-law had elected to handle *this* situation without his advice. Oh sure, he recognized the same traits in his son-in-law that he'd seen in himself at that age but, nonetheless, Skye should have confided in him.

Granted his daughter was not faultless, but she and Skye had made a damn fine match, and the rest would have worked itself out... to one degree or another. You had to take the bumps along with the smooth ride. He'd done it, hadn't he, and look at him now. He stopped short but pushed away his misgivings.

"Look at me, Delaney." He knew this would be a difficult conversation, so he began slowly. "You know, Doodle Bug, everything is not always about you." She lifted her misty green eyes toward him, and he relented. "But most things are. However, some instances involve others, like when we forgive people for making mistakes, we reap the rewards they give us for being kind." He cleared his throat and continued awkwardly, "You understand that applies to personal interaction not business links."

"Yes, Daddy," she hiccupped pitifully.

"In the corporate world, we must remain strong, but your personal partnership with Skye is different, and you must be patient and allow time for him to fix this, um'mm, uncomfortable state of affairs."

"Bad choice of words, Chucky." Terri Sue Ellen put the drinks on a side table with a slap of glasses that sent liquid spilling over. "Ah said bad!" She glared at her husband. "Enough of this mind-numbin' jibber jabber. Spit it out like a man. We're dealin' with a malfunction."

Charles ignored her and continued to hold his weeping daughter. He spoke softly, "Sometime, Doodle Bug, a little honey on your words is better than being so blunt. Of course, we all know Skye was wrong, and I'm sure he's just as distraught as you are but..."

Big Sur, California
Stone House

Same night

Skye looked peaceful when his mother came outside. She asked, "Wasn't Monique adorable in her pinafore?"

"Cute as a cookie," Pete replied.

"Nathalie was a beautiful woman."

"Someday, son." She put her hand on his shoulder and continued, "I want you to tell me about her. Not now. Timing isn't right, but someday it will be."

Nodding, he spread his hands. "Okay."

"Then I'll leave it there."

Skye pushed himself up. "Think I'll go to bed."

Dark puffs of clouds began to move in, smothering the twinkling stars. Melissa put her head on Pete's shoulder, and they watched as the moon pushed through an opening, appearing noble and remote while it cast shadows randomly across the land.

Big Sur California

Stone House

Following day

That morning, the call came from "Chuck" who identified himself as Charles Covington in a cool tone of voice and Skye immediately tensed up. *Oh shit! This is it.*

Charles wasted no time on amenities. "Do I understand that the wedding is on hold for now?"

"Yes, sir."

He talked about his daughter's broken heart and the numerous repercussions of the break-up, both emotional and financial.

"I'm sorry. I wish I could fix this faster, but I can't." Skye shook his head. "I have to work this out before my life can go forward."

"Take some time away from the job." It was a curt reply, and Skye felt a wave of coldness shoot through the phone.

"Yes, sir. I will, and I will call Delaney as soon as I have some news."

"Don't wait too long." The phone went dead.

Feeling the need to get away, Skye spent the rest of the morning outside. This time he let the warm softness of early summer cling to him as he walked around the stone house. He realized with some surprise that the booming sounds of the surf were not as annoying as he remembered.

When he returned home, he stopped to look at the trailing vines and wondered if the ollalieberries were still as sweet as he recalled. *What an odd thought. Next I'll be wanting to plant some myself and maybe grow tomatoes in pots on the nineteenth floor of my condo. Wait. It isn't really my condo. It's actually Delaney's condo.*

By the time he appeared at the kitchen door for lunch, he'd admitted to himself that the phone call had carried a measure of relief. It seemed too bad that Chuck was once again Charles, but a soon-to-be father-in-law would be called Chuck...a man to share a cigar with. An ex-employee would refer to the boss as Charles and hope for a decent referral.

Yeah, as if that would happen after screwing up the wedding of the century!

He raked his fingers through his hair. Instead of waiting for the axe to fall, he was pretty sure it had happened. After all, there were lots of ways to say 'you're fired.' Now he was free to get on with his life, even though it was no prize at the moment. Or, his hope sprang high for a second, had it been just a warning call from Delaney's father?

Same Day
Late Morning

Melissa noticed that her son had some healthy color in his face for the first time since he'd arrived home. She smiled to herself, thinking that the visit was good for him, even if he didn't know it. He hadn't bothered to shave but had changed into his clean clothes...a definite step in the right direction. His shirt was still wrinkled from the dryer, and she made a mental note to press it then reminded herself he was no longer a child.

He watched his mother's face as it changed expression for no reason. "Mom, you okay?"

"Of course." She hesitated, not wishing to pry into his life, but losing the battle, she asked, "Are you?"

"Yeah, sure." He shifted his weight from one foot to the other. "Can I camp out here for a while?" He hadn't meant to spit out the question like that, but there it was. He joked, "I really don't mind the house tilting to the north."

She rolled her eyes. "That's surely a comfort to my heart."

Resting his hand on her shoulder he added, "You might as well hear it from me first. I'm on official leave."

She nodded. "Do you want some lunch?"

"Aw, mom." He lowered his head glumly. "Is feeding me going to make it better?"

"Yes."

"Well," he looked up and grinned sheepishly. "I can always eat."

Chicago, Illinois
Covington Home
Same Day

"Just what do you mean you gave Skye *personal* time!" Terry Sue Ellen squealed. "How do you think all those German castles got built if mah royal relatives went around givin' personal time to their staff?"

"He's not staff, mother. He's my finance."

"Same thing."

"Calm down, sugar."

"Ah will do no such thing! As ah am clearly the only one who has the thorough knowledge of this debacle, ah must take command. Truth be told, the boy needs us to help him cover-up his escapade with the floozy."

"French girlfriend, mother."

"That what ah said!" Looking at her husband, she glowered, "What's happenin' here?"

Charles nodded tiredly at his wife. "Skye has to make some choices."

"You bet he does, but not without us in the driver's seat! Who else is goin' marry our daughter?" The screech in her voice escalated, "If you give Skye personal time, he could have babies all over this world!" She shook her head and scowled "Ah declare. Here ah was worried about his sexual proficiency."

"What, mother?"

"Nothin'."

She leaned closer to Charles. "See here, that boy should be on a plane headin' to Chicago with a box of chocolates and a bouquet of roses beggin' our little girl to take him back. Ah've got it! You send him a bonus check so he can buy an expensive please-forgive-me-item-of-jewelry for Delaney. Why is it ah have to do all the thinkin' in this family? Maria, get me a valium!"

Charles nodded at Delaney who sat quietly next to him. "No, mother. I need time, and Skye does, too."

"What! That's the silliest thing ah ever heard." Her voice turned into a wail, "And wrr-oo-ng." She pulled extra syllables out of the word before turning back to her daughter. "Who gave you an idea like that?" Putting her face close to Delaney, she hissed, "You haven't told anyone about this, have you?"

"I really don't have any close girlfriends to talk to."

"Good! " She made an effort to pull herself together and reached over to hold her daughter's hand. "Ah have mah own story that ah'm fixin' to put out. Ah just haven't perfected it yet but..."

Delaney interrupted, "I've thought about it, and Skye and I need a hiatus in our relationship"

"Your daddy can buy you one of those. He can get you whatever you need." She reached up and held her daughter's face in both hands. "Now, honey, let's just stay on point here. Don't go wanderin' off 'cause that kind of thinkin' confuses the hell out'ta the real issue."

She ignored her mother's outburst and continued, "I'm upset because Skye remained with his mother to work on the adoption idea, and he's mad at me because he thinks I've overstepped the boundaries of our relationship. What I'm saying, mother, is there's a lot to work out. We both have opinions that must be addressed."

"Chuck, honey, are you listen' to this?" Terri Sue Ellen stood up and gulped the pill then dismissed Maria. "Off you go, now. Attend to something else." Looking wildly around the room, she seemed befuddled. "Why are we askin' Skye's opinion, anyhow? Where'd all this righteous do-goodin' come from?" She backed up and pointed at her chest. "Certainly not from mah side of the family. Truth be told, it doesn't amount to a hill of beans what Skye thinks."

"Yes, it does." Delaney smiled weakly. "Because it takes two people to make a relationship work."

"It does not! It takes power to make a match and bushels full of money to keep it rock solid. You can buy your way into anything. All successful people know that! Oh, for goodness sake, get me mah maid. Ah've no idea why she runs off like that. " She walked over to the door and shouted, "Maria, bring me a cold compress for mah head. All this agitation is bringin' on a hot flash. Step lively!"

"There, there, sugar," Charles murmured. "You need a nap."

Key West, Florida
Robert and Evelyn Covington Residence

Evelyn rolled up her yoga mat, put it away, and walked into the kitchen. "You should try it, Robert. Just because we're eighty doesn't mean we can't do the simple stretches. It's an excellent way to achieve a healthy flow of energy throughout one's body."

He put the cell phone on the counter and faced his wife. "That was Charles. He spoke with the young man and gave him time off to think."

"Good idea."

Robert poured a glass of orange juice and offered it to his wife. "Terri Sue Ellen got on the phone; she wants to sue for wedding costs."

Evelyn let out her breath. "Was she sober?" She took a sip and put the glass down.

"I also spoke with our granddaughter. She's distraught that her fiancée is staying in Big Sur with his mother and her gentlemen friend. However, he's looking for someone to adopt the baby."

"All that sounds reasonable as long as Terry Sue Ellen isn't involved."

Robert's brow's knit together. He removed his glasses and pinched the bridge of his nose. "Ahh, it seems there's also a young woman who is helping out with the child."

"That makes sense."

"She has a nose ring and purple hair that's shaped into points. They refer to her as a Pottery Nanny."

"Huh?" She stared at her husband.

"You're up to speed." He smiled. "Care to join me for a walk?"

The Florida sunshine spilled between white clouds, heating the day. Robert held the door open for his wife then reached for her hand. "You know, Evelyn, perhaps I will try some gentle yoga."

Big Sur, California
Stone House
Same Day
Noon

Skye carried the glasses of tea to the table, "I'd like to see Duane again and meet Sandy."

Pete looked up from slicing tomatoes, "They're drivin' down for dinner and usually spend the night in your old room."

Skye winked. "Oh. I get it. You want me to give up my bed." Melissa turned toward Pete, and Skye added, "No problem. I can camp on the floor. Besides, it'll be nice to see a happy couple...especially one without major issues."

"Pete!" Melissa raised her head, giving him a long look. "Speak up. Now's the time."

Clearing his throat, Pete smiled. "Your mom wants you to know that she's fixin' chicken and dumplings tonight. It'll be real good. Mark my words on that."

"Peterson!" Melissa hitched her thumb toward Skye. "Tell him." She looked stern. "You're sliding on the issues."

"Missy, I don't slide on issues." Pete finished slicing the last tomato and carefully set the knife aside. "Skye, you should be advised that these are store bought tomatoes. Good ones, mind you, but not as sweet as the ones we grow."

"This is your last warning." She placed both hands on her hips.

"Well now." Pete straightened his shoulders. "If that's the way you're goin' be, I'll get right to it." He hitched his fingers into imaginary suspenders and posed.

"Quit your foolin' around. Talk to him."

"Come over here, Skye." He motioned toward two chairs. "Why don't you sit down? Your mother feels that we should talk some about Sandy and Duane."

"Not yet. Let me cleanup for lunch. I might even tuck in my shirt." He grinned at his mother. "Oh, I saw the look you gave me earlier, but at least I'm in fresh clothes." He glanced down and added, "Though slightly wrinkled." Bending over, he kissed the top of her head. "And I promise to look for my belt." Raising his hands in surrender, he added quietly, "You know that Delaney is very upset, and official leave really means..." He left the thought hanging.

"The job goes with the girl." Melissa smiled sadly.

"Yes. I think that's a good assumption." He pushed two fingers against a spot over his eye and released them as if to rid himself of the pressure that was building. "I could also lose a lifestyle that I worked hard to get." Turning to go, he added, " I have a lot to think about."

Pete spread mayonnaise on the toasted wheat bread and added lettuce and tomato as Skye walked down the hall to his room. "Well, Missy, maybe we'll wait till after lunch to tell him."

"Uh-huh." Melissa generously layered crisp slices of bacon on the sandwiches. "Sandy and Duane will be here about five o'clock" She glanced at Pete and narrowed her eyes. "That's something you'll need to remember in your timeframe." Carrying the plates to the table, she paused and added. "Isn't that so?"

She set the dishes down and picked up the bowl of thickly sliced potato chips, distributing them among the sandwich plates.

"Now Missy, you aren't going to be a stickler for punctuality on this. Are you?"

"I do believe that I am." She moved toward the sink, stopped, and turned to look at him. The small gesture was not lost.

Skye was back within minutes. He sat down and started to eat at the kitchen table. "You know BLTs are a favorite of mine; plus I've missed these homemade chips." He wiped at his mouth and added, "Ah, don't take this wrong." He glanced up. "But I looked in on the baby, and, mm, she's sleeping. I guess that's good. Right? Anyhow, you should know...she's, ahh, got some green, ugly shoes on her feet."

Melissa raised an eyebrow, and Skye shrugged.

"I can't imagine why she'd be wearing anything like that. The gypsy had on similar boots," Skye said. His brows knit in puzzlement. "Some kind of special shoe, maybe?" Turning to his mom, he asked, "Maybe they both have foot problems? Damn!" he sat back looking surprised. "I probably shouldn't have picked on Angie's shoes. Her feet are deformed! That's why she got so upset and called me names."

Melissa looked from Skye to Pete. "What's he talking about?"

"I got this one." Pete turned to Skye. "Neither Angie nor Monique have foot problems. No health issues of any kind."

"Yeah. Well, that's good 'cause you want that baby to be in top shape so people will like her." Skye shivered. "She can get real loud. She's powerful for a little person."

"Thank you, Skye." Pete cut him off and continued, "Now here, have some more of those chips. Your mom does 'em up, oh, maybe once a month or so. Fries 'em in avocado oil and tosses 'em in Black Lava salt."

"Whoa! Cholesterol, carbs and salt–not good for a body."

Melissa watched her son dig into the chips and start on his second sandwich. She commented, "It's always good to be informed. And you seem well versed on a number of subjects."

"He is, indeed." Pete nodded.

"Oh, I almost forgot." She continued to look at her son with a half-smile. "I was to give you a message from Angie."

Skye held the sandwich halfway to his mouth and stiffened. "What did she want?"

"Why, she wanted you to know that she had an early lunch." Melissa looked muddled as she continued. "I can't imagine why she wanted you to know that."

"Yeah. Well, that's 'cause she's strange." He rolled his eyes. "She makes me very nervous. I don't like that." He glanced around. "Where is she now?"

"Pottery class."

"That's a good place for her. She can take out her frustrations on the clay. Truth is that short people can be pushy and bossy. She tried to stand up to me earlier. Pete can tell you."

"Yup. She did."

Melissa shook her head as Skye wiped his hands on a paper napkin and continued, "You always used cotton napkins."

"Yes, but times have changed." Glancing at him, she teased, "I've got a lot on my plate. Living on the edge, inviting frightening people into my home, searching for bullets... I had to table the cotton napkins. Couldn't risk more stress with all that washing and ironing."

"I hear you." He crunched a potato chip. "It's good to know your position on cotton versus paper."

Melissa nodded causally at Pete. "Did you follow that conversation?"

"Best I could. Business phrases are difficult for me to keep up with." He pushed back from the table. "Why, Missy, I had no idea you could talk like that... throwing around those thirty something catchwords."

"I'm just chock full of surprises. And speaking of surprises..." She focused an intense glare in his direction. "Peterson, I think you have a little something you want to say."

Skye wiped his mouth and looked up from his plate. "Let's skip to the bottom line."

"Good by me." Pete gave Melissa a playful glance. "That means getting to the end of the subject."

"I know that!"

"Just checkin'." His blue eyes shined with humor. "Your boy has somethin' he wants to add before I get down to sayin' my piece." Leaning forward, he continued, "This is the second business meeting he's had in the last couple days. Truth be told, I haven't seen this much commotion in your kitchen since you lost your datebook, and the ladies from the B. S. Garden Club came on the same day you were having Church Circle." He faced Skye. "Sorry for the cuss word but your mom is into some radical groups."

"Stop it! Skye knows B.S. stands for Big Sur. Don't you?"

"Ahh. Sure."

Taking a deep breath, her eyebrows arched as she gave Pete a final look of warning. "Might be I'll have to step in here."

"Mom, look. I've got something that needs to be said." Skye carefully placed his napkin next to his plate. "Delaney didn't leave me because I had a child by someone else. She left because I couldn't act on a decision about the baby in a timely manner. Mom." His deep brown eyes looked directly at her. "A child needs parents who are young enough to raise a baby to adulthood... strong enough to go through the ups and downs of whatever it takes. Look at me. I was trial and error, but you were fresh and could appreciate the challenge. A little girl in this day and age could be a lot of trouble. You know how stubborn girls can be; you were young once."

Melissa's mouth dropped open, and Pete commented dryly, "Say again."

"What I'm telling you is that a girl could develop radical thoughts, date undesirables, and come home late at night. Whereas, when I think back, I was nearly perfect."

Melissa's eyebrows flew up. "Who are you talking about?"

She had more to say, but Skye continued, "If Sandy and Duane are interested in adoption, then you and Pete would still be a big part of Monique's life." His voice sounded empty. "It's probably the best I can come up with for now. I realize I sound selfish, but I'll need to put my life back together. And wherever I'm employed, I'll be away from home for weeks at a time." Shifting in the kitchen chair, he reached for his mother's hand. " It's laughable, isn't it? I can't fix my career or my life, but people pay me damn fine money to straighten out theirs." His brows knit. "The truth is I can't offer my expertise in what to do with a child, which I realize wouldn't be worth much anyhow until I got the hang of it. Oh, I know..." He waved his hands dismissively and continued, "There are a lot of sites I could visit. But even then, I'd still be gone most of the time." He shrugged. "Sure, I know I could email you my words of wisdom, but that's probably not the same as being here."

"Really." Melissa shook her head. "A few weeks online and you'd know how to rear a child." She blinked at Skye with an expression bordering on amusement. "And you could email me advice. Did I get that right?"

"I think so."

She let his words settle around her and smiled. "There's a lot to consider even when I toss out most of what you just said. But you need to realize that it's important to understand that I have a say." A thoughtful expression settled across her face, and she finished with, "I'm going to think about it some more before I answer you."

He was relieved that no immediate discussion followed as he helped clear the table.

Pete whispered in her ear, "I had no idea he was a flawless child. Weren't you the lucky one?"

Big Sur, California
Stone House
After Lunch

"Guess I'll take a drive this afternoon. You know, check out the old haunts? What time should I be back for dinner?"

Melissa rinsed the dishes. "Duane and Sandy will be here around five, so dinner won't be 'til late. Maybe six-thirty or seven."

"That's not late, mom." He laughed. "Trust me."

Cheerfully she replied, "Late enough. Sandy is going to bake a pie, and that will take time."

"Hey, good to know she can bake!"

"Peterson! Come here," she shouted down the hall then faced her son. "Pete has a little something he'd like to talk to you about."

"How about I catch him when I get home?"

She smiled wearily as she watched her son leave, wishing he had put on socks and ironed his shirt. *Adult children are... well,* she reasoned, *they still need work.*

After the screen door shut, Pete appeared from around the corner.

'Well, now," she added sarcastically. "Isn't that just miraculous how you showed up after Skye left?" She began to load the dishwasher. "Didn't you hear me call you?"

"I did." He leaned forward and kissed her cheek. "Here let me do that for you."

"Peterson!"

"I got here fast as I could."

"Where were you?" She folded her arms across her chest. "The ends of the Earth."

"Nope. I was in the bathroom."

"Oh Pete!" Making a face, shook her head. "You should have told him." She ran water over the clean sponge and started to wipe the mayo off the table's surface. "Skye went to check on his old hangouts. That's showing some interest in his childhood in Big Sur." Looking imploringly at Pete, she added, "Don't you think he's made progress?"

"Yup. I do." Pete's sunny blue eyes shined with pleasure. "I'm glad we're both heading toward the adoption idea. Sooner or later we've got to face that we're not exactly spring chickens." He folded his arms across his chest and did a Do-si-do around her. "On the other hand, we're not old geezers either. Heck, I still work full time."

"Oh Pete." She sat down at the table. "You should be at the school now, instead of babysitting me."

"Nope. Not today. Got two student assistants taking over and my chief potter monitoring them. All's well at the school."

"Then I'm glad you're here." She rested her head in her hands, "I feel... well, vulnerable."

He massaged her shoulder, "It's going to be okay. You know, Missy, the party ain't over 'til the fat lady sings. Tell ya what we'll do. Let's take the little one out to the rocker and give her some Big Sur cuddlin'."

"Don't you mean B. S. cuddling?"

"No, ma'am. I'm cleaning up my words so the baby's ears won't pick up any of this blasphemy you're tossing around."

"Really, Pete?"

He grinned as she shook her head and smiled back. "I'm glad we shared the news of the baby with Duane and Sandy early on, even if it was difficult to fill them in on Delaney Covington and Nathalie LaVeron."

"Yup. It was best to get it all out in the open."

"When your son asked if we planned to raise the little one and you said 'sure enough,' well, Pete, I heard Duane's pause. It was clearly an expression of concern."

Handing her the wrap-around glasses, he nodded. "So it was. But when I talked with him about adopting Monique, it's like I said, there was hesitation in his voice."

"Yes, but he sounded better this morning."

"He and Sandy discussed the idea, and of course, they're in favor of adopting, but they're worried Skye will change his mind. After the surrogate decided to keep her baby, it was real rough on them." Pete shook his head. "Oh sure, it made 'em stronger the way a tragedy will, but still in all, they've been together six years, and they want children...not more heartache."

"I understand." Melissa closed her eyes and spoke thoughtfully, "Having everyone meet tonight will tell the tale."

"Your boy's come up with a sound plan."

She moved toward the kitchen door and turned with a thoughtful expression on her face. "I do believe that would make us "official" grandparents."

"Until your son has babies."

She smiled woefully. "If he marries Delaney, I don't think she'll share grandchildren with me. She doesn't want to share my son with anyone other than her family so I imagine it will be the same with any children she would have. I think she's insecure and compensates by associating only with the people who support her one hundred percent." She grimaced and looked at Pete. "In good conscience, I cannot do that."

"Well now, that's a piece of truth I agree with, but this old world is a strange place. Things can get switched around then straightened out. Delaney Covington has a lot to learn. Let's not fret about it yet. What say I call Duane and give him a heads-up on the situation? When I talked with him this morning, he told me that they're bringing Monique a special present." Her tiny waking cry rang through the air. "We need to get us one of those baby monitors. They're very popular."

"Oh poo. I can hear my granddaughter just fine. House isn't that big."

Pete nodded. "You go on out and get comfy. I'll change our little one and bring her along. Then I'll make that phone call."

****

Fat trumpet vines looped through the overhead trellis, offering a tangle of orange blossoms that shimmered in the freckled sun light. Melissa settled comfortably in the old rocking chair and listened to the music of the ocean. The serenity of the moment melted into the herb scented corners of her front porch.

Pete carried Monique outside, gently placing her in Melissa's arms. The baby's pretty brown eyes held an enquiring look. Tiny hands reached up to grab the stuffed doll Melissa held out.

Pete asked, "You make that?"

"I did. Found some material in my sewing basket and stuffed it in a sock, stitched on a face and, voila, created a little doll."

He joked, "It's no Barbie."

"No. It isn't."

"I don't think it's a learning toy, either."

"Well, I differ with that thought. Little girls cuddle with their dolls. It's a might difficult to snuggle up with a toy computer and give it kisses." Monique cooed cheerfully causing her grandmother to smile. "Learnin' comes in all stages. Oh, I know it's an old fashioned thought, but the old and the new should meet, don't you think?"

Wisps of clouds mingled in idleness within the blue sky, and a lifestyle of the past settled comfortably into the day.

"As soon as you make that call to Duane, come on back and sit down."

She patted the chair next to hers. "We'll practice doing nothing."

Nodding happily, he added, "That's a concept I like."

****

Skye pointed the rental car in the direction of the local watering hole. He admitted only to himself that he'd felt odd when he'd used the word "Monique." It had created a feeling of protectiveness toward the infant. That wasn't right! Caring about a baby was definitely an emotion he didn't want to develop. His father's words came thundering through his mind, "A man's worth is measured by what he does."

Big Sur, California
Joe's Saloon and Eatery
Afternoon

With the early summer heat holding for another day, the cool dark interior of Joe's Saloon and Eatery was a welcome relief. Skye inhaled the smells of malt and beer and thought about the Moose Lodge where his dad had taken him when they'd had a manly day out. He remembered himself as the little boy with scuffed knees who would climb onto a bar stool and order a soda. It would come in a tall frosted glass filled with ice cubes. Refills were free.

Smiling, he walked up to the bar of the modern day saloon and sat on a red vinyl stool, letting his legs straddle the metal frame.

When Joe Campbell heard the bell ring announcing a customer, he came out of the back room, holding a bar towel and paused in disbelief. "Skye? What are you doing here grinning like a fool? What the hell's on your mind?"

"Joe!" Skye extended a hand to his high school buddy. "Joe Campbell! You look good, man. Better then you should!"

Joe slapped Skye on the shoulder. "Long time, no see. Come here." The men exchanged a hug and laughed. "Hey, I heard you took up city life with gusto. Much like quarterbacking at Carmel High."

Skye laughed. "Yes and no. As I recall the old football team finished last in their league."

"Shoot, man. Someone's got to be last."

"Guess that's so." Skye hesitated before responding, "I never thought about it like that." Turning the conversation to a less problematic subject, he added, "Hey, what's with you running your dad's bar? What happened to the restaurant?"

"We call it an eatery now. Better wording, gets more business." He nodded toward the back. "We're in the process of another update to the outside dining area. Besides, this is my second job. My accounting office is in Carmel,. but I've got an office staff and two other CPAs who can run it after tax season when my folks take off in their RV." He laughed. "That's when I become their official hired hand. It's their idea of pay back for the student loans that I don't have, thanks to their generosity. Anyhow, they got themselves a pooch and took up cruisin' the back roads of America."

Skye had a concerned look on his face as he leaned forward. "You ever hear them talk about New Zealand?"

"Hell, I don't think so." Joe grinned, "Truth is, you try to raise your folk's right. Give them the best years of your life, and look what happens. They reach a certain age and get unruly. No telling where they'll go off to."

"Isn't that the truth."

"So, I heard that your mom's been teaching some classes about Big Sur history at the college. She always knew her stuff. You remember the stories she'd tell us?"

"Sure. But that was when we were kids, and everything seemed interesting."

"Some things still are." Joe tossed the towel next to the sink behind the bar. "You got yourself some color, but you still look like shit. Wrinkled shit."

"What are you? A fashion consultant?"

"Hey! When I saw you come in, I thought you'd lost your belt. Did you also give up shaving?"

Skye laughed. "I'm not wearing socks either."

"Damn, you used to look good, man."

Joe looked about the same...tall, lean, and still sporting an easy smile. When was that? Seven or eight years ago? For a moment, Skye wondered how his mother let him out of the house looking so sloppy. "Hey, let me explain my appearance..."

"Nah. I can see you're a bum." Laughter followed. "Heard you're engaged."

"Not exactly." Forcing energy into his tone, he kept going, "But what about you? Family?"

Joe beamed, letting the happiness he felt fill the room. "Married Susan Franklund."

"That's great" Skye thought for a minute. "Our homecoming queen. Right? At'ta way to go!"

"Sure enough." Joe reached for a framed photo under the bar. "Got twin daughters."

"Whoa. Two, huh?"

"That's the way twins usually come. Here, take a look. Alexandra and Abigail. Prettiest little things you ever saw. Three years old this summer."

Skye experienced a feeling of self-reproach as he held the picture that was extended to him. He studied the faces of the little girls, as a deluge of emotions flooded through him.

Joe penetrated his thoughts. "You drinkin' beer?"

He forced his hand to be steady as he handed the frame back. "Beautiful children."

"Thanks. Susan's just started to work again...a part-time teaching job so she can get out of the house. She can also meet her friends, go shopping, and be in adult company. Our parents are great baby sitters, when they're around. I never thought my folks would be so into traveling." He added with a sigh, "And then there's Susan's parents. Shoot, they plan to spend a month in Europe this fall. Where's that coming from?"

"Huh?" Skye sucked on his bottom lip as he considered what Joe was saying. "You'd sort of think they'd stay home and appreciate the peace and quiet they never had when we were around. His laugh was unsteady. "Recently I learned that my mom was thinking of buying a sports car. I can't figure it out."

Joe shrugged. "So how about that beer?"

"Got wine?"

"Nah. Don't go there." He pointed in the direction of a box labeled red.

Skye nodded in understanding. "Draft?"

"Good choice."

While Joe poured frosty mugs, Skye recalled how their college discussions of wine versus beer and tequila would end with both of them drinking too much and being carried back to the frat house by their dates. He wondered if Joe ever recalled those innocent college days when they thought they had all the answers.

"Hey, wake up." Joe set the mug in front of him, "You with me or spaced out?"

"Not only am I with you, I can still do a shot and a beer and see you two to one."

"Bull! Joe went over to the door and flipped the closed sign toward the outside. "Let's see you put your money where your mouth is, city slick."

"Can you do that? Just close up?"

"It's not every day an old friend wanders in here and challenges me to a drink-off that he's going to lose." He moved behind the bar and looked at Skye with a grin. "Get ready to taste defeat."

Chapter Eighteen

Chicago, Illinois
Covington House

Terri Sue Ellen woke from a nap to an empty bedroom. She felt cranky and her head hurt. The drapes were drawn to shut out the light, but Maria was working in the closet folding fresh clothes and quietly sliding them into built-in drawers.

"Maria! Prepare mah bath. Wait! Find mah husband first. No, hold on. Help me up."

"Si, Mrs. Covington." She moved toward the bed and grabbed her employer's arm to pull her to a sitting position.

"Not so fast!" Terri Sue Ellen sounded cantankerous as she leaned forward. "You go on and fix mah bath, and I'll look for mah husband." She got out of bed with great effort and headed toward the door. "Chuck!" She yelled irritably, "Where are you?"

He responded through the bedroom intercom, "Right here, sugar. In the second floor library."

"Where?"

"Two doors down at the end of the hall."

"Ah know where it is! Just hold yourself there and listen real good." She faced the intercom as Maria helped steady her balance. "Chucky, the situation with Skye needs some tweekin' before we can turn it over to our daughter. Ah'm about to join you. Maria!" she screeched over her shoulder, causing the maid to jump. "Oh, there you are. Get me something for mah head! It feels too big."

Terri Sue Ellen shook off her maid and stumbled down the hall, entering the library where Charles looked up from his book.

"You have not handled this well, Chucky. Not at all. Encouraging Delaney to think Skye had a say in things was wrong! It was out and out misleadin'. We got us enough problems with our daughter without givin' her an incorrect idea. Are you hearin' what ah'm sayin'?"

"We need to stay out of it."

"We do not!"

Charles stood up and moved toward the window. "I'm going to the office to catch up on work. Delaney has gone home, and she'll handle whatever happens next with Skye."

"Have you gone crazy? Ah'm through mollycoddlin' you with this ongoin' confusion about who's in charge of what." She sank into the nearest chair as Maria appeared with water and aspirin. "Give that to me and stop fussin' with mah bath. Do as ah tell you, and lay out mah clothes. Go on now." Turning to her husband she continued, "Delaney and ah will join you."

Maria was in the doorway when Terri Sue Ellen stopped her.

"Just where in tarnation did you think you were headed? Honestly, Maria, pay attention. Ah want you to call mah daughter quick-like. Tell her to meet me at the company compound. This here is a family emergency and requires our sprightly attention."

Charles looked at his disheveled wife and sighed noisily.

"This embarrassment is pressin' unkindly against mah southern heritage. A cancelled weddin' makes me look stupid, and ah will not be havin' any of that! Chucky, do you realize that Skye could be telling other people about us?"

"No. I don't think he'd discuss this with anyone other than his mother. It's not exactly dinner party conversation."

"Well, no worries there," she huffed. "Ya got'ta think farther then the end of your nose, for Pete's sake. It remains a good thing that ah studied history. Indians don't throw dinner parties unless it's late in November."

Big Sur, California
Joe's Saloon and Eatery

After a few beers and a few shots, the men were buzzing, but still in control. Joe knew about the 'surprise' baby and Delaney's anger, the questionable engagement, and the potential loss of Skye's job.

Skye wasn't through talking, "You haven't heard this part. When I first got home, I walked into my mom's kitchen, and she wasn't alone. There was this short, bald guy there cutting expensive cheese."

"So you think he was a bad influence?"

"Oh, shit yes! Way bad." He leaned forward in a confidential manner. "You see, there was no reason for anyone to be at her house. She hasn't been exposed to a lot of men because most of her time was spent being my mom, and I like to think that was heartwarming and gratifying as well as enjoying."

"Well," Joe scratched at his chest. "As I remember, you provided lots of entertainment for everyone."

Skye focused on his friend's blurred face and grumbled, "The guy in the kitchen was Pete Bailey." He belched into his hand. "S'cuse my poor manners. Point is, now get this; they're living together. Can you believe that crap?"

"Yeah. Everyone knows that."

"Damn!" He finished the beer, sitting the empty mug on the bar with a thump. "That's wrong on all levels."

"Why? I lived with Susan. You lived with..." Joe's thoughts were garbled. "Well, let's just say more than one lady." He drew two more drafts and cut fresh limes for the tequila.

Skye's eyes narrowed. "This is my mother I'm talking about. I hold her to a higher set of values."

"Higher than what?"

"Higher than ours for damn sure!"

"I don't understand." Joe leaned forward and his elbows slid off the wet bar. "Can you be more precise?"

"Sure I can. There's a parental code of ...hmmm...proper behavior that needs to be... give me a minute, Joe." Skye straightened up. "It needs to be maintained for the family concept to remain, umm," he hiccupped, "...strong." His shoulders slumped forward as he looked out of blurry eyes. "As I see it, my mom hasn't thought of anyone other than herself."

"Huh." Joe wiped at the water rings. "So, other than your mom is living with an old time family friend, how's it feel to be home?"

Skye wearily wrapped both hands around his beer. "To tell you the truth," he blew air through his lips, "now that I'm back here, I feel..." He massaged his forehead. "Like there's been something missing in my life." He placed a hand over his heart and leaned forward unsteadily.

Joe poured them both another shot of tequila and asked, "What?"

"It's the kind of peace that comes from deep within. If you have it, you know you can handle anything." Skye's sampled the cold beer. "My parents had it. They were happy here in Big Sur." Shaking his head to clear his thoughts, he added impatiently, "But not me. No sir." He wiped the foam from his lips with the back of his hand." When I was a kid, I wondered if I was adopted."

"That's bull."

"Yeah. I know."

"You moved on, man. You did your own thing."

He nodded with a lop-sided grin. "But now that I'm back, I think I've been substituting power and wealth for what's missing in my heart." Pausing, he frowned. "Did I just say that?"

Coming around the bar, Joe sat on the stool next to him.

Feeling that he might have the spinning sensation under control Skye looked up. "You see," he leaned his elbows on the bar. "I thought I was right on track. You know, perfect job, perfect woman. Shit, there's even royalty in Delaney's family."

"Get out."

"Yeah." He tipped his head to the right. "But it might be all in her mother's head. She used to be some kind of fruit queen back in the day. Now there's a southern belle you don't want to meet."

Joe waved him on. "Let's hear the rest of this."

"I've got a Mercedes in the garage, great seats at the theater. Hell, we even had plans for an African photo safari next year." Skye stopped as if to play back what he'd said. "But I'm pretty sure it's all gone now." He looked at the dusty light as it filtered into the bar through half drawn shades. Reaching for the tequila, he downed it in one swallow. "Ahhh." He felt tears sting his eyes and wiped the corner of his mouth. "Whoa! Good stuff."

Joe nodded. "We've had worse." He raised his glass and knocked back the shot. "Damn!"

Shaking his head, Skye still felt the burn of the alcohol as Joe started to talk, "You're bullshitting me, right? I mean you're just telling me stuff like this 'cause I'm here in sleepy Carmel and you're in the big corporate world in Chicago. You do know that influential people from all over come here to play golf, right?"

Skye leaned forward. "Let me tell you a secret. I don't even like the sport, but I have to play it 'cause that's where the big deals are done... on the golf course."

Joe sat back and blinked at his friend. "I may be a small town guy, but, hell, even I know that. Seems to me what you got'ta decide is are you in the big city fast lane or here in Big Sur, what we call God's country." He grinned and sat up straighter. "I may have said something very profound just now."

"What if I need to be both places?"

"Then I guess you'll work it out."

"Yeah, well... I don't want to talk about it. Besides, I've got to get home. My mom's got company comin' for dinner." He turned to stand, but the room began to spin. "Or maybe I'll just sit here for a while longer."

Joe rested his head on the bar. "Now that's a good idea. I might even catch forty winks. Can you work the bar if anyone comes in?" He held up his index finger, "Oh yeah. That's right. We hung up the closed sign."

Both men sat in sluggish silence until Skye spoke, "Did I tell you that Duane and Sandy are coming for dinner? You remember Duane Bailey?"

"Yeah. Sure." Joe turned to face his friend but remained seated. "You two ripped out good plants the year you decided to be business men. Shoot, man, we still laugh about that!" He sat straight and looked at Skye. "Duane's a pediatrician, now, up in the city." He slapped the bar with his hand, "Now there's a boy who's here and there."

"I want Sandy and Duane to adopt my daughter."

"You want them to do...what'd ya say?"

Did I just say daughter again? Damn. He looked hard at Joe until he could pick out only one face. "Have you met either of them?"

Joe articulated slowly, "Yes, I have." Time passed while he thought about his options. "My grandma once told me that you shouldn't say anything about a person unless it's good. You know... keep your words sweet just in case you have to eat 'em?"

Skye gave a restless shrug. "So..."

"Don't confuse me." Joe gazed at his longtime friend. "Okay. Here goes." He raked his fingers through his hair and took a deep breath. "My wife says Duane is a lovely man, and Sandy has real nice taste. Is into cookin'."

"It's a comfort that Susan likes them." Skye waited, and when it was clear that was all Joe had to say, he asked, "What do you think of Duane?"

Joe fished for words as he turned the shot glass around. "Guess I'd have to say... very well educated. A caring person. He stopped in the bar with Sandy a few months back, and we got to talking. I mentioned how the twins had a cold, and he said he'd look in on them. It was a real nice thing to do. "

"A good doctor, huh? And Sandy?"

"The same. A caring person."

"Anything else?" Skye was leaning forward at an awkward angle.

"Ahh..." Joe struggled to focus clearly. "Both of them wear expensive shoes."

"I got expensive shoes."

"The ones you got on look like crap."

"Yeah, well, that's 'cause I keep the good ones in Chicago." Skye attempted to stand up but not without the aid of his hands pushing himself from the bar. "Understand they can't have children of their own." He tipped his head and asked, "You hear that?"

"Yup. That'd be about right." Joe straightened himself on the stool. "I got more to say."

Skye was finally on his feet. He felt a bit shaky as he turned to look at his friend. "What's the problem here? You said they were a loving couple."

"Seem to be, considering..."

"Considering what?" Joe hesitated, and Skye spoke, "No matter. I'll met them myself tonight."

"Okay." Joe paused with a thoughtful expression on his face. "That's the best idea, anyhow."

"Give me a high five. I'm out'ta here."

"I'd offer to drive you, but I'm in no condition. I'm gon'na have to call Susan." He frowned for the first time that afternoon. "Oh shit! I won't hear the end of this for a while. And Susan will tell my mom." He pointed a wobbly finger at Skye. "You're in trouble with the women in my life, and that's not a good place to be."

"I know that." Frowning, Skye moved in the direction of the blinking Miller Beer sign, "You could walk. I'm gon'na." The hot air blasted through the open door causing him to step back. "It's a hot one!" He pulled up the waist band of his pants and moved forward. "This will sweat the beer right out of me. I'll feel better in a hurry. What do ya say, Joe?"

"You need yourself a belt."

"Wan'na take the walk with me?"

"Nope. Gon'na make that call."

"That's it. No words of wisdom?"

"Hydrate." He put his head back on the bar and muttered, "Take a bottle of water from the cooler."

Big Sur, California
Highway One
Late Afternoon

Forty-five minutes in the late afternoon sun had a sobering effect on Skye, creating a headache that felt as if a jack hammer was pounding inside his skull. He couldn't remember the last time he'd done beers and shots but knew it had been years ago. *And I swear to whatever's holy, I'll never do it again.* The words became his mantra as he lumbered along the side of Highway One where cars shot by him going too fast for the curves. The smells of gas fumes mixed with hot air caused his stomach to rumble.

Even though he'd tried to take only small sips of the water, it was gone, and his thirst was overwhelming. He glanced down at his feet and reaffirmed that his city shoes had worn blisters into both of his heels and they hurt like hell. Shaking his head, he longed for a cool shower but would gratefully settle for some basic shade.

He knew if he arrived home ahead of the dinner guests, he'd have time to clean-up, and that would be important if he wanted to impress them favorably. After all, they were going to adopt his daughter and he would be demonstrating his advanced leadership skills with the emphasis placed on proper protocol, but first he needed to rest.

Coming to a halt, he stared at the summer sky, a bright blue bowl embracing the surrounding hills. Golden sunshine dazzled the day with intense light, and he squinted as he looked up, wishing he had Pete's wrap-around glasses. As far as he could see, the road shimmered in a maze of heat waves causing his eyes to tear from the glare.

Taking a deep breath, he continued moving. *I've got a life....soon as I piece it back together. Gon'na do what's right for my daughter.* Stopping abruptly, he shook his head. *Why do I keep using that word?*

Closing his eyes, he welcomed the immediate blackness. *Okay. I got'ta think sharp and stay within the parameters of the problem. Chair this activity, get the prospective parents to understand my point of view, and wrap up the outcome on a positive note. After dinner someone will take me back for my rental car.* He opened his eyes slowly. *Okay. I got a plan.*

Wiping at the sweat on his forehead, he realized his arms were streaked with dirt.

****

Sighting the road to his mother's home, he let out an audible sigh. It wound steeply down, but he could manage it. As he rounded the final curve, he saw Pete's truck, and parked next to it was a dark purple Ferrari. It glowed in the late afternoon sunshine, demanding his attention. Stopping short, he tripped over his feet. *Where's the Toyota?* He squinted at the sleek car, feeling perplexed.

Oh, I get it. This is his sports car. What a show-off! Duane's probably short and chunky, just like his dad, so a Ferrari screams I'm mean and lean. Good thing I got height on my side. It's an advantage.

A sudden burst of sharp pain sliced behind his eyes, and he rubbed a spot above his eyebrow. *I need more water.* He continued down the drive thinking,

Would the owner of a flashy Ferrari make a good father? Doctors have big egos so is his girlfriend just eye-candy on his arm? These seemed like important questions, and he'd address them as soon as his head stopped throbbing.

As he climbed the porch steps, he took a deep breath and pulled on the front door. He could hear voices bubbling with pleasure and knew that they were admiring Monique. A sudden pop of anger shook his body. They had started without him! He should have been there, supervising, running the show, not coming home from a bar in the middle of the afternoon. He felt a moment's empathy with the Ford Taurus, dusty and rejected, left in the parking lot at Joe's Saloon.

Lowering his chin, he began to rub the tight muscles on the back of his neck, and the smells of spilled beer from his shirt assaulted his nose. His stomach flipped unpleasantly, and he leaned heavily against the hall table. Water splashed out of the chipped vase. *Damn! Why can't I be more careful?*

He centered on his main goals; get a shower, find clean clothes, and treat his blisters. He kicked off his shoes and grabbed them in one hand as he started down the hall.

His escape was short lived when a tall, slender man came through the back screen door. He looked casually sophisticated, as if he'd stepped off the pages of an Italian men's magazine. Skye squinted in confusion as the stranger addressed him with a warm smile.

"Skye! Haven't seen you in years. What a lovely little girl you have."

"Who are you?" His neck leaned forward at an awkward angle, and he sucked hard on his bottom lip. "No way! Damn it, Duane?"

His mind told him that Duane had never been that well-dressed and shouldn't look so trim and muscular. He, Skye, had been the school jock, athletic, buffed, and dressed in the style of the day. He smiled weakly, thinking that Duane must have favored his mother.

A foul stench rose up from his shoes as he shook hands. Duane's expression didn't change, but he took a step away. A second man, carrying an hors d'oeuvre tray, walked out of the kitchen, and Duane moved toward him. "Skye, I'd like you to meet Sandy Waters."

Setting the tray down, Sandy stepped forward, "Hi. I've heard a lot about you." He, too, was wearing smart, casual clothes and offered a sincere smile.

Two men! Where was the girl? Skye was vaguely aware that his body had begun a tilt to the north. *Oh shit! Same as the house.* "Where's Sandy?" he demanded. "I want to meet the nurse."

The man with the tray of food smiled. "Over here. I'm Sandy."

With an effort, Skye righted himself but continued to stare at the stone walls, letting the facts invade his blurry thinking. Sandy was a man! He felt his mouth open and waited for words to tumble out, but he belched instead.

"Look guys. I've got to shower and, you know, ahh, clean up." He carried himself upright by placing his free hand on the wall as he moved awkwardly toward the bedroom. He stopped suddenly and slapped his forehead as if he'd just remembered his manners. It took another moment for the throbbing to stop before he could speak, "Ah, it was nice to see you, meet you...you know what I mean."

The two men nodded. They were genteel, comfortable with themselves, and clean. Yes, definitely clean and, if he wasn't mistaken, they're concern was directed at him. That was ridiculous. He was fine, wasn't he?

Chapter Nineteen

Chicago, Illinois
Tech World International
Evening

"Do you think Skye will find someone to adopt his daughter?" Delaney asked her father. "Other than his mother? Because that's just a bad idea."

They sat in the corner office of Tech World International sipping coffee. Far below them, as if in another world, the lights of Chicago were softened in a wavering mist.

Terri Sue Ellen was lying on a sofa that faced the window. "His mama all but tossed me out. Indians are supposed to be more polite to potential family members." She sat up and pointed at the wall to the left of her husband's desk. "Y'all see where ah'm a' pointin'? That's where we could ov' hung one of her works of art. Ah'll bet she knows how to paint a donkey and an elephant...on separate velvet pieces, of course. See here, Chucky, you could switch out the animals dependin' on whether you're entertain' a Democrat or Republican.

"Where's some paper? Ah should be writing this down. Why, that acceptance of a picture might ov' kept the peace with Skye's mama, and then he would have been obligated to marry our little girl. Ah think Indians still do things that way. It's tribal. What do you think Chucky? Is that an idea worth exploring?"

"No," Chuck replied, thinking of the tall elegant woman who lived in the stone house. He faced his daughter. "I feel that a nice young couple will step up, and Skye will sign the paperwork. It's my opinion that baby will be raised in a normal household."

"With the good Lord willin' and the creek don't run dry, that's exactly what will happen." Terri Sue Ellen took a deep breath. "Amen." Placing her feet on the floor, she continued, "With that havin' been said, ah believe it's time for dinner.

"Chucky, call for the car. Ah want to dine at the club and have mah favorite waitress pamper me half to death. Phone ahead and be sure Lorraine is on duty tonight. If she's not, have somebody call her in 'cause she'll want to be there for me." She clutched at her heart as she wobbled to her feet. "Ah feel the need to be surrounded by old friends."

Delaney looked out the window. "Adoption is best. I hope you're right, Daddy."

Charles stood up and nodded. "This will be a problem of the past. I'm sure Skye's professional sense will dictate his behavior."

Big Sur, California
Stone House
Same Day
Late Afternoon

When Skye got to his bedroom, he drank three glasses of tap water, too fast. He felt his insides rumble and just made it to the toilet. The after taste of beer and tequila made him gag. He longed to lie down, but there was no time for a nap. The party had started.

Looking at the old tub in his bathroom, he shook his head. He needed a shower, not a soak and decided to use his mother's bathroom, which had been remodeled and now had a large glass enclosed area with water jets shooting from the walls. It must have been Pete's idea. His mother had been content with a small shower...or had she?

Leaving his clothes on the floor, he stepped into the rainfall area and turned the knob to cold, letting the gush of icy water penetrate his body. When he could take it no more, he switched to hot, soaped up, and took a long shower. In a final attempt to sober up, he decided to turn the knobs back to cold. After a minute, he was breathless and reached for a towel. *I'll never drink again!*

He noticed that although his body odor was gone, he now smelled like some kind of flower. Squinting at the label on the lavender colored dispenser he groaned, "Lilacs in Spring. Of course, it's my mother's soap!" *I smell like Easter.*

He turned the hot water back to high in an effort to get rid of the sweet fragrance, but only cold ran out, and he realized that his body could not handle another icy spray. His college days of out-drinking his buddies were gone forever.

The blisters on his heels continued to throb. He spotted a pair of his mother' fuzzy slippers and shoved his toes in them. Muttering to himself, he pushed his arms through the red velour robe he'd used yesterday and stepped over his dirty clothes. He felt his feet flop against the floor as he walked into the kitchen.

Duane was opening a bottle of wine and looked up. Skye stopped short, stumbling over the slippers, and catching himself on the counter. "Hey, I can explain."

"No need." Duane picked up a bottle of wine and joked, "You couldn't build a fort worth shit, but you always had taste in clothes...that is until today." He moved toward the screen porch, adding, "But on the up side," he kidded, "your mom frequently said red was a good color on you. I'll see you outside."

Looking for soda crackers and ginger ale in an effort to calm his upset stomach, Skye mumbled, "Good color, my ass." He started back down the hall talking to himself, "I did so know how to build a fort!"

Back in the bedroom, he checked the medicine cabinet for aspirin. Beginning to think that he might live, he searched drawers that he'd used years ago. Kicking off the fuzzy slippers, he stuck one leg into jeans that were too short, but in his haste caught his heel and winced in pain. *Damn!* He danced around for a second, then showing great care, slid his other leg into the pants. He found a wrinkled T-shirt that said, in faded letters, "Dude, Beer" and put it on.

In his bare feet, he made his way to the back porch where everyone had assembled. Pausing, he listened to the chatter coming from outside and let his questions flow around him. Why hadn't anyone told him that Duane and Sandy were gay?

The family scene was hospitable, but Skye held back, feeling ill at ease. He could see that wine glasses were raised in a general toast, and Monique was lying in a new cradle, cooing sweetly, taking her part in the conversation seriously.

Damn it! His daughter's future was at stake. As a father, he should have been told there was a gay couple involved! *Whoa, strike the father word!* He shook his head sending pain searing across his temples.

His mother looked up. "Come on out, Skye." She waved him into the center of the porch. "Duane and Sandy brought Monique a little present." She was beaming as she pointed toward a small bed. "Every little girl should have a pink cradle to embrace her. Do you see the little rose buds that have been craved in the wood?" She motioned him to come closer. "Step over here. See how pretty it is." Tipping her head, she looked at her son's appearance. "I see you found the old clothes you left here. I meant to clean those drawers' years ago. But I guess it's good that I never got around to it." Looking toward his feet, she laughed lightly. "I must have tossed all your old shoes. Huh?"

"Got blisters." He added sheepishly, "Real bad ones."

"You want me to take a look at them?" Duane asked.

Skye started to raise his foot but put it down. "No. I can handle it." Trying to cover the faded lettering on his shirt, he acknowledged Duane and Sandy with a nod. "Shirt's from my college days. I used to drink beer. Well, I still do...but only from boutique breweries, you know, designer beer." He hung his head. "But not today." He wondered how long before the aspirin would start working. With everyone looking at him, he paused, confused by what he should say next. "Ahh, I'm actually into wine now."

He looked at his mother, and she replied, "Yes, that's right, Skye's been drinking whatever wine we open."

He added quietly, "But not a lot." *Did my mother make a joke at my expense? That's just mean.* Sweat trickled down his neck, "I did have a beer this afternoon, with an old friend, Joe Campbell. He was minding the bar for his dad." He waved his hand. "It doesn't matter."

Duane nodded. "I remember Joe. You guys used to do beer and shots. How'd that work out for you today?"

"Not so good."

Everyone laughed, and Duane continued, "Joe married Susan Franklund. I've seen their twin daughters. Pretty little girls, but they're a handful."

Feeling the pressure building, Skye's stomach growled with a vengeance as he faced Duane and attempted to smile. "Nice Ferrari."

"Thanks. We're enjoying it. Unfortunately, we don't take it out on the open road often enough. Usually we drive our SUV." He nodded in the direction of Melissa. "Visiting Dad and your mom allows us the opportunity to blow the dust off the Italian beauty."

Pete quipped, "Good thing he's got himself a steady job so he can afford the pretty automobile. It's built in Italy, not even American made, but it guzzles our gas like there was no tomorrow."

"Come on, dad." Duane smiled. "You know you enjoy a ride."

"Maybe." Pete adjusted his wraparound sun glasses. "Missy and me might take us a spin in the purple plum after dinner." He paused, his brow creased. "But then, maybe not. We gave Angie the day off so who would watch our little one?" Turning toward Duane, he added, "Say, you'll want to meet Angie. She's real good with Monique, and she'll be back later."

"She sounds like a sweetheart."

Skye noticed his mother was wearing dark-blue mirrored sunglasses that matched Pete's, and a pair of tiny sunglasses, shaped like stars, were sitting close to the new baby bed. Could they possibly be for Monique?

Duane tossed his dad the car keys then turned back to Skye, "Plus there's your mom's cooking that always brings us back to Big Sur."

Melissa spoke with affection, "You're a smooth talker, just like your father." She held her hand out. "Peterson, I'll be taking those keys. You drive too fast."

"Do not."

"Do so."

Laughing, Duane stretched his legs, crossing them at the ankle. He smiled at Melissa. "Is he going to buy you that little Audi R8?"

"Says I have to give up my Chevy." Her whisky colored eyes danced with good humor.

Sandy laughed. "Might be a good trade. What do you think, Skye?"

"Audi R8? For my mother? I don't think so." He looked sharply at both men and noticed their shoes. Duane was wearing a Bottega Veneta loafer, timeless styling, very classic. He had a pair in Chicago. Sandy had on San Marco Crocodile loafers by Zelli. Delaney had ordered some for him. He looked at the fuzzy slippers on his feet and groaned. "So, ahh, my mother has a car." He noticed Duane and Sandy had no pretenses. He shifted again in his chair. "It's a Chevy. And she likes it...a lot."

Melissa smiled indulgently. "I may give it up. Or maybe Angie would want to buy it? She'll need transportation if she moves here permanently."

"We'll ask her," Pete answered.

"As to my getting a little Audi R8..." She smiled. "It all depends if they have my color."

"You've picked a color?" Skye's voice was clipped, "I wish you had talked to me first."

"Metallic black with red interior that has the baseball stitching." She looked quizzically at Skye. "Why should I have talked with you first?"

"Well, there you are!" He swatted at a honey bee. "Mom, they only make that interior in a convertible."

"I can feel the wind on my face now. I might even tie a red kerchief around my head to keep my hair from blowing out of control when I cruise down the highway." Laughing, she reached over to push the hair off Skye's forehead. She sniffed at the air quizzically and asked, "Why do you smell like flowers?"

"Used lilac soap."

"Because..." She paused, waiting for his answer.

"It was in your shower."

Pete nodded, "Right next to it was a bar of Old Spice."

Skye shook his head wondering which was worse. He changed the subject, "What's important here is that you understand that convertibles are dangerous." He spoke firmly, "Mother, do you realize there is no support on the top?"

"Is that a fact?"

"Yes, it is." He flipped his hand at another bee.

"Well, I promise to be careful." She patted his arm affectionately. "You do know that bees are attracted to flowery scents?"

"I know that." He answered tersely. "I rinsed off several times, but some of the smell stayed put."

She leaned forward and inhaled. "You needed to rinse your hair, too."

"I thought I had," he replied impatiently. Pushing his hands in front of himself, he looked toward the ocean and took a deep breath. "Sorry. I didn't mean to sound gruff."

"Excuse me." Sandy got up. "I want to check the olallieberry pie." He turned to Melissa. "I tried your recipe for the crust. Let's hope it's as good as when you do it." In passing Skye, he commented, "Your mom works so hard, I like to help out by preparing the dessert."

"Yeah." Feeling self-conscious, Skye squirmed and added, "As a kid I used to dry the dishes."

"He did." Melissa nodded thoughtfully. "Just last night, he cleaned the burners on the range."

Pete reached over and slapped him on the back. "And he tidied under the big oven hood this morning."

"Even though it wasn't dirty," his mother reminded him firmly. She pointed toward a glass. "How about some wine?"

Shaking his head no, he managed a weak smile and sank into a shady chair next to his daughter. He let his hand fall over the side of the new cradle. "Are those sunglasses for her?"

"Yes, they are," she added cheerfully. "Angie bought them on our shopping trip, but Monique doesn't want to keep them on."

"Oh." He looked at the baby who was grabbing her toes and babbling.

Conversation flowed around him, and he wondered if he was going to make it through the evening meal. He still felt unsteady and needed more water. Just not too much, too fast.

Without warning Monique grabbed his finger, squealing with delight. She held on tightly as he looked into the cradle where her soft brown eyes met his in an even stare. He noticed the golden specks, and felt his heart beat faster as a flow of love passed between them.

"Motor reflexes," Duane replied to Skye's startled look. "She's developing them. Got a good grip, doesn't she?"

Not having much exposure to children and none to babies, Skye couldn't understand why his hands reached into the cradle to gather up his daughter. She seemed to be evaluating him as he lifted her.

"Skye?" Melissa's voice sounded far away. "Skye, are you all right?"

The baby's weight felt good against his body. She wasn't wet and slippery as she'd been when he picked her up earlier that morning. He'd expected something light as a feather, but his daughter was firm and smelled fresh, like spring air that had mixed with sunshine. She gurgled softly as she rested her head on his shoulder. Was she talking to him? This small human being was his creation. He had to do the right thing for her.

Melissa, alarmed, started to rise. "Skye?"

"I'm fine." He gently moved Monique from his shoulder so that she was cradled in his arms. He couldn't take his eyes away from her. "She's so perfect." For a moment in time, no one else existed in the world except the two of them.

Melissa sat down, and Pete moved to her side. Duane watched the scene unfold as his breath caught in his throat. It was going to happen again; another baby would be taken from them.

Sandy let the screen door shut behind him and smiled. "I think the pie is going to be..." He paused when he saw Skye with his daughter and stood very still.

Monique turned her head and peered into her father's eyes. Skye saw himself in her face. Her mouth was shaped like his. He remembered Nathalie had high cheek bones. Would Monique? She had her mother's chin and skin tone. Why hadn't she told him she was going to have his child? Maybe she was trying to tell him when she'd called Tech World International, but he'd refused to take her calls. Even if he had known, what would he have done? Would he ever know the answer to that question? What would he tell his daughter about her mother?

Thoughts whirled around his head as the baby gave him a toothless grin and waved her short arms in circles. Her chubby legs lengthened into a satisfied stretch before she relaxed again. He was held in awe of her tiny performance and felt a tear slide down his cheek.

People were talking to him, but he couldn't make out their words. This little person was his daughter. He felt his heart melting with love. The feeling kicked in with a wallop leaving him weak in the knees.

Duane's look of fear mixed with cold disappointment, and he knew that Sandy shared the same feelings. They moved closer to each other for support.

Skye stood slowly, cradling his child in his arms. A man's worth is measured by what he does. His father had been right. Taking a deep breath, he carefully handed his daughter to her new parents.

Duane hesitated, not understanding what was happening, but he accepted the baby tenderly. Skye felt a corner of his heart break away and deposit itself somewhere deep within his little girl. It would be forever hidden away, but always there. He offered a silent prayer that Nathalie would understand, and he asked her forgiveness.

Facing the people gathered around him, he announced, "This is my little girl, Monique LaVeron Topple." He nodded his head a couple of times as if to reassure himself and everyone else. Looking into the eyes of Duane and Sandy, he continued, "But you're going to be her parents." He fought to be brave, but his voice caught. He took a moment and spoke softly, "My heart is breaking, but for the good of this baby, it's the right thing to do." More tears stung his eyes. He needed to be alone with his emotions, and he turned to leave. "Please excuse me."

Melissa followed him into the garden and opened her arms. She whispered, "Life's lessons can be so very difficult." She held him tightly. "I'm sorry you hurt so much. I wish I could make it better."

"I know, mom. I know you do."

****

Angie arrived back at the stone house shortly after dinner, and Duane and Sandy got on with her right away. They didn't seem put off by her appearance, and she chatted with them like they were old friends. Skye maintained a pleasant attitude as everyone discussed what would happen next. His mother and Pete were eager to be grandparents and stay involved in Monique's life. They offered many ideas, which Duane and Sandy barely heard because they were doting over their daughter.

When it was time to turn in, they refused to let Skye give up his bedroom. They had brought sleeping bags and would use them.

The night seemed endless. Skye felt a rush of emotions; had he made the right choice? It felt right, but another part of him wanted to reconsider even though he knew that wasn't possible. His decision was firm, and the legal papers would be binding. Sometimes doing what was right was the most difficult call.

Chapter Twenty

Big Sur, California
Stone House
Next Day

After a happy and noisy family breakfast, where Melissa and Pete pointed out everything Monique liked and disliked and Angie voiced her own set of comments on proper care, Duane and Sandy left for San Francisco. Monique was staying with her grandparents for a few more days until Duane made legal arrangements, and Sandy arranged for time off from the hospital.

Skye's emotions were mixed, and he wasn't sure what to do next, so he made a plan to stop and see Joe, let him know what had happened and probably go to his house and apologize to Susan. He owed them that. But first he had to make the call. It was only fair to tell Delaney what had taken place.

He was sitting in the kitchen, looking at the old wall phone, when Angie walked toward him dressed in a tangle of clothes ranging from a brocade vest over her peasant blouse to a skirt that dragged across the top of her boots. He said nothing as she placed Monique in the new pink cradle that sat next to him by the table.

She settled the baby and gently kissed her forehead. Looking at Skye, she spoke simply, "I admire you for making that choice." She gave the cradle a gentle push. "I'm glad your mom is keeping the original Drawer Bed. She can use it when Monique comes to visit." She walked down the hall but turned around and added, "Not for long, though 'cause Mr. Pete is right...she's growing like a weed. However," she held up a finger. "You could open the ends for length and expand the sides of the drawer." Her brows knit in concentration, and she muttered, "But then it would be a new bed." Shaking her head, she walked down the hall.

Skye watched her leave and thought he understood what she'd said and that made him feel oddly at peace. It was time to place the call.

Delaney answered on the fourth ring, just before her machine picked up. Her voice was cool and professional until she heard him speak. He felt her breath catch, "Please don't hang up," he pleaded.

"No. I wasn't going to do that. It's just that I didn't recognize the phone number."

"Cell reception is bad so I'm using my mom's land line. I, ah, well I want to talk to you. Tell you where I am. Are you okay with that?"

"Yes. I want to know." Her voice turned softer, "I'm glad you called."

He explained his decisions quietly, hoping she'd understand his responsibility as a father, knowing it was important for her to comprehend what had taken place. As he told her about Duane and Sandy, she listened intently.

"And they're gay? I mean that's fine. It's sort of the 'in' thing right now. Even my father has someone in his family who's gay." She added quickly, "But that's different." She inhaled and continued, "So, I guess, that means that your mother will be a part of the baby's life." She paused, her voice cool. "That's good, too." *She's going to be there for that child. Always interfering.*

Skye added, "Yes, it works out best for everyone." Silence filled the air, so he continued, "Duane gave Monique a pretty thorough physical. Says she's perfect." Looking at his sleeping daughter, he felt good. "Her medical records were in an envelope, and he took them home. He'll check with the hospital where she was born. There may be more details."

"That's nice." Delaney's voice was calm. "I really mean it. I'm glad it worked out." *After all, adoption was the idea that me and mother had come up with to fix this problem in the first place.*

"She's still here." Skye reached in the pink bed and ran his finger across the baby's soft cheek. "It gives my mom and Pete time to adjust. Of course, they'll see her a lot. Duane and Sandy are getting ready for Monique now. Lots of stuff to do. Get a room painted pink, buy baby things." He felt himself tear up and changed the subject. "The crazy gypsy is going with them to help for a few weeks or however long they may need her. She said something about visiting her family so, hopefully, she won't be coming back." He took a deep breath. "And that's good in my book."

"Yes. It's probably best."

"But mom and Pete will miss her, so I'm really not that sure what will happen."

"Guess you'll have to wait and see." *That Pottery Nanny was such a messy person. Purple hair, clothes askew, piercings. Uck.*

"Yup, that's about right." He cleared his throat and continued, "Sandy is going to be a stay-at-home dad. They're nice guys. They love Monique, and they've waited a long time for a baby. They'll be wonderful fathers." He paused, taking a deep breath, and plunged ahead, "I'll be submitting my resignation to Tech World International today. You know..." he cleared his throat. "To make it official."

"You don't have to." Sadness permeated her words. "You were good for the company."

"It would be best," he paused, running his hand over his unshaven chin. "Umm, could you pack my clothes and send them to me?"

"I don't hate you, Skye. I just need..." He knew she was close to tears. He let the moment go, and her voice rallied, "I don't know what I need."

"It's okay, Delaney." He heard her sigh and said quietly, "There's no rush."

"I was awful." She sniffed and took a deep breath. "I'm so sorry. Can you ever forgive me?"

He spoke guardedly. "I understand." She was spoiled and manipulative, but he still enjoyed her company. *I must have a weak-spot in my personality. Everyone has shortcomings that can't be explained.*

"Well," he could hear her nervous laugh and wondered if she was brushing her hair. It was an annoying yet endearing trait. He pushed the thought aside as she continued, "Maybe you could come in person to get your things. Not right away...." She added quickly, "But whenever." Her voice held a flicker of hope.

"Guess, I won't be needing my business suits for a while. I'm going to house-sit while mom and Pete take a trip Down Under. Besides, I need to get comfortable with where I am. On a personal level." He ran a hand across his forehead and allowed himself a deep breath. "I guess I've been pushing myself in lots of directions."

"I think I get it."

"Are you nodding your head?"

"Yes."

"Thought so." He grinned. "I wish you and my mom had gotten on better."

"I do, too." She frowned, remembering the short visits she'd had with Melissa and shuddered.

"Ah," he felt the need to ask, "How is your family handling this?"

"Well, mother's playing lots of golf. Daddy spends his time at the office. My grandparents are taking it in stride. Grandmother Evelyn didn't seem surprised by the announcement of our broken engagement, but mother says she's old and doesn't understand everything."

"I'm sorry, Delaney."

"Me, too. We all need time." The memory of roasting meat and family stories caused her to scowl.

"Well, for now..." His eyes traveled affectionately across the parlor, stopping at the swan sofa. "I'll be at my family's home. Truth is, in the middle of this chaos, I can find peace." Shaking his head he added, "Go figure." When she offered no comment, he continued. "When I find a position, it will require travel, so I'll move closer to the city."

Her words were earnest, "That sounds like a positive plan." *You leaving that stone house is a good call.*

"I can make it work." His voice filled with fondness. "I want to stay in touch, Delaney." He realized that even when her moods swung out of control, he still enjoyed how she doted on him. *People aren't perfect. I'm not.*

"Good idea." Her voice was warmer. "I'll be in Paris next week. My team will present the strategy. Niles Rand and his group will handle implementation." She paused. "It won't be as good as your approach, but it will have to do."

He laughed, allowing Delaney to finish her thought, "Maybe when I get back, we can talk again? We could, ummm, even celebrate your birthday. You know, on the official date." He could feel her smile, and she added, "After all, I've still got your stuff."

"Yes," his tone was firm. "We should do that." A pleasant feeling settled into place. *Who knows what the future holds?*

Made in the USA
San Bernardino, CA
18 March 2018